Coping with Demons of War:

A Novel About Combat PTSD

Dr. Ari DeLevie

D1713839

"The treatment of combat PTSD is complex and difficult...This book, based on the rich experience of the author in the treatment of PTSD victims, offers a unique and substantial contribution."

Dr. Ofir Levi, Lieutenant Colonel
Director of the Unit for Combat Reactions, Israel Defense Forces (IDF)

"...in the book the daily struggles and pain of those suffering from combat PTSD is clearly elucidated, side by side with the efforts to rehabilitate their lives. The wide array of therapeutic techniques presented in your book is likely to assist therapists who treat those who suffer from this disorder. Many thanks..."

Dana Ben Reuven, Director of the Office
Office of the President of the State of Israel

"This book is very impressive, written in a clear and understandable manner, despite the suffering of PTSD victims. No less important is the manner in which methods for overcoming emotional crises are presented. I particularly appreciate this point, because...I'm aware how emotional breakdown can lead to severe physical illness."

Dr. Daniel Yam, Disease Prevention Specialist
Formerly at the Weitzman Institute, Rehovot, Israel

"This book shows the author's desire to lend a hand in times of war and its aftermath, and demonstrates professionalism of the first order."

Dr. Gad Lubin, Colonel
Former Chief of Mental Health Services, IDF

"I am pleased to tell you that I enjoyed your book very much. I find it excellent...as it is written in an interesting, flowing manner, combined with the excellent description of the characters and the fascinating therapeutic interventions. I've personally benefited from it, as it's enriched me professionally."

Eli Perkal, CSW
Director, ERAN Mental Health Hotline, Rishon Lezion, Israel

"....therapeutically, the description of the group sessions is very inspiring and interesting. I've given it to colleagues who treat high-risk children."

Dr. Shmuella Guissin, Special Education Teacher

This book is dedicated to my three terrific daughters,
Sharon, Rena and Tammy,
who supported me during a difficult period in my life.

To my sister Ayana "the one and only," without whose efforts and
resilience the book would not have come into existence,
to her husband, Shalom;
and to my extended family for their hospitality, support and love.

And, most especially, to my beloved late wife, Joan,
who allowed me to be absent from her life for five long months, thus
making it possible for me to fulfill a wish I yearned to accomplish.
She had hoped to see the book in print – but to my sorrow
she was deprived of it, passing away after a nearly three-year long
courageous battle with lung cancer.

CONTENTS

ACKNOWLEDGMENTS

My deep thanks go to my sister Ayana for reading and correcting the manuscript; and

To my daughter Sharon, first reader of the English version, for her advice and editing.

Thank you to Ora and Oded Manor, in whose home I stayed during my long period of volunteering; and to Ahuva Cohen for going over the manuscript;

To Colonel (Retired) Dr. Gad Lubin, psychiatrist, former Chief, Mental Health Services of the Israeli Defense Forces (IDF), who made it possible for me to volunteer;

To Lt. Colonel Dr. Ofir Levi, social worker, Chief of the Unit for Combat Reactions (a PTSD clinic), who guided me patiently through the maze of professional challenges;

To Major Eran Golani, social worker, who was encouraging and supportive in difficult moments;

To my friend, Susi Lowenheim, a gifted therapist, for her professional advice and support;

To my first editor, June Fox, who helped shape the book;

And to Heather Quist for her meticulous final editing.

Ari DeLevie
White Plains, NY
2012

INTRODUCTION

One could compare a soldier suffering from Post Traumatic Stress Disorder – PTSD – to a pebble tossed into calm waters, creating concentric circles of waves that spread further and further. Where the pebble hits, small and sharp waves are created, and as the distance from the center increases, they become shallower, and eventually fade – yet they continue to exist.

Why the comparison?

The soldier who is suffering from the horrors of battle directly affects those surrounding him or her: parents, siblings, boyfriends and girlfriends, spouses, children, employers and friends, army comrades and many more. Those who are closer are more directly affected and those further away, less so. But even a casual passerby, witnessing an unexpected outburst, might be affected.

Frustrated parents watch with anxiety and grief how their son or daughter, returned from military service, simply isn't "what they used to be."

Spouses and life partners are depressed because of the lack of interest shown to them, and the physical and emotional distance they experience.

Young children do not understand why daddy, who used to be so sweet to them, is nervous and impatient and no longer wants to play with them.

Employers and friends anxiously track the shifting moods of the veteran, their reduced productivity and the apathy they display, the "I don't give a damn" attitude.

Friends who used to be close to the veteran, quietly whisper to each other in sadness how they have lost contact, how there is no reply to their phone calls, and how evasive their friend has become.

The medical establishment is affected by endless complaints about unexplained pains in various parts of the body, about sleep problems, loss of interest in sex, and a general deterioration in functioning and health.

The circles are huge and keep expanding.

To all those who suffer from PTSD, this book is dedicated. It is a work of fiction, based on true events as relayed in stories from Israeli veterans, who (like American soldiers and others from around the world) have experienced the horrors of war. All stories in this book are composites of several soldiers' stories, and all characters are fictional, representing a cross-section of society.

It is my hope that PTSD survivors, and those surrounding them, will benefit from reading this book. It is not a scientific book and does not presume to give professional advice to any one person, but it contains a number of therapeutic interventions that have proven to be helpful in ameliorating the suffering. Even after many years have passed since the traumatic event, it is often possible to achieve relief, even if incomplete.

My deep thanks to those veterans who opened their hearts to me and courageously allowed me to share their anxieties, fears, their hopes for the future, their struggle with their "demons," their night terrors, their fear of noises, their apathy toward life.

There were some among my clients who confided to me that talking about the events was no less intense than experiencing them; that it required heroic courage to talk about them. Often, it was the first time they directly confronted their suffering in a professional setting.

My thanks to those who trusted me and my ability, to help them move from a "frozen" condition to one that is more optimistic with improved functioning. I hope that readers will benefit, whether they are in the inner circles or the wider ones of PTSD, and that it will assist them to successfully cope with their demons.

ZEV

Balding and wearing glasses, he is of average height and relatively slim. He is in his seventies, but looks younger. He wears an Amish-style beard, no mustache. What is left of his formerly black hair is now white, and his black-and-white beard is evidence of his body's battle to retain youth in the face of reality.

Zev's parents were from Germany and immigrated to Palestine before the war, when they were in their twenties. His father, Fred, was a businessman. He was successful in his job and had just been promoted when Hitler rose to power. He and Ruth had only been married a short time when she declared sharply that Germany was no place for Jews to live, and insisted on emigrating to Palestine; and at the beginning of 1935, they boarded a ship and sailed to Haifa. One year after docking, Zev was born, his parents having settled in a small, newly-built apartment in the Hadar Hacarmel section of Haifa, on the slopes of Mt. Carmel.

Ruth, used to read him Bible stories in German, because until she had lived in *Eretz Israel* for several years, she knew too little Hebrew to read in anything but her native tongue. In his early years he spoke German with them, but after the other kids teased him on his first day in kindergarten, he switched to Hebrew. Clearly, he didn't learn it overnight – he knew Hebrew, but for some reason had failed to use it on that first day of school.

When he was nine, Zev's sister Aviva was born, adding much joy to the small family that had no relatives in Israel. He quickly took to his role as "big brother," playing with her and occasionally getting into some mischief (which once resulted in her requiring a few stitches in her chin). But she was a good-natured child, and forgave him.

Zev's mother was clever, creative, and deeply committed to helping others. She had planned on becoming a nurse, but due to the political situation in Germany, she only managed to receive a diploma as an "Infants' Nurse." She engaged in that profession for many years and developed a reputation as one of the best in Haifa. Young couples registered with her practically "the morning after," and she had great success nursing healthy babies and restoring to health those who were sick.

His mother's love for helping people in distress apparently attached itself to Zev, and at the age of 14 he showed up at the local first-aid station, *Magen David Adom*, hoping to become a volunteer. The person in charge looked at him pityingly and suggested he return after he had "wiped the milk off your lips," pointedly hinting at his youth and lack of maturity for such a responsible position. Insulted but getting the message, Zev returned the following year, this time with an upper lip on which – with a magnifying glass – one could discern the beginnings of some hair growth. He lowered his voice and announced that he was "ready."

He was accepted and took many courses in first aid. He learned to bandage wounds, treat broken bones and sprains, administer artificial respiration, and carry injured people on stretchers and on chairs in tight spaces. He rode in an ambulance for nearly four years and dealt with the survivors of hundreds of car accidents, electrocutions, falls from scaffolds, and drownings in the untrustworthy Mediterranean Sea. He suffered through a failed attempt to revive a drowning victim. He saw gunshot wounds, deep gashes, limbs distorted by open fractures, and burns of every type.

Zev accumulated a great deal of knowledge in anatomy and physiology, subjects that fascinated him. He recalled that, in addition to Bible stories, his mother had read to him from a huge book in German with wonderful illustrations called *The Human Being: in Health and in Sickness*. She had explained to him such physiological functions as breathing and digestion.

Volunteering in first aid, Zev quickly learned that, as critical as it is to stem bleeding or stabilize a fractured limb, psychologically calming and encouraging a suffering victim was equally important. Being fluent in German, within weeks he was able to learn Yiddish and to speak it with immigrants from Eastern Bloc countries, for which it was their mother tongue. He discovered that there are many expressions in Yiddish to describe pain, such as: *"Es brent"* (it's burning), *"Es schmerzt"* (it's painful), *"Es reisst"* (it's tearing), *"Es drickt"* (it's pressing), and many more.

And most importantly, he learned that "connecting" with people, in a way that worked for *them*, was vital to the healing process.

He went on to study clinical psychology, gaining knowledge and methods to help him effectively work with people who needed emotional support. And he acquired a doctorate in psychology from a prestigious New York university.

In his off-hours, he enjoyed listening to music, a love he'd inherited from his father. Without any musical education, his father understood music and was one of the earliest listeners to the brilliant works of Gustav Mahler, which were rarely played or appreciated back then. Zev's first major purchase in fact, when he was 20, was a state-of-the-art Garrard record player for his father.

His sister had followed him into the healing professions, first becoming a volunteer at Magen David Adom, and then going on to become a nurse. And music was also a bond – though she learned to play the clarinet and became a member of a youth orchestra..

Eventually, Zev met his future wife, and they had three daughters.

Now, at age 71, retired with seven grandchildren, he decided to volunteer once again. This time it would not be Magen David Adom, but helping soldiers who were suffering from combat-related Post Traumatic Stress Disorder.

FIRST SESSION

"I haven't picked up a phone to my friends ever since...."

"I haven't either," adds Avi, a short muscular man, with a serious expression.

Gil joins in nervously: "I prefer talking to no one. I don't feel like talking to anybody."

Zev: "Does anyone else feel that way?"

Some of the guys nod. Hesitantly, Yossi offers; "Years – it's been years. I no longer have friends. They've had it with me. At the beginning they used to try, but I wouldn't respond. I knew who was calling; I saw the number on the screen. It's so strange, because when we were there... contact with them was the most important thing in the world. We'd call out to each other, 'Brother, are you ok?' And now, zero."

Gil begins to speak, his voice tense. "I tried. I would dial but then hang up before anyone could answer. I just don't want to be reminded of it."

Zev: "Reminded of what?"

"You know! How can you even ask?" His face reddens with anger.

"I'm sorry that this is so hard. It is a delicate question. Could you say, anyway, what would happen if you did speak with them?"

Yossi, who is very thin and bearded with curly black hair, starts weeping quietly. He sits deep in his chair, cupping his narrow face in his hands, a tear creeping down his cheek. A heavy atmosphere of tension engulfs everyone in the room. Eight stories that have not been told are circulating in the minds of eight fighters who experienced traumatic events during their service. Ron, the first to talk, and Avi aren't the only ones avoiding their friends since they lived through their experiences. It seems that no one has been talking.

For years.

Not even to their close friends, their wives or girlfriends.

Avi is biting his lip. When he is by himself, sometimes he cries, out of rage, out of mourning. But he swore that he would never cry in front of others; he thinks it isn't manly, indicates weakness. He has never even cried in front of his wife – but here he is, crying in front of other men, strangers. He, the hero who received the "Medal of Valor" that he is ashamed to show to anyone, even his father. He knows that his father received a similar medal for his actions during one horrible night, thirty years ago, on the rocky slopes of the Golan Heights. His father had never shown him his "Pin," yet Avi knew of its existence. As a young child he had accidentally discovered it deep within a night table drawer. He didn't know then what he had discovered; and because he wasn't supposed to dig around in his father's belongings, he never asked.

At home, Avi sometimes takes out his medal and strokes it with his fingers, just as he did the cheek of his close friend, Rami, when he rescued him. He had evacuated him under fire, determined to save his life.

But now, whenever Avi looks at the pin, he feels guilty, since he survived but, ultimately, Rami did not. He continues to wonder whether he should have treated Rami more thoroughly on the spot. Yet if they had remained there even a few more seconds, both would have been wiped out, as they were in the crosshairs of snipers. He did apply a tourniquet to Rami's smashed arm, but had remained unaware of his second injury…

* * *

It is the first group meeting. The guys have just started looking at each other. Aside from initial clues, the personal stories are as yet unknown. The participants don't know exactly what is bothering the others, but Gil's remark: "I don't feel like talking to anybody" has provided the first hint. The thought is familiar to everyone here, although only three have admitted to it; when Gil angrily confronted Zev, the others remained silent.

"Good evening, my name is Zev, and I am a psychologist. I'll be leading our group. We have eight participants, and we'll meet 12 times. At the beginning, I'll tell you something about myself, and then everyone will introduce himself in a few words so that we'll know each other's names and can start to get to know each other."

Nine men sit on nine identical chairs arranged in a circle, in a classroom-sized space. On a table near one of the walls sits an electric kettle, already plugged in and boiling. Next to the kettle stand nine mugs, upside down on a paper towel, as well as a package of hot-drink cups. A glass jar holds instant coffee and another, powdered Turkish coffee. There is sugar in a third glass jar, and little pink packets of artificial sweetener in a fourth. At the front of the table is a large, flat plate holding an assortment of inexpensive supermarket cookies. A small collection of paper plates, napkins, and plastic spoons completes the refreshment offering.

The room has two large windows. Curtains that have seen better days hang on each side of the windows, their color difficult to define, something close to beige-brown, boring-looking and nondescript. Dust-covered white metal Venetian blinds that have been pulled to the top of the frame complete the window treatment. One of the windows looks out on a group of ugly concrete buildings several hundred yards away. The second reveals a neglected meadow, empty except for a few low trees and two huge eucalyptus trees that look to be at least 60-70 years old. Weeds fill the meadow, in countless shades of green, some wilted, and some having just sprouted after the last rain.

Low-flying birds pass by from time to time, and one can hear dogs barking outside and – from a distance – the roar of passenger planes poised at the end of a runway, awaiting takeoff. The roar increases to a whine as the planes lift off, on their way to faraway lands. The sirens of ambulances can be heard, sometimes with great frequency. At other times, the area is tranquil. The mental-health clinic where the group meets is near a large hospital, accounting for the sirens. The occasional roar from the runway suggests that the clinic is situated in the center of the country, not far from Tel Aviv.

A small sign outside the building indicates that smoking is not permitted, according to a recently passed law that forbids smoking in public places. Yet the undying craving to smoke is evidenced by the scores of crushed cigarette butts that line the walkway leading to the entrance. The addicted suck their last precious drags before entering, satisfying their craving while still respecting the injunction. In the room, there is no trace of the ashtray that, until recently, was commonly found and generally expected.

Some of the light illuminating the large room comes from the windows, but with the setting sun, overhead fluorescent lights get turned on. Next to the kettle, a small tabletop lamp with a straw lampshade emits a pleasant light that softens the room's atmosphere. Combined with the comforting aroma of the coffee freshly prepared by the participants, the room – where one can anticipate hearing difficult things – feels more welcoming and pleasant.

"I'll start with myself," opens Zev, "and everyone can choose what he'd like to tell us now, and what he chooses to add in later sessions.

"I am 71 years old, married, the father of three daughters, and have seven grandchildren. My wife, a former schoolteacher, is now retired. I have been a psychologist for more than 40 years. I have experience with individuals, couples therapy, families, groups and children. I've specialized in physical injuries and rehabilitation. In recent years I've been working with people who have experienced traumatic events, such as rape, accidents, and disasters. Many years ago I worked in rehabilitation with Israeli soldiers. I'll add more details as time passes, but now, let's hear from others. Who is ready to start?"

No one opens his mouth. Everyone waits for the others, and not out of politeness. There is palpable concern about revealing more than is comfortable to this group of strangers, some of whom have less-than-sympathetic faces, some who even look wary or suspicious. They are reluctant to reveal their identities, their life history, to divulge painful secrets, yet they had all agreed to join this group. Each had done so after having an individual session with Zev, during which he explained the purpose, the process, and the advantages and disadvantages of short-term, focused, group psychotherapy. They had been carefully selected, and everyone who had promised to come had come. Everyone who had arrived in this room knew that he would be expected to tell the others what was troubling him, what symptoms he would like to rid himself of. And each had been told that sharing his story and experiences could help others.

"Somebody has to jump into the cold water – might as well be me" puts in a rather tough-looking man, with olive skin, a round face, bushy eyebrows, and a noticeable scar on his chin. "I'm Yariv; I am from a kibbutz in the north. I'm 29, married, father of two, and I am a farmer. My hobbies are swimming and weightlifting. What happened to me... I'll talk about that at another time. Is that enough?" He turns toward Zev with a questioning look.

"Yes, certainly, thanks for paving the way."

"I'm Uri, 23," offers a tall, pale man with a high forehead and rimless glasses, in a soft, diffident voice. "I'm a musician and teach music in a high school. I'm from Haifa, married, no children. As you have already surmised, I'm a *Yekke*, so I might as well put it right out on the table so that you can't tease me later on..." Everyone burst out laughing.

"You're a man, you are, Uri, to expose your family background so early on" says a smiling blond man with blue eyes and a friendly face with delicate features. "And since I've started talking, I'll continue. My name is Sergei, and as you have probably figured out, I'm an immigrant from the former USSR. I'm 22 and have been in Israel since I was nine. I came with my mother and sister. We live in Raanana, where we have a bakery, and do some catering. I am also in school, where I study cinema, a real passion of mine. But now I'm unable to sleep at night. Bad dreams and nightmares haunt me." His voice becomes swallowed up in a wave of emotion, and he falls silent.

"Thanks, Sergei. You told us a lot. Wasn't easy, was it? Who is ready to go on?" asks Zev searchingly.

"Ah...It's...well...I'm Avi...and...I'm sort of...I don't know what to say. I came here because I have those thoughts, you know...bad feelings...that something awful will happen to me

10

and my family, that I have no future...and that...I can't think of anything else except that these thoughts keep jumping into my head, and I would like someone to help me with these," Avi concludes gravely.

"Thanks, Avi," Zev replied, understanding full well how difficult it is for him to reveal these things. "Could you tell us some more details, like, how old you are, married? Things like that."

"Ah...yes. I'm 35, and I have a metal shop in the Moshav, a collective settlement. I'm married with four children. I'm unable to play with them. I have no patience for them, and that upsets me. Because...as I said, you know, these thoughts, these bad thoughts..."

"Again, many thanks, Avi. A lot of information, and you had the courage to say things that aren't easy to say. Who's next?"

Gil sits quietly but it is evident from his expression that he is dying to enter the circle. He is about 5 foot 6 with coarse brown hair, and sits tensely at the edge of his chair, his legs slightly spread apart and his lips pursed, as if words are about to spill out of them. Zev gets the message and turns to him.

"Yes, let's hear from you," he says encouragingly.

"I'm...I'm 22, single. I live in the center, near Petah Tikvah. I deal with heavy earth-moving equipment, like bulldozers and such. I repair them."

"Thanks, and could you also tell us your name?" Zev asks. A broad smile appears on several faces of the group members. Gil blushes, clears his throat and blurts out a short syllable, "Gil, my name is Gil."

"Welcome Gil."

Zev feels things are moving along well. Within minutes, more than half the group has introduced itself. Only three more names and everyone would be part of the circle.

A tall, intense-looking guy appears ready to join, and Zev motions encouragingly with his hand to invite him to talk.

"I'm Ido, a Jerusalemite." He speaks slowly and deliberately, and his black-rimmed glasses add to his serious demeanor. "I am a lecturer at the university, in history, and I'm a nature lover. I still guard my bachelorhood, but I have a girlfriend, and we both love to cook. I was involved in some incidents that left a deep impression on me, and I've tried to cope with them on my own, but not successfully. That is why I agreed to come when Zev invited me to join the group. I have doubts and hesitations about participating in such a group, but I'm also open-minded. I'd like to return to being the person I used to be. I'm not the way I used to be."

"Thanks, Ido. You've shed light on some important problems, and I can assure you that everything you are experiencing is also being experienced by others who are here. You are not alone."

"My name is Yossi," hesitantly offers the skinny man with the thin beard who had cried earlier in the session. He wears a *kippa* – a skull cap – and khaki shorts, moves about in his seat, and sounds uncertain, almost apologetic.

"Yes, Yossi, could you also say something about your life? How old you are, what you do, and anything else you'd like to add."

"Yeah. I'm Yossi from Rehobot, married, with a four-year-old daughter. I'm not working. I can't."

"Thanks, Yosssi. And now we have one member remaining, and we'd love to hear from you," said Zev, turning toward a good-looking man who had not introduced himself.

"OK. So, I'm Ron. I was born in the USA and made *Aliya*, immigrated, several years ago. I'm a medic, single, and my girlfriend is in Boston, as is my family. I also have family in Tel Aviv. I'm 24. At the present time I'm a student. I served in the Gaza Strip and I lost an injured soldier. I think about him all the time. It makes me crazy. I cannot concentrate on my studies. I used to be a good student, but now I'm not doing well. It's a big problem."

"Thank you, Ron." Zev started summing up the opening phase. "Thank you all for this information. I know that at the beginning it's confusing to remember everyone's name and details, but don't be concerned about that. Shortly we will gel into a coherent group, and everyone will know each other well."

Suddenly the room is completely still. Nine men who had been total strangers to each other a mere hour ago have started the process of getting to know each other, and their curiosity is mixed with uneasy concerns. What will they be expected to say next time? Who will reveal his traumatic experiences first? And what if the emotions become so intense that it feels unbearable, and it becomes impossible to talk about what had happened?

Zev continues with his explanations. "We are meeting here to deal with everyone's troubling issues. We will grapple with the problem that everyone here has in common: Combat-Related Post Traumatic Stress Disorder, or PTSD, as it is known today. It has a long history, and the lack of understanding as to its significance is reflected in the various names by which it has been described in the past. During the Second World War, it was known as "Battle Fatigue." In the First World War it was often referred to as "Shell Shock." And there is even evidence that Napoleon's soldiers knew of it. Yet for a long time, there were people who believed that this wasn't a real, debilitating phenomenon, that there was some pretense involved, and that people who seemed to suffer from it should just move on and "get over it."

"Since the Vietnam War, people have started to understand that these sufferers aren't imposters, but rather a group of people who have been deeply affected by the events of war, and who suffer from a group of specific symptoms related to their experiences."

"For example?" Ido inquires.

"For example, intrusive thoughts that are very difficult to get rid of. They repeatedly invade one's mind and refuse to leave. Another example is night terrors."

"That's familiar," Ron acknowledges.

"And also avoidance."

"Avoidance of what?" inquires Gil.

"For example, avoiding places that remind one of events that occurred there. For instance, some soldiers who were in the Second Lebanon War might avoid travelling north, even to picturesque places like the popular tourist areas, with their delightful bed & breakfasts."

"And what about not visiting friends…in other words, avoiding social contacts?"

"Yeah. These are all examples of these symptoms. And another one that is very common is trouble sleeping: trouble falling asleep, or trouble staying asleep all night."

"Say, Zev, what about the problem that I cannot remember important events that happened to me during the war? Is that related?"

"Certainly is, and we will talk about it and the means we have of overcoming it."

"I have problems with my girlfriend. I'm just not as interested in her as I used to be. I still love her, but not like before. She hasn't changed, it's me, and she doesn't understand why I'm acting so strangely."

"That too is part of the same issue," responds Zev. "You see, there is an entire list of emotional experiences that one who hasn't experienced them would find impossible to comprehend. Or they might think that they aren't genuine, are just some fabrication or set of excuses made by a returning soldier. And it can even be the result of events that occurred many years ago. It's confusing and frustrating to loved ones, and at times it spoils perfectly good relationships – even marriages."

"Yes," sighs Avi, "I noticed."

"Other symptoms that are also related include physical reactions, such as a pounding heart, sweating, shaking, muscle tension, and sudden outbursts of anger, at times for no obvious reason."

"You are describing aspects of me, and of a good friend of mine. It just isn't possible to talk with him without him starting to argue and bicker about complete nonsense. He bursts out screaming, even slams doors, and I just stand there looking at him as if he had gone nuts."

"That's sad, but it's a very accurate description of what often happens," Zev responds. "We'll deal with all these matters as they come up during sessions, and I'm asking that you be frank. Sometimes things will sound embarrassing and might cause a feeling of shame, but here is a place you need never feel ashamed. You'll be surprised to hear things from your colleagues in the group that they have been sitting on for a long time and never wanted to share with anyone in the world. But here is the place to tell."

"You've given us a long list of symptoms. But does it include everything?" inquires Ido. "Is there anything else?"

"There is. Did I mention difficulty concentrating? That's very typical, and also irritability and being hyper-alert, such as jumping from noises to the point of hiding, even in public places that are safe. For example, in shopping malls, when hearing a helicopter fly by, or metallic noises."

"Oh! You are getting closer and closer to areas I never wanted to touch. I thought of myself as a psycho every time I had a reaction like that."

"The important thing to remember is that these are normal reactions, that they are part and parcel of the PTSD syndrome. The trouble is that those who have not experienced them sometimes don't understand how real they are, and that it at times makes us feel like we are crazy, even though that's entirely false."

"That's actually very comforting," mumbles Avi between his lips, and others nod their heads.

"Is there someone here who has separated from a girlfriend, or whose marriage is shaky since the events?"

Silence pervades the room, but the eye rolling of three members suggests that Zev has touched on another sensitive area. It is simply too early for them to deal with it, although it is clearly a vital subject that would have to be explored thoroughly in future sessions.

"I'll lead the group, and I will add my comments, thoughts, questions, and ideas, but you will be doing most of the work, each of you, for yourself. We are going to meet here every Tuesday, from 4:30 to 6:00, for the next 12 weeks. This is a closed-end, symptom-focused group: its purpose is to bring your symptoms to a manageable level in order for you to return to a normal life. No one will forget what happened to him – that isn't the goal. The goal is to bring your memories to a level where they will not interfere in your day-to-day living to a significant degree. That is what we are striving for.

"And everything that is said in this room stays here. We must completely respect the privacy, thoughts, feelings, and facts of everyone's life, so that we can trust each other and feel safe enough to talk freely."

"What? I can't even tell my wife?" bursts out Uri.

"No. Whatever is said in here is confidential and private."

"But Karnit is the one who pushed me to get here. I didn't want to come. I don't think I even need this!"

"She actually did a good thing by encouraging you to come, but that doesn't give her the right to know about the *other* group members. You can tell her whatever you wish about yourself, but not about the others. Ok? Can everyone agree to that?"

Silence.

Faces turn from one to another.

There is a mingled sense of both doubt and discomfort in the room.

Yariv is thinking to himself, "Will everyone really be able to respect this agreement? How can I trust Uri not to tell his wife? He's behaving as though he is entitled to talk openly with her. So, I'm not saying a word." And indeed, he keeps silent.

Zev asks again: "We must get everyone's commitment. Is everyone able to do that?"

Three men nod their heads; others sit stone-faced.

"Is there a problem here? If so, let's talk about it now. Obviously that includes me as well. It might be that I will consult with a professional colleague if I should need assistance, but no names, no identifying details. You have my word."

Sergei: "Ok. I'm able to keep a secret."

"Me too," Uri says quietly, still betraying a sense of reservation.

"Good, but we must hear from each and every one of you. If there is someone who cannot commit to this, it's ok, but then this isn't the right place for him. We can deal with that in another framework," concluded Zev.

But no one wanted to be excluded from this framework. "Separated from others, scared to death, unsure of myself, constantly reliving my worst feelings during battle, even if only for a few seconds – I never, ever want to experience that again." Thoughts like this pass through everyone's mind.

Three out of the eight are still not committing to maintaining the privacy of the others. Zev is puzzled. He is an experienced therapist and has led many such groups. He is the graduate of a well-known university and received certificates from several psychotherapy institutes, and is very experienced in treating PTSD. In all his previous experience with groups, there was already a full agreement to confidentiality among group participants at this point, and he is wondering what has led to the current resistance. He furrows his brow.

"I am hearing commitments from Ron, Avi, Yossi, Sergei, and

Uri. What about the rest of you?"

"This is all new to me," Ido says slowly, "and I'm a cautious person. I don't sign up for things easily. I need to know more about what will happen here."

"As I said when I invited you to join the group, we'll deal with the things that are disturbing to you, such as, 'to be myself again, like I used to be.' And that is true for everyone here. We shall talk about events and feelings, even embarrassing things. But nothing will take place unless we can trust each other," emphasizes Zev.

"OK, I'm in." Ido decides. "That's what I thought; I just needed to hear it once more, clearly laid out."

At this point, Yariv nods his agreement.

That was sufficient for seven out of eight. Only Gil still remains silent.

Zev is starting to sense that this may be a particularly challenging group. "Of course, every group presents its challenges, but there is something here that seems to be different. We'll see," he thinks to himself.

Yossi, who has been tearing up since the session began, suddenly stops. He doesn't wipe away his tears, just ignores them as if they never happened. Abruptly, he sits up straight, turns to Gil, and addresses him in a menacing tone: "Are you with us? Yes or no?"

"Yeah, I am, but don't expect many words from me, all that girly talk..."

Eight pairs of eyes snap toward him at once.

"*Girly talk*? Is *that* what you said?" Avi replies angrily. "I've been sitting on this for *four years*. I can't sleep, I wake up with nightmares about Rami, and you dare to refer to that as *girly talk*? What are you thinking...this is *girly* talk...?"

Zev wants to diffuse the emotions. "We'll talk about that next time, but for today we're going to conclude. So, where are we? We are planning to meet here next week, but is there someone who needs more time to consider this? We have a whole week to think."

"I still need to think about it," Gil whispers, and Zev decides to offer him another individual session.

Gil feels unable to commit himself to the group at this point, because he cannot yet imagine telling others why he is so anxiety ridden. He knows that – in the end – everyone else will have to tell his story, and then what will he do? By avoiding committing himself, he hopes that he is leaving an escape hatch for himself, similar to the door of the D-9 armored bulldozer, through which he had always been able to escape. He feels his emotions may explode at any moment. The event he experienced has been on his mind for the past 18 months, and it is probably time to come clean. But he feels as ashamed as when he was a child, and had stolen coins from the coin jar but was never caught. That has also stayed in his mind. He never had the occasion or the courage to confess that, either.

"I'm thinking, I'm thinking," he says, somewhat frantically.

"We still have until next week. You can call me any time and we'll talk. Everyone else ok?"

Yossi and Yariv know each other from the battle in the Lebanese village of Debel. They had both experienced similar moments of horror and powerlessness when the anti-tank missiles were aimed toward them. Now Yossi approaches Yariv, and asks quietly, "Do you really want to do this? I've put it all behind me, don't really want to reopen it."

"I must, I *must*. It's been haunting me, all of it, the scorched smell, the stench of blood on the shirt, on my hands, on the flack jacket. I can't even look at a piece of meat, let alone eat it. It makes my wife crazy."

Zev remains behind, and turning to Gil, offers: "Want to talk?"

"No need, I'll be here," Gil responds in a low voice.

Although the session has formally ended, the participants seem to find it difficult to leave the room. The preparations for this session had been lengthy, and were filled with tension and anxious expectations. And after this initial meeting, at least for some, many of their concerns have melted away. Zev seems like a calm and balanced guy, he didn't push and he allowed anyone to talk if they wanted to, and indeed, everyone had participated. There were those who quickly found themselves able to go into some detail, and there were others who protected themselves by saying only the most basic things. But everyone had offered something.

Two of the guys rise from their chairs and start milling about; two others return to the kettle. They talk to each other in quiet tones, so the others can't hear what is being said.

Zev stays in the room and waits until the group has dispersed, saying "good bye" to each one personally on their way out. Most leave singly. Yariv and Yossi leave together.

RON

Ron comes from a highly educated, accomplished family. His father, Steve, is a professor of Jewish studies at Boston University. His brown hair shows glimpses of silver strands, also visible in his goatee. Ron's mother, Miriam, is a physician whose specialties are genetic research and hereditary diseases. Her appearance is delicate and diminutive. Ron has an older brother, also a physician, an orthopedic surgeon. His sister Ruth, a lawyer, is an expert in tax law. Ron is tall like his brother and thin like his mother, with green eyes, rather like those of a cat. He and his sister are close.

At home, as Ron grew up, Jewish traditions were observed, but with greater emphasis on its academic aspects than spiritual ones: the history of Israel and the Jewish people, biblical literature, and Zionism. In Hebrew school, Ron learned to speak the language. He wore a skullcap – a yarmulke, kippa – while at school, but quickly removed it when school ended and he was on his way home. He never wore it at home, and his parents did not object. The school's policy dictated wearing one, but his parents agreed with Ron that it wasn't necessary to openly demonstrate one's Jewishness in public. And although most of his friends were Jewish, none wore a kippa, so he did not stand out.

His father had his own, peculiar rituals regarding the kippa, signaling ambivalence. He carried one with him and wore it when he lectured, then removed it and put it away. He wore it when he sat alone in his study preparing a lecture or studying new material, when he wrote a chapter, or researched some aspect of Judaism. Ron knew his father's unusual habits, and certain messages sank in over the years: respect for Jewish tradition, yet a certain disdain for its customs. His father's habits telegraphed the idea that everyone was free to follow or disregard customs as he pleased. These messages eventually boomeranged on Steve and on his relationship with his son.

Ron passed his first years in Hebrew school uneventfully. He was smart, learned to read and write easily, and liked his classmates. He also liked sports and after school he'd go out and shoot baskets over and over until he became an excellent player. The neighborhood kids, some Jewish, others not, often joined him at his house, where the sports equipment was state of the art. Everyone found his mom, Miriam – who loved to see other children playing with her own – to be a lovely lady. Ron's father was seen only on rare occasions. It was understood that he traveled frequently and gave seminars in distant places.

In high school, Ron's friends included kids from the basketball league and others from school. In eleventh grade, he spent many hours filling out applications to various colleges, both near home and distant ones, with steady help from his mother. The essay, such an important part of the application, went though many drafts, of which only the final one was meticulously examined by his father.

Ron's SAT scores were high and he easily got into Yale, his school of choice. There he joined the basketball team, and had a good freshman year. He was still pondering his major while enjoying his liberal arts studies.

But when he had finished his freshman year, Ron surprised his parents by announcing that he wanted to "make *Aliyah*": to immigrate to Israel and join the army, the IDF, as a combat soldier. Steve was shaken and opposed to it. He had aspirations for his son – to continue the academic tradition, like all other family members – and Ron's sharp departure from this vision upset him terribly.

Urgent consultations transpired between his parents, but Ron's resolve did not falter. His older brother Bill, the surgeon with pragmatic views, tried to convince him that it would be better to study first, and perhaps make *Aliyah* later. Ron, familiar with his

father's machinations and suspecting that Steve was behind his
brother's suggestion, could not be persuaded. He quietly
discussed his plans at length with close friends and spent many
hours thinking, pondering and fantasizing, picturing himself as a
brave combat soldier – manly and courageous.

Ron tentatively tried to discuss his wishes with his mother,
engaging in sort of a game: "What if I was to…" But he never got
a clear answer. She dealt with the frightening prospect by
dismissing it and changing the subject. Because she never voiced
an outright refusal, he concluded that – when the time came –
she'd be the easier one to convince.

Relations between Ron and his father had always been tense. It
had never been easy to approach his father, a fussy researcher
with stiff manners and strange habits, a man who only rarely
expressed his emotions and never hugged his children.

Ron had often longed for expressions of warmth and closeness
from his father, especially when he did well at school or when he
was sick. What he did receive were strongly held opinions and
intellectual declarations, "lectures" of one or two sentences: "I told
you to take care of yourself, and here you are, sick." Or, at best
(and rarely): "See! It paid off to be well prepared, so you could do
well on the test." The warm embrace and kiss that a typical father
would give his son at such times never happened.

Ron tried to impress his father with his studies and continued
to do well at school, but had finally concluded that he could not
expect any positive feedback or encouragement from this distant
and rigid man. His decision to make *Aliyah* – to "ascend" to the
land of Israel – was partly driven by the desire to "descend" – go
away from – his father; to live in a faraway place where his father
could no longer interfere or hurt him, and where he could be free
and independent. Meeting his father's expectations was a lost
cause, he concluded, because his standards were both
unachievable and very different from Ron's.

As expected, Miriam cried over his decision, but she did not
openly object. She knew her son well, and in her heart she
understood that he needed to distance himself from his
disapproving, rather arrogant father. Although she did not openly
express this to Ron, in private conversations with Steve, when he
expressed his fears and opposition to Ron's tentative plans,

Miriam did her best to respond honestly, while trying to soothe her difficult husband.

"What? Aren't I a good father? What do you mean, 'he has to find himself and his own place?' We all did that, but we did it *here*. Why must he move 5,000 miles away from his family? Isn't it good for him here?"

"Of course it's good for him here. We are a close-knit family, but he is attempting to find his own place in the world, and it's hard for him to compete with you and your achievements. You have always told him that he has to 'prove himself,' to 'be someone.' Ruth is a successful attorney, Bill a successful surgeon, you are a professor, I'm a researcher, and Ron has his own interests, which are different. He has found a way to express his wish to follow his own path. Of course, I worry about his safety. Of course, I wish he could do something right here to prove himself. Of course, I'm afraid for him. But I don't want to stop him.

"He has thought about this so much. And wasn't it you and I who taught him about the importance of Israel in the life of the Jewish nation, who conveyed our pride in an Israeli army that is strong and a deterrent?"

"Yes, yes, but he is still young. He should study something serious first and then perhaps rethink the decision to leave."

"This is not an impulsive decision. It didn't occur to him yesterday. He has discussed it at length with his friends for at least a year and with me too."

"He's been discussing this with *you*? And I haven't been included?"

"I wanted to, I tried, but you are always so resistant to new ideas – especially if they aren't yours. Each time I started to raise the subject, you changed course and started talking about a new article you published, about a conference where you were invited to be the keynote speaker, about someone in some distant university who is seeking your advice about some academic question. But about Ron you did not want to talk."

Steve was quiet. He had no answer to his wife's words. He knew she had not invented this scenario – conversations like that were common fare between them. She had pretty much stopped discussing sensitive subjects with her husband, including her own achievements. Steve was so much more interested in his own accomplishments, and in those of his surgeon son. In fact, he was not particularly impressed by the accomplishments of his daughter, although she impressed many others in her field. She had earned a reputation as a sharp and accomplished lawyer, but in his eyes, she was "merely" a woman. In his heart, Steve knew his wife was right – he hadn't wanted to hear about Ron's plans, which represented such a departure from everything he considered worth pursuing.

Ron and his sister Ruth were seven years apart. As he grew up, she had often played the role of babysitter, taking care of her little brother. The family employed a nanny who was devoted to the kids, but Ron was particularly close to his sister who spoiled him. When the idea of *Aliyah* had first occurred to him, he called her.

"Ruthie, I need to talk with you."

"Okay, Ronny, but you sound tense. Everything ok?"

"Yeah, all's well, but I want to speak with you. When do you have a break in your meetings?"

"I'm the boss. Anytime you want. Want to meet tomorrow for lunch?"

"Great. Thanks Ruthie, you're the best."

They settled on a time and place – an upscale restaurant near her office. They had met there before on several occasions, and Ron always felt privileged and happy that his sister had invited him to dine at such a prestigious place.

"What is it?" inquired Ruthie the next day, after they were comfortably seated.

"You know that our parents always made a big deal of the importance of Israel, of how strongly they feel connected to it, the trips to Israel for Bill and my Bar Mitzvahs and your Bat Mitzvah and all of that…"

"What are you trying to tell me?" she interrupted, sensing that something big was brewing.

"I want to make *Aliyah*," he blurted out quickly, as if to prevent changing his mind about telling her.

"Yes. I'm not surprised. I've been expecting something like that. Mom will worry but will manage, but for dad it will be difficult."

"Really? He only thinks about himself and his own

achievements – his books, his lectures. You think it will be especially hard for *him*?"

"Yes, and that's the reason. He only thinks of himself, and considers you a part of him, and your decision will demonstrate that he actually has no control over an important part of himself, and that will upset him. And the truth is, that under that stern facade, he's crazy about you. I've heard him brag about you to his colleagues."

"Really?! So why doesn't he ever say a good word to me?"

"That's just him. That's how he's built, how he functions."

Ron hung his head, looked sad, and concluded: "I've lived with it so long, I'm just going to go ahead and follow my dream." His sister reached her hand across the table and softly stroked his

When Ron was 15, he had met Alice at the Bar Mitzvah of a mutual friend. She was a lively girl with a long single braid, brown hair, and a family background similar to his. Her intelligence and sweet-tempered nature appealed to Ron. They lived in the same area and were in the same grade, and they started seeing each other frequently, especially on weekends.

When Alice chose a college, she selected one that was only about 100 miles from Ron's. They continued to see each other almost every weekend throughout their freshman year. When Ron decided to make *Aliyah*, he found it painful to tell her, but she understood his decision and accepted it with grace and understanding. Although sad, she understood that he was leaving to fulfill a dream, taking a huge step toward self-fulfillment, toward an inner calling. It would be hard being 5,000 miles away from him and worrying about his safety, and she had a thousand other thoughts about his leaving. But Ron had raised the topic before, discussing his plan to immigrate to Israel with her on several occasions, and these conversations had lasted many hours. She had tried to prepare for this decision, while hoping it might never happen.

"When, Ronny, when?" she asked, as a tear formed.

"In August, I think. I'll go home at the end of the semester and stay for a few months. That way I can start my military service together with the Israeli high school graduates, and it should be easy for me to get in synch with them. They usually start basic training around then, and I'll be an integral part of the class." Ron felt grateful and relieved by Alice's philosophical acceptance of his plan.

"That's reasonable. I know you've thought about this a lot," she said, wiping away a tear. "Have you told your parents yet?"

"No. You are the first one. Next I'll tell my sister, Ruthie, who I know will support me, and then my mother."

"And what about your father?"

"Mother will tell him."

"Are you serious? You won't talk to your father about such an important matter?"

"He won't want to hear about it. He will only react with anger and rejection, and there is no point trying to persuade him."

"And what about your brother?"

"He is in the same league as dad. He can hear from mom, or perhaps from Ruthie."

When Ron's decision not to return to school could no longer be comfortably concealed from his father, it indeed fell to Miriam to deliver the difficult news. It took courage, because she knew full well how he would react, but she had no choice. She took a deep breath.

"Ronny finishes the semester in another week and is coming home. But he will not be returning to the university for his sophomore year," she announced to Steve on the phone. He was in Cleveland, far from home, at one of the professional conferences in which he so often participated. He had just finished delivering a lecture on a topic in which he was considered an international expert and was feeling especially pleased with himself when he was confronted by this unwelcome news.

"Why not," he responded in a tense voice. "I always knew that he was immature, kind of a 'loser.' Actually, I'm not surprised – has he failed his…" and he might have continued with a series of imaginary failures and accusations if Miriam hadn't cut him off sharply, in an uncharacteristic manner.

"Steve, listen! He completed his freshman year with honors, with a grade point average of four! He failed nothing. He is an outstanding student."

"So…what is happening here?" Steve sounded confused and embarrassed. The stream of accusations that he had begun to lob at his son with no justification caused even him a degree of shame.

"I don't understand. Is he into drugs? Was he expelled? Did he offend his professors somehow?" He clearly preferred to spew angry questions rather than to simply listen to his wife, who obviously knew the answer.

Her husband's arrogance and intolerance had been bothering her for a long time, but in the past, Miriam had chosen to ignore them, always feeling that their life together would be easier this way. However, now she became angry. The volley of baseless accusations against her beloved son infuriated her. Her husband had gone too far, and she felt here was an opportunity that must be taken to finally rebuke him for his self-centered unreasonableness.

"Since you are unwilling to listen, and have all the answers without any facts, all based completely on fantasies in your own head, you'll have to get the answer for yourself. You ask Ron why he won't be returning for sophomore year." And before her startled husband could answer, she slammed down the phone.

Steve was shocked. Such a heated confrontation had never taken place before between him and his wife. She had always acquiesced to his demands, obedient and respectful. How dare she slam the phone in his face?! Anger started boiling up. He paraded in his room with rapid strides, circling the table in sharp turns, reaching the window and returning to the bed. He was like a caged animal. He had never encountered a situation like this. Ron, his son, had succeeded in his studies – so important to his father – yet for some reason didn't want to pursue them. And his obedient wife screamed at him and slammed down the phone. What nerve!

Yet, in some corner of his heart, doubts had started creeping. Perhaps his behavior had been inappropriate. His wife told him how well Ron had done at school, and all he had been able to do was launch into a series of accusations. Perhaps she was right in saying he was "unwilling to listen," and maybe it was his obligation to find out about Ron's plans, and in a manner that is more respectful toward his wife. He felt ashamed, and began looking for a way to get out of the thicket without looking like a fool. He decided to call her back and pretend he thought the call had somehow been interrupted for technical reasons. He was anxious to know what was happening with his son, and worry had started creeping into his heart.

"Oh, God! What if he has a serious disease, cancer, lymphoma, perhaps AIDS, God forbid!" Horrible thoughts coursed through his mind. A new wave of shame washed over him. Not only had he accused his son unjustly, the poor guy could be deathly ill and might not even recover.

He dragged himself to the desk. He picked up the phone, his hands shaking, and dialed Miriam's number. He worried that she might not answer, that she would continue to punish him for his abominable behavior – that she would deny him the information he was now craving so badly. That she might not be home. In his imagination he saw her out walking the streets, trying to calm down after the way he had spoken to her. The tremor in his hand increased. The phone rang for what seemed long minutes.

"Hello?" He was relieved to hear Miriam's voice.

"Miriam...it's me...I – I'm sorry I did not listen to you."

"Are you ok, Steve? You don't sound good."

"Yes, yes, I'm ok. What's the matter with Ron? Is he well?"

"Are you ready to listen? And will you let me finish what I'm saying?" She used a confident tone, the kind she employed professionally in her genetics lab when giving out assignments to her assistants. Previously, that strong and confident voice would disappear when she interacted with her tyrannical husband.

"I promise. I will listen and won't say a word until you let me. I'm so worried about Ronny."

"Ok. Steve, do you remember that from time to time I tried to talk to you about Ronny's idea about making *Aliyah*?"

An enormous sigh of relief emerged from Steve's throat. This was more palatable. So, Ron wasn't expelled, didn't fail, and wasn't sick. He is merely disobedient. He is doing what he wants, paying no attention to his father's wishes. Ron is young, cocky, undisciplined, and unwilling to listen to his wise and experienced parents. The shame and embarrassment that Steve experienced just minutes ago were being replaced by a mounting rage.

"That nervy guy! I knew that..."

"Steve. I haven't finished, and you promised to listen, right?" Miriam pulled him back on track.

Steve mustered all his energy, clenching his teeth so as not to burst out again. He not only felt angry at Ron, but at Miriam as well. He did recall the late-night conversation in their bedroom, when Miriam had gently alluded to Ron's thoughts. But he had been unwilling to contemplate such a frightening scenario. The idea that his son would go to such a distant place, and even into a dangerous situation, without completing his education, was too much at odds with his own aspirations for his son. He had put it out of his head, and Miriam hadn't brought it up again.

"Yes, I'm listening."

"Ron completed his freshman year successfully, but he felt unsatisfied. He thought he was wasting his life on insignificant matters. He felt he needed to respond to his inner calling, to go to Israel, to contribute his share, fulfill an aspiration: to implement the very things we had inculcated in him during his childhood years. He heard from us morning, noon, and night about the history of Israel, about the Maccabees' wars and Joshua's battles. We traveled and fulfilled the mitzvah of Bar and Bat Mitzvahs for all our children, in Israel. Would you like me to continue, Steve?"

"I understand. It is the fruit of the tree we planted, and it has now ripened. I must accept his decision, be proud of his choice, support him, and not criticize, but it's hard, it's painful. I really think that he should complete his studies, and then maybe he can…"

"Steve. Steve! I'm not finished. You promised me."

In a low voice, almost a whisper, he agreed to continue to listen to his wife.

* * *

Ron arrived in Israel at the beginning of August. He settled at the home of his uncle in Tel-Aviv – Avraham, his mother's brother. He'd always felt at home with his aunt and uncle whenever he had visited them. He expected that they would be happy to see him and would appreciate his decision to make *Aliyah*, to join with them both in body and spirit, not only in words and ideology like his father. With them he had a solid runway from which to take off to his military service and where he could land and find comfort during furloughs and times of stress. He anticipated that such moments would come.

SECOND SESSION

"You also mentioned something like: 'not the way I used to be,' right?"

"Yeah, that's what my wife said. But you know something, she's right. I really don't feel the way I used to, so I understand her completely. The trouble is, I don't know what I can do about it."

Zev joins the dialogue between Ido and Uri.

"That feeling that you're not the way you used to be, which a few of you have mentioned, what's it like? How would you describe it to somebody? How would I, for example, understand that this is how you feel? What is different?"

"Well, it's like this: I don't have the desire for things I was once dying to do," responds Uri.

"Such as?"

"I don't straighten out the things on my desk. I don't care that the room looks messy. I don't have the desire – maybe don't have the energy – to get out, even just going to see a movie. I used to look at the paper before the weekend to see what's playing, and where, and make plans to go out with friends – to go see a film, have a bite, and scarf down a cold beer."

"And now?"

"Like I said, I don't have the energy to move my ass, I don't care what movie is playing and I don't mind missing it. Just want to sit quietly at home. Don't want to go down to the noisy streets and fight all those crowds at the movie complex, a million people, everyone pushing and yelling and stuff. Who needs it?"

"Does that sound familiar to anyone?"

Eight pairs of eyes focus on Uri. Familiar? Very. Everyone else felt exactly that way and had said so many times to anyone willing to listen. And, upsettingly, those who initially seemed glad to listen, who hoped their listening might help you to "get over it," all seemed to have ultimately lost their patience and their desire to hear about your feelings. It had become an "old script," repetitious and tiresome, and it seemed to irritate people, even your best buddies, because it interfered with their own plans with their wives, girlfriends, and friends.

"So it affects many aspects of daily living, doesn't it?"

Nods from different parts of the room encourage Zev to continue without the need for verbal permission.

"Then how does one move on from here? We've been stuck in this mess already for quite some time and nothing moves, so what's next? It sounds to me like this is a serious problem for almost everyone here, not just Uri – maybe for every single one of us."

Again, nods of agreement give Zev the green light to start tackling this problem. "Has anyone attempted to overcome this?"

"Yes, I tried," comes from Uri.

"And...?"

"It wasn't so good."

"Which means what?" Zev gently prods.

"I said to myself, 'So, move it already, force yourself, don't disappoint her, in your life you've done harder things, so just get going."

"And? Did you move?"

"Hardly. I put on my coat, and we started going toward the door, and truly, I had good intentions, and I didn't think it was a big deal, was sure that I could do it...but then I couldn't."

"What couldn't you do?" Zev questions.

"We reached the door, I hesitated, I mumbled something, and stopped."

"And what did she say?"

"'So? Are you coming? What's happening with you?'

'Don't wanna go.'

'But you promised!'

31

'Yes, I know, I promised, and I really wanted to go, but now I'm too tired, and I just can't. You go and tell me how it was.' 'Are you crazy? I should go by myself? And what shall I say to Itzik and Dalia? I'm not going without you. You've spoiled my evening. I only have one evening a week when I can go out, and look what you are doing to me. All week long I'm working like a dog, my boss is completely disorganized, the clients drive me nuts, the air conditioner in the office isn't even working properly, and I'm dreaming about the weekend when I can go out with you to a movie and a nice dinner. And then, *I don't feel like it.* That's just great! What about me? How long can this go on?'

"And she started to cry, and ran off to the bedroom and slammed the door. That's what I meant by 'It didn't go so well.'"

"It really didn't, that's clear," confirms Zev.

"Ya know, I also had something like that, but not quite," Ido joined in. "With my girlfriend. She was more patient than your wife, but the words were similar, just that she didn't slam the door and she didn't run away. After we exchanged some words she stood in the doorway and said: 'Let's try. Let's go down the stairs, to the street level and we'll see how it goes for us.' She put her hand on my shoulder and pointed me to the door. I felt like escaping but didn't have the guts to do it to her. The fact that she said, 'Let's see how it goes for *us*,' and not 'How it goes for *you*' – that was something! She didn't throw it all on me. She was there *with* me, and that gave me a boost; and also, by saying 'Let's see how it goes,' she left me an opening. She left space that if it didn't work, then maybe another time, and she didn't press. I knew she was dying to see that film, and actually I wanted to see it too, so that combination moved me."

"And how far did you go?" Zev inquires.

"Downstairs, to the entrance to the apartment building. Then we stopped. Actually, *I* stopped."

"And then?"

"She placed her hand on my shoulder and said something like, 'Good beginning. Look, we left our apartment. Wanna go on? Not the end of the world if we don't see this film tonight, the main thing is, we're together.'"

"And from then on, what happened?"

"We started walking into the street. At first just a few steps, real slow, but then we turned onto the next street, crossed it, and continued. We didn't talk, but we walked. I felt that she was watching me very carefully, but she didn't ask any questions. Suddenly, a woman passed by pushing a baby carriage. We both followed her with our eyes. It was a bit late at night for something like that, but who knows what was up with that woman. So my girlfriend says to me: 'Look, a mother with a baby, that's great,' and I replied, 'Yeah, really nice.' There are people, who have normal lives, and maybe we'll be normal someday, go out to movies, we'll get married, maybe we'll have children. For me it's like a distant dream.

"At that moment she snuggled up to me and whispered, 'It will be ok, you'll see. We are already walking in the street, and last week you didn't even want to hear about that. It'll be ok, be patient; I'm with you.'"

"Wow!" blurts out Uri. "You have a girlfriend who's a ten. I wish Karnit would feel like or behave like her. With us, that's still so far away."

Zev re-enters the conversation: "Correct: Nava is truly supportive and understanding and that's terrific, but everyone has his or her own agenda. We must remember that Uri's wife might feel a little trapped, because they're married, they depend on each other economically; they've been together for years, and she feels an obligation toward him. It is frightening to her to see these changes and she doesn't know how to help, or how to get out of it. She too needs help, and her outburst indicates how frustrated she feels. So it turns out that there are two important factors here, one interwoven with the other. First, what is happening inside you, and secondly, how the environment influences what's going on. Uri has internal pressures, like everyone here, as well as external pressures: the frustration and anxiety of his wife. Ido also has internal pressures, but Nava, his girlfriend, is more understanding, more patient and supportive, and all that helps. We must find a way to help Uri's wife to help both herself and Uri. Each of us is attached to someone outside of ourselves."

Moans and nods by others confirm his words.

A strange silence comes over the room…a rather painful pause. Everyone is tired from the intensity of the subject and the uncomfortable sensation of "I'm not what I used to be," with all its worrisome implications.

The guys move about in their chairs. No one utters a word. Ron gets up from his seat, walks slowly over to the corner of the room, and prepares a cup of coffee. The hot drink gives off a calming aroma. In measured motions he scoops a spoonful of sugar and tilts it toward the mug, watching the white grains flow from the spoon into the mug. He plays with the angle of the spoon, speeding up and slowing down the flow, making the simple process last as long as possible. The transition from pouring the sugar to stirring the coffee is slow and deliberate. Finally he lifts the spoon sharply and shoves it into the mug. In his mind's eye he sees the grains melting away in the hot brew. With the mug in his hand, he turns to the container that holds the milk, lifts it slowly then pours the cold milk into the hot liquid. If he can drag this process out to the end of the session, he muses, he might not have to deal with this difficult subject. In the end, having prolonged it for a minute that seems like an eternity, he returns to the group and sits down. He lifts the cup to his lips but doesn't drink. He inhales the aroma of the coffee and fills his lungs like someone taking in fresh air on a spring day. The others look at him approvingly. They too wish to escape the continuation of this ordeal.

At last he sips from the cup, licks his lip, and begins to talk.

"This is what happened. We were in the Gaza Strip, at night. There was that eerie silence. Dawn broke and the sun started to rise over the hills. We were lying there all night and it was damned cold. My muscles were tight from the chill and from fear. I moved a bit to get out of the stiff position I was in. Suddenly, there were explosions and a volley of machine-gun fire. Then silence again. We looked at each other. Apparently something had happened. We didn't know. We continued to lie there quietly, perhaps a minute or two that felt like forever. Suddenly, over the radio we hear 'Medic! Medic!'

"My heart jumped. That's for me! I'm the medic. Something *did* happen after all. But where? Where should I be going, what do I do? My heart is pounding like a machine gun and I'm wound like a spring. As I'm lying there, thinking, a dust-covered Jeep comes tearing in, makes a sharp turn, nearly flips over and shrieks to a stop. 'That's it,' I say to myself. 'They brought someone. Jump! Do what you're supposed to be doing, what we have trained for twenty times. This is the moment you have been preparing for during the entire track of the combat medics course, all the lessons in anatomy, in physiology, in reviving, stemming blood flow, intubating under fire, this is it, jump, do, *act*' – it's as if I'm giving myself an order to unfreeze. And what would happen if I raised my head, and got up to do what I need to do, and that son-of-a-whore fires another volley? And I'm in his crosshairs? But I'm a medic, and I'm forbidden to think of myself, I am obligated to help the one who was brought in by the jeep. They endangered themselves in the vehicle to bring somebody who needs me, and I'm shivering here. What's happening to me?

"Two dusty soldiers are beginning to drag a wounded soldier from the jeep. He's fat and heavy and blood is pouring out of him. He isn't moving. Now I'm jumping up and begin to assist them. I lay him on the ground and check his pulse. I'm not successful. I *hate* fat people – it's impossible to find their pulse. Why didn't he eat less? His face is ashen and quiet. At least he isn't suffering any pain. I check his breathing, and am unable to detect any. He is wearing a heavy army coat, he is all soiled and it is difficult to discern what's happening here. I check again, at the neck, can't find a pulse. I'm convinced that he isn't breathing. Artificial respiration! I must revive him. Now! There is no more time for checking. The seconds are precious. These two guys risked their lives to get him here so that I could save him. So it makes no difference if I like thin ones or fat ones. To save, to *save!*

"I hover over him, partially rip open his coat so that I can reach his chest. I place one hand over the other, count and press. He is a large man and I'm pressing hard, one-two-three-four-five, steadily. I must get his heart going. I want to feel his pulse. I change to breathing. I pinch his nose and inflate his lungs in a long, deep breath. I lower my ear to listen to the escaping air, return to the heart, and so it continues, for many minutes. I'm getting tired. His face is still white. His eyes are open and he's looking to the sky. What is he searching for? What does he see? Why isn't he talking to me? I press again and begin to feel nauseous. I'm exhausted and a thought is beginning to seep in that perhaps it's too late, that perhaps what I'm trying to do here is futile.

"Another medic arrived. 'Come, I'll spell you,' he said, and we changed hands. I sat next to the wounded man and looked at him more objectively. The thought again pierced my body, deeper, more demanding, and a wave of sadness washed over me. He isn't injured…he is dead. I failed. I did not rise to the occasion. I disappointed myself and everyone who trained me. And him. He relied on me to save him. His mother and father trusted me to save their son. And I did not save him. I wanted to cry, but only bit my lip. It is unbecoming for others to see a medic cry; it destroys morale.

"I was still unprepared to say that final, awful word. I am a medic, I *must* save him. Who is he? What will I tell his mother? And suddenly a horrible thought crashed into my head: I didn't check his entire body when he arrived. It had seemed so urgent to massage the heart and get him breathing. And after all that there was still no change. What if there was another injury, and I made it worse with all my pressing? Fear and horror spread all over me. Surely by now I must have been as pale as him.

"We lifted him into an ambulance. A torrent of blood poured out and covered my boots. I felt like throwing up. It now became clear to me that the bullet – or bullets – that entered him from the front had ripped a main artery, and that the loss of blood was so massive that no revival was possible.

"A physician arrived, examined the body and looked at me. 'Don't be disappointed; he was dead when he arrived. There was nothing you could have done. You made a valiant effort, but judging by the location of the wounds and their size, when they brought him here it was already too late. What a pity.'

"And since then," Ron adds in a soft voice, uttering his words slowly, "I feel like I'm not the way I used to be."

A terrible silence envelops the room.

He has been the first to tell his story – the event that brought him to the group; the story that he had shared with no one but his mother, over the phone, far away in the USA. He hadn't even been able to get a consoling hug from her, just a few words of comfort via satellite.

Now Gil sits up, moves about in his seat…but keeps silent. He takes a deep breath and it appears that he is about to enter the conversation…but he doesn't. He sits motionless, as the eyes of the other men start to focus on him. Then he moves again, folds his upper lip over his lower lip then rolls the lower one on top of the upper. A lip-smacking sound can be heard, but still, no words. He takes a deep breath, and everyone expects him to begin to tell his tale, but no words come.

Zev turns toward Gil, tilting his head toward him, opening his eyes wide and spreading his hands apart in a silent gesture, "inviting" him to participate in the discussion without saying a word. Gil still doesn't talk, although his entire body broadcasts tension and conflict. Finally, he looks at Zev, and – almost in a whisper – says, "I thought I could talk about it, but I can't. Perhaps next time. I can't, I just can't," he adds softly, dropping his gaze.

"Whenever you'd like, whenever you feel you are ready, we'll listen to what you have to say, Gil," responds Zev, in a calm and encouraging tone.

Zev was experienced in the phenomenon the group had just witnessed. One member would open a subject, another would join, others would simply sit and listen, while some pondered when – and if – they should join the conversation. There were moments when some felt almost ready to let their fears and other painful feelings come out of their mouths, to finally allow others to know the terrible facts, but who were somehow unable to utter the words that were at the tips of their tongues. Some feared the actual words themselves – words they had thought about dozens, perhaps hundreds of times, but never said out loud. The silence had a magical, protective quality, as if maintaining it could mean those horrors had never really happened. The moment one said them out loud, there would never again be any choice but to face and struggle with the demons. And so it was better to keep quiet, despite the continuous, gnawing stress.

Zev knows that the group leader has to be sensitive and walk a thin line – finding the balance between encouraging someone to speak and protecting a man who isn't ready to do so at that instant, while leaving a door open for the moment he might be. He has to be alert to the possibility that there might be a strong emotional reaction once the dam of feelings is breached. There might be an outburst of crying, of rage, of almost uncontrollable body movements, of shivering, even curling up in a fetal position, of irregular breathing, of screaming. He has witnessed all of these reactions, at times with anxiety and uneasiness, but he knows that all of them are normal. He also knows that most group members have never witnessed anything like that before, and may become alarmed or frightened.

They wouldn't know how to react, and witnessing so much visible suffering might cause them to conclude that it is better to keep quiet than experience such agony themselves. Zev's job is to allow the words to emerge and to change course if things went awry, protecting those who might become scared. Zev would have to draw on his previous experience and skills to navigate this narrow path.

He turns to the group to offer reassurance. "What Gil is experiencing now is normal: wanting to say something, yet being unable to do so right now. This might happen to anyone and is no reason for concern. There are some among us who are ready today to discuss difficult matters, and others who need more time. I want to be sure that everyone understands that he can speak whenever he wishes and that there will be a receptive, respectful ear from all of us.

"We'll return to the subject that Ron has brought up in the next sessions; and in order for us to begin to cope with the demons, I'd like to explain the goal we shall be striving to achieve in the coming weeks.

"There are all sorts of psychological interventions that can be used to treat post traumatic stress disorder; each has its adherents and its detractors; each method has advantages and disadvantages. I personally prefer the 'cognitive-behavioral' approach, and I will explain to you what that is. I like it and have had good therapeutic results, and it is hard to argue with success. A therapist is generally more successful working in the method he or she feels most comfortable with, and that's a great advantage.

"When you talk with others, you will surely hear about therapists who use different methods – for example, 'dynamic treatment.' I will explain what that is as well. Dynamic therapy is a time-honored treatment modality, but I feel the method I will use for us is preferable for the following reasons.

"The cognitive-behavioral approach is highly focused, and can be used quite effectively in a short term of therapy. We have only 12 sessions; so in comparison to other methods of treatment, ours is definitely short-term. I mentioned that it is a *focused* therapy: this means that we do not explore the past in great detail. Instead, we focus on what is happening now and how to change it."

"So, let's go, sounds good!" blurts out Gil.

Zev continues calmly: "In contrast, dynamic treatment means deep, extended treatment – surely not 12 weeks – that sometimes goes on for years. And very often the meetings take place more than once a week. It definitely digs in deeply and examines the past, the client's family background, and the feelings that arise between therapist and client. It does not necessarily set goals that can be used to measure therapeutic success – or the lack of it. It is harder to measure what comes out of it, but clients often report favorable changes in their lives."

Yariv cuts in: "Like what?"

"Improvements in day-to-day functioning and in happiness – good things. This form of treatment originates with the thinking and particular techniques – such as the interpretation of dreams – of the famous Sigmund Freud, who developed the method known as 'psychoanalysis.' Since then, psychoanalysis has undergone numerous transformations, but Freud's basic approach is still in use."

"Interesting. So, what's wrong with that?" asks Ron.

"Nothing is wrong with it. It is definitely a good technique, but in my opinion, not for here and not now. You will soon understand why I think so."

"So let's hear," grumbles Yossi impatiently.

"Cognitive behavioral treatment is very different. It focuses on changes in behavior that can actually be measured in an objective way. And it requires direct and active intervention from the therapist. In dynamic therapy, the therapist is often much more passive."

"So what exactly is 'cognitive'?" interrupts Yossi.

"Yes. Explain! I don't understand what it is." Gil joins in.

It is starting to seem to Zev that the group is ganging up on him. "Okay. The origin of the word is 'thinking.' It derives from the word 'cognition,' as in 'to recognize' or 'to identify.' So it is something that can be understood based on thinking. The meaning of this idea, in relation to our particular situation, is that what very often happens in post trauma is that we are still thinking and reacting to what happened when the trauma occurred, even though currently those thoughts are no longer relevant, correct, realistic, or helpful. They may have nothing at all to do with our current situation. But because thinking is so powerful, it still drives our behavior even if it is based on the past and not the present. And this can cause problems".

"For example?" Uri chimes in.

"You may continue to think that your life's circumstances are dangerous and threatening, and you behave accordingly. For example, you hear a whistling noise and think that it is a mortar shell coming at you, and you jump and hide under the table. The reality is that there is no shell, that nothing here is dangerous other than the painful memory. Does that make it clear?"

"Sort of."

"So the second word is 'behavioral,' and what is that? Can someone explain to me what "behavior" means?

The guys shift in their chairs as if the question thrown into the air is so basic, it would be insulting to respond to it. Could there be anyone who doesn't know what "behavior" means? After all it appears even in school report cards, where the teacher notes if someone's conduct is okay or not. It is so elementary! Everyone knows what it is. So what is Zev fishing for?

"So? Is anyone brave enough to take a chance and offer a definition?" This time it is Zev who is challenging the group.

"Um...ah...well...so, if you hit someone, that's not good behavior; it's violent," says Yariv.

"Good example. Anyone else?" The challenge continues.

"So, if a wife screams at her husband and he screams back at her, this is behavior, isn't it?"

"Also a good example. Next? "

"If a guy gives a girl a present, that's also a form of behavior ".

"Right. Then what is the common denominator among all these?" Zev continues to prod, trying to initiate a line of thinking among group members.

Again, a tense quiet pervades the room. *What is this egghead searching for? Let him start being practical, I have no patience for his 'lectures.'"* Such are the unspoken thoughts of the guys in the room.

No response is forthcoming, as the men feel restless and stymied by Zev's inquiry. So he starts to summarize.

"What's common to all these examples is that behavior is something you can see with your eyes, hear with your ears. You can photograph it and record it on a tape recorder. It is external rather than internal, and it doesn't matter if it is 'good' or 'bad,' 'nice' or 'not nice.' If I can see and hear it, and therefore photograph and record it, then it is behavior."

"And what, let's say, if I feel fear or anger? asks Gil."

"Good question. Did anyone ever *see* fear or anger?" asks Zev.

"Sure. All the time. When I'm angry you can hear it. Isn't that so?"

"No. Speaking angrily or shouting are behaviors that may result from anger, but if you are angry and hold it inside, and you don't shout, then I may have no idea that you are angry. You see the difference?"

"Oh...yeah. I do." Uri is beginning to understand and acknowledges it, nodding deliberately. Others are also starting to get it, but are more cautious in their reactions.

"And if you think someone is coming to do you harm, is that behavior?" asks Avi.

"No. But if I do something physical to him, then you will know what I am thinking. Right?" explains Yariv.

"Right. And until you do something that I can observe, I do not know what is going on inside your head," adds Zev.

An audible "hmmm" comes from several of the men.

"And our behaviors can be measured quite accurately, and they are divisible into two groups: too many or too much, and too little or too few." Zev continues.

"What is 'too many' and 'too few?'" A new wave of questions floods the participants.

"Let's return to the things that we are dealing with here: We have guys who do not pick up a telephone to call their friends, do not go out socially, and don't visit their family. Right? These are examples of 'too little.' There are guys who often start arguing about nonsense, have outbursts of temper, throw a chair in anger, and watch television until 4 a.m. These are examples of 'too many' or 'too much.' And all these are measurable. For example, someone has temper outbursts three times a week. That's easy to count and write down. Or, someone is able to read only one page in a book. That's also easy to measure, and on and on".

"So what?" inquires Yossi.

"This is valuable information, because everyone has his own agenda of things that bother him, things he would like to change, improve, get rid of, and get back to 'how I once was.'"

"Oh, now I get it. It's beginning to make sense to me. That's why you want to measure our behavior."

"No. Not that *I* want to – *you* are the one who wants to, and I'll help you. And after some time we will be able to know if we are moving in the right direction. You are here because you are not able to sleep, and that's in the category of 'too little.' You also told me that you feel anxiety many hours during the day and at night. So that falls in the category of 'too much.' What if I told you that by the end of 12 weeks you will feel anxiety only an hour a day instead of 8 hours a day? Would that be appealing to you?" Zev is gently shaping their understanding that behavior can be measured and changed, and is starting to suggest some objectives.

"So, that kind of measurement...yes, interesting," muses Gil out loud.

"Is it clear what I mean by changes in behavior? Don't take this personally, as if someone is judging you. The word 'behavior' is not a great word in that respect, but it does explain the idea. Remember, it doesn't matter if behavior is 'good' or 'bad,' we just want to know what it is, and – if we decide we want to – to change it.

"Now let's talk about cognition, or thinking. What does that have to do with behavior? Turns out that thinking – even at times when we are not aware of it – controls our behavior, the way we act. The idea here is that we need to examine what we think, figure out where that thinking is coming from, and then compare it to the reality of the present moment."

"What?!" exclaim two guys, almost in unison.

"Let's suppose that you turn down a good employment opportunity because you are sure that after what happened to you in Gaza and the West Bank, you are 'just not able'; and that by doing so, you lose an excellent job, with good employee benefits, in an area in which you are well trained and in which you are interested."

"Yes. This is exactly what I did and I now I'm sorry. There was a great job, which I turned down, and someone else took it. And here I am – sitting at home without work."

"But if you had been given the opportunity to evaluate where your thinking was actually coming from, and then to compare that with your current reality, would you still have rejected the job offer?"

"Perhaps not."

"This is what I'm trying to illustrate," explains Zev, continuing to summarize the process. "In each session, we will talk about certain situations, and we'll describe them in great detail. Anyone can bring up any situation that causes him distress, anxiety, or feelings of shame, or complaints others level against him – for example a spouse, friend, or parents. We will not be able to discuss every subject in each session, and if we don't finish in a certain session, we will return to the subject in the next one. Anyone have a question about what I just said? Is there anything vague? Any objections? Confusion? If there are, it's understandable and normal. The more we progress, the clearer things will become, but it's always permissible, and encouraged, to interrupt if you have a question or a problem. Okay?"

"So one topic could be what I started with: that I don't pick up a telephone to talk to friends?" Uri interjects, wanting to verify that he is on the right track.

"Exactly. I may add questions, such as 'when was the last time you *did* pick up the phone to talk to a friend? And why *this* friend, and not another? And what was the reaction that you received?' And more details like these. That is what I mean when I say 'in great detail,' because a more detailed description will help you to set objectives and to measure changes. Is that clear?"

Various murmurings can be heard throughout the room. Some participants are not surprised by what Zev has explained. Others had arrived knowing nothing at all about treatment methods, except for a brief mention during their initial individual sessions with Zev before joining the group. Now things are clearer, which arouses some uneasiness and discomfort.

Anxious thoughts are buzzing through people's heads. *"What? I have to sit here and tell these strangers what I go through every night?*

About the fights I have with my wife? How I felt there in that Lebanese village? And what if they see me as a coward, or laugh at me? No! I won't do it. Let the others talk, let them pour out their souls. I'm not telling anyone that I look at my girlfriend when she is showering and nothing happens to my body. That she exits from the shower and comes to me and all I can say to her is 'come, let's go and watch some TV.' I'll never talk about that! And that therapist, what does he know? He wasn't there. He just sits here in his chair, spouting knowledge that all came from books. No missile landed on him! How can he possibly understand me? How could anyone who was never in battle? And he's going to tell me how to act? Bullshit!!"

Yet, no one left the room. An air of "perhaps" had started to crystallize. Maybe there is something here that could help. And maybe, just maybe, "that one over there" knows something that will help me to deal with my nightmares. And maybe what I feel, others also feel, and if I fear it, maybe I am not the only one. Then "maybe." And maybe I need to give this a chance.

SERGEI

Sergei was a quiet man. From time to time, he let out a short remark that shed some light on his past.

During the first session, he had alluded to nightmares. At the second session, he nodded when the subject of sleeping problems was mentioned, and on another occasion he added "me, too" but it was difficult to know what he was referring to. Aside from his love of the cinema, his flashbacks, and his problems with clanking noises, he had exposed little about himself.

* * *

Sergei was born and raised in St. Petersburg, Russia. His father, Nikolai, was a forester and was rarely home. He stayed in distant places for many months, and whenever he came home he was grumpy and hot-tempered. He screamed at his wife Maria, slammed doors, and was capable of polishing off a bottle of vodka in one evening without any help from others. After finishing a bottle, he'd usually fall asleep in the rocker, or sitting at the table if he couldn't manage to get himself from there to the rocker. He would mumble unintelligible words and his snoring was evidence of his deep sleep. Actually, from the perspective of his two small children, there was little difference between his being awake or asleep as he uttered only few words, and paid so little attention to them. For all practical purposes, it was as though Sergei and his sister Miriam grew up without a father. The little that Sergei learned from observing his father was how to be introverted, tense and non-communicative.

By the time Sergei was nine, Maria concluded that there was no point waiting for her husband to change his ways. Together with many others, she immigrated to Israel with her children, though she herself was Russian Orthodox. Her husband, however, did support her in this decision. It was the first and only time that Nikolai had a serious conversation with his son. He told Sergei that he was Jewish, and that his own great-grandfather had been a Rabbi. He personally had little interest in religion, yet in the depth of his soul there was something left from the Jewish practices of his youth. He also understood that the future of Jews in the Soviet Union was dubious. So it seemed to him that immigrating to Israel was a reasonable move, and an opportunity to improve the family's standard of living. He even bent down and kissed Sergei on his cheek (which Sergei could not remember his father ever doing before), and wished him a good trip. He hinted that he might join the family there one day, although he made no promises.

Sergei always remembered this event quite clearly, as it was the single warm encounter between father and son that he could remember. He also recalled that after this kiss from his dad, who on that occasion was sober, he overheard his parents talking at length in their small kitchen. This time they talked in a whisper, and there were no screams, no acrimonious words. The talk was apparently not intended for the ears of the children. Sergei could make out that his mother was crying softly, and he thought he heard her mumble something like, "Thank you for helping." Later he learned that Nikolai had accumulated a sum of money over many months in order to help his wife and children to carry out this revolutionary plan. He was surprised by his father's support, by his kiss, and especially by the effort Nikolai had made to save money out of his meager earnings, so his family could emigrate.

Although Sergei was always aware that his father was Jewish and his mother was not, in one way or another he always thought of himself as a Jew, perhaps because kids in his class occasionally tossed the disrespectful term *"Yid"* at him. He was surprised that his mother would want to emigrate to a faraway land about which she knew very little. He was not, however, surprised that she'd move away from her husband whose rare visits were always accompanied by screams and tension. Sergei secretly felt that not being in Nikolai's presence might bring an improvement to all their lives.

His mother directed Sergei and Miriam to pack only their most precious belongings; only what they could fit into a medium-sized suitcase. Sergei chose carefully. There was the ball with which he played with his friends, a few shirts he liked, and two books: the one he had received from his mother for his eighth birthday, and the one that had been a gift from his Aunt Sonya, his father's sister. These and a few practical items were all he really cared about, and he did not want to cause his mother stress by dragging along unnecessary things.

For years after leaving, he longed for his hometown of St. Petersburg. He missed the wide, gently-curving canals lined with one palace after another, the former residences of the Romanoff Tsars. Aunt Sonya always came on Sunday mornings to take him on excursions in one of the many tour boats that leisurely plied the twisty Neva River and the canals emanating from it. When he was still little, he would snuggle in her lap as she recounted tales of the city's history and described the vision of Peter the Great, the tsar who dreamed of founding a modern city in the style of famous European cities. Sergei soaked up the stories with relish.

These excursions made history come alive for the young boy. They visited the Winter Palace of Peter the Great on several occasions. Sonya explained that the Romanov Tsars did not understand the "people," and lived shockingly wasteful lives, until the people rose up against them and toppled the regime. Every Sunday, she took Sergei to a different area in their gorgeous city and told him of her own childhood memories, when the city had still been known as Leningrad.

They frequently visited the Hermitage Museum, where they always began their tour in the cafeteria with hot chocolate and some delicious dessert. They explored the many galleries, once the giant ballrooms in the palace designed by the famous Italian architect Rastelli, following the directives of Tsarina Elizabeth. In Elizabeth's time, opulent balls took place, with slow dances to Baroque music. Listening to Sonya's descriptions, Sergei imagined himself as a little prince in royal attire being escorted by his aunt.

As the fantasy faded, he would find himself standing in front of famous oils by Rembrandt, Cezanne, Matisse, Renoir and other greats. Sonya explained what the paintings were about, and Sergei absorbed their beauty and this knowledge. At the end of their tour, they would slowly descend the wide steps of the famous staircase made of carrera marble, the architect's pièce de résistance. On the way home, on the street next to St. Isaac's huge church, Sonya bought ice cream cones, and they savored them as they walked.

When Sergei missed St. Petersburg, he was really missing Sonya, the soul closest to his. His mother took care of his physical needs, but she was emotionally distant and did not shower him with love. He knew she loved him, but she rarely expressed any physical affection. Sonya was entirely different. She understood that her brother was a hard and distant man, and that Sergei's mother was also emotionally limited. The affectionate aunt made it her task to fill the gap and sweeten the life of her nephew, whom she loved deeply. She noticed and appreciated his intelligence, his searching questions, and his eyes that scoured the environment with curiosity. She was unmarried and had no children. Her nephew was the son she always yearned for, but never had. So when he moved to Israel, the separation was particularly painful for both of them. They exchanged only a few short words of goodbye, and his eyes pleaded with her not to let him leave. He tried to be a little man and not cry, but inside he was heartbroken.

In Israel, Sergei, his mother, and his sister settled in a modest apartment in Raanana, a well-established town north of Tel Aviv. Maria took a job in a local bakery, owned by other Russian immigrants. After a few months, she stopped wearing the cross that hung from a gold chain, and started studying at an *Ulpan*, an adult Hebrew school for immigrants. In a relatively short period of time she learned sufficient Hebrew to hold a basic conversation. As she continued to work behind the counter interacting with customers, her language improved. Two years later, she was fluent, although listeners could still immediately identify her Russian origins. Many of the customers were also Russian immigrants, and the conversation often shifted from Hebrew to Russian. A native Israeli visiting the bakery when it was full of patrons might have thought that he was in Moscow.

Maria was a private person who did not share her emotions. At home she watched Russian programs on TV, and rarely exchanged more than a few sentences with her young son. She took care of the simple, daily things like clothing and meals, but showed little interest in his studies. She had little reason to worry, as Sergei quickly acclimated to school and picked up Hebrew as a sponge would absorb water. He started reading books in Hebrew. The subjects that attracted him most had to do with cinema, music, and theatre. He read biographies of famous actors, directors, and dancers: Charlie Chaplin, Alfred Hitchcock, Martin Scorsese, Rudolf Nureyev. He could tell stories about the lives of Marlon Brando, Brigitte Bardot, and scores of others. His mother did not share his interests, but she was willing to listen to his descriptions. This was her way of communicating with her son without having to deal with emotions, which were uncomfortable for her.

Sergei faithfully corresponded with Aunt Sonya, and when he was 12, he received a letter from her that mentioned an encounter with his father. Meeting him accidentally on the street one day, she had suddenly been struck by how old and lonely her brother looked. The veins in his nose were swollen, his face red and blotchy. She concluded that his heavy drinking was showing in his body. She did not share these details with Sergei, but she did write that Nikolai had said he was thinking of going on a visit to Israel; not as a precursor to moving there, but from a desire to see his wife and children again.

She was surprised to hear the words "I miss my children, and Maria, too," and even more by the tears she saw in Nikolai's eyes.

Sergei read Sonya's letter many times. He was at a sensitive age, approaching his Bar Mitzvah without any of the parental support that most young boys have for such an important event. He had observed his friends working hard to prepare for the chanting of their Torah portion, and the Haftara – a reading from the later books of the Old Testament that relate to his Torah portion – that followed, and he had no one to help or direct him. His mother knew the importance of the event, but she was Christian and knew very little about Judaism and its customs. Finally, as the event grew closer and her son voiced his anxiety, she enlisted the help of a religiously observant Russian-Jewish woman.

To Sergei's happy surprise, his father did indeed visit, in time to attend his son's Bar Mitzvah. He had coordinated his arrival with Maria, and had even brought nice clothes, a sharp contrast to the usual sloppy attire that was his trademark. He stayed for a week and Sergei heard none of the quarreling between his parents as in years past. Nikolai did drink a lot of vodka, however. He participated in family meals, but said little.

After dinner one night, Sergei noticed his father in a huddle with his sister – an unusual event. Miriam confided later that Nikolai expressed worry about Sergei and his safety as he was approaching enlistment in the army. Although there were still some years before this would happen, Nikolai wasn't certain he'd still be alive when it did, and he wanted to have some input. It didn't escape Sergei's notice that his father shared his worries with his daughter, rather than with his wife. It had always bothered Sergei that his father so clearly lacked any respect for Maria. He had never taken her seriously, and on the rare occasions he discussed anything, he preferred his daughter, a diminutive girl with a sharp mind, to his wife.

A week later Nikolai returned to Russia. He gave Sergei a gold pocket watch, a rare emotional gesture for the type of man he was.

* * *

Miriam was three years older than Sergei, and during his childhood, she often filled the emotional gap their mother left. His sister wasn't close to Aunt Sonya as Sergei was, and at times even perceived her aunt as a rival. Miriam looked after her little brother, babysitting, reading books to him, and putting him to bed. Her mother was quietly relieved that her daughter was so devoted to her brother.

Miriam graduated high school three years before Sergei and enlisted in the army. She completed her service before he started his, and was soon developing a catering business from their small kitchen. While still in school, she had worked in the same bakery as her mother, learning cooking and baking from a Ukrainian woman who worked there. Her beginnings in her home kitchen were modest, consisting mostly of birthday cakes and prettily-decorated cookies for family affairs. Next came salads and hors d'oeuvres for festive occasions. Her mother helped guide her with shortcuts in baking and food preparation, although they did not speak very much. Miriam dreamed of opening her own catering establishment and was delighted that Sergei often joined her in the kitchen, exhibiting an artistic flare and sharing her love for cooking and baking.

The siblings were close, with mutual concern for each other's well-being. Kitchen conversations were great opportunities for Miriam to keep abreast of her brother's life. "Say, Sergei, how goes it at school?" she would ask as she was kneading dough. "It's okay, I'm doing, I have friends and the work isn't difficult" was a typically reassuring response. He would talk to her about his teachers, particularly his art teacher with whom he got along especially well, and about his interest in art and movies. It relieved Miriam to know that the transition from their country of origin hadn't been too difficult for him. His disposition was more easy-going than hers, and he tended not to get riled by small matters. Although he felt strong emotions, he kept them to himself. In that sense, he was like his mother.

The two looked out for each other, with Sergei keeping an eye on the boys Miriam dated, although he trusted her judgment. The two did for each other what a mother, more typical than theirs, would generally do. They did not discuss their mother, and they loved her, but they both understood her emotional limitations. During his brief visit, their father had noticed their closeness. It may have been one of the reasons he chose to talk to his daughter rather than his wife about how his son was managing in Israel.

Toward the end of high school, in the kitchen where most of their talks took place, Miriam turned to her brother and asked, "What are your plans, Sergei? Where do you plan to go in the army?" She had an uneasy suspicion that he would volunteer for a dangerous unit. From the few remarks she had heard him make to his friends, she had surmised that he was thinking of joining a commando unit.

"I'm thinking paratroopers..." he responded hesitantly. He knew where her questions were pointing and wanted to put her mind at ease, but not to lie. His close friend, Ivan was also planning to be a paratrooper, and they wanted to be together. "What do you think?" he asked.

"Look, I knew where you wanted to go; I'm not surprised. But you have to prepare mom. Don't drop it on her in the last minute. She doesn't talk much, but she has thoughts and feelings, and she worries. And you know, even dad is concerned. Years ago, at your Bar Mitzvah, remember when he took me aside and spoke with me?"

"Yes, and what did he say?"

"He tried to convince me to persuade you, when the time comes, to do something safer. He knows you are smart, so he said, 'Why not Intelligence?'"

"I thought of that as well; but, for one thing, that can also be dangerous. Anyway, I want action."

"I understand." And at that, the conversation ended. Miriam understood that a day might come when she would have to deal with the consequences of her little brother's decision.

* * *

After returning from his last stint in the service, Sergei developed some strange gestures. Nearly every time he was about to speak, he would clear his throat, then pause. He often sat with his right hand on his neck, fingers spread apart, thumb gripping one side and fingers gripping the other. It was as though he were pulling on something invisible that was choking him. He was completely unaware of doing this, but his friends were all very aware of it, as was Zev. None of the group members pointed it out. Zev continued to accumulate observations in order to come to an understanding of this unique behavior.

THIRD SESSION

"Today I want to dedicate some of our time to a demonstration, to give you a little instruction in a couple of psychological methods that will become tools for our tool box: techniques we can use anytime to cope with troublesome occurrences," Zev begins.

"When we experience stress, tension, anger, fear, or pain – any unpleasant sensations – we think about them and translate them into descriptions. We use words like: 'I feel like shit; I can't sleep; I feel tense; I have a pain here; my jaw is clenched,' and on and on. Still, the unpleasant sensation persists. It won't go away. It disturbs our sleep, can cause stiff and jerky body movements. It contributes to being short-tempered, to muscle tension, and to restlessness. It causes trouble for us, and it is very desirable to get rid of it, even if only for brief periods of time."

"If we only get rid of it for brief periods and the crappy sensation returns, why even bother?" asks Yariv.

"A good question and here's the answer. When we learn to use relaxation techniques, two processes will occur simultaneously. One is that for however long the relaxation occurs, even if it is brief, we feel no tension. It is like an overheated engine that is cooling down. Second, these methods start to become a way of life, a mode of behavior that gets reinforced and eventually becomes a habit: one that replaces our previous way of functioning. This leads to a more relaxed, pleasant way of life. It challenges that tense way of living, and raises the question, 'Do I have to feel like that? Couldn't I feel different in spite of the difficult situations I've lived through?'"

"It *is* difficult," Uri affirms. "I walk around with tight lips, and my jaw hurts from clenching my teeth all day. Sometimes I look at my hands and they are clenched into fists, and I wasn't even aware of it. And I'm exhausted from all this anxiety and think and pray, 'When will this be over?' But I've given up. It's been like this for several years now, so except for a few occasional moments – like after a cigarette or a beer – I just live with constant tension."

"You're describing exactly what I want to address, so let's try to change it," Zev continues, satisfied that he has prepared the ground for the first demonstration. He had anticipated resistance from these tough fighters, a reluctance to close their eyes in front of the group, or to appear vulnerable in the presence of others. He expected that some of the men would feel shy, would find the exercises childish or too dramatic, and would come up with a reason not to participate. He knew it was important to get at least some confirmation and encouragement from the group before he started a demonstration.

"Let's take, for example, the things that Uri just explained so clearly: tight lips, clenched fists, muscle tension, and fatigue. I'm going to take you on a brief journey, and I encourage everyone who can, to participate. There will be things that will seem a bit strange, but you'll see that there is logic behind them. Let's start.

"Close your eyes and listen to your breathing. Is it smooth, calm, and deep, or is it shallow and jerky? Notice that the chair you are sitting on supports your body and holds you in place, so that you don't float in midair. Additionally, your sitting bones are pressing on the seat and putting weight on it. Notice that there is a reciprocal relationship here: the body presses on the seat, and the seat supports the body.

"Now, start to notice: are your fists clenched? Are your *teeth* clenched? Is there tension in any particular part of your body?

"Our body has three different types of muscles: first, there are *voluntary* muscles, the ones we operate at will, like our arms and legs and head. The second group is *involuntary*, like our intestines and heart, which we cannot control: they are independent, automatic. The third is a single big muscle, the diaphragm, which is both voluntary and involuntary. When we simply breathe without thinking about it, the diaphragm works automatically. But we can also voluntarily decide to take a breath, to deepen it, perhaps to hold it for a few seconds, to breathe faster or more slowly. And we can hold the air in for as much as perhaps a minute. We have some *control* over our breathing.

"We also know from experience that when we are alarmed, our breathing is fast and shallow and our heart rate increases. We may also become pale, and our hands may get sweaty. We can't control these phenomena, and there may be other physiological changes as well.

"So we have no control over the involuntary muscles. But we can control the voluntary ones precisely, and the diaphragm partially, for brief moments that can be repeated. When Uri is sitting here with clenched fists – and I'm sure he's not the only one – he may be unaware of it, as he told us. The voluntary muscles in his hands are tightened in an unnatural manner, he is experiencing tension and feels tired as well. But it doesn't have to be this way.

"Here is the procedure: take a deep breath, and hold in the air for five seconds, counting one one-thousand, two one-thousand, and so on." Zev pauses. "Now let the air out, slowly, in a controlled fashion, and notice how expelling the air slowly actually reduces tension in the body. Repeat this cycle a few times, and deepen the breath a little each time – just a little, to avoid getting dizzy." He pauses, to give the men a little time to try this.

"Now, let's go over the muscle groups to demonstrate how much control we have over them. After we become more aware of this control, learn this technique, and have practiced it several times, our hands will no longer be clenched, unless we decide to shake a friend's hand or grab something."

"Let's start with the head. This might sound strange, but work with me. Perform each action I describe three times. Let's start with the muscles in your face. Imagine that you're about to hear some bad news or something frightening, and scrunch up your entire face: eyebrows, forehead, lips, nose, cheeks, feel a deep tightening of muscles, like 'making a face'; and after five seconds, relax completely. Don't forget to breathe normally. It's easy to forget to breathe when you're concentrating on something else.

"Next, the neck. Raise your head slowly and tilt it backwards until it presses on the upper part of your back. When you're doing this at home, you can do it sitting in a chair; just leave yourself some space for the head movements.

"Now the back. Press against the back of your chair. Then relax. Next, raise your shoulders to the level of the ears, like a small child who is saying 'I don't know.' Then release them. Do this three times; then return to deep, controlled breathing.

"Next are the fists. Clench them very tightly (don't forget to breathe), keep them like that for five seconds, and then relax. Do this three times.

"Now raise your forearms to the shoulders as if 'making a muscle,' and imagine someone wants to pry something out of your hand and you won't allow it. Hold for five seconds, breathe, and then relax.

"The abdomen: remember what it's like to be punched in the stomach. Get ready, as if this were about to happen, turning your belly into a hard, flat surface for five seconds. Breathe, and then relax.

"Next are the thighs, which have the strongest muscle group of the body: the quadriceps. Sit deeply in your seat and raise your feet 90 degrees to level position. Imagine that someone is placing ten pounds on each foot but you won't permit your legs to bend or sink. Three times, five seconds each. Breathe! (You've been forgetting that, right?)

"Now your feet: this is similar to clenching a fist, only with your toes; but don't overdo it – avoid spasms."

"The buttocks: tighten them strongly, hold for five seconds, then relax. Three times.

"Last are the calves. Raise your heel so only the tips of your toes are resting on the floor. Do this carefully also, to avoid muscle cramps; then relax.

"And that's it…we've covered the entire body, top to bottom. Here is a summary of what we did: we contracted and then relaxed every muscle in the body that can be contracted at will – every such muscle that has been contracting on its own without our awareness, causing us tension, discomfort, and fatigue. We've decided that we're going to rule, not them.

"Also, when our heart is beating like crazy because we are fearful or anxious, by relaxing our breathing and our muscles, the heart also relaxes and slows – even though it is an involuntary muscle. With the slowing of our pulse, there is a reduction in anxiety. With the reduction of anxiety, there is an increase in our own sense of control. With an increase in control, our self-confidence increases.

"And with that, comes a return to more normal life, better sleep, fewer muscle aches, less fatigue. It's a magic circle."

It delighted Zev to see that some of the members had followed him during the demonstration, and those who had, looked significantly more relaxed.

"I strongly recommend that you do these at home. Some people prefer to do them alone, others like to have a friend or partner present; it doesn't matter. On average it should take between one and 15 minutes, and the more you practice it, the greater the benefits you will experience. Even once a week is good, twice is better, and so on.

"Now I'd like to demonstrate another method that has a remarkable ability to solve physical problems. Its ability to do this is rooted in neurology and physiology. It is a type of "guided imagery," which we will talk about in detail. It is particularly efficient at getting rid of unpleasant body sensations, like headaches."

"I have a lot of those," puts in Sergei. "So pull it out, I'm dying to know how it works."

"I'm interested too," joins Gil. "I've got these pains in my neck and back, and no matter what positions I try, they won't go away. How much aspirin can a person take?"

It was obvious that there was great interest in this promise of relief; nearly everyone in the group suffered from unpleasant physical sensations that persisted for hours. Most had despaired of finding any relief, resigning themselves to living with their discomfort.

"Who'd like to volunteer for the demonstration?"

Sergei raises a hand and slides forward in his seat.

"Ok Sergei. Could you get into the middle of the circle? That will make it easier for everyone to see what's happening."

"No prob." He moves his chair to the center. At this stage of the group's interactions there is no longer much hesitancy and shyness. Sufficient trust has developed among the guys to try new things, even some which seem strange and unfamiliar.

"Sit with your eyes closed and take a deep breath," Zev begins. "I'm going to ask you a series of questions and will ask you to give me precise answers, even if they sound a bit peculiar. Ok?"

"No problem," and Sergei closes his eyes, sitting comfortably.

"Sergei, look carefully at your headache and describe to us where it is. Exactly where do you feel it? Where is it located?"

"Um...ah...I don't know. A headache, y'know, a pain in the head."

"Exactly where?" presses Zev. "It's important to be very precise with this method to make it work best."

"I don't know, in the forehead...and also in the upper part of the head."

"Excellent. Now you are approaching a description we can work with. Next, what is its shape?"

"What's its *shape*? That's a peculiar question!" Sergei blurts out.

"I know. And there will be other peculiar questions, but let's work together."

"Alright. It's like a long band."

"Great. Where does it start and where does it end?"

"Starts on one side of the forehead and goes across, and also on top of the head to about the middle," Sergei explains.

"So it's about seven inches from side to side, and about four inches to the middle of the head?" asks Zev, honing the description.

"Yeah, something like that. I've never thought about the size of a headache."

"How thick is it?" continues Zev, ignoring Sergei's remark.

"Thickness...thickness...maybe ¾ of an inch."

"And the color?"

"Black, dark, sort of."

"Can one push a finger through it?"

"Finger? Push a finger through a headache...No, I don't think so, it's dense and hard, like a piece of wood."

"And its edges: smooth and sharp, or soft and undefined?"

"Like the dull side of a knife, clearly defined."

"What is its size now?"

"Um...that's interesting – maybe a little less, about ½ inch to an inch shorter at the ends!" Sergei replies, surprised.

The other group members exhibit interest, leaning forward in their seats and being very attentive.

"And the color?"

"A bit lighter, maybe? What's happening here?"

"And the thickness?"

"Less than ¾ inch, perhaps ½ and there is one spot that seems even thinner."

"And the edges? Sharp?"

"No! They are beginning to be soft, like, let's say a picture that's out of focus," replies Sergei, moving in his seat.

"Can one push a finger through it?"

"Yes, with a little pressure I think it's possible."

"Can one get through it to the other side?"

"Um....ah...yes, and it's looking much brighter now, sort of bluish and a little white."

"And the size?" Zev continues the therapeutic marathon.

"Maybe half of what it was when we started," replies Sergei with increasing astonishment.

"And the thickness?"

"This is crazy!! It's beginning to be like a thin piece of cardboard."

"And the edges?"

"Like cotton candy – soft, difficult to define, blending into its surroundings."

"And the size?"

"Only, maybe, three inches in width and 1½ on the head."

"And the color?"

"Gone, there's no color. I don't see any color."

"Dense?"

"No! Sort of soft. You could push your finger through it from one side to the other for sure, like passing a finger through water."

"Thickness?" Zev is pushing to get to a conclusion.

"There is no thickness, its like tissue paper."

"Size?"

"Size...I no longer see a shape, so there is no size! I can't believe it, I think it's gone!"

"What's left from your headache?"

"Nothing! It's gone! No shape, no color. My headache disappeared, there's just a dull, mild sensation; it's amazing!"

Zev falls silent and allows everyone to digest this information. The silence in the room is one of amazement, in contrast to other times when the silences were filled with tension. Zev is always surprised anew by the effectiveness of this technique and eager to pass it on to his clients. It is one of his favorite therapeutic tools, although he has never quite understood how it works. But he comforts himself with the thought that it is still not completely clear how aspirin or other wonder drugs work either, yet they are effective and widely used.

"Wow! That's something, this method!" Uri chimes in, cutting the silence. "Does it always work like that?"

"Nothing always, *always* works, but often it does. It's definitely worth using, but one must pay attention to all the nuances, so let's review it again briefly, to anchor it in our heads.

"We begin by looking decisively at the pain, penetrating it with our mind's eye, focusing all our attention on it, and concentrating on the physical sensation. We localize it precisely – where is the pain? Estimate its physical size; see its boundaries – its thickness, shape, color, and density.

"We estimate its hardness, softness, and then its location again, because it may have migrated to another location, verify the size, thickness, etc. repeatedly, until there isn't anything more to describe."

Zev sits up, satisfied with the success of the demonstration. He fervently hopes that the guys will take it home and use this unique type of guided imagery.

* * *

"And now for another subject that you've been waiting for: medication.

"Who here is receiving medications to help manage the PTSD?"

Several hands go up.

Yossi explains that a doctor prescribed sleeping pills for him. Three others also say they use them.

"Does it help?" asks Zev.

"Sometimes more, sometimes less. If I take one and don't fall asleep after an hour, I sometimes take another pill. But the trouble is that the next day I feel a little groggy, so I tend to avoid doing that," explains Avi, who has been suffering from night terrors.

"There are many different drugs for that purpose. You have to experiment until you find the one that works best for you," adds Zev. "And after a while, it should be alternated with a different sleep medication."

"I take Paxil for depression. I started with Prozac, but it wasn't doing any good, so the doctor switched it. It helps," Ido adds.

"I have a lot of anxiety," joins Gil, "and the doctor prescribed Xanax, and it works well. I keep a few pills in my wallet, and if I have an anxiety attack anywhere, I take one, and within half an hour I'm much calmer."

Zev begins to summarize: "So you see, there are three categories of medications that help in our situation. One is for sleep, both for falling asleep and for staying asleep. The second group is for calming down and relieving anxiety, and this type of drug works very quickly, usually within half an hour. Anti-anxiety medication can be taken as needed, or on a regular basis.

"The third group is the anti-depressants, and these must be taken very differently: consistently, with no interruptions, just as prescribed, because it takes four to six weeks before they kick in. If you were to stop taking the medication and then start it again, it might take even longer to work, or might not work as well as before. There is a large array of medications and it's worthwhile to keep in mind that they are there when needed. I don't believe that avoiding taking meds is a sign of masculinity: it just causes unnecessary suffering. At the same time, no need to go overboard. And along with medications, we must use the therapeutic techniques we already demonstrated, and others, to cope with the demons."

Zev's last words fell on fertile ground, because about half the group was being helped by medications while the others either avoided them or put off using them. Zev is well aware that, even today, there are objections among certain segments of the population, people who insist, "I don't believe in drugs," and he believes that this is often to their detriment.

* * *

Suddenly Sergei looks tired and tense. His blue eyes are quite bloodshot, and the guys try to guess if this is the result of weeping, or perhaps an allergy. But neither of those has caused his suddenly weary face. The culprit is flashbacks and nightmares that rob him of sleep and steal his nights. These are common events for Sergei. Shortly after he had returned from battle, he started experiencing them several times a week. As weeks and months passed, their frequency declined, but they never completely disappeared.

Miriam, Sergei's older sister, has become very concerned about his welfare and his disturbed nights. One evening as they were sitting together in the kitchen of their apartment, she asked what was wrong. He explained about the nightmares, and told her that he preferred sleeping during the day, for an hour or two here and there. It seemed to him that daylight was easier for him than darkness, maybe because in the dark the colors of the nightmares were so vivid, and the bright flashes of light and explosions thick with smoke were more alarming. He slept restlessly, tossing and turning from side to side, moaning, and sometimes sitting up sharply, mumbling unintelligible words. He would find himself clutching an imaginary submachine gun, aiming it in all directions. At other times he'd be raising his arms in a defensive position, protecting himself from an unseen enemy. Miriam listened anxiously. She knew she could not possibly imagine how powerful and terrifying these dreams were. It was no wonder, she thought, that her brother did not want to go to sleep at night.

* * *

Someone in the group has started to talk about something, but Sergei isn't listening. He gazes out the window at the setting sun. The wind is lapping at leaves and making them dance in circular motions. He hears people speaking around him, but they sound far away. He is seeing images of wounded lying on stretchers, some screaming, others silent. He hears the cries for medics, sees a physician walking among the stretchers and motioning a medic to cover one with a blanket, over the man's face.

Sergei leaps from his seat, raising his arm to cover his eyes. He is unaware of his actions, and only after he hears Zev repeating:

"Sergei, are you alright?" does he understand what has happened: he has once again experienced one of those flashbacks. He had felt as though he was right there at that very moment, in the battalion field hospital, having just encountered a group of armed Hamas fighters. There were casualties, and he had tried to help as much as he could. The sight of the wounded soldier, who was no longer wounded, who had moved beyond injury into the final category, marked by the doctor's hand motion, was too much to bear; and Sergei covered his eyes.

"Yes, what? Where am I?" he awakens with a start, slowly comprehending that he is with the group, that Zev is talking to him, that the guys look worried. He feels a sense of shame and embarrassment. Zev calmly explains what Sergei already knows – that he was experiencing a flashback of a terrifying event, and that, for a few seconds, he was detached from reality. That in fact he had drifted away from sitting in a chair, among friends, with a group leader, in a safe and protected place, where others were concerned with his well-being.

"I was hoping that this would never happen in the presence of others. It's so embarrassing, I'm sorry."

"Not at all, you've nothing to be ashamed of. Unfortunately, this is one of the disturbing occurrences that we must cope with and it's no different from being startled and upset by noises, or not wanting to answer the phone. How often does it happen?" asked Zev gently. He wants to return Sergei to the present moment, to explain the event, and to calm and encourage him.

"From time to time, like twice a week. It was worse earlier on, right after I returned from Gaza and Lebanon. It's less often now. It's always frightening and confusing, as if I'm not here. When I come to, I have that awful feeling, as if I've lost control over my life. I hate it," and he avoids everyone's eyes.

AVI

Avi joined the conversation from his corner: "That's also a problem for us" and fell silent. What he was referring to was excluding his wife by not telling her his story.

At 35, Avi is the group's oldest member. He is married and the father of four children. A "*Kibbutznik*" from the north and first-generation Israeli, he grew up in the kibbutz, becoming a shepherd. The son of a mechanically talented father, he eventually learned welding and metal works, which he developed into a thriving business years after he left the kibbutz. He is short, stocky, and muscular with strong hands and short fingers. He tends to have a serious expression on his face, and although something of a "macho man," he has a soft side, which can reveal itself unexpectedly.

Avi is one of a small group who still has an interest in stamp collecting. The many hours he spent tending his sheep allowed him to do a lot of reading about foreign countries, which led to a fascination with stamps. He subscribes to the Philatelic Society and once a year he pampers himself by buying the annual "Israeli Stamps Album," the complete collection of stamps issued that year, in a posh binding with elaborate explanations. On the day of its arrival, he would examine each page and sink into a reverie, sailing to the ends of the earth on the coattails of his beloved stamps, imagining himself floating about in those wondrous locations.

His parents, Zigo and Sonya, had immigrated to Israel from

Bulgaria in the 1960s, part of a group that arrived with the help of "the Jewish Agency" (the largest organization in charge of immigration to Israel). They had been married for a number of years and had thought about leaving Bulgaria for some time, but had delayed their departure to complete the liquidation of Sonya's parents' family business, which had been thriving for two generations.

Sonya and Zigo met when she was still a high school student, and he, at age 20, was a company clerk. Zigo was stocky with a head of thick brown hair, an endearing smile, and a touch of shyness. Sonya was vivacious, with grey-green eyes, sandy-colored hair, a shapely figure, and an exuberant laugh. She exuded warmth.

He courted her for weeks before she accepted his invitation to coffee in a local café. Sonya enjoyed the attention he lavished on her and played hard-to-get, but inside she knew he had caught her. Both of them came from a middle-class Jewish background, from well-established and affluent families. They shared the same values, and had an easy time connecting emotionally with each other.

It wasn't clear who brought it up first, but within months of dating, the subject of emigrating arose. They met with a man from the Jewish Agency and agreed to think about it seriously, which indeed they did.

The tension around selling the family business, saying goodbye to their families, and dealing with several sets of raised eyebrows in reaction to their decision, led to their first arguments. But they were deeply in love and these spats quickly subsided with a kiss from Zigo to which Sonya readily responded with her own passionate kiss.

They settled in a Kibbutz in the north. The transition from being businesspeople in Sophia, the capital of Bulgaria, to farming, was not an easy transition for them, physically or mentally. Fortunately there were other Bulgarian-speaking people in the Kibbutz, so their social life continued with new friends and people who shared their ideology. Zigo quickly learned how to operate a tractor and other farm equipment. After just a few years, he became a farmer in body and soul. His European garb; dark suits with conservative neckties and carefully pleated slacks, gave way to crumpled khakis in the summer and spring. Love for the land and the culture captured him, and he soon found himself humming Hebrew songs that only a short time ago he had never heard.

Sonya had a good ear for languages – she already spoke Yiddish, German, and Russian – and she learned Hebrew with amazing speed. The workers in the Kibbutz's business office soon recognized that she had intelligence and strong administrative skills. Initially she had been assigned to the chicken coops, which were an important source of income for the Kibbutz; but after a few months, the secretary, Moshiko, who was also a Bulgarian, approached her about working in the office.

* * *

Despite more Spartan living conditions than they had been accustomed to and hard work, their romance continued to blossom. The subject of children emerged, but they weren't quite ready to become parents. They wished to spend a few more years just enjoying each other and their freedom as a couple.

Within a few years they both spoke Hebrew well, and during "Communal Meetings," they began voicing their opinions about the direction the kibbutz should be taking. Drawing on their professional skills, they suggested a plan for creating a commercial enterprise. There had been a gradual decline in the importance of the chicken trade, and the income it brought in had shrunk. It was therefore scaled down to cover the needs of the Kibbutz and that of two neighboring Kibbutzim. Aided by Sonya and Zigo's business acumen, the chicken coops were ultimately replaced by a modern factory that manufactured brass water valves of superior quality and contemporary design, inspired by Italian styling. Much of its production was aimed at exporting these goods throughout Europe. The fact that Sonya spoke fluent Bulgarian, German and Russian, and had managed to add English to her repertoire, propelled her to a high position within the factory. She became the assistant to the factory's business manager, spent hours on the phone talking to Europe, and had a hand in setting prices. Her days in the chicken coops were behind her.

Zigo also advanced in his work. He loved the tractor, and in his free time he liked to read professional magazines about agricultural equipment. Initially, he could only study the pictures and mechanical drawings, but over the years he took some courses in English and gradually started reading the text.

At times, as he was leafing through the journals, he'd suddenly jump off his sofa and hurry to the equipment shed to check out a technical detail in one of their machines. Then he would go to Micha, who was in charge of all the mechanical equipment, with an idea to improve a machine's functioning. Micha was also a mechanical nut and was open to Zigo's ideas. Often they would hurry over to the welding torch and modify the equipment. Gradually, other Kibbutzim started adopting their innovations. As time passed, the Kibbutz developed Zigo's and Micha's inventions into a thriving commercial enterprise they named "S.A.E.": "Sophisticated Agricultural Equipment." It soon became a name in the agricultural industry and orders for their products came streaming in. Zigo still enjoyed working on his tractor, but eventually he came to devote more of his time to technical innovations and less to plowing. He took on the Hebrew name "Yirmi," which derived from the prophet Jeremiah.

Twenty years after his first invention, a brief article he'd written about the S.A.E. (with assistance from an English-speaking American immigrant) appeared in one of the technical journals that he used to leaf through without understanding a word. When the article about S.A.E. appeared, Yirmi's achievements became a great source of pride for the entire Kibbutz.

In Sophia, Zigo and Sonya hadn't observed many Jewish traditions, hadn't attended Friday night services or lit the Sabbath candles. In fact, they worked at least half-days on Saturday, the Jewish Sabbath. But on the Kibbutz, Friday nights were special. Zigo's filthy work clothes gave way to a long-sleeve white shirt and well-fitting khakis. His festive attire was preceded by a warm shower and a long, meticulous shave. His hair was carefully combed and his entire appearance was one of tranquility and respect. Sonya's Friday-night clothing was equally special: an embroidered blouse with a delicate collar and a pastel-colored skirt. Everyone looked their best.

The Friday-night meal was richer and the tables were covered with white tablecloths. Traditional Jewish foods, including chicken soup and chicken dishes, appeared on the tables. Sabbath candles flickered in the corner of the large communal dining hall. Although this Kibbutz was not a religious one, it did observe some traditions and the Sabbath candles were part of them. At the conclusion of the festive meal, Nissan would pull out his accordion and everyone would burst out with modern Israeli songs. The unique atmosphere of *"Erev Shabat,"* "Friday Night," exuded a sense of togetherness, security, pride and calm.

* * *

"Yirmi," whispered Sonya one evening.

"What?" he asked, sensing something different in his wife's voice.

"Yirmi..." and she hesitated a moment, lowering her voice, "I have something to tell you."

The hesitation in her voice confirmed his suspicion. He was shaken, fearful she might be telling him some bad news.

"What is it, Sonya, what?" he asked, alarmed.

"No, no, nothing bad, all's well, don't worry, it's only that..."

"What? Say it already" he muttered impatiently.

"It's been several weeks that in the mornings I'm a bit nauseous."

"Did you eat some bad food? Do you have a stomach problem? Did you go see the nurse?" he asked.

"No, sweetie. My stomach is just fine. It's something else..." and a huge smile spread across her face.

"No!!! Really? Is that what you mean?"

"Yes. I think I'm pregnant, sweetheart. We're going to have a child, a Sabra" – an Israeli-born child.

"When?"

"I'm still at the beginning, just a month or so. I guess by the end of the summer" she replied proudly.

He leapt from his chair to hug her. A wave of joy and pride swept over him. He'll be a father, like his own father, like his grandfather, and here, in their new home, their new life, in the Kibbutz!

He was also a little shaken by the idea: What does one do with a baby? Someone would have to guide them. He was glad they were living within this framework of group life: someone there would surely be an expert with babies, he hoped.

Avi was born at the end of the summer. He weighed 7 pounds and 13 ounces, and had a lock of hair over his forehead and thick, dark eyebrows. He didn't scream as most other babies did, and seemed to be calmly observing his surroundings. Zigo tenderly kissed his newborn son and his wife, and a tear of happiness and gratitude crept down Sonya's cheek. The young couple had accomplished one more goal they had been striving for: to bring a child into this world, to the homeland, to the Kibbutz.

Avi was only the third child to be born there.

Children grew up in the Children's House, where they slept and were fed and cared for, rather than sleeping with their parents, implementing the then-prevailing philosophy of communal childhood rearing and education. Ofra, one of the veteran members, had a lot of experience in dealing with babies, since she was the oldest in a family with many children, and she had been put in charge of the Children's House. The kids were in each others' company 24 hours a day. Their early schooling took place at an educational institute on the grounds of a neighboring Kibbutz, similar to a regional school. In the afternoons, after completing their homework, they'd play ball, tag, and hide and seek in the yard near the school. Toward evening, they would visit with their parents and sometimes have dinner with them, especially as they got a little older. After dinner they'd return to the Children's House and spend the night there.

Avi's handwriting was rounded and clean. On those occasions when his mother spent time with him, she insisted on good penmanship. She found herself wishing she could spend much more time with her son, but being a loyal Kibbutz member and adhering to its ideology, she accepted its authority and made do with what little time was allotted to her. In her heart of hearts, she didn't believe that separating children from their parents was the best way to raise them, but she was inexperienced in child rearing and complied with the rules. In the little time they shared, she made an effort to influence Avi's upbringing and personality, even if it could only be to a small extent.

One rainy winter night when Avi was seven, he came down with the flu. He was boiling with fever, coughing severely, and nauseous. His joints ached and he felt miserable. He was unable to speak coherently, and drifted in and out of sleep. Ofra, the woman in charge of the Children's House, gave him a warm, sweetened drink and a pill to reduce his fever, covering him with an extra blanket. She took care of his physical needs but she didn't sit at the edge of his bed as his mother would have, didn't stroke his burning head or comfort him. She merely said a few practical words, such as "tomorrow you'll feel better, drink your tea," then hurried off to look after the other children. She didn't think it was necessary to let Sonya know that her son was sick, feeling it was her own responsibility to see to him. Ofra was from the ilk of women who can "do it all" and who rise to any challenge, but who show little emotion.

Avi started hallucinating with fever. In his disturbed sleep, he was yearning for his mother and wished she'd come and hold him, cover him with kisses, and say soothing words in her gentle voice. At times he felt so terrible he wanted to cry out "*Ima, Ima*," but he didn't want his friends to think of him as a crybaby, so he bit his quivering lips and sobbed quietly under the blanket.

Avi felt abandoned, frightened, and alone. He thought with envy about his cousin who lived in Tel Aviv with his parents. When David was sick, his mother would sit at the edge of his bed, stroking his head and singing soothing songs to him in a soft, calming voice. He would be receiving pills and hot tea like Avi, but the emotional medicine of a loving mother was even more important, and that's exactly what Avi didn't get. He feared that if he were to complain and request his *Ima*, Ofra would feel offended and respond unpleasantly. So he didn't ask. He had reached the conclusion that Ofra was unlikely to help him in his distress, and this made him feel even more lonely and anxious. Finally, in desperation, he nodded off.

* * *

Yirmi reached the rank of major in the army. This was due in part to his outstanding knowledge of mechanical matters, which his commanders relied on. During the Yom Kippur War, he participated in the fierce tank battles on the Golan Heights. The engine of one of the tanks stopped, exposing it to Syrian fire. Yirmi's commander looked for him.

"Yirmi, in the third tank in front of you, the engine has stopped. Take a look and see what you can do."

Yirmi left his own tank, and under cover of his comrades, crept to the immobilized tank. He identified the problem and felt sure he could restart the errant engine. But at exactly that moment, the tank was hit by an anti-tank missile, and Yirmi was sent flying. When he woke up in Rambam Hospital in Haifa, Sonya's scared face hovered above his. He recuperated in a few weeks and returned to his Kibbutz.

Years later, he started becoming irritable and short-tempered. The sound of the missile hitting the tank came back to him in his dreams, and sometimes even when he was awake. As Sonya became aware of the change in his temperament, she tried talking to him about it. "It's nothing, it's from the hot weather, it has nothing to do with the Golan," he blurted out, then changed the subject.

And though Avi was aware of the events his father had experienced on those infamous cliffs, the Golan Heights, before he was born, they never spoke of them.

FOURTH SESSION

"Had you ever heard of guided imagery before I mentioned it during our last session?" asks Zev.

"I hadn't," answers Yariv.

"Anyone else heard of it?" Zev scanned the group. Since it included people from all walks of life, and varied backgrounds, it was possible some of them might be familiar with this psychological technique.

"Guided imagery is a category of treatment methods in which we imagine events that could happen, without actually experiencing them. The idea is to create an imaginary scenario and combine it with relaxation techniques, which we've already used. In this way, we can take a frightening situation, an unpleasant memory, or the anticipation of an unknown event that is potentially upsetting, and gradually, gently, defuse it of its sting. This might sound a bit abstract, but I'll demonstrate it, and explain it to you in detail."

"I don't get it," says Avi.

"Is anyone prepared to volunteer so that I can demonstrate?"

Gil suddenly shifts forward in his chair. At this point, he has acclimated somewhat to the group and seems more willing to participate.

"That depends," he says now, narrowing his eyes. "If it is suddenly going to become scary, I don't want to; but if I can trust you to guide me slowly, that's fine."

"Thanks. I promise to try. But what you expressed goes to the heart of the method: that is, the pace of the exercise will depend solely on you, and I will be taking my cues from you, not the other way around. So, are you game?"

"I guess." Gil moves his chair to the center of the circle.

"Choose a scene, an image, a mental picture of something that is bothersome to you, something that you find yourself unable to cope with, and whenever you try to do it, you run away from it."

"That business of not wanting to travel south, because it reminds me of the incident in the Gaza Strip, and how I almost didn't get out of there."

"Good example; but, first tell us *why* you want to go there. Why couldn't you just decide never to go there again?"

"Two good reasons: first, I have an aunt I love, who lives in Nahal Oz, a kibbutz very close to Gaza; and I can't expect her to always come to Petah Tikvah, where I live. And second, what kind of man am I if I can't overcome my fears and travel to the southern part of my own country?" answered Gil, his tone irritated.

"I asked the question because your motivation is a major factor. It would be difficult to lead a person through guided imagery that will include tense moments if he or she isn't motivated to achieve results. No one likes to jump into a cold shower, unless you stink and there is no warm water. Something has to motivate you from within."

"Ok, I get it."

"We'll start by assessing the degree of tension you are experiencing right now. We'll create a "Units of Distress" scale which will tell us how stressed you feel at any moment. Starting at zero, meaning no tension at all, like being almost asleep and going all the way up to ten, an unbearable level of tension; where would you place yourself right now?"

Gil rolls his eyes, shifting in his chair, and grumbles something under his breath. Finally he looks around at the others, then back at Zev and offers: "maybe around five, something like that."

"Very good. In other words, just in the middle, neither particularly calm nor particularly tense. Now I'll start weaving a story that is connected to your goal, and the moment you feel the slightest change in tension, you'll raise your finger to let me know the level has changed, and give me the new number. You understand?"

"Yeah. It already jumped; the moment you said that you'll be 'weaving a story', I tensed up and could feel my heart beating."

"So your tension bumped up to what number?"

"Maybe seven or eight."

"Okay. Now take a deep breath, calm yourself down, and when you're back at five or six, raise your finger again."

Gil shut his eyes, made himself more comfortable in his seat, and took a deep breath. Silence fell on the group. The guys all looked curious to see what would happen. Gil raised his finger, and his face seemed to relax.

"And the number?" inquired Zev.

"Six."

"Good. The story starts with you wanting to visit your aunt... "

Gil's finger flew up as though triggered by a tightly wound spring.

"The number?"

"Eight!"

"You know what to do, right? Deep breath, inner calming, relaxation of the muscles that feel tight." Zev guided Gil, while explaining the process to everyone.

Seconds passed that felt like minutes. Gil finally raised his finger.

"I've returned to five – six."

"You intend to visit…what is her name? in Nahal Oz."

The finger jumps, Zev falls silent.

"Hanna, my sweet aunt. I'm at seven."

Zev waits quietly until Gil raises his finger again and announces: "Five." It is clear that he is understanding the method and using it successfully.

"You are planning to visit Hanna…" and Zev waits. Gil's finger is still.

He continues, "You are picking up the phone to call…" The finger snaps up. There is visible tension in Gil's face.

Zev waits. When the finger goes up signaling calm, he gently continues.

"You are dialing to call Hanna." He pauses to see if Gil is tolerating this development. It seems that he is. "You are about to tell her that you miss her…" The finger jumps. After Gil has calmed himself, Zev repeats, "... about to tell her you miss her." He pauses briefly, then continues. "And she's happy to hear from you, and asks 'So, when do we see you here?'" – the finger just about jumps off the hand.

"Gil, what's the number?"

"Eight, even higher."

"Calm down before we move on, ok? We'll only continue when you're back at five."

Moments pass. The guys look quietly from Zev to Gil, absorbing the method. The demonstration evokes a combination of curiosity, tension, and hope. A minute ago, Gil wasn't even able to contemplate a trip, and now he's having a conversation about it with his aunt.

"Five, let's go on."

"Hanna wants to know when you might be coming south." Here Zev deliberately inserts the word 'south.' "She proposes that you come in a week or two." Nothing happens. Gil is sitting quietly, listening.

"You reply that that's too soon, but she continues to press you..." and the finger flies up into the air.

Gil signals to continue.

"Hanna is pushing you to come in two weeks... " he pauses, watching for a signal from Gil, then continues: "and you're saying that you'll think about it."

Gil looks tense but does not raise his finger.

"What's happening? You look tense but you're not signaling to me. What's up?" Zev asks.

"Not sure, a little tense but I don't think the number has gone up," explains Gil.

"It's important that you listen to your body. Pay attention to any muscle tension, rapid breathing, pounding of your heart, and observe it, but don't try to interpret it. Your body is what determines your level, not your thoughts, ok?" Zev adds this additional clarification because it appears that Gil may have veered off track and returned to his original unsuccessful strategy of trying to handle his discomfort by using his thoughts, rather than the new coping tools.

"Ok, so it's six-seven," admits Gil.

* * *

Zev waits, and soon Gil signals that he can resume.

"You are making plans with Hanna to arrive by bus at six in the evening... " The finger jumps up. When Gil has calmed himself, Zev starts to pick up the pace.

"The bus is leaving Petah Tikvah at 4:15, so you have to be there at four to buy a ticket and get a good seat..." Zev waits. The finger stays bent. Now, even though the details are very realistic, they are no longer evoking the same anxiety. It appears that Gil can use the method effectively. The kind of stimulus that made him jump just a little while ago has lost its power. He no longer feels threatened and scared.

Zev continues filling in more and more details, such as packing pajamas for the nights at his aunt's, selecting a present to bring her, explaining to his boss that he has to leave work half an hour earlier to catch the bus, and other details that are even more challenging. He adds a guided-imagery description of a trip around the area with Hanna during his stay, even going to see the fence around the Gaza strip – getting even closer to the site of Gil's traumatic experience.

Gil smiles and winks toward the other guys, looking as if he has escaped from a den of lions. The others are also smiling, and a couple of them laugh and shake their heads in disbelief. Zev takes a moment to explain that this method is useful for all kinds of situations that arouse anxiety or fear.

"It works for social events with family, friends, and employers," he notes.

Yossi, stroking his thin beard absentmindedly, can be heard mumbling, "I'm going to try to use this for that business of clanking metal..." and as others turn to look at him he remains deep in thought, ignoring them. Zev smiles.

"I see that you've gotten the idea and are starting to work with it on your own," he addresses Yossi. "Good. Continue, and next week you can tell us how it worked."

Yossi, startled out of his reverie, looks up, a bit embarrassed. "Yes, ok, I'll be working on it."

Avi straightens up, raising his hand like a child in a classroom. "I'll try it, too. I have recurring nightmares about Rami."

It is obvious that this mention of Rami is a hint to the headline of Avi's story. The others sit quietly, waiting for him to continue. Avi hesitates, than continues.

"We were in the West Bank, in a casbah, one of those old neighborhoods like you see in a movie; a maze of narrow streets, high walls, shuttered windows, and always people watching from every corner. We were looking for men wanted for terrorist acts. Our force entered with jeep-style vehicles, which are quite wide, and the streets and alleys were very narrow. There was a bad feeling and a lot of tension. The night was particularly dark as there was no moon. The darkness gave us good cover, but it also made it difficult for us to see where we were going. Some of us had been there before, for others it was the first time. My friend Rami and I left our vehicle and started to go from house to house. We had a list of suspects we were looking for. One was a grocer, and we started by going to his store. He wasn't there. The guy behind the counter whistled the moment we appeared, and the other workers looked at us strangely. One leapt toward the rear door, as if to block it. I looked at Rami and he winked at me. It was obvious they had been expecting us, and the whistle was a signal for the wanted man to get lost. He managed to escape, but we had his home address, Intelligence had supplied us with it, and we left the grocery. Again, there was a bad feeling, and there was fear. The narrow alleyways, the darkness, the hostile environment, and the fact that our arrival had been anticipated and the men there were ready for us, all increased our tension.

"Rami and I had been together in the army and the reserves. He was my closest friend in the entire service. There were times when I'd had it with the training and the commanders, with battalion comrades who got on my nerves, and Rami always calmed me down and encouraged me. I'd visited his home a thousand times. His mother, a widow, always greeted me happily with a smile. She'd call me Avi'le, affectionately. She'd put out coffee and homemade cake, and then she'd disappear, giving us the freedom to chat about anything we wished. Rami smoked a lot, and that worried her. She begged him to stop, 'Because it's not good for you,' but he'd wave her off with a hand gesture. From time to time, when we were sitting together, I'd light one as well. Her face would fall, and she would leave the room – she'd lost her battle. Rami would get up and go over to her, hug her gently, and whisper in her ear, '*Ima*, it's not so terrible, it's just a cigarette, I won't die from it, don't believe all the media reports," and he'd kiss her on the cheek. And I remember she'd say, 'Just be well, my Rami.'

"And he came to my house, too. We'd sit in the living room, smoke cigarettes, and talk and talk. My wife was usually at work, and if Rami and I met up in an evening, she'd come in, say 'hi,' and leave the room. She didn't play hostess or interfere. She knew he was important to me and she gave us our space."

Avi stopped talking, took a deep breath, and prepared himself and his listeners for what was coming. No one rushed him. Everyone understood that whatever was next, wouldn't be easy for him.

"We left the grocery going to the man's home. Behind us, the other guys followed in pairs. We walked in a row, looking in all directions, necks straining, weapons cocked; tension and fear hanging in the air. We arrived at the grocer's apartment. The television was blasting, there were kids running around, women gabbing. We reached the door and suddenly there was complete quiet. Someone shut off the TV, the kids and women fell silent. I guess they had been alerted right after we left the grocery. They have a system of communication, from one mouth to another, and they are very sophisticated, sending messages quietly and efficiently. It is impossible to surprise them once you arrive at the *casbah*. Everyone there is alert, ready for anything. We knocked on the door and one of the women opened it. 'Where's Abu...' I don't remember his name exactly.

"'He not here'," she replied in broken Hebrew with an Arabic accent. 'Where is he?' I repeated the question, knowing full well that any answer we'd receive would be useless for finding him.

"'We not know' she mumbled, but it was obvious that she was nervous and lying.

"It is clear that Abu, or whatever his name was, had escaped and certainly not into his own bedroom. We decided not to search the apartment and to return to our vehicles. Perhaps someone else would have better luck, but we doubted it, because someone had alerted everyone to our operation before we even arrived. We walked back through dark alleys, tense and disappointed by the failure of our mission."

Here Avi pauses. He has a faraway look in his eyes, and when he continues, it is as though the room has fallen away and he is somewhere else.

"We are about ten feet from our vehicles when there is a huge explosion. A vehicle flies into the air, flips over, and lands on Rami. He lets out a long, blood-curdling shriek, then falls silent. He is pinned under the vehicle and he's moaning. The darkness is horrible. I must free him but I don't know where to start. The blast threw me and I'm leaning against the wall of a house. Adrenalin is coursing through my body. Suddenly there is an outburst of shots from submachine guns and explosions from hand grenades coming from all over. We've been ambushed! They simply waited for us to return to the vehicles, knowing that we were stuck in these narrow alleyways, not knowing all their twists and turns, easy targets. My fear is gone. Now I'm furious. Someone is calling for the evacuation helicopters. There are others who are injured, not just Rami. There is the smell of gunpowder and smoke in the air and the cries of the injured come from all directions.

"I call out, 'Rami? Rami?' and hear nothing. Just more gunshots, bursts of fire, explosions, flashes of light, and another big burst of gunfire. And I'm thinking of Rami being stuck under the car, and my mind is going crazy. I pull out the flashlight, breaking the rules, and in a split second of light I find him. He is looking at me, whispering faintly 'I can't feel my arm…' I crawl under the vehicle – and see the blood flowing from where his arm used to be. It isn't there. I feel the urge to vomit, but I know he will bleed to death within minutes – unless I save him. 'Rami, I'm getting you out of here, it'll be ok.' My flashlight makes me a target and I turn it off. I call for help and two other guys come rushing. I gather all my strength and we manage to tilt the heavy car a few inches and I pull Rami out. He is silent. I lay him on the sidewalk, tying a tourniquet on the stump of his arm. The bleeding stops. I inject him with morphine, and gently stroke his cheek, fire coming from all directions. The smell of burning flesh chokes me. I hear the helicopter above me. We lift him off the sidewalk. His body is limp, heavy, shapeless – not the body of a young, fit fighter lifting such weights in the gym that others watch in amazement. Now he's like a rag, dripping blood, silent. He's

79

not even moaning. I'm looking at him, and I know he recognizes me. His lips are moving but I can't understand what he's saying. 'Rami, we are on the way. A few more minutes and we'll be at the hospital. Hang in there, buddy, hang in!' I plead and encourage him, still stroking his cheek. Another soldier and I manage to load him onto the helicopter. I run back to the overturned vehicle; rescue another injured guy lying next to it. We load him onto the chopper as well, and it immediately takes off while hellish fire is directed at it.

"I drop to the sidewalk. 'I saved Rami, I saved Rami,' I moan as bursts of fire continue to hit the walls of the houses, splattering chunks of stone and concrete. I'm covered with dust from head to toe. The smell of burning flesh is overpowering, and I understand where it's coming from. There is no lamb being roasted here... there is no barbecue going on... these are my friends... and I push the thoughts out of my head.

"I don't understand how or why, but no bullets hit me. Chunks of stone hit my helmet with ominous sounds, sharp, short 'pings.' My back hurts, and I know it is from lifting the car. I'm numb and exhausted; but I had managed to save Rami. His lips were moving when we loaded him on, and his chest was going up and down.

"Minutes later, everyone has been evacuated. During that eternity, we returned fire in every direction, but who knows if we hit anything. I climb into the helicopter in which I am finally evacuated and two bodies lie next to me. There had been no one to save these unfortunate guys. I grab a blanket and use it to cover one of them. I turn my head away because I can't look at the second one. Such a young kid, surely not even 20 years old. What will become of his mother and father when they hear what has happened? I close my eyes. Suddenly I feel a thump. We've landed. We arrive at the hospital and are immediately taken into the ER. I drop onto a gurney. I don't remember what happened afterwards."

The silence in the room is palpable.

"You did something, you really did!" Yariv finally exclaims. "You saved your friend under hellish fire, and you endangered your own life for him. More power to you."

Avi does not react. The others are puzzled. All's well that ends well. Why doesn't he even nod his head?

Zev starts speaking. "What Avi hasn't told us, is that Rami was unconscious when he arrived at the ER and died within a week. He never regained consciousness. Avi also hasn't told us that the second soldier he freed, survived and recovered. And what we also haven't heard, is that Avi was awarded the Medal of Valor for his heroism."

A sad and heavy silence engulfs the room. Now it is obvious why Avi is so unhappy. They don't know, and never will, that in the privacy of his room he strokes the pin he earned, in the same tender manner in which he stroked Rami's cooling cheek.

*   *   *

Touched by Avi's revelations, Sergei feels encouraged to begin telling his own story. "When the war was over, I went to school. I started the semester eagerly; it was about time to return to normal life. I had taken the entrance examinations before I was called up, and I was accepted into the cinema department at the Beit Berl Academy. It's a great school. I always loved the cinema, and I saw lots of movies as a child with my mother and my sister, who also loved them. So when I told them of my plans to study film, my sister said, 'Good!' And she wished me luck. But she also warned me that there is a lot of competition, and it isn't easy to make a movie, so I should think about earning a living in another way." With these words, Sergei begins his tale.

"So now I'm starting my studies. I'm sitting in class and the teacher is discussing the history of the black-and-white film, and in my head I'm completely somewhere else. I'm in a jeep in my flak jacket, driving along the "Philadephi Axis," the road that separates Gaza from Egypt, at four in the morning, worrying about how to keep from being blown up by a landmine.

"The lecturer is talking about Marlene Dietrich and Charlie Chaplin and I'm concentrating on that one turn in the dirt road that always makes my throat go dry as I approach it, because you never know what's ahead. And the professor is talking about the celluloid from which film is made, and how it used to dry out and become brittle and how it was necessary to re-glue pieces, and in my head I'm making that turn in the road, holding my breath, and I know that the three other guys with me in the jeep are also not

81

breathing at that moment.

"Everyone is always frightened by that spot. Every single morning. On the way to the tunnels. Those smuggling tunnels, from Gaza to Sinai.

"And the lecturer continues to blab, and the others in the class take copious notes, because this material is sure to show up on the test, and I'm just not there. Marlene Dietrich and ancient celluloid are juxtaposed to that turn in the road, it's nuts, how can one even compare... "

"Comparing is not the important subject," Zev cuts in. "The topic here is this: how will you pass the final exam in another nine weeks at the end of the semester? You invested so much effort to pass the entrance exam, to get accepted to college, to receive a partial scholarship, to find the room in Herzlia, to buy your little scooter, to obtain the used books. And now it looks as if all this effort might go down the drain."

"It's a problem. I am simply unable to concentrate. In class, my thoughts are always in the Gaza Strip, in the jeep, on that mine-laden dirt road, on the snipers who hide behind the walls we left standing after we took down their houses. Three of my friends were killed there, recently, and two injured. And at home I pick up a book and after half a page, I'm again in another world, in the Strip, and I can't concentrate at all. This unnerves me, and it's starting to frighten me, because in the first weeks of the semester I said to myself, 'Look, this is only the beginning, it will be okay, this is a transition. And...and... but now I don't see any change, and the weeks are flying by."

"So, what's your plan?"

"I don't have one. I have lots of good intentions. I pick up the book, I'm lying in the corner of the room, I turn on the radio and start reading and within seconds, it's over. I don't remember anything I read even though I know that I finished the page, because my finger is on the last line. Ask me even half a question and I won't know the answer. It's very scary."

"Is Sergei the only one here who has this problem?"

"What, are you kidding? The only one? This is a problem for all of us; at least that's what I think."

"I no longer have this problem. I had it initially but it passed."

"Just like that, by itself? Without you doing a thing? "

"Not quite," says Avi.

"Then how?"

"I grabbed my head, and I told myself that it's time to put everything behind me and if I wanted this job – and I wanted it very much because it paid good money – then I'd have to pay attention to every detail."

"And that worked?"

"It was hard. But every time I noticed my thoughts drifting back, I'd go back to thinking about the money. I made an equation in my head between concentrating and earning money. And I told myself, *either you think about what happened in Lebanon or you stay focused on the money that you'll make if you succeed,* and these thoughts battled it out. But, I imagined myself getting that metal gate job and walking away with 8000 shekels, and that helped me to push the other thoughts away, at least temporarily. It's not that I forget anything that happened," Avi pauses, "I don't believe that I will ever forget; but at that moment I needed to conclude that deal, which required many calculations, and my determination actually worked. When I completed that task, bang, Lebanon jumped right back into my head; but during the time that I needed to concentrate and to deal with the job, it worked."

"Sergei, could you use this model?" asked Zev.

"Maybe. But for me it's not a question of making money. I'm a student, and for me the problem is how to finish studying a textbook, how to sit down and do a project, how to prepare for an exam and the like, not to get money. Money is easier, because it's measurable. Money can be measured in shekels, such as: ten minutes worth of concentration will get me 20 shekels. Simple."

"Really? Do you think that it was simple for me to come up with my method and make it work? I had lots of screw-ups, opportunities that I lost, until I started to understand this equation that concentration equals money. Until I combined these two, I was lost in thoughts of what had happened, always felt sad, believed I got screwed, asked 'why me,' protested constantly that this isn't fair, and more."

"Good. So what Avi is telling us here is worth a lot, both in money and in other desirable goals. What he is saying is this: in order to get out from under these reveries, these difficult memories, from upsetting sounds that clash with our ability to concentrate on what we need to accomplish now – we have to come up with an opposing force, one that is as strong as the one that pulls at us and keeps us from doing what we need to," explains Zev.

"Could you say this in understandable language?"

"Sure. You have to establish a goal, in your case – to pass a test in the history of black-and-white film. From what you told us, that seems to be a crucial goal for you. And you're also telling us that you have good intentions and a task-oriented desire to accomplish this. And you're also telling us that you open a book on the subject, and within a page you're already 'not there,' rather you're deep in thought about the painful events, the upsetting memories, the sorrow, the mourning, the anger; and to hell with the history of film. Is this accurate? "

"You couldn't have said it more accurately."

"Ok. So what exactly is your task?"

"To study the book and reach a level that would enable me to pass the test."

"Is that all? Just to pass one lousy exam? All this effort just for that? "

"Of course not!"

"What else then?"

"Don't pretend that you don't know."

"Right. I do know, but you need to hear it in your own voice: exactly why you're doing it, why you must make this tremendous effort. My telling you in my words will not make the same impression on you. You need to hear your own inner voice spoken aloud. Are you ready to say to all of us here, in your own words, why you need to pass this exam?"

"What is this, kindergarten? Fine, never mind. It's something like this: I want to be a filmmaker and to earn a living from it. In order to get a job in this profession, I need a diploma in film from a serious institution such as Bet Berl. In order to receive this diploma, I must pass tests and complete projects. And, in order to pass the tests, I must study, among other things, a tedious and boring book on the history of film, as if anyone gives a damn about it."

"Now, may I quote *you?* You couldn't have said it more accurately!"

Everyone laughed, including Sergei.

"Again, we need to return to the transition from problem to solution that Avi found for his problem and compare it to your specific issue. Don't laugh: at the end you too will arrive at money, when all is said and done, but there are many interim steps until you get there, and therefore it's more difficult. It is actually impossible to pinpoint exactly how one exam in one particular subject, regardless of whether you like it or hate it, will lead to earning money. We must see the total picture: every exam adds to the successful completion of a course. All the courses and the projects of each semester add up. Every two semesters equal a year and after 3 or 4 years, voila! There is a certificate and a degree. It's a long journey with a final stop."

"You know what?" Yariv joins the conversation. "I actually have a good analogy. It's like a race in which, from the first second on, you can't afford to lose time, because in the end it will cost you. I once participated in a mini-triathlon. We had to swim one kilometer in the sea, change our clothes quickly, jump on our bikes, ride 24 kilometers, drop the bikes and run 8 kilometers. Initially, I didn't take it too seriously and didn't make much of an effort while swimming, but suddenly I started to see others jumping out of the water onto their bikes, and I understood that I wasn't with it. And then I started to compete in earnest. In the end I finished honorably, but if I had started out more seriously from the first moment, I would have done much better."

"Interesting. But what's the analogy?"

"That exam on film is like the first ten meters of my swimming. If he doesn't pass it, it will cost him in the end. And he won't pass it if he can't read and study the book, and he can't study the book if he doesn't finish the first page! This, exactly, is the analogy."

"Sergei, do you see the parallel?

"I see, I see. But how do I make the transition from holding the book in my hand – while in my mind, I'm in a faraway world – and get to the point that I read and finish an entire page and can answer questions or write an essay on the subject?"

"It's like the first 10 meters of Yariv's swimming in the sea."

"Which means?"

"You choose a quiet corner of the room, next to a table. You don't look out the window. In fact, if there's a window, you close the curtains or the shutters. You turn off the radio, unless you're truly one who learns better with music in the background, then ok, but at a low volume and only as background. No stirring music, you understand, right?

"And the light must be good, not something like a dim lamp on the other side of the room. Light that falls straight on the book. Next to you is a writing pad and a pen or pencil or, if you prefer, a computer. And you set one of two goals for yourself: either I finish a page, or a certain small number of pages, or I study for five minutes. If you choose time, then you set a timer for five minutes, and you don't get up from the chair until you hear it ring. Or, if you decide on a fixed number of pages – just a few initially – then you don't move until you finish studying these pages.

"You don't lie comfortably on the floor, with dim light and the cat snuggling against you, etc. etc.... You are serious, focused, you concentrate and finish the "first ten meters," no fooling around.

"Boy, that's a whole story. How did you know that I am on the floor with the cat and all that?"

"Actually, I don't know, I'm only imagining a situation that makes studying more difficult. Studying is not a joke; it requires effort. If you're going to extricate a car from deep mud, you must straighten the front wheels, take off heavy loads, and remove obstacles that are in the way. It's basically the same thing."

"I'll try that. There are some decent ideas here."

* * *

"I'm not a student, and studying is not an issue for me. I have other problems," Yossi announces.

"Tell us," Zev responds.

"I can't get to meetings on time, I miss doctors' appointments, I don't pick up the phone to make a call even after I've sworn that I will. I forget all these simple things that everyone else remembers without a problem."

"Yes, that's a problem, but it's not as unusual as you might think. Other people also have problems like that, but that won't help you, other than just knowing that you're not the only one. For you the important thing is to return to normalcy, when tasks like that were not a problem. Right?"

"Exactly. How?"

"After what you've gone through, things got jumbled inside your head. That's part of the total picture. So you can't assume anymore that having good intentions means that you'll succeed in carrying them out, just because carrying them out wasn't a problem in the past. I'm sorry to tell you that things have changed, and the sooner you can accept that, the sooner you'll be able to start coping with it. It's frustrating to think that at your age you already have memory problems like your grandfather, whom you've heard complaining for years, "Damn it! My memory is gone."

"You have a grandfather like that, too? Mine says the same thing, and then my grandmother comes in and announces, "You think you forget? Look at me, I hardly know your name," and then they start to fight over who has the worse memory, and in the end everyone laughs."

"However," continues Zev, "for you this isn't funny. It's really embarrassing to miss a doctor's appointment, or fail to arrive at a meeting. So, tell us what you do to help yourself keep your appointments."

"Sometimes I write them down, sometimes I try to remember, sometimes someone reminds me, and sometimes I try very hard and keep repeating to myself: 'Don't forget! You have a meeting today at ten...' and suddenly it's noon, and then I remember it, but it's too late, and I curse, and bang my hand on the table, but, in fact, I missed the appointment."

"Does that seem like an efficient way to operate?"

"Apparently not."

"So, what's not working here?"

This is a crucial topic for the group, the problem of impaired memory, of being disorganized and missing important things. These are familiar problems with unpleasant implications. Almost everyone is encountering this in some form. A few have been unwilling to admit to it, while others are very troubled by it. Several have developed methods for coping with the issue and have achieved a degree of success. For Yossi, at this point any improvement would be a blessing.

Zev continues. "The first thing that strikes me is the word

'sometimes.' Sometimes you do this, and sometimes that...there's no consistent method. That is part of the problem, but there's more.

"Let me explain, through an example, what I am driving at. Does anyone here have a friend who is habitually late and always keeps you waiting? And everyone knows it and seems to accept it: 'He's always late, that's the way he is'. But actually, you feel angry and swear that the next time he's late, you'll just leave, and he can go jump in the lake?"

"Absolutely! My brother's like that. He drives the family crazy. It's impossible to depend on him, and we're always mad at him. And he sincerely apologizes again and again, but he keeps on doing it."

"What do you think is the reason for this behavior?"

"I really don't know. It's maddening."

"Here is a possible answer and with it, an idea for a solution. Your brother believes, wholeheartedly, that he is going to arrive on time without a problem. He tells himself something like, 'after all, it's close by, and everyone knows you can get there in ten minutes.' But then, every single time something happens, and he's late. 'Too much traffic, the weather got messed up, I forgot my hat and had to go back' – there's always a good reason, but the final result is that he never arrives on time.

"The problem, in my opinion, is his unrealistic blind belief that he'll manage to arrive within ten minutes. Then reality smacks him in the face, repeatedly proving him wrong. And it doesn't actually matter why. The moment that your brother starts to believe that he actually needs twenty minutes, not ten, and acts accordingly, even though it sounds excessive and silly, he will start arriving on time. Because if he suddenly hits heavy traffic, or the weather gets messed up, or he forgets his hat – doesn't matter what the reason is – he'll have time to spare, and in the worst-case scenario, he'll arrive a little early."

"Very well, correct, but what's that got to do with me?"

"Ok, so about you: prior to the war events, you arrived on time because you functioned in a particular way. And you still believe, very sincerely, that now, because you have good intentions, you can continue exactly as before and get the same results. And you're unwilling to believe that this is not the case. Due to the events you experienced, there's a 'new normal,' which means that things are a bit different from what they used to be. That's the connection."

"How frustrating!"

"Yes, it is frustrating. But haven't you noticed that in other ways you are also functioning a little bit differently, but somehow it doesn't bother you very much?"

"Like what?"

"You are more tired and therefore sleep more often."

"True."

"And also, you suddenly have those images in your mind that you didn't have before. You don't like them, but you manage to cope with them and with other things as well. Now, let's get back to the subject we started with: keeping meetings and appointments, and doing things at specified times, on specified days. Things have changed, and you must believe that, and act a little differently, in accordance with the new normal.

"For example; if someone breaks a leg and is forbidden to put weight on it, he will get a cane and lean on it until the leg mends. Usually it is easy to accept the need for this change, because it's so visible and obvious. It's much harder to believe that our memory doesn't function well and therefore needs a cane to lean on."

"Use a cane for our memory? Are you making fun of us?"

"Absolutely not. I have a long list of 'canes' that can assist memory, but none will be of any help if they aren't used. And, as we have already seen, if one doesn't believe there's a problem with his leg, then one doesn't use the cane and might slip and fall. And in a parallel way, this applies to missing appointments and forgetting things."

"Memory canes? I'm dying to know, let's hear it."

"There are two types: things that are written down, and things that make noise and get your attention."

"Ah, like an alarm?"

"Exactly. Most homes have several kinds: a sleep alarm, which no one is shy about using, and others like the clock on a microwave, or the alarm function of a wristwatch."

"And you'll tell us how to implement them?"

"Sure. First let's talk about written things. The most common item, which many have used since childhood, is a diary, or a calendar. Most organized people use one. It may hang on a wall or on the refrigerator, there are also pocket organizers, the size or shape doesn't matter; it's all the same idea: to jot down a date and a time.

"That's the easy part. The difficult part is, no joke, to look at it frequently and be sure not to miss these dates.

"Another technique is the daily list. I personally have been using one for years, and it works like a charm. I take a lined piece of paper and fold it lengthwise, and all day long, I jot down things to be done, and relish every time I cross one out. I keep it in my shirt pocket, and at night, near my bed. When it gets filled on one side, I flip it to the other. When it's no longer easily readable, I transfer the remaining items to a new list and discard the old one. If there are useful telephone numbers, e-mail addresses, etc. that I have jotted down on the list, I transfer these to a more permanent place.

"Sometimes, for my own enjoyment and a sense of accomplishment, I will write on it something I have already done, so that I can cross it out. This is an old-fashioned method, but it doesn't depend on batteries, it costs nothing, takes up no room in our pockets.

"But what if you lose it?" challenges Yossi.

"Yeah, that has happened, and it's annoying. At times I didn't actually lose it, just put it someplace where I couldn't find it when I needed it, but sometimes I've had to reconstruct the list. Nothing is 100% foolproof, but it's still better than no list."

"In this day and age of electronic devices, there are desktop computers, laptops, iPods, Blackberries, cellphones, smartphones, iPads that have ringing and buzzing reminders, a plethora of variations. In short, there are many aides available: 'canes' that can help with memory, with being organized.

"The problem is that many people feel ashamed to use these helpful tools, because using one reminds them that something isn't 'right.' They think that only someone who is disorganized needs them, or they think, 'I'm okay, I don't need this stuff.' The question is simply this: what's more important, to continue to fail and then feel like a failure, or to make use of one of these simple methods. Often they're needed only temporarily. I'll describe what's available and how to implement it."

"So how *would* you use one of those fancy devices? How do I get from having an iPad to not missing my physical therapy, which has already happened several times?" asks Yossi.

Zev throws the question to the group.

Ido: "Yossi, when is your PT session?"

"Tuesday and Thursday. Tuesday at 9:30, Thursday at 2 o'clock."

"How do you remember when to go?"

"That's the problem...sometimes I remember, other times I forget, and then they are angry with me and I don't feel like going back."

"When you remember, how do you do it?"

"No system – just luck. Actually, when my knee hurts, it reminds me. And with luck, that happens before the appointment," says Yossi.

"That's a problem," frets Ido. "Wait – don't you have a calendar?"

"Yes. But it hangs on the wall. I can't keep it with me."

"Do you write on it?"

"Sometimes."

"So that's what Zev means by 'no consistency.' You've got to write it every time."

"Okay, but what does that have to do with an iPad?"

"After you write the appointment on the calendar, you enter it in your iPad for that day and time, and you take it with you. You set it so it rings 30 minutes before your appointment. And when you finish with your appointment, you enter the next date right then and there. That's how." Ido sits back in his chair, visibly pleased with himself for figuring this out.

Zev smiles; this is what he was hoping for. Then he adds: "If someone isn't interested in using this method, then maybe he can come up with one of his own. We have a creative group here with a lot of brain power and we could help each other out with ideas that have worked for us."

* * *

Uri nods and squirms in his seat, and it is obvious that he is dying to get into the conversation.

"The problem for me is different. It's not a problem of keeping appointments. It's more like Sergei's problem: I can't concentrate. I'm in a masters program in music, and for my final I have to compose a piece of music. Every time I start to compose, the shriek of a mortar shell enters my head and completely fills it and I can't get back to the musical notes. I feel stressed, sad, and unfocused." Uri is complaining to Zev, almost pleading for him to solve his problem.

"What are you trying to compose?"

"Something cheerful, pleasing, a piece of about ten or fifteen minutes that will impress my professors."

"I'm identifying two problems here," answered Zev. "I'm not a musician, but I love music and do know something about it. My answer is not professional, but practical. First, why must the piece be cheerful? In your current mental state, this in itself is an unrealistic task. It is difficult to write something cheerful when you feel sad. It makes much more sense to write something that is compatible with your mood, and there are many wonderful examples of that from history. You surely know of Tchaikovsky's *Symphony Pathetique*, which he wrote when he was depressed. Do you know the funeral procession, the *Marche Funèbre*, the second movement of Beethoven's third symphony? Did you ever hear *The War Requiem* that the English composer Benjamin Britten wrote to commemorate the bombardment of the city of Coventry during the Second World War, where hundreds of citizens were killed? And Verdi wrote his famous requiem grieving the death of Manzoni, whom he revered. Brahms wrote *A German Requiem* after his mother's death. Mozart's *Requiem*, his last piece, was composed when he knew he was dying, and he never even completed it. There are numerous examples of such works. Imagine how these great composers would have reacted to a request to compose something cheerful when they were suffering?"

"I understand. I didn't think about that aspect. Maybe I'm trying to do something that is illogical and so I shrink from the task. I feel more like writing something sad, in a minor key, so maybe that's a better approach. And by the way, why was Beethoven so depressed that he composed a funeral march?"

"Some think he was shaken by the huge number of soldiers

who lost their lives in the Napoleonic wars. But that's just a conjecture."

"Interesting. But what's the second problem you identified?"

"The second problem, it seems to me, is the length of your piece: it's too long. A ten- to fifteen-minute piece of music is a tremendous challenge, and a shorter creation, at this moment in your life, would be more attainable: something in the order of four to seven minutes."

"Too short, too short," replied Uri.

"Really? I will give you examples of famous short pieces known to everyone in the music world. The first one that jumps to mind is *Finlandia*, by Jan Sibelius, a Finnish composer who hated the Russians. The piece is seven minutes long and is so stirring that the Russians forbade its performance for fear that it would incite nationalistic demonstrations. Just seven minutes!

"Here is another example: *Fanfare to the Common Man*, by the Jewish-American composer Aaron Copland. The sound of the trumpets makes listeners jump out of their seats. It is played hundreds of times a year, can be seen on TV, heard on the radio, and performed in concerts by famous orchestras and even high school bands. It's length? Three minutes! Just three minutes long!"

"It's impressive, and I certainly know these works, they are very famous and I admire them. But I am no Copland, I'm no Sibelius, and I'm certainly no Beethoven." Uri sighs.

"True, but so what?" replies Zev. "Does anyone here have something to add to help Uri to overcome his block?"

Yossi jostles forward in his chair, until he reaches the edge, raises his hand, and says, "I'm surely no musician, but I think that what Zev is telling you is that you're trying to do too much. That you're trying to do something that you're simply 'not into,' so you get stuck and end up doing nothing. So you feel disappointed and frustrated. I have a similar scenario. Since the war, I haven't been working. I just can't. I'm always thinking that I'll get up in the morning, get dressed, jump into my truck, and make a delivery, make some money like I always did. I have customers who are waiting for me to come back. I can't pull it off. I stay in bed, I don't get up, I don't get into my truck. I do nothing. And I feel like shit."

"Yes, that's similar," Zev confirms.

"Each of us has his blocks," adds Yariv. "For Uri, it's composing music, for Yossi it's getting into his truck to make a delivery, for me it's growing my business. Seems it doesn't matter exactly what the job is, it's the same problem. Some of us have succeeded in moving on and have managed to get it together. Yossi, Uri, and I, and some others – we still haven't returned to normal life. We're still stuck. I can't even imagine how anyone composes music, to me it seems like a task for geniuses, but for me, just to return to my regular day-to-day work – or for Yossi, to make a delivery – even that's too much. How are we going to overcome this?"

Zev has a plan to help move things along, but he purposely sits quietly and doesn't respond. He allows some tension to arise without offering solutions, hoping that from this skilled group of people, with its creativity and life experience, solutions will emerge.

The silence continues. One looks at the other, some look at Zev, waiting for an answer.

Zev persists in his silence and directs glances at several group members, shifting from one to the other without focusing on anyone in particular, his facial expression suggesting, "Now what?"

Ron suddenly moves. "You know what?" he offers. "Zev taught us all these coping mechanisms at the very beginning, remember? Relaxation and all that, what do you call it? Something with imagery, and we're not using them here. Until now we've gotten by with just talking, but now we seem to be stuck. It's like my own situation: as a medic, I see blood gushing, and I have to stem the flow, so I take a tourniquet, a really important tool for me, and I use it and it saves the day. We have situations here that require tools, but we're not using them."

Several pairs of eyes open wide, heads move, and lips tighten, signs the men are considering this. Several *hmmmmms* are heard. Ron seems to have hit on something.

Uri speaks up. "Ron has an idea. What's the point of walking around with your toolbox if you never open it? Zev won't always be with us. We've made progress in a number of problems and we still have more sessions, but at the end of 12 sessions we will have to take care of ourselves; so we might as well begin."

That was the response Zev had been hoping for. So far he had been giving answers, offering suggestions and proposing solutions, and now he had decided that it's time that group members start to depend more on themselves, and to implement the techniques he taught them.

"That's it, well said, both of you. So for example, Ron: how would you take what we learned regarding Uri or Yossi, and apply it to yourself?"

"I was speaking in generalities, in principal, but I really don't know how to move from idea to action."

"Can someone help here?" Zev inquires.

Again, heads turn and mumbling is audible.

Ido straightens up. "I have an idea that comes, in a way, from my background studying history. With history, we always search for a connection between one event and others that offers us clues as to why something occurred. Uri, you're telling us that the whistle of the shells is buzzing around in your head and interfering with your ability to compose. What would you think of taking that very whistling sound – we all know it well: whining, shrieking, high-pitched and frightening, because you know what is about to happen in just a few seconds – and instead of fighting the sound, enlist it for your purposes. Turn it into the sound of some musical instrument. You could turn that nasty whining into a melody, a musical theme. Prokofiev, if I remember correctly, in 'Peter and the Wolf,' assigned one particular musical instrument to each animal so that the listener immediately understands that this particular sound means the wolf, and that one stands for the bird, and so on.

"There are wind instruments that produce a high pitched sound, like a whistle. Do you remember the opening sound of the 'Rhapsody in Blue' by Gershwin? A long shrieking sound? Why don't you use such a sound for your purposes?"

Uri was intrigued. He felt relieved that members of his group were supportive of him in his stress. They did not seem to be put off by that unique task, although it was strange and unusual for them, and that they started to come up with solutions that might be helpful to him. He was afraid that the task of composing music is so elitist that others would turn their back and would not take his dilemma seriously. He was thinking of Yossi who wasn't even able to enter his truck, and here he is, struggling with such a complex academic subject.

URI

He is tall and thin, with high cheekbones, pale skin, and black rimmed glasses. His appearance is one of "Excuse me for being here."

His ethnic background is a crazy salad, with ingredients from many countries. Some of these countries no longer exist, having fallen victim to political upheavals, territorial exchanges, and shifting borders. Even their names are now only part of history. The Austro-Hungarian Monarchy was a phenomenon that today can only be found in history texts or on antique maps. Czechoslovakia disappeared and was replaced by Slovakia and the Czech Republic. And the USSR with its 15 member states was dismantled, each piece becoming a proud, independent country.

Once-mighty Germany was sliced in half in 1945; a piece of it becoming part of Poland. The portion that became East Germany remained in a state of virtual paralysis for 40 years, suffocated under the Soviet blanket of secrecy, terror and poverty until 1989, when the infamous Berlin Wall was finally smashed by sledgehammers. Only in recent years has it begun to recuperate.

Uri's background is tied into all these places. On one side of his family he qualifies as a *"Yekke,"* a slang term for a person of German origin. On the other side are elements of other European countries, among them Hungary and Czechoslovakia.

There are differences of opinion as to the origin of the term *"Yekke."* The most widely-held explanation is that it refers to the German male intellectuals who immigrated to Palestine to escape

Nazi persecution: the doctors, lawyers, and professors who accepted jobs as construction workers in their new home because they could not find work in their respective professions. It is said that many of them wore their business suits while doing manual labor, insisting on continuing to dress as professionals. As a jacket is a *"jacke"* in German (pronounced with a "y"), these men came to be called *"Yekkes."* Who in his right mind would wear a jacket and neatly-ironed slacks while mixing cement and laying bricks...unless he was a Yekke?

That humorous reference to this rigidity is joined by a second explanation, one that is less gently mocking and more insulting: that the word is an acronym for *Yehudi Ksheh Havanah,* a Hebrew expression meaning "a Jew who is dense." Behind that derogatory expression however, there is an air of appreciation for being honorable and respect for the accomplishments of this group of people. If one wants to accomplish something, needs to rely on someone, wants to be certain that he is working with a reliable and non-corrupt person – then he should be dealing with a Yekke. But all that comes at a price; it is best to anticipate a degree of rigidity, not too much bending of rules. "Ordnung muss sein" – "Things must be done in an orderly fashion" is their motto. That is how the Yekkes managed to acclimate to their lives in a strange and difficult new environment.

Uri's grandfather and father both referred to themselves as Yekkes. His mother was Czech, born in the beautiful city of Prague, known to its admirers as *"Zlata Praha,"* the "Prague of Gold."

After having emigrated from Germany in the 1930s, great-grandfather Gerhard Lehman struggled to find work. In Germany he was a wholesale grain dealer, but since it was difficult for him to learn Hebrew, he was unable to get into business again, and after some disappointments and failures, he opened a small hat shop on the main street in Haifa. Most of his customers were also Yekkim – the Hebrew version of Yekkes – as they could not part with their customary attire despite a radically different climate. Lehman made a modest living but his Hebrew did not improve. He continued to speak German with is customers and therefore had no need to strain himself, learning that strange and complicated language, which was difficult to pronounce as well.

One day, however, things changed.

"Gerhard," whispered one of his customers, a man in his forties, a veteran who was already established, in terms of those years.

"Yes, Jozeff, what is it?"

"My name now is Yossi, you know, it sounds much more Hebraic."

"Ach so" he replied.

"Have you ever heard of the 'Haggana'?"

"No, what's that?"

"You know, we are having trouble with the Arabs. They don't want us here. They set things on fire, shoot, murder, make life miserable for us. But we have in the Yishuv – our community – an organization that responds to them, the "Haggana" – that means "Protection" – but we must operate quietly. The British who are governing Palestine at this time don't want trouble, so they don't support us and we are not allowed to act too openly."

"You don't say! A military organization? With weapons? Do you belong?"

"Yes, and we need you too. We need anyone who is capable."

"I don't speak Hebrew, you know, how could I be with them?"

"You'll learn. I also learned. I still make mistakes, but I manage. On Thursday evening just before 7, I'll come pick you up for a meeting at our local fire station on Pevsner Street. Don't talk about it. Tell Ilse that you are meeting a friend."

Gerhard changed his name to Gid'on shortly after he joined the Haggana, did what he was assigned to do but never discussed it. It was said that he learned to use a pistol and throw a hand grenade and that he went for training sessions and possibly participated in some actions. Ilse, who did not change her name to the day she died, never knew exactly where her husband disappeared to from time to time. She was astute enough not to ask and quietly happy that he was part of the system.

* * *

Uri was born in Haifa, in Carmel Hospital on Mount Carmel. A week after his first screams, he cried again for a few seconds, when he was entered into the covenant of Abraham. Tears of joy, mixed with worry about his well-being, streamed down his mother's cheeks, as the proud father and grandfather showed off their newborn to the guests. At last she grabbed him from their hands and declared "Uri had a tough day, he must sleep," and they disappeared into the bedroom. She breathed a sigh of relief as both mother and baby got their much needed rest. She exposed an engorged breast and nursed her baby with great love.

At a young age, Uri showed an affinity for music; in kindergarten he particularly enjoyed singing, drumming, and playing castanets. This was no surprise to his parents, as his grandmother on his mother's side was a well-known classical pianist in Prague who taught numerous students. Tragically, she was among the Jewish artists and musicians deported to Auschwitz, where she perished. This talent and love for music skipped over Uri's mother, who had no particular interest in it. His father did have an appreciation, and often hummed melodies from classical music although he did not play an instrument.

Uri grew up listening to classical music. His grandparents had brought with them a pile of thick, heavy records from Germany, which were played on an old, odd-looking record player that had to be cranked by hand. He loved listening to Italian operas, though he did not understand a single word. As he listened over and over, the evocative melodies, and even some of the words, became etched in his mind, filling him with strong emotions. He was soon able to hum and whistle whole sections from many of these, among them Verdi's *"La Forza del Destino,"* "The Force of Destiny." This title turned out to have a symbolic, prophetic meaning for him, as it unfolded that music was indeed his destiny. From time to time, especially in later years when life was burdensome, he returned to this music for solace.

At age six, he started piano lessons with a private teacher, immediately enjoying the sounds he was able to produce. His skinny legs dangled from the bench and it was difficult for him to reach the pedals, but his teacher helped him manage. At home, he played the melodies he had learned for his mother and father, reveling in their applause. These little performances awoke feelings of nostalgia in his mother, who recalled her own mother giving lessons to children of Uri's age. Her mother had tried to interest her in the piano, without success. Now, listening to Uri play, she felt the generations reconnected.

In high school, Uri befriended a classmate named Doron, a handsome fellow whose goal was to become a fighter. Once, during a class trip to the north, Doron had slipped across the border into Lebanon – hostile territory – in the dark of night with two friends on a dare. The counselors remained unaware of the deed until morning, when the three kids straggled back to camp.

The two boys were quite different: Doron knew nothing about classical music and Uri was not the least bit interested in becoming a fighter, but both were intelligent and appreciated each other's good qualities. Toward the end of twelfth grade, Uri invited Doron to join him for a free classical music concert in a public park, and Doron gladly accepted.

The program that evening was Verdi's "Requiem," a composition based on a prayer for the dead, a Catholic mass sung at memorial services. The music ranged from nearly inaudible whispers to hair-raising, blasting crescendos. Trumpet sounds were heard from players behind the scenery, while soloists and a large choir intermingled with the orchestra. Uri was mesmerized and surreptitiously glanced over to Doron to see his reactions. He could see that Doron, too, was captivated by this new experience and by the beauty of the music. On their way home, as they took the steps two at a time down the hill from Mount Carmel to their Hadar neighborhood, Uri explained to his friend that Verdi composed this piece in memory of Alessandro Manzoni, "the Father of Italy," whom he admired, for the anniversary of his death. "So it had a very special, deep meaning for Verdi," he added.

That concert was the last time Uri saw Doron.

Immediately after graduating high school, Doron enlisted in the army and fulfilled his deep yearning: he was accepted into the paratroopers and became a fighter. A few months later he volunteered for a military operation, where he led his company in storming the enemy, and was killed.

Verdi's requiem acquired another layer of meaning for Uri – it became Doron's requiem.

* * *

Over the years, Uri mastered both classical music and jazz. During his last two summers of high school, he was employed on a cruise ship, playing piano in the bar. In this way, he got to see many European cities. And although he was shy, this turned out to be a good way to meet girls from different countries. His unique position as a musician in the bar, with his shift ending after midnight, led to many exciting experiences, both cultural and romantic.

In addition to being musical he was smart, and graduated high school with excellent grades, paving the way for him to go into the academic reserve corps. This special arrangement with the armed forces allowed military service to be deferred until after graduation from college, at which point Uri was inducted into officer training immediately following basic training. He completed a bachelor's degree at Haifa University, majoring in both classical music and jazz, and then registered to study for his master's.

One night while on a furlough from the reserves, Uri went to a downtown bar to spend time with friends. Shortly after their arrival, their attention was diverted by a group of girls laughing and talking at an adjacent table. One particular girl, with a long black ponytail and twinkling dark eyes, caught Uri's attention. He tried to be casual, making an attempt to hide his interest from his friends, but unsuccessfully. Nor did his interest escape the vivacious young lady. She was also glancing at him, and likewise trying to hide this from her friends, with the same degree of failure. "Karnit," a girlfriend asked, "Do you know him?"

Uri stood out somewhat from the group he was with, looking more quiet and thoughtful. Karnit noticed his calm eyes and long, graceful fingers, and thought he looked smart and cultured. For a long time, she had been hoping to meet someone with those qualities. She found most boys to be loud and silly, and interested in "just one thing." She continued to glance at Uri, and her friend finally suggested, "If you want to meet him, just go to the next table and introduce yourself."

"Just like that? Go to the table? That's a bit crass."

"Don't be silly. I'll arrange it," and turning to the next table, her friend raised her glass and addressed the guys with a confident, "*L'chaim*, good things to you all." They were surprised by Zafrira's openness, but delighted to have the opportunity to meet several cute girls with such ease.

Uri's two friends raised their drinks in return, and Amos added: "All the best to you!" He winked at the girl with the ponytail, pointing his thumb backwards toward Uri. He then turned to him and whispered: "I think she's waiting for *you*." Uri blushed.

With the spark between the two now out in the open, their friends were curious to see how things would develop. All kinds of chatter started passing between the two tables, and within a minute someone pushed the tables together and created one big, noisy celebrating group.

Uri bent toward the other table and introduced himself to the girl closest to him. "I'm Uri, nice to meet you." Then he glanced toward Karnit, and the girl he'd addressed winked at him, saying with a smile, "I'm Vered, come, I'd like you to meet my friend, Karnit," which broke the ice.

By the end of the evening, that included some beer and wine, Uri and Karnit had exchanged cellphone numbers. They had chatted a little about themselves, establishing that he was from Haifa and she from a neighboring village, and that he was on furlough from the reserves and had two days before he had to return to his base.

Karnit was a senior worker in a high-tech company, an expert with computers who had, more than once, rescued her boss, Regev, from screw-ups and thus had an excellent relationship with him. When she notified Regev that she wanted two days off to "take care of some urgent matters," he replied, "OK, Karnit, no problem."

Uri and Karnit spent the next two days almost entirely together. His parents were disappointed that he did not spend more time with them, but from the broad smile that covered his face, they understood that something important and wonderful was happening. They recalled how wiped out and depressed he had seemed the last few times he came home, and they were relieved to see him in such high spirits and good health. His mother had particularly good intuition about her boy, and she felt quietly happy for him.

Uri and Karnit spent much of the time talking nonstop and

learning everything they could about each other. Uri explained that he was a music teacher, and that his reserve time had been scheduled to coincide with his school summer vacation. He shared that he was a pianist, but "not at concert level." He talked about his grandmother in Prague, one of the few who did achieve that level: well-known in her time and appearing in the famous concert halls of Vienna, Budapest, and Prague.

"I did not reach her level, and in our tiny country there is a great deal of competition and very few spots in orchestras or chamber groups. It seems like every second Russian immigrant that comes here is a superb musician, and I have little hope of competing. Fortunately, I enjoy teaching kids the beauty of music, classical and jazz. Sometimes I discover a talent, a child who has music in his or her blood. A girl puts a flute to her lips and within a minute I can hear that her soul is playing through it. Or a boy sits at the piano and I close my eyes and enjoy the level to which I've brought him. The girls, in particular, have good musical sense and great power of listening."

"I could tell right away that you are crazy for music: both classical and jazz, right?"

"Yes. How did you know?"

"From the way you talked about both forms, so sensually and enthusiastically."

"Oh, I'll have to be careful with you and your x-ray vision. What else did you discover about me since yesterday?"

"You're a Yekke, right? And you are close to your mom and dad, polite, not a braggart, and a bit sensitive. I thought your friends would have you for lunch in that bar."

"Oh! Are you sure you're not a psychologist? And what about you? What turns you on?"

"I adore computers, so sophisticated and with such endless possibilities. And I like my boss, it's fun working with him. He has unique ideas and a great mind and there's always something new to learn from him, and he's advanced the company a lot. A few months ago he received a patent and an American company is interested in it. If it goes through, we'll make a fortune, the company, that is. But we are only eight people, and everyone will get something. I deserve it," she smiled. "I save him a tremendous amount of time. He is so disorganized, he couldn't even remember where he filed the patent application..." and she burst into laughter.

There was something in Karnit's throaty laughter that ignited Uri. He found it so sexy that he couldn't get enough of it and kept thinking of ways to make her laugh – funny questions and words, even resorting to silly faces. She found his antics totally charming. They talked for hours; anyone catching a glimpse of the happy pair could see they were falling in love, and would have guessed they had known each other for years. All shyness had vanished. The night before Uri's departure was spent together in Karnit's tiny, cozy apartment.

After Uri's return to the reserves, the two texted each other at every opportunity. He sent no army details, but his messages were filled with endearing words and plans for activities they would share when they could be together again.

With the end of summer, Uri returned to his work as a high school music teacher, and his studies at the university. Weekends often found the pair at the Sea of Galilee, on the Golan Heights, in a bed and breakfast in Kibbutz Kfar Hanasie, and in restaurants near the beaches, which they both loved. Weekdays kept them both busy with work and school. Uri's master's level courses were more difficult than he had anticipated, and the workload at his job caught him by surprise.

* * *

From time to time he awoke from violent, frightening dreams, in which he was trying to run away from danger, but his legs would not carry him. He awoke drenched in sweat, his heart pounding. When these occurred, mornings found him tense and exhausted. When the dreams failed to subside, he noticed himself becoming irritable. He was taken aback by this change, because he had always been gentle and even-tempered. He knew that friends and acquaintances all perceived him as a sweet, calm man with a lot of patience. He had never been one to raise his voice, and he was someone people knew they could count on to be logical and balanced. What surprised, even *alarmed* him more than anything, was his discovery that he was becoming less interested in listening to music. He no longer cared when a favorite piece of music was playing on the radio; in fact, he sometimes found himself turning it off.

Karnit noticed that at times he would just stare into space. But they both avoided talking about these strange behaviors.

One day Uri shocked Karnit by announcing that it might be better if they "took a break." This pronouncement was devastating for her, and she questioned him about it for a long time. His explanations were vague and evasive. She suspected he had found someone else, and sadness descended on her. The sadness was followed by anger, then confusion, as she decided that perhaps she was wrong after all. Eventually she just decided to let things go their way, and agreed to the break, trying to convince herself that it would be brief and temporary.

Uri went on several dates with other women, but none spoke to his heart. He did not enjoy their company. Even sex was unexciting, and he felt that he was walking numbly down a directionless path. During the entire period of their separation, he kept thinking of Karnit and missing her, yet he did not feel ready to contact her. She, too, kept her distance. One day Uri ran into Karnit's friend Zafrira. She told him that Karnit was not seeing anyone and that she missed him, but that she had dignity and pride and wouldn't contact him. In turn, Zafrira reported to Karnit that Uri looked tense and sad and sent his regards.

Months passed. Finally Uri broke down and called.

"Karnit? This is Uri." When she heard his voice, she was stunned but quiet. She was afraid to be seen as too eager, and was uncertain how to respond.

"Are you OK, Uri?"

"Yeah. I'm fine, and I miss you. I had a tough time and couldn't include anyone, not even you. I'm better now, and I'm dying to see you." If anyone had been listening, they would have heard the heavy weight drop from her heart.

Uri managed to suppress the things that were still bothering him. He was busy at work and with his studies, and tried to spend every spare minute with Karnit. He was very much in love and could foresee a joint future.

Karnit was equally crazy about him. She decided it was time to invite him to dinner at her parents. The evening went well; her parents were impressed by the modest Yekke and his good manners. Her father, a well-established businessman who owned a contemporary furniture store, was pleased that Uri had a steady career and felt the young man was ambitious enough that he would always be able to take care of his daughter, the apple of his eye. His wife, a bookkeeper at Bank Hapoalim, warmed up to Uri within minutes of meeting him.

The evening with Uri's parents was a little tenser. It was difficult for the Yekke couple to accept the fact that their son might marry someone of Iraqi ancestry. Like many mothers, his mother felt that Uri's obviously deep feelings for Karnit were a challenge to her own dominance in his life. But both parents were impressed by Karnit's beauty, her intelligence, and her career. His father was drawn to her abundant charm. His mother understood that if she made the mistake of competing for her son she would lose, and she acted warmly and tried to be open-minded. Karnit understood the situation and maintained her composure.

Six months after these family meetings, Karnit and Uri became engaged, and they married within the year.

FIFTH SESSION

Zev opened the session by throwing a general question into the air.

"Does anyone have something to report? Have there been any changes, good or bad?"

It quickly becomes obvious that several of the guys are eager to answer this.

Gil, who was initially so skeptical that he refused to promise to actively participate or honor the confidentiality of the group, bursts out with an unexpected reply.

"Do you remember how I would not pick up a phone, even for my closest friends? I'd hear it ringing, glance at the screen, and ignore it. And after a while the phone stopped ringing, and I understood that my friends had gotten the message. I guess they gave up on me and decided not to waste their time, or they just didn't want to bother me. At first I breathed a huge sigh of relief. I no longer had to be in the position of ignoring people who were simply concerned about my welfare. I didn't have to lie to them anymore, saying I was okay when I wasn't. Well, after a few weeks I started feeling neglected and ignored, and feeling that nobody really gave a damn about me, that all that talk about 'we'll look after you when you return' was just talk. They probably had never really cared much about me."

"I certainly remember," replied Uri, but the look he sends Gil is impatient.

"And you are surprised that your friends gave up on you?

Really? Don't you understand that it was you who sent the message, loud and clear: 'Get off me,' and that they heard you, and that's when they stopped? They may even have discussed this with each other, and I can just imagine how their conversations might have sounded."

Gil reddens. He hadn't expected such an aggressive answer. He had hoped for something more along the lines of 'You don't deserve this,' and other words of that sort. He is taken aback, confused, and a little embarrassed. He isn't sure how to react, but he's curious to know how Uri imagines such a conversation among his friends might have gone. He looks toward Zev as if asking for a life raft, but Zev is quiet and looking at him expectantly. When no help is offered, he looks anxiously toward the other group members, and finally directly at Yariv, who has gained the respect of the group and become something of an unofficial leader, hoping for rescue. Yariv returns his gaze, but says nothing. Gil understands that no one is going to come to his aid; he will have to deal with Uri's response by himself.

"I...I was really surprised. I had figured that even if I didn't respond to them, my friends would continue trying to reach me, so I dragged out my lack of communication longer and longer. Maybe it was kind of a test to see if they really loved me, how much they cared..."

"Oh, so you are playing mind games with them! You put them to the test and when they give you a clear answer, you get insulted and start blaming them. Come on, really!" Uri is on the attack, and the tension in the room increases.

Up to this point, there had not been any open confrontations among group members; everyone was trying to be supportive, friendly, and generous to each other. But Gil's self-pity got under the skin of the usually polite and soft-spoken Uri. He disapproved of the psychological game Gil was forcing on his friends, and to a certain extent felt as if he, too, had fallen victim to it.

Gil didn't want to believe that he actually caused the outcome that was now upsetting him: the silent withdrawal of his friends. "No, I swear, I didn't mean that at all. I love my friends, and it was never, ever my intention to insult them or play games with them," his voice rises defensively, and he reddens again. Now he feels more isolated than ever, and he is hoping that Zev – or someone else – will come to his rescue.

There is only silence. When Gil finally breaks it, his voice is subdued and placating.

"So tell me, Uri, really: how do you think a conversation among my friends might have sounded? I'm apparently missing something important here." He hopes that asking this direct question will fend off further attacks.

"You want to know? Seriously? You might not be happy to hear this," replies Uri. But he immediately adds, "You understand that this is just my supposition, and it's entirely possible that no such conversation ever took place." He tries to relax his tone and retreat from his aggressive stance.

"Yes, I would still really like to know," replies Gil, his voice quiet, almost pleading.

"Ok. So you understand this is just from my imagination. The way I picture it, a friend of yours from the reserves who fought alongside you, let's call him Moshe, picks up the phone to call Yigal, a mutual friend. The conversation goes something like this:

"Yigal, this is Moshe, from the 51st, what's happening?"

"Ok, it's happening. Not as well as before August, before the battle of Bint Jbail, but it's going."

"You working?"

"Yeah, not full time like before, I don't have the same amount of energy, but I'm managing."

"Good, good, I'm also somewhat affected by what happened. Say, have you heard from Gil?"

"No, he never calls. Not only that, but I've called him many times and he never answers. I know his phone is working, because it rings and I get his message: 'This is Gil, leave a message, and I'll get back to you.' So I wait a few days and try again, and I get the same message again. At first I thought that maybe he went away or something, and he'd call me when he got back. But he never did. Then I started to think that maybe something's wrong, and I actually got scared, but I don't know how else to get in touch with him. I don't know if something is wrong, or if he just doesn't want to talk to me."

Moshe replies, "Yeah, well, the same thing happens to me. I call, I leave a message, and I never hear from him. Days pass, and I have the same concerns as you, but you know, in the end, if he doesn't want to talk, he doesn't want to talk! I figure that we're such a tight group that if, God forbid, something terrible happened, if he had died or something, I'm sure we'd have heard about it – bad news always travels fast. But I haven't heard anything, so I really don't know. Maybe there's something else: maybe he's angry at me, or I said something that insulted him, maybe I didn't pay enough attention to him, but if he won't tell me, what can I do? I decided that if he doesn't want to stay in touch, then the hell with him! What are you going to do about him?"

"Don't know. It's actually kind of irritating. I mean if something really happened to him, wouldn't someone have let us know? I stopped worrying about him, and now I'm thinking that all his talk back then about 'let's stay in touch,' and all that, was just talk. He didn't actually mean it. But, you know, I also had thoughts that maybe I did something to upset him, but I can't think what, I don't remember any incident or anything, I just can't figure it out. I don't know. Maybe we should just forget about him, and that's it."

"Just forget? That's hard when we were so close that we hugged each other, and called each other 'brother,' and then he just disappears. It's maddening."

Uri sighs, concluding his imaginary conversation.

Gil looks embarrassed, upset, and on the verge of tears. He had not anticipated the eventual withdrawal of his friends. He had gambled that even if he did not reply for some time, his close friends, his comrades in arms, would continue to be concerned about his welfare, and that if he ever decided to pick up the phone again, all would be well. He had not really considered his friends' feelings, or reasoned that they might move from frustration to worry, from concern to anger, and finally decide he was a lost cause. It alarmed him to hear that they might, in fact, be suffering from feelings that maybe they had done something wrong and this was the reason he was ignoring them. He had never contemplated such a possibility. But now, after Uri's imaginary but convincing explanation, it seemed clear that he had better change his behavior, and fast, if he didn't want to permanently lose his friends. He was seeing that his behavior had consequences, and possibly had already caused significant damage to his relationships. He just hoped that if this had happened, it was reversible.

Yossi joins in. "So Gil, you get what you have to do? Your friends were probably very concerned, but everyone has his limits, and if you don't start to respond, you'll lose them. None of us can afford such a loss. Did you ever think about why you don't reply?"

"Yes, of course I did. It's on my mind all the time! Every time I see a number lighting up the screen, I have an inner war. I want to respond, but I'm afraid, and I can't."

"Afraid of what?" Yariv enters the discussion.

"Afraid that I won't know what to say."

"What do you mean?" Yariv coaxes.

"They'll surely ask me, 'So, how's it going,' and such."

"True, it's reasonable to assume you'll hear that. So what?"

"I don't want to lie and say that everything's fine, when the truth is that it's not. I don't function like before, I'm in a therapy group of post-trauma survivors, I can't work like I used to, and I feel like shit; and who really wants to hear things like that?"

"You explain it very well. I'm sure most of us feel like you're describing, but just like we have to make an effort to start getting back to work and to studying, we have to work at getting back to our families and our friends. At the beginning it's very hard; it's much easier to avoid them and to hide, but the price is way too high. The more time passes, the more the pattern solidifies and the harder it becomes to change. Which friend has called you most often?"

"Eliyahu. Eliyahu, a very dear friend. We were together at the worst times..."

"Can you try to imagine having a phone conversation with him?" Yariv inquires, in a gently encouraging tone.

Gil is frozen in his seat. He has tried to imagine having a conversation with Eliyahu many times. Now that he is being questioned about it by a new, supportive friend in this sheltered environment, surrounded by others with similar problems, he finds he is completely unable to respond.

"So listen to what happened to me," Yossi says urgently. "My friends used to call too, and I wouldn't answer. A week ago, I'm walking in the street, and bang! I run into Israel, the one who called me the most. I was startled and nervous and tried to pretend that I didn't see him, but he immediately caught on. He smiled at me, stopped in his tracks, but didn't say a word. It's as if he was inviting me without words to take the next step, and we both understood that was the agenda.

"So I stopped. I couldn't run away, it wouldn't be nice, and I certainly didn't want to offend him, he's such a good friend. So I'm recalling what we learned here, in the group, the deep breathing, relaxation, and all that. And my heart is pounding, I can feel the veins in my temples bulging and a sharp headache is beginning to develop. And I'm noticing all this. I'm translating it all into Zev's words: 'anxiety causes bodily sensations and overreactions.' And I decide right on the spot that hard as it is, right now I'm taking the step I've been managing to avoid since I got back. So I take a deep breath and start walking toward him, very slowly, about ten yards. Israel understood what's happening, instantly, and he too started walking over to me, slowly. Finally we stood next to each other, and suddenly he gives me a huge hug, still not saying a word. The ice was broken. The encounter I feared so much had happened at last. And he was perfect – he totally got it.

"We stood there, hugging for almost a minute, which felt like forever, and then he let go and said, 'So happy to see you. Espresso? There's a Café Joe right around the corner.'"

"We sat there, for hours and talked and talked. As if we had never stopped talking. And he never threw me any, 'why didn't you answer my phone calls?' I was so lucky to have run into a friend as sensitive as Israel. He helped me to overcome that tremendous hurdle.

"So here's what you have to do. Wait, I don't mean that you *have* to, I mean that it might be a good idea for you to do it: choose the most sensitive friend you have, one who's not going to accuse you or blame you, who'd just be happy to hear from you again. Take that deep breath, prepare a few opening sentences, and pick up the phone. Don't apologize that you haven't answered the phone when he called. Start as if you're continuing a conversation from yesterday."

Gil responds with a heavy sigh. He feels envious of Yossi. He can't think of any friend he has who is like that; there is no one who seems as sensitive or understanding as Yossi's friend Israel seems to be. He wishes he had such a friend; but since he doesn't, he continues to think about what he will say if the phone ever rings again and he finds a friend on the other end. If he were to hear 'Where have you been?', he'll answer 'I'm here now, and I'm happy to talk with you,' and he'll move on.

"What did you talk about for hours?" He finally asks Yossi, as if trying to imagine a scenario he might be able to use for himself.

"About his family, my family, his work, economics, whatever, it's amazing how fast the time passed. He had a tremendous amount to say. Since I saw him, his mother had passed away, a niece got married, he changed jobs, and he's taking engineering courses now. We're meeting again next week."

"So much news and so much living. I guess that as time passes, things just happen to people," Gil muses.

Zev remains silent. He didn't intervene when Uri confronted Gil, didn't broaden the topic when Yossi described how he had implemented the technique he had learned in the group. Zev had merely introduced the subject in broad terms then stepped back to let the group carry the ball. He saw that the group had become sufficiently coherent, and some of its members had learned techniques well enough, for the guys to help their fellow sufferers whom they understood so deeply. Warm bonds were beginning to form.

Now Yariv softly clears his throat, signaling that he's preparing to speak. He is among those members who have reached a modest degree of success, and he is eager to share his gains with his new friends. Zev's invitation to report on changes had given him all the encouragement he needed, but he had chosen to wait respectfully until everyone else who wanted to talk had said their piece.

"For me, it wasn't that I didn't answer the phone, I actually did; but when the conversation rolled in the direction of 'let's meet,' I always found a reason why it was inconvenient: I didn't have time, the car was being serviced, my dog had a cough...and so on, because I, like Gil, was afraid what would happen after the first words. Would they want to talk about the events we experienced? I certainly didn't. Nor about my recuperation after I got injured, and definitely not about the political situation and the security threats – God forbid. So I found all kinds of excuses to postpone invitations and refuse them. But with my wife Anat's encouragement, last week I finally agreed to go with her to visit some friends on Saturday. When the day came I had a huge headache all morning, I was tense and irritable, quarreled with her, asked why I had to accompany her, asked her to go with the kids and without me, and more nonsense. She put her hand on my shoulder, and calmly assured me that everything would be fine. She hinted that our friends were aware how difficult it might be for me to discuss painful subjects. In other words, she had prepared the ground. She hadn't expected me to initiate the visit, even though Yoel is my friend, and so she had done it. All she hoped for was my participation, even passively. She assured me that I was not expected to be entertaining or tell stories, that I could just listen, and maybe talk a little bit; I wasn't the lead actor on the stage. She just wanted to break the cycle of avoidance that I had pursued for the last several months."

"And how did it go?" asked Yossi.

"We drove there, to Modiin, where the officers' residences are. There was some tension in the car, which I could tell even the kids sensed, because they didn't act wild like they usually do. They actually whispered among themselves and didn't even fight as to who would sit next to the window and all the normal silly stuff kids do. My wife chatted a little about something she had purchased on sale, and I understood that she was just trying to dissipate the tension; she knows perfectly well that she never needs my "permission" to buy something; I trust her completely and support anything she wants to purchase.

"When we arrived, we were warmly received. We sat on a terrace overlooking the surrounding mountains – very beautiful, very relaxing. Yoel brought out beer and the kids had slices of cold watermelon, which they love. The women, always watching their diets, skipped the hors d'ouvres and waited for the meal. Yoel and I talked about this and that, and nobody brought up any sensitive subjects. Yoel let me lead the conversation and essentially just reacted to things I said. After about half an hour, my headache disappeared, I calmed down, and felt at home. It didn't feel as though nine months had passed since I had visited anyone's home. The beer might have helped a little, but I was sipping it slowly, not throwing it down to use it like a tranquilizer, so I think its effect wasn't significant. What *was* significant was the receptive atmosphere, not having to play a major role, just visiting good friends like the old days. We got home about nine p.m., which was much later than I had expected; I had set a two-hour limit before we even left in the morning, but time passed so easily that I didn't even notice."

Nodding heads among the guys indicated understanding and satisfaction at Yariv's progress. He had successfully broken the cycle of isolation, which gave hope to the others that they might do this, too.

Silence settled again throughout the room, like a collective deep breath. The tension had eased and there didn't seem to be much to add, at least for the moment.

After a lengthy pause, perhaps a minute long, Zev concluded that it was an appropriate moment to summarize all these reports and to try to draw conclusions from them.

"So what do all these descriptions have in common?"

"It seems that the fear of the unknown turns out to be worse than the event itself. I had built myself a wall to hide behind, afraid that I wouldn't be able to stand up to the demands of socializing, and it turned out not to be a problem," said Yariv.

"And another thing is that it's important to pave the way, that is, to choose someone to be with who is easygoing and sensitive to our needs. Luckily for me, it was Anat, who was able to prepare the ground in her own way. She organized the get-together; she arranged with the hosts ahead of time what subjects not to bring up; and she was calm and encouraging to me."

Yossi adds his own conclusions: "True, like Yariv said, I had the good luck to run into a friend who was sensitive to me and didn't press me to discuss things he knew I might not want to talk about, and he wasn't on my case about not having answered his calls. He made the unexpected meeting pleasant and lengthy."

"And what if I don't have anyone like that?" Gil burst out in a more aggressive tone than he had used earlier. He felt that things were easier for the others, who seemed to have more friends to help them, whereas he had only himself to depend on.

Zev chimes in. "It's hard to believe that among all your family and friends, there isn't one who could pave the way for you.

Think for a moment about all the people who know your situation. I believe you'll discover that such a person exists, possibly someone who at first glance you might not think of. Here's an idea: do you remember that at the beginning, when you returned from the war feeling sad and needing support, you mentioned that several people said something like, 'If there's anything I can do, please let me know?' And you always responded with, 'No, thanks, I don't need anything,' right? Well, now is the time for you to cash in one of those chips and say to someone who offered, 'Remember when you offered to help me and I said I didn't need anything? Well, now I would appreciate it if you could help me with something…' And then you outline for him exactly what you would like. For example, set up a meeting between me and one of my friends, one in which he too would participate, or call another friend and report to him on what's happening with me and arrange for him to call me. There are many possibilities."

Zev hopes his words will help Gil to move forward.

*   *   *

Yariv is sitting quietly now, looking thoughtful. Uri's earlier aggression toward Gil had surprised him, and he is suddenly aware that Uri has revealed very little about his own problems, or about the events in his life that had brought him to the group. From his occasional comments, it is clear that he feels he has changed and that he's having difficulties with his wife. He has acknowledged having some of the same symptoms as the others when they have brought them up. But he has given few details about his issues and none about what had actually happened to him. Yariv wonders if Uri might be hiding something extremely painful, and if the reason he was so confrontational with Gil was partly to avoid talking about himself.

He turns toward Uri. "Uri, I noticed that you're on Gil's back, and I understand why, you've explained it well; but I get the feeling that behind all this there is something tormenting you that we haven't heard about. I've been wondering: what is it that brought you here?"

Uri blushes. He's been dreading this moment, engaging in

evasive maneuvers to avoid confronting his own issues. But now the moment has unavoidably arrived with this challenge offered by Yariv, and he feels that he owes his friends an honest answer.

"True. Until now, I haven't been straight about what happened with me. The reason is that I'm ashamed of it, and I haven't had the guts to bring it out into the open. So, as much as I worry about what you will think of me when I'm done talking, it's probably good that you are pushing me to the wall."

Haltingly, he begins his story. "After I was in the academic reserve, I enrolled in the armored corps. I went to the officer's course and came out with a rank of Second Lieutenant. I enjoyed the job, and was surprised how interesting I found the innards and workings of a tank. As a musician, I had never thought about such technical matters. I participated in a number of operations, gained experience, overcame challenges like communicating among all the chaos and noise, and I felt good that I could be contributing to the overall effort at an officer's level. The operations I participated in always ended well for us, and although we were shot at, I had no serious problems and the level of danger seemed tolerable. This one time, though, things were different.

"Like some of you, the Second Lebanon War changed everything for me. This time we were shot at with armor-piercing missiles that sliced through the tank like it was butter. The armored walls stopped nothing. A small hole, even two inches in diameter, caused havoc. Sagger Anti-Tank Missiles flew in all directions and as tank commander, with my upper body out of the turret, I saw incredible horrors. There was a row of tanks ahead of us, moving slowly, and suddenly there was an explosion and in the row of tanks a big gap opened! The tank that had been there a minute ago just disappeared, as if it had never been there! There was just a cloud of dust to offer a hint as to what had happened. And the radio chirped, 'Flower, Flower,' the code for injuries, and actually it was much worse. There weren't only wounded, some guys just completely vanished! I was terrified! I might be the next one, and as I'm trying to gather my thoughts, bang, we're hit! My tank shuddered and moved sideways, as if someone had given it a little nudge, not too powerful, but I'm hearing awful cries from inside. My loader-radio operator gave a long wailing shriek then fell silent. The driver tried to turn us around, but couldn't. Thick smoke started to rise from the inside and covered me so I couldn't see what was happening or where to go. Over the radio, I yelled, 'We're hit!' and at that very moment, I don't recall how, I leaped from the tank and started running away. I ran like a madman, not knowing where I was going. I was scared to death. There were explosions, people screaming, medics running all over, and I'm running too. Suddenly I stop and I realize that I've simply abandoned my post as tank commander! I'm responsible for that tank, and I'm not doing what I'm supposed to. I started to turn back to it, and then it gets hit again - and it explodes! I cup my face in my palms, my hands are shaking. It's not as though I could have prevented the missile from hitting my tank, but I wasn't commanding! I just left! I felt horrible. I had disappointed my guys. I let them down. I failed . I should have stayed, should have acted like a commander, but I ran. I was in charge of the tank, it was my obligation to remain, and I didn't..."

Uri slumps back in his seat, looking agonized. Tears are streaming down his cheeks.

Silence pervades the room, as it had on many other such occasions.

Everyone was trying to digest the content of Uri's experience. Everyone had heard of such events before joining the group, but this time the story had come from the mouth of one their fellow group members, and it contained deeply troubling aspects. There was the horror Uri described; the empathy they felt about what Uri and his crew suffered; and there was also the aspect that Uri was so upset about: that he might be seen as a coward. Here was Ron, who attempted to save a soldier with all his strength yet felt ashamed that he did not succeed, as opposed to Uri who should have stayed in his post, but instead abandoned it. They all understand why Uri feels shame and embarrassment. Some want to console and support him, but several others just nod their heads in agreement with Uri's own assessment of his actions. The ongoing silence intensifies the conflicting feelings. Some believe that they might very well have acted exactly as Uri did in those horrendous moments, and just try to survive. Others feel that his actions did not befit those of a commander; and although no one was prepared to say this out loud, there was really no need to: the silence spoke for itself.

Zev came to Uri's aid. "You've experienced an awful situation and it's easy to understand why it has been so difficult for you to talk about it. You're judging yourself, and we're our own harshest critics. We all need to absorb and digest what you've told us, and that won't happen right away. We'll talk about it next time. And if you'd like to talk to me during the week, you always know how to reach me."

The quiet continued for some time. Two guys walked over to Uri and patted him on the shoulder, without speaking. Others just nodded in his direction.

* * *

Sergei broke the silence.

"Yesterday I was walking on Herzel Street and a bus passed by. I have been seeing this bus my whole life, it's not a surprise, but when it stopped and the driver opened the door and that whistle of compressed air was heard, I jumped like you wouldn't believe! People on the street turned around to see what had happened and looked at me as if I was nuts. I wanted to disappear, to evaporate into thin air. I was hoping that nobody I knew had seen me. It was just terrible."

Sergei sinks deep in his chair, sounds exhausted and emotional. This confession is difficult for him. He had been sitting on this problem, his sensitivity to noises, afraid to bring it up, fearing he would sound childish and weak.

"So, the noise of the doors made you jump?" asked Zev.

"Yeah, stupid, isn't it?" replied Sergei.

"No, not stupid at all, but definitely frustrating. And it's easy to understand why you'd feel it was embarrassing."

"All kinds of noises drive me crazy. Even something as simple as washing silverware in the sink. Imagine...the ordinary sound of a piece of metal clanking against another one reminds me of the sounds I heard in the tank. There it was metal chains, tools, extrication equipment, the sound of a hammer hitting the track, and the sound you hear when a shell hits something while you are loading it into the canon. Even the sound of a water canteen hitting something. There were always sounds of metal hitting metal. But even so, silverware? That's insane! My mother says that instead of sitting at home all day, at least I should be doing something there, like washing the dishes. I'd like to, but that sound...it jettisons me right back to my room. I simply can't take it. I know this is idiotic, and I'm ashamed of it, and my mother thinks that I'm just lazy and want her to wait on me all day – but that's not true at all! I *don't* want that. I used to be the king of dishwashing. I've been doing the dishes since I was five, I was an expert, a "specialist," but now it's a totally different story. It's not just silverware anymore: it's like the noise one second before one of those things explodes..."

"Want to learn how to deal with it?"

"Of course! It drives me insane."

"Why?" Zev questions him more intensely.

"Why? What am I, a psycho? I can't do a simple thing like wash dishes? I'm 22 years old. I vote, I can drive a car, even a tank, know how to shoot a canon, screw women – but I can't wash the dishes!"

"Technically, it's not true that you *can't* wash dishes. You've already convinced us that you are a "specialist" in that. It's that the noise produced by a fork hitting a spoon in the sink, or the knife smacking the ladle, the sounds of cooking utensils mixed together and banging against each other and producing metallic noises – this all reminds you of a very scary event, a truly alarming experience, a situation in which terrible things happened. And right now you're in a state where these noises automatically take you back there – far away from the familiar and safe kitchen sink in your own apartment, which you ordinarily wouldn't even think about twice. At that moment, it seems to me, you have no control over this automatic response...because it is exactly that: automatic."

"So, what does one do?" Sergei asks.

"Here, again, is a good example of a change that has taken place in your perspective about what is happening: where reality is replaced by what is going on in your imagination. The situation is this: the banging of metal on metal is instantly translated into the perception of a dangerous situation, which you must escape in order to survive. Of course, when the fork hits the spoon in the kitchen sink in your own home, the reality is that there isn't any danger at all. But by the time you figure this out logically, the escape action has already occurred, and so you feel a sense of failure, 'I'm a rabbit, jeez, I just can't, what happened to me...' and so on."

"Well, yeah, we've heard all of that before, so what does one *do*?" Sergei says impatiently.

"Let's start with your wish to go to the kitchen, let's say to prepare a cup of hot soup. Okay? Reasonable?"

"Sure, so what?" is the curt reply.

"So you start looking for ingredients: a pot, the soup, a spoon, and whatever else you might need. You have to heat up the soup, no problem, but the spoon isn't in its usual place. You can't find it. Turns out it is in the sink together with all the breakfast dishes. So you are searching among the utensils to find it, rinse it, and prepare your soup. Right?"

"Yeah, and..."

"You rummage through the silverware and the utensils make that metallic sound – and, boom! You're outside the kitchen, back in your room, and you're telling yourself, "I'm not hungry. I didn't really want that soup anyway.'"

"Yeah, something like that. But you're still not moving me forward." Sergei is twitching in his seat as if he's ready to jump up and leave.

"Just a second! I'm constructing something here. Before you even enter the kitchen, stop!"

"What? Why, are there land mines in there?" Sergei asks sarcastically, with a smirk.

"Don't laugh! For you, there are! Not the kind that cut off your leg, the kind that destroy your morale."

"What are you babbling about?" Sergei throws a verbal punch.

"The mine is the automatic explosion inside your head, which is connected to the noise of one spoon banging against another and signaling that there is danger from which you must escape. And when you've fled, you feel like shit, feel that you failed. Isn't that a kind of mine?"

"Ok, I get it. Again, what do I do?" Sergei retreats from his aggressive stance, sounding more like his usual friendly self.

Zev continues: "Back to the entrance of the kitchen. You stop. You don't enter. And you think: 'I need the pot, the soup, and the soupspoon that is always in the drawer, but there is a good chance that if it isn't there, it might be in the sink, where there are often lots of other utensils as well.' Ok? 'And if I have to reach the spoon by rummaging through the sink, then metallic sounds will come from things banging against each other.' All this, while you are still at the entrance to the kitchen and you have not yet set foot in it. Still far away from your soup. And you start to imagine that noise, the banging, the scraping, the clanking sound of something hitting the metallic sink when something is jarred or falls to the bottom of the sink. And as you stand there and imagine it, your heart begins to race..."

"Which is exactly what is happening right now, as you speak..."

"Yes. So you take a deep breath, exhale it very slowly, and you still don't move. Are you listening? You *don't move!*"

"So?"

"So, do it now!" commands Zev.

"Do what?"

"Take a deep breath and exhale it slowly, imagining that scene in the kitchen doorway. And when your racing heart has slowed down to a reasonable level, lift your finger to let me know."

Five group members start to do what Zev has asked for. They are thinking of their own particular anxiety-causing scenarios, and experiencing some of the physiological discomforts associated with them. They no longer feel any embarrassment in front of Zev or their friends; they are simply eager to learn the techniques that can ease their pain.

"Yeah, it's working. I've calmed down," affirms Sergei.

"Back to the entrance of the kitchen. Are you with me?"

"Yes, go on."

"You are visualizing, paying attention to your heartbeat, your tension and fear, and you think: 'It is a soupspoon in my kitchen, in the sink. I'm hungry and want to eat a bowl of soup and that damned spoon will be making that hateful sound.' And probably your pulse leaps up again. And you do not enter the kitchen until you bring it down to a reasonable level. Only then do you enter, slowly, knowing what to expect. You know how it will sound, you know there are no mines, no shells, that you are not in the tank and that you're going to act bravely, and despite the fear – you make that soup. You find that spoon and manage your fear; you make the soup, pick up the spoon, overcome your anxiety, and eat your soup. Sound simple enough?"

"Yes and no. Right now I'm imagining what will happen in the kitchen, and I'm managing my anxiety, and planning to try this tomorrow."

"That's the 'yes,' what's the 'no'?" asks Zev.

"Here, now that I'm with you and my buddies, I'm confident. But I don't know what will happen when I'm at home by myself and the fears come flooding in, and I can't stop them despite all good intentions."

"That's what I thought that you would say. But don't forget, this is a learning process and one doesn't always execute everything perfectly on first try. That's normal. You may have to try it several times and in small steps. There's no shame in that. Do you swim?"

"Yes, of course. What about it?"

"Did you just one day at age six jump into the water and swim away?"

"Okay, okay, I get the point."

"Maybe nothing bad would happen next time if you just walked into the kitchen, but why risk it? If you move too quickly without being calm and prepared and then you fail – that is, you run out of the kitchen again – your failure might reinforce the very feeling of fear that you are trying to avoid. The heroism here is in taking measured steps, because as everyone here knows, overcoming fear is every bit as difficult as overcoming physical pain. A small step can require a lot of courage. For example, it takes great determination to stretch a rubber band in a physical therapy session when you have a painful joint, or to make a fist with swollen fingers. Have any of you ever had orthopedic surgery and then undergone rehab? If so, you know exactly what I'm talking about. The courage required to go for those treatments is sometimes no less than that required to face a dangerous situation in battle. I understand that you feel impatient, and that perhaps it feels childish to you to stand at the entrance to the kitchen and not enter it 'Until I'm ready,' but believe me, the time you put in waiting is a good investment."

"You're probably right," agrees Sergei with a sigh. "And I

suppose I do the same thing with that bus?"

"Something very similar," confirms Zev. "Can you figure it out?" Zev leans toward Sergei in a supportive gesture.

"Just thinking that the bus is coming makes me crazy!"

"Anyone have some advice for Sergei?"

Gil rubs his hands together nervously, pulls his shoulders back, clenches his teeth, and takes a deep breath as if preparing to jump from the diving board into a neighborhood's pool. It's never easy for him to join in the discussions without worrying that he'll say something silly or stupid, but he feels he has something to contribute now, and is unwilling to succumb to his shyness.

"Can you imagine that you're sitting at home," Gil begins, "and you say to yourself, 'I'm gonna go out to Herzl Street, and then the bus will arrive – cause it comes every 20 minutes – and then it'll stop at the corner and the driver'll open the door, and the compressed air that opens the doors will make that awful shrieking sound like the one you hear in the battlefield, and it reminds me of one of the guys screaming 'Shell coming, shell coming,' and the shell lands very close to me and I'm scared to death, and I'm jumping like mad and running to save my soul. And now, on Herzl Street, I'm waiting for the bus and I'm feeling like it's the same thing. But I know it's Herzl Street, and that there's no shell coming, and there are no shells, and nothing…"

"Yes, I can," Sergei interrupts, "but my heart is still pounding and my hands are wet, and there's sweat on my forehead…"

"Yeah, so you take a deep breath, you close your eyes, you imagine the bus, you wait inside your head for the air to whistle, take another deep breath, like Zev said, and you don't go out to the street until you do it enough times, until you hear the doors in your imagination, and it no longer does anything to you. Only then you go out to Herzl…"

Gil sighs deeply and sinks into his chair, as though he has completed a challenging task and is greatly relieved that it's over.

"More power to you, Gil! You really said something helpful," Zev says approvingly. "That's exactly the idea. Sergei, will you give it a try?"

The group sits quietly. The wall clock indicates that time is up for today's session, but no one is moving. Zev is pleased by the deep silence and stillness. He knows that wheels are turning. He is confident that the techniques they worked on in today's session will be taken home and used. People will attempt to tailor them to fit their own personal demons. He's curious and filled with anticipation for the next session and the feedback he hopes to receive. Everyone understands what he is hoping for, because everyone is thinking the same thing. There is a mixture of anxiety, hope and eagerness for their next meeting in the air.

"Next week! Homework, everyone." says Zev without the need for further elaboration.

IDO

Ido is a tall, lanky 30-year-old. His face almost always wears a serious expression, and his daily attire consists of wrinkled khakis held in place by a thin, somewhat shabby brown belt whose end is often left dangling loosely. He is generally disorganized and conveys the impression that he doesn't attribute much importance to his appearance. However, behind this solemn expression and apparent carelessness about his attire lies a complex personality that he prefers to conceal.

When the Shachar family in Jerusalem gave birth to their first baby, they wanted a name that reflected their feelings. For years they had dreamt of dwelling in the holy city, of having a child, and now their dreams were realized. They were encouraged, filled with hope, pride, and contentment – and they named the baby Ido, a play on words suggesting the Hebrew word for "encouragement."

In the first years of his life, Ido developed physically like any other child. He was a normal boy, yet not quite: at ten months he started saying words, and within a few weeks, short sentences came from his tiny mouth. One morning in the kitchen with his mother, he suddenly said: "Ima, food Ido." His disbelieving mother whirled around to look at him. When he went on to say, "Ima, eat" there was no denying that the surprising request had come from her small son. From then on, he was never quiet.

In the first grade, he argued with his teacher, managing to convince her that the break between lessons was too short and that she ought to allow more time for her students to gather their belongings and prepare for their next subject. His powers of persuasion were impressive and he used language like a child twice his age.

In the second grade, he discovered history and was fascinated to hear – and later on to read – about the Roman legions. He asked his father numerous questions, then he wanted the answers repeated over and over. The story of Masada captured his imagination. His parents were delighted by his interest in this historic national site, where 400 Jewish fighters committed suicide rather than fall captive to the Roman legions.

In the third grade, he read constantly, devouring books at a sixth-grade level, and he was able to recall almost every detail from his readings. He began to draw connections among facts and events from different periods and to pose challenging questions. One evening, the eight-year-old boy turned to his father and posited the following: "Aba, if the Babylonians succeeded in destroying the First Temple and expelling the Jews from *Eretz Israel*, the land of Israel, and then after a few hundred years the Romans succeeded in destroying the Second Temple and exiling the Jews, what would prevent our enemies now from overthrowing our state? After all, doesn't history repeat itself?"

Ido's father was surprised and impressed by the intellectual power of his son. In fact, this very question had been rattling around in his own head and in the heads of many other adults he knew, troubling them deeply. He found it hard to believe that such a young boy had already succeeded in conceptualizing their long, painful national history and was asking something that most of them were reluctant to voice aloud. And here was this little guy, with his still-childish voice and innocent eyes, raising the most worrisome issue of all: the continued existence of the state.

After taking a deep breath to regain his composure and buy himself a few seconds of time, his father gave his son a thoughtful and detailed reply, one the boy never forgot; in fact, it became a perpetual light that guided his thinking on the subject from that day forward.

"You've asked a very difficult question, Ido, and you deserve an answer. It seems to me that if you are able to ask it, despite your young age, then you are probably ready to hear the answer, and, after some thought, to digest it. This question has been niggling in many of our heads for years, although it is rarely discussed. There are many people who are sure that Israel is always in great danger and that therefore we must be ready for all eventualities. And there are others who think – or more correctly, *believe* – that God will protect us, and that faith and good deeds are the answer. Your mother and I belong to the first group, and therefore we believe in a strong Israeli Army, in the power of deterrence, in constant vigilance, and not in miracles. We believe that Israelis need to train, gather intelligence, and be outfitted with the most modern and sophisticated equipment. We have faith in the power of science and in the Jewish-Israeli brain to deal with any threats, plots, and schemes that are aimed against us. And at the same time, we want to live in peace and quiet with those we consider our 'cousins.' There are thousands of examples demonstrating that such coexistence really is possible."

"Aba, now I'm going to play with Danny. Call me for dinner," announced Ido, and he disappeared into the yard.

Clearly, Ido felt that what he had heard was enough. After all, he was only eight years old. This long and complex answer was a tall order for the little questioner, and while he was with his friend, his father's words continued to percolate in his head.

Ido's one friend, Danny, was a quiet, bespectacled boy, introverted and book-loving like Ido. They spent many hours together. But rather than play games, they preferred doing homework, reading, and talking. Often they settled themselves in the comfortable home-office of Danny's father, a lawyer. There, deep sunk in two dark-brown leather armchairs, Ido delved into his history books while Danny immersed himself in science. Like Ido, Danny's knowledge was well beyond that of a typical eight-year old. Already he understood how an elevator works, how a radio receives waves over the ether and transmits them as music and speech, and how a computer stores information and spits it out with a few keystrokes. Now and then, Danny and Ido would share their knowledge of their respective areas with each other.

"Would you believe?" Danny would exclaim.

"What?" replied Ido, anticipating a morsel of information on some scientific subject that was actually of little interest to him. He knew how delighted Danny was whenever he learned something new, and he understood their tit-for-tat exchanges.

"When a satellite ends its life, its track shortens, the speed decreases, and then it drifts into a whirlpool and gets sucked in, moving toward earth, disintegrating in flames on its way down. Wow!"

"That's really interesting. How long does a satellite survive in space?"

"Years and years" replied the little professor, "but none of them lasts forever."

"Hmmm" responded Ido, wanting to support his friend, but not wanting to encourage him to go further.

Danny, in turn, sometimes had to suffer from historical facts being tossed out at him from the other armchair, from which Ido's two skinny legs were dangling.

"Hannibal did amazing tricks with his elephants."

"For example?" asked Danny, who was not at all interested in Hannibal's elephants' tricks. But he also understood the rules – if he wanted Ido to continue to listen to the wonderful scientific minutia that he was feeding him, then he would have to listen to the historical events that stirred Ido.

"Well, he crossed the high, freezing Alps with elephants. Elephants live in warm climates like India and Africa and cold weather is hard for them. I don't know how the elephants survived."

"Maybe Hannibal fed them a special diet that gave them energy," Ido suggested, searching for a scientific answer to the question plaguing Danny.

"Maybe popsicles…" he added, and they both burst out laughing.

Although Ido was a serious child whose friendly smile was seen only rarely, Danny would easily burst into laughter that was so refreshing and contagious that others, Ido included, would join in, often without completely understanding why.

Ido had blue eyes and sandy blond hair, a reflection of his Russian heritage. He had a small nose and a wide mouth, and his eyes expressed curiosity and intelligence. Danny was of Eastern descent, with darkish skin and black eyes. A lock of hair hung down playfully from his high forehead. His hands were small and to the casual observer, the sight of this young boy with tiny hands holding a large and heavy scientific book was comical.

Ido's father, Alex, managed a bank branch. He was a fussy man, careful with words and meticulous with his clothing. He said little and his facial expression often left the observer wondering whether he was preoccupied or worried.

Actually his life was orderly and he had no particular problems or concerns. He made a good salary, got along well with his superiors who appreciated his work and advice, and ran a branch whose income was among the highest in the system. Businessmen respected his professionalism and turned to him for advice and for private and business loans. His work hours were moderate, and after he returned home he did not have to engage in work-related activities until the next morning.

When Alex returned home, he would remove his jacket, undo his tie, take off his starched long sleeved shirt, and slip off his polished shoes. Every item was put in its proper place. He got great peace of mind from his routines, and he didn't like surprises. He was often thrown off-balance by the startling and provocative questions Ido raised, like the one about the destruction of the First and Second Temples. He would need to take a deep breath, compose himself, and carefully formulate his answer himself before responding to his young son.

Alex Shachar was known among colleagues and friends as a man on whom one could rely, but also one whom it was best not to confront. In contrast, Ido's mother Chaya, short and chunky at 51, still had an open, girlish smile and was much easier to get close to. Unlike her husband, she did not particularly revere order. Her house wasn't spotless, and dishes were not always in their cupboards. At times, some were left in the sink for awhile after meals. To her way of thinking, why rush? Chatting and watching television had a much greater appeal for her than household chores.

Chaya was a clerk in the local clinic of the national health insurance system, and all the patients loved her. She was sensitive to their suffering and more than once succeeded in sneaking a patient into the doctor's office at the last moment, just before the doctor's shift was over. Staff liked her too, and many turned to her with their personal problems. Chaya organized farewell parties, birthday celebrations, parties for a new grandchild: all those events that sweeten a workplace and create personal closeness.

She was also good at her job. Over the years she learned to use the computer and gently pushed the staff to follow in her footsteps, including the elderly doctor who was the most difficult to convince.

"Chaya, I have been writing scripts by hand for 30 years and all is going well, so I'm not changing."

"Yes, but 30 years ago we had only 1/10 of today's drugs."

"OK. OK. I get it," and he relented.

Conversations between Ido and his father were intellectual, dealing with history, the Bible, and politics. Dealing with feelings was left to Ido and his mother. The boy inherited his serious expression from his father and his occasional friendly smile from his mother.

In high school, Ido participated in the obligatory athletic activities, but was not a sports enthusiast. He still enjoyed reading about the history of Israel, memorizing places, names, and dates with ease and connecting them in his head. But when he was 14, he found another love: field trips. He especially liked exploring places whose history he had learned. These excursions began close to home with the annual class trips and outings with his Scout troop. Later they expanded to include more distant destinations, like the Golan Heights and Eilat. He particularly loved to stroll through the neighborhoods of Jerusalem. He was perfectly happy to make these excursions on his own, and soon he knew the city from one end to the other. On Shabbat mornings he would set out with a copy of "The Jerusalem Guide" to "conquer" one neighborhood after another. He would scribble notes in the margins and make small sketches to add details the author had not included.

He was particularly fond of Emek Refaim Street, the main road in the German Colony. For some reason he found himself drawn to its straight, orderly streets, a characteristic that made it unlike other neighborhoods that had developed in a more helter-skelter fashion. Emek Refaim Street became one of his favorite walks. He would peek into its cafes, the bookstore, the grocery store, then make a sharp left into one of the small side streets, named after Émile Zola. This modest little pathway had only a few houses and the shrubbery growing on its fences was so thick that it was impossible to read house numbers. Many years ago, his grandfather had lived in one of these homes, and he used to tell his grandson stories about his romantic escapades inside its walls. Ido searched for it several times but was never able to identify it.

Burrowing through the neighborhood in this manner deepened his love for the city, and he became adept at finding his way despite its many turns. His grandfather told him that he, too, used to walk there on Shabbat, all the way to the border of the divided city, where he would then be forced to stop at the barbed wire near a stone wall covered with layers of sandbags and dotted with lookout posts. As a young man, his grandfather would sometimes wave toward a Jordanian soldier who stood guard less than 150 feet away. There was a measure of *chutzpah*, of hubris, in this, bordering on provocation, but it was also intended as a message that it might be possible to be friendly neighbors, and that a handwave could be an alternative to the deadly sniping.

Without the limitations imposed on his grandfather, Ido continued his walk through Emil Zola Street and at its end turned into Smaats Street. He then took a right turn into Lloyd George Street, proceeded to the end of that tiny alley, and thus arrived at the major road, Derekh Beit Lehem. Just a short stride further brought him to the old railroad station that his grandfather used to talk about. From there, the Old City was visible in all its glory.

The neighborhood of Mishkenot Sha'anim (the first neighborhood built outside the ancient city walls) lay there in front of him, and if he understood his grandfather's description accurately, that was another spot where the city had been divided for 19 years. Ido continued down the slope on The Jerusalem Brigade Street, the Cinematek to his right, and a few steps further, the Scottish Guest House with its cross mounted high up. All these places were out of reach until 1967. He marched further down the street into the lowest point of the valley, over the small bridge across the valley and then started the ascent toward the Tower of David. To the right he could see the Church of Dormition, which his grandpa remembered with a destroyed and burnt roof. It now stood there proudly, fully restored as if nothing had ever happened. Just a short distance further up the steep slope, he arrived at Jaffa Gate. Like King David, millennia ago, he stood there at the entrance to the Old City. Breathing deeply (as the steep incline taxed the energy of even a young, strong man), he inhaled Jerusalem's fresh air, taking in its history. Every time he reached that spot he felt a small shudder.

At times, Ido chose to get up early in the morning for his jaunts, a cool breeze wafting up the Judean hills from the valley of Jericho, to see the sun rise over the Golden Dome. On other days he chose to arrive there at dusk, when the sky reddened, bathing that wondrous edifice in a glistening, pink hue. The sounds of the muezzins, the Muslim clerics, calling the believers to prayer, filled the air from a distance, reminiscent of Verdi's behind-the-stage trumpets in Aida.

After graduating high school, Ido enlisted. Although still not particularly athletic, his frequent excursions climbing up steep hills and along narrow paths helped him in the bivouacs during basic training and the courses that followed. There was rarely a trip or excursion with which he wasn't already familiar, and his experience made him helpful to his comrades on these exhausting hikes. His love for nature and his eagerness to reach historical sites overshadowed the physical effort involved. As he had on his youthful trips into Jerusalem, he continued to take notes, and if he had spare energy, he'd add a quick sketch of a rock, a spring, or the hidden entrance to a cave. His knowledge of geography, of paths leading to unknown places and as yet unexcavated historical sites kept accumulating. Ido had become an expert, and his commanders often consulted him about which paths to take. Soon the Army Intelligence Service became interested in his skills.

"You seem to know Jerusalem and its neighborhoods well."

"Yes, why?" he responded to the Intelligence officer who had set up a meeting with him.

"And the surroundings, too."

"Yes. I love to explore and get to know unfamiliar locations, and to connect them to our history."

"We've noticed that you research things carefully, that you don't jump to conclusions until you're sure of the facts, and…"

"Who's 'we'? Am I being followed? What's going on here?" Ido felt puzzled and a little apprehensive.

"You're needed in Intelligence."

"Ah! So that's why you came to meet with me! All that talk about researching the Bible and all that…"

"Yes, that's it. That's why we think you would fit this particular assignment, and in three weeks, at the conclusion of basic training, you'll be assigned. Alright?"

"I hadn't planned on becoming a spy. I'll have to think about it. I just love to travel and learn."

"They go hand in hand. You'll have opportunities to go to places that would otherwise be out of your reach. And the contribution you can make, don't underestimate it!"

"We'll talk," Ido said hesitantly, with a sigh that intimated he had already accepted his fate, and was quietly pleased to have been selected for this coveted position.

Ido easily completed officers' training. He learned the material quickly, got along with his commanders, and was helpful to his comrades. At his graduation ceremony, his parents beamed with pride as the insignia of Second Lieutenant were placed on his shoulders. Alex produced one of his rare smiles, and Chaya wiped away tears of joy.

* * *

Toward the end of high school, Ido had become aware of Nava, a girl one year younger than him. She lived in the same neighborhood, and he'd bump into her on the street when he'd return from the grocery store, or from one of his hikes. She was usually surrounded by her girlfriends, but one day he spotted her walking home by herself, and, despite his shyness, he felt it was the right moment to approach her.

"You live in this area, right?"

Nava stopped in her tracks, surprised by the unexpected question.

"Yes...yeah...why do you ask?"

"Me too, here on Achad Ha'am, corner of Keren Hayesod."

"I'm on Smolenskin. You often take walks around here, right? I've noticed you many times, with a book in your hand."

"Yes, my guidebook. I like to explore the neighborhoods, especially on Shabbat, when it's quiet, not much traffic. Would you like to join me? I'll show you places that you surely haven't seen, didn't even know that they exist."

Nava was again taken aback by the assertive approach of this stranger. 'He barely knows me and is already asking me to join him in God-forsaken places.' But that side of him was intriguing and seductive. He looked well-built and masculine, and his wild hair and casual clothes piqued her interest. Unlike all the other guys his age, who spent a fortune on clothing, this guy showed more interest in the environment and nature than in his looks. He also appeared to have romantic potential, one who didn't flaunt his emotions, but rather let them out gently and quietly. She was interested in spending time with this strange adventurer, but was slightly apprehensive. She started to search for ways to say yes, without coming across as too eager, and agreed to a short stroll on Saturday.

The excursion took place just as planned.

"Hi, where to?" she asked, partly out of curiosity and partly because she truly had no idea where they would be going. She trusted him to know where to go, and all she wanted was to be with him. "All the rest will evolve," she thought.

That trip was the first of many, not only on Shabbat mornings, but also on holidays, and even at the end of a short school day. Ido led confidently, knowing his way and making sudden turns. At times he'd surprise her with unexpected views from a high point, telling her the names of the surrounding hills, teaching her how to use a compass. Nava never thought that she might be interested in this subject and discovered she was enthusiastic and curious. After a few such excursions with her newly found guide, she confidently identified places that, only a short time ago, she didn't know existed.

On one occasion she announced:" I'm tired, I need to sit down."

They sat at the foot of a large rock, observing the distant mountains to their left, Hadassah Hospital to their right. They were deep in the woods, trees branches shading them. Ido sat down next to her, back to back. "Want to lean?" he whispered, his heart pounding. She didn't respond – but she did lean back. And with each providing a backrest to the other, they sat there a few minutes, enjoying that moment when a friendship changes into something more.

"You're so cute, you know... " he filtered between half-closed lips as he began to turn to face her. "You too" and her head slumped into his neck. Without further words, they exchanged kisses. They sat there for long minutes, not showing any interest in reaching their original destination, just being together, as the small forest offered convenient and inviting shelter. They didn't return home till sunset. Both had some explaining to do on why they had returned so late, but neither set of parents inquired too deeply, understanding and just winking to each other, each in their own home.

When they had clearly become a couple, their families were pleased. Nava was Ido's first serious girlfriend, just as he was her first real boyfriend. She had dated a few times, but her relationship with Ido had greater intensity and content. Their parents knew each other, and both families felt comfortable with the partner their child had chosen.

* * *

Ido enlisted after they had been together for a year. His recruitment by the Intelligence Corps meant that he sometimes disappeared for lengthy periods and couldn't be in contact with her, or even his parents. Hezbollah and Hamas became very interested in his whereabouts, and because of this he was forbidden to reveal his identity or location. His parents and Nava respected the need for secrecy, and as much as they feared for his well-being and wished to know more – they didn't ask.

They also knew that he would have just glanced at them obliquely, tilted his head and whispered; "..so, really, you know that I don't talk, so why put us all in an awkward position? When you need to know, you will."

What they didn't know was that he was assigned to a secret, elite unit. His vast knowledge of the hills of Judea, the winding alleys of the Old City, and of other places that he had managed to sneak into without being discovered, placed him in a unique position. Ido was an expert in the history of the past hundred years and understood the significance of things that the average observer wouldn't. He was able to connect family names to particular locations; to understand the interpersonal relationships that emanated from these connections. He was able to tell his commanders that a member of a certain family clan who lived in a place such as Ramalla, a major Palestinian town in the West Bank, Arafat's previous headquarters, was a sworn enemy of another clan that lived in Sur Bakher, an Arab neighborhood of Jerusalem, and that he would be willing to share information, out of revenge.

This knowledge was vital to scuttling terror attacks and preventing suicide bombings. When army forces were operating in the territories, Ido could lead his unit along mysterious paths, arrive at destinations via shortcuts, and save precious time that reduced the chances of being discovered. Even when he wasn't familiar with a location, his knowledge of the terrain allowed him to make quick calculations in his head. Just as history gave clues to the future, so did geography, he discovered.

After his discharge from the army, Ido was admitted to Hebrew University and graduated *magna cum laude* with a B.A. in history. He started teaching while he was still a student, and often his instructors had special requests for him. His background as an amateur explorer and the knowledge he had accumulated made Ido more of an expert in certain subjects than his professors. Wanting to become a lecturer and researcher, he continued toward his M.A., obtaining it with little effort. He then enrolled in a doctoral program. He was given the position of lecturer and taught two courses in Jewish history while conducting his research and writing articles. He was at work on an article entitled: "The Historical and Symbolic Significance of Names of the First Neighborhoods Outside the Walled City," one of his favorite areas of interest, when he was suddenly called up to the reserves. And that changed everything.

By now, Ido and Nava had been living together for three years, in an apartment in Gilo, a neighborhood in Jerusalem that his parents had helped to purchase. Nava's parents bought furniture for the young couple. There was talk of marriage, and anyone who knew the devoted pair waited expectantly for an official date, but none was announced. Both of them were cautious by nature, and they agreed to live together for a few years before deciding to marry.

* * *

One evening at home with Nava, he asked with interest, "What are we going to have for dinner?" Cooking was one of their favorite activities; Ido having learned from long hours watching his mother. He had always found it relaxing – forgetting the outside world in the warmth of the kitchen. Nava replied, "I looked at the recipes in the 'Weekend Section,' and I'll surprise you."

The radio was playing classical music; Ido was sitting in the living room contentedly leafing through the newspaper; Nava was cooking. At seven o'clock, the shrill beep of the time signal sounded and the news came on. Ido was listening with half an ear when he heard: "A unit of the IDF encountered a group of armed militants in the vicinity of Ramalla and suffered casualties. A first sergeant was critically injured and was evacuated to Hadassah Hospital…"

Ido was overcome by vertigo. Danny, his dearest friend, had been serving in that area, and Ido had known there would be a special operation that night.

Danny's injury shook him to his core.

SIXTH SESSION

Uri hurries into the room. He is a little late, and keenly aware that the sessions always start within minutes of the scheduled time. He is anxious not to miss anything since the sessions are important to him, and he's spent a tremendous amount of time thinking about his revelations during the previous meeting. He also has some news he wants to share with the group. In this he is like all the others; everyone has come to value their camaraderie and Zev's guidance.

He takes a seat, his body language and expression indicating that he is eagerly waiting his turn to speak.

The group is having a lively conversation revolving around the issue of sensitivity to noises. Yossi announces, with a bit of pride, that this week when a tractor passed his house with a shovel loaded with metal parts, he simply stood outside and watched it as it went further and further up the street. The potholes that marred the road's surface had yet to be repaired, and the sudden clanking of the metal was quite loud, but this time they caused him no anxiety or any physical reaction. He didn't enjoy the grating noises, but he was not shaken by them. He smiles with satisfaction when he has finished reporting this positive development to his friends.

The expressions on the group members' faces show that they are happy for him, and some look over toward Zev with a smile, as if to acknowledge that his work has borne fruit. They all want to be able to use what they learn in the sessions for their own positive changes, and a development like Yossi's is proof of that possibility and an encouragement to everyone.

After waiting for a short lull in the conversation, Uri jumps in.

"I just met with my adviser in the music department to discuss the progress of my studies. My course grades aren't an issue, but he wanted to know what was happening with my final composition.

"I started to mumble something about working on it, that it wasn't easy to select a theme, and that I was struggling with questions of style, and suddenly I remembered what Zev and some of you had said about this. I pulled myself together and told him that I had decided to compose something that focuses on the war, with instruments that include a recorder, trumpet and timpani, in a minor key.

"And how did he react?"

"He liked my line of thinking and felt that with the current circumstances, the war having just recently ended, the idea is an excellent one. Then he asked if I had started the composition. I told him that I had some initial sketches of the opening and the conclusion, but that the middle is still missing."

"And what did he say to that?"

"He wasn't bothered by the gap in the middle. He praised me for having a plan that could be implemented, but he did remind me that I don't have much time, since the semester ends in six weeks. I told him that I was aware of this and would try to finish on schedule."

"And how did you feel after that meeting? Sounds like an important one."

"I felt very encouraged. Clearly, I still have a long way to go, and time is short, but now at least I have a direction. The discussion we had here about both the length and the topic helped me a lot. Before that, I felt overwhelmed and didn't know where to start. So, we'll see. My little composition won't garner The Israel Prize,' but hopefully it will get me a passing grade so I can continue next semester – that's the goal. I hope that sometime in my life I'll compose something a bit more monumental, but for the moment, that's not my aim. Our discussion in the group helped me to put things in perspective."

"Glad to hear," said Zev, and others nodded.

* * *

Avi sits quietly in his chair, and he appears noticeably sad. His expression is always somber, so only those who know him well are able to discern a subtle change that might be significant. Now he speaks up.

"I'm happy, Uri, that you are making progress in your task, that's encouraging. The news from here isn't as good. My four-year-old daughter fell off her bike. She hit her face on the ground and cut her lower lip open. There was a lot of blood, and she was screaming and sobbing. My wife asked me to take her to the local clinic since Shlomo had a high fever and she was busy taking care of him and didn't want to leave. I wasn't crazy about going to a place with injured people, but I agreed to do it. I drove her downtown to the clinic. When the doctor on duty saw the condition of her lip, he decided she had to be seen by a plastic surgeon, and he sent me to the ER.

My heart started pounding like crazy. On the one hand, I wanted to do anything for my little sweetie, my Gilat, but on the other, the idea of going to the ER terrified me. But I had no choice. On the way, I took deep breaths, talked to myself to try to calm myself down, spoke to Gilat and tried to soothe her, promising her ice cream and all sorts of goodies after we were finished. And she finally relaxed and put her little head in my lap, and just whimpered quietly. It broke my heart. In the meantime, my tension kept rising.

"I parked at the ER and carried Gilat inside. Her mouth and lips were covered with blood and her blouse was soaked with it, too. I lay her down on the gurney that the nurse pointed to. All around me I could hear the moans of injured people. Doctors and nurses were rushing about and my heart was pounding like an air hammer. It was hard to breathe. I wanted to escape. Me, the battle-hardened paratrooper, with my Medal of Valor, a warrior in the best army in the Middle East, and I can't give my four-year-old the basic support she needs, without practically passing out!

"The ER was humming like a beehive, because of a terrible accident in which many people had been hurt. Memories of the evacuations from bloody battles were flooding into my head. I could smell scorched flesh, the stench of bloody clothing; I could hear the cries of the wounded, and a helicopter hovering outside, attempting to land, then taking off....

"My face must have been white, and my hands were shaking like crazy, and a male nurse passed by. He looked at me and kept going, then he stopped and came back. "Are you ok?" he asked, "What happened to you?" Clearly he thought I myself was hurt. When I tried to answer, the words stuck in my throat. I felt humiliated. I tried again to answer him, and finally, in desperation, I just pointed to Gilat and her injured lip.

"That's all? Is she your child? And you're so pale and shaky? Are you ok?" He's completely puzzled, and I'm dying inside. My little daughter is injured and I'm the one falling apart! I was so ashamed. After all our sessions here, the explanations, the techniques, the cognitive methods and all that, and the moment I'm in an emergency room with my daughter, I collapse."

"Frustrating, isn't it? And embarrassing." Zev interrupts Avi's painful narrative in a sympathetic tone, trying to rescue him from his extreme agitation and to calm him a little. "Have you heard the expression that Rome wasn't built in a day?"

"Yes. I have, but what does that have to do with failing my daughter in the ER?" answers Avi angrily.

"The parallel is that you were put to a difficult task and you weren't able to succeed yet at the level you had hoped to, and you're beating yourself up about it. It's true that if you had been able to react in a more relaxed and confident manner, you'd feel better about it, but it seems that you just need more training, more preparation, and more self-confidence. It's frustrating that Gilat's injury occurred so early in the process, and that you didn't have enough tools yet to cope with the challenge, but it doesn't mean you won't cope with it better the next time. We're still working on all this, improving things and adding more tools. I'm sorry you are disappointed, but I do understand it. We'll continue working, ok?"

"That's not the end of the story."

"No? What else was there?"

"I couldn't breathe, the pounding of my heart was driving me crazy, my hands were dripping with sweat, and I was completely overcome with anxiety. I tried to calm myself, but I couldn't, and I had to get out of there! I asked when Gilat would be seen and got a derisive answer from that same nurse: 'Do you see what's going on here? Serious injuries, a state of emergency, we're terribly busy, you'll just have to wait. It will be at least an hour before anyone looks at your daughter.'

"I barely made it to the chair next to Gilat's gurney. I was close to passing out. The thought that I would have to stay in this atmosphere for at least another hour terrified me. It felt like the time in the village of Bint Jbail, when I thought that my soldiers would all die because the evacuation helicopter turned around and fled to avoid being hit by enemy fire. Now all the strength left my body and I slumped into my chair. With a tremendous effort, I managed to pull out my cell phone and call Nili.

"'Find someone to watch Shlomo and come take over for me at the ER. I can't stay here!' I shouted, and shame covered me from head to toe. Me, the strong man, asking his wife for help with this simple task. What's happened to me? I feel that I'm even worse off than when I started here!"

"I understand, it's not a comfortable situation. You feel ashamed that you weren't able to cope and had to ask for help. Someone who has never experienced anything like all that you've gone through might look at you contemptuously and not understand, which is exactly how you're looking at yourself."

"Right! Exactly like that."

"How much of what that ignorant nurse said to you is connected to the way you are viewing yourself?"

"It didn't help. You'd think that someone who works in an ER would be trained to be sensitive to patients and their parents, but that one certainly wasn't."

Yossi spoke up, his voice hoarse with emotion.

"People don't even try to understand. They look at me sometimes like they think I'm insane. They make insulting comments and have no idea what they are talking about, and it hurts. I was in a mall with my wife and daughter, and suddenly a helicopter passed overhead, flying very low, making very loud thumping noises. Without even thinking, I suddenly found myself under a rack of bathing suits, the best cover I could find. I was sure I was again under attack and my body just reacted completely automatically.

"I just stayed there until everyone who had seen me jump had moved on, then I pretended I had dropped something that rolled under the rack and I was looking for it. The shame was eating at me. My wife understood immediately, and when I got up, she hugged me without a word. She's experienced situations like that with me many times, and she's always great about it, thank goodness, she is hoping it will pass, but she never says a word. I know it's difficult for her. I know her girlfriends ask her what's happening with me, and I imagine she's told them about it. Avi, I understand exactly what happened to you. For me, it's not the sight of blood or hearing the screams of the wounded; for me it's the helicopters and the booms of artillery."

"Me too," Yariv adds quietly. "You have no idea how often I avoid being in a situation where I think there may be loud noises. Independence Day, with the fireworks that everyone loves so much? I run away from it, staying home with the windows and doors shut and disappointing my children.

"They say to me, 'Come Aba, come, its fun, it's pretty, don't you want to see them? Come on, Aba, come with us.'

"And what can I tell them? 'Udi and Liat, the last time I saw something like that, I was scared to death. My friends were hurt. I saw a tank explode from a missile hit in Lebanon, and all those beautiful colors in the sky that you want me to see, they remind me of the guys I knew that were hurt and burned, and I don't want to be reminded of all that..

"Is that what I should say to them? They are five and seven years old, and they deserve to enjoy a celebration like all their friends do, and they shouldn't have a father who is such a coward that he's unable to see fireworks, who runs and hides."

"So what *do* you tell them?" Yossi asks. "How do you explain why you don't want to go? That you have to disappoint them, that they should go, but only with Ima?"

"It's a dilemma. I don't want to lie to them and say something like 'Fireworks are just a waste of public funds.' I've heard people use that explanation, but it wouldn't be the truth. And I'm not ready to tell them the truth; it's too awful to describe to anyone, especially small children, and it might scare them to know that their father almost got killed, like the father of one of their friends who actually did get killed. I'm afraid they might start dreaming about it, and that's all they and we need. They are great kids, happy, lively, and well behaved, why spoil their innocence?"

"So what *do* you say? You must say something!" Yossi pressed.

"Ah! You noticed that I'm avoiding the question, you son of a gun. Ok, you deserve an answer, because I know you have the same problem and you probably don't know what to say to your kids either, right? I told them that during the war, there were explosions that hurt my ears, and therefore I'm sensitive to noises, and so while it's true that the colors are pretty and exciting, and the designs of the fireworks in the sky are fantastic, I need to protect my ears. At least that's partly true."

"And they accepted that?"

"Sort of. Udi made a face and told me to stuff cotton in my ears because the fireworks are so pretty it would be a shame to miss them just because of a little noise. Liat is seven, and I think she understands that there is more to it than just noise, but she doesn't push. She just looks at me with sad eyes and says, 'Maybe next year,' and I answer, 'Yes, maybe next year.'"

"And do you believe that you will be there next year?"

"I don't know. But I hope I will. That's why I'm in this room every week. I hope to overcome it."

* * *

"Zev!"

Avi turns to Zev with a piercing question. "I've heard people saying that post traumatic stress disorder never goes away, that it's there for life. Is that true?"

The question falls on the group like a hammer blow.

It had been swirling around their heads, but no one had dared to raise it.

Everyone has heard something like that and no one wants to believe it. Everyone is terrified that there is a degree of truth in it, and the thought of never being able to rid themselves of their anxiety, fears, and stress feels too painful to discuss. Everyone knows someone who is still suffering from the syndrome long after the traumatic event occurred. One guy tells a story about somebody's grandfather who fought in Sinai more than 50 years ago and is still struggling with the symptoms.

Another one knows a man who fought in Europe during World War II and *still* has flashbacks and nightmares.

Someone knows a friend of his father who was fine for many years, and then suddenly something happened to him and he started suffering all over again.

Everyone fears that they suffer from a disorder that can never be permanently overcome.

Zev, too, knows people who have been suffering for many years and have not been completely cured. He has been anticipating Avi's question for a long time.

He also knows from his studies and from professional colleagues that part of the problem is that until relatively recently, even though many people suffered from it, PTSD had not been recognized as a very real, intensely serious, emotional disorder. For years, the symptoms had no specific diagnosis or treatment. It wasn't until 1980 that it appeared in the *Diagnostic and Statistical Manual of Mental Disorders* ("DSM") of the American Psychiatric Association, the "bible" of psychiatric disorders relied on by many countries, including Israel. Thus, society had essentially ignored the problem until just a few years ago. And then, even after the disorder was recognized and included in the DSM, it was years before the helping professions paid serious attention to it. Consequently, those who suffered from combat-related trauma largely failed to seek help; and if they did, they often could not find a therapist who knew how to treat it.

"Today," he explained, "there are more therapists who are familiar with post trauma that has resulted from *civilian* events, such as car accidents, plane crashes, rape, or natural disasters. And the number who do know about combat PTSD is increasing all the time. Fortunately, America, which often paves the way in many medical areas, accepts combat PTSD as a serious, disturbing, and very real phenomenon, as does Israel. While there are still some medical doctors who dismiss it, they are usually from an older generation. Younger doctors have been trained to deal with it, or at least they know enough to take it seriously and to refer patients to mental health professionals who are skilled at treating it. Many younger doctors in Israel have been in combat themselves, and have personal knowledge of it. Those who suffer can now find treatment relatively quickly," Zev's voice continues to be reassuring. "Sometimes they even get help the same day. This shorter time lapse between trauma and treatment is an enormous advantage."

"That's encouraging," Yariv murmurs.

"So anyone seeking help is no longer viewed as a malingerer or someone trying to 'pull something' for his own advantage. The complaint is usually taken quite seriously, and professional help is much more readily available. In addition, society at large has become concerned about the issue, as reflected by almost weekly media coverage describing the phenomenon, discussing its implications, and detailing methods of treatment. The general view is no longer of sufferers as 'crazies' or 'complainers who should just snap out of it.' Society now recognizes soldiers whose emotional injuries are every bit as valid as physical injuries more visible to the naked eye."

Zev continues to explain that many of those whom they know or have heard about who are still suffering are people who may have walked around for years with no understanding of what had happened to them. "Some feared they had gone insane, and many were viewed by others, including family members and doctors, as malingerers. Many received incorrect diagnoses or were told, 'it's all in your head,' or 'you can snap out of it if you just decide you want to,' both ignorant and dismissive expressions. No wonder most sufferers didn't seek help when no treatment was offered and other people tended to greet their complaints with skepticism. They suffered alone and in silence. They *still* suffer."

Ido speaks up, looking at Zev piercingly through his black-rimmed glasses "The new approach is encouraging, but I have two friends who *did* receive treatment, and are still receiving it, and by respected professionals and their issues persist. They still haven't recovered."

"Yes," answers Zev, "I also know of situations like that. The question is whether they are still at the same level of discomfort as they were before treatment. Are they a bit better, or has their condition really not improved at all? Obviously I can't answer that, but I think there is a good chance that things *have* improved for them, even if they are not completely healed.

"Let's return to Avi's issue: the fear that things will never get better. The current situation is this: it is quite possible that some residual symptoms might linger for a long time. It is possible that post trauma, in our present state of knowledge, is a condition that cannot be completely eradicated, although there are professionals who claim that it can. But think about other medical issues, like diabetes, muscle diseases, asthma, and cancer: despite the most advanced treatments, they have not been completely eradicated or cured. Nevertheless, they can be treated, and are often treated successfully. Do you remember what I said to you in the first session? I said then – and this hasn't changed – that our goal here is to improve things, not to feel like 'psychos' as someone here put it, to learn to live to the highest possible degree of healthy functioning and happiness with the abilities and techniques at our disposal. As a physician friend of mine once said about a mutual friend: "He has prostate cancer, and he will die *with* it, not *of* it."

"It is very possible that you'll continue to have feelings that are connected to the trauma, and at the same time will live a nearly normal life. And at the end of the day, if sensitivity to noise has improved, just hasn't disappeared entirely, that's a condition that isn't wonderful, but it's much better, and you can adjust more easily to living with it. An amputee gets up every morning and understands that one of his legs is still missing. It's sad, but he puts on his prosthesis and continues with daily life. An asthmatic gets attacks from time to time, experiences a choking feeling that is frightening and frustrating, but he inhales his medication, calms down, and goes on."

"What about those horrible dreams? I heard they never go away," questions Sergei.

"It's a stubborn problem and not easy to treat. But remember, things are always developing. There are new treatment methods, like Somatic Experiencing (SE), developed by Peter Levine, that look very promising for treating the effects of trauma. There is a lot of research going on to improve treatment outcomes, so while there might not be a perfect answer to the problem right now, there is a good chance there will be one soon. There is medication, which we discussed, which does not completely eradicate the symptoms but gives great relief in sleeping. The medications for asthma do not eliminate it, but they allow a person to breathe. Medications for diabetes do not cure it, but allow one to live a nearly normal life, eat tasty foods, and avoid losing a foot to gangrene. The same is true for anti-anxiety medications."

"We covered a lot of ground today," Ron observes. "We started with Yossi's improvement with noises, then Uri and the piece he is composing, Avi and his troubles in the ER, Yossi's anxiety in the mall, Yariv's problem with fireworks and then Avi's troubling question about getting over all this – which worries all of us – and Zev's extensive answers. There is a lot to digest in one sitting." Ron, in his soft-spoken and intelligent way, is attempting to give order to the myriad of subjects covered, to acknowledge their wide range, and to deal with the emotional swings between hope and despair. He and many of the others have begun to understand that not every issue has a completely satisfactory solution, and that all of this will require not only a lot more thought and discussion, but hard work.

Zev has been able to allay a few of their concerns. But he has also conceded some of the limitations of treatment. He has gently implied that they may all have to learn to live with a number of unresolved issues.

YARIV

Zev: "Let's return to what Yariv said, that he doesn't tell his wife a thing and that he's frustrated that she doesn't understand him. How could she? How could she explain to herself or to the kids why Aba wakes up at night, sits up straight as a rod, and yells incoherent words into the darkness of the room?"

Yariv had been particularly bothered by the question: "Why did we report for duty?" during the first session. He had always responded to "Order #8," the annual order to report for military reserve duty, without question, with the same sense of obligation that had guided him all of his life. When he received the call that last time, during a time of war, he was startled, he understood its implications – but once again he did not hesitate for a minute. How could he not show up? What would his father have said were he alive? He had never refused a call to arms – and that's how he had raised Yariv.

* * *

In the 1960s, his father, Moshe, emigrated from Morocco together with his family. He was fifteen years old, spoke French and Arabic but not a word of Hebrew. The beginnings were difficult: a leaky tent in a Ma'abara – a temporary refugee camp, a "transitional settlement," – unemployment, small rationed portions of unfamiliar food.

Living space was limited and did not allow for privacy. His

parents were short-tempered and high-strung, and more than once he heard them arguing "Why did we come here? Why did we leave what we had? It wasn't so bad in Morocco, and here, now, we are in a freezing tent that leaks, lousy food, not enough work. Why did we come here?"

Yet, at the end of such arguments, Moshe's father would straighten up and look at his wife, "You know exactly why. We had agreed. We talked about it. We must build this country, and we are part of this building, we could not have stayed there. We'll make it."

He would then don his torn raincoat and go out into the stormy weather, the pouring rain, and report to one of the temporary jobs allotted to him. He dug trenches, erected fences, fortified the roofs of metal sheds that were ripped off by the high winds, and gritted his teeth. But inside he felt good to be part of a large and important undertaking of building a country, of being a participant in an historic event.

These thoughts helped him to overcome the fatigue, and sometimes hunger. After eight months in the Ma'abara, they moved into a small metal shed which presented a great improvement over the rain-soaked tent. Now, however, they were fried in the summer by a blazing sun baking the metal roof. At least there was a water spigot nearby, and from time to time they'd stick their head underneath it to cool off.

Over time, the family's situation improved, but Moshe was still trying to find a place for himself in this new country. Doubts about his future bothered him. Then one night he decided the time had come to enlist in the Israel Defense Forces, the IDF. He was strong; his Hebrew was still imperfect, but he learned new words every day. After basic training, he was accepted into the paratroopers, an elite branch of the army, and took part in some combat operations. He finally felt that he had "come home."

At the end of his three years of mandatory service, he signed up for more time, and over the course of years he became an experienced commander. His eastern background, command of Arabic and understanding of the Arab mind pushed him up the military ladder, and he reached the level of Lieutenant Colonel. Moshe had found his place and no longer wondered "Why did we come?"

Yariv was born when Moshe and his wife, Haviva, were living in the army officers' residences, a privilege given to those who stayed in the army beyond the mandatory years. Moshe by then was a Major, and felt that he was contributing to Israeli society. His brother, too, was in the same position, and the families frequently visited each other, the brothers huddling in the corner to talk about military subjects. Thus, Yariv's background included both a father and an uncle, both career officers, dedicated to the service. It is possible that even his name, Yariv (from the root of "to quarrel"), was derived subconsciously from his father's view of life; an unwillingness to give up an inch of disputed land.

He was right in the middle of five siblings, with an older brother and sister, and a younger brother and sister. He had black hair and dark brown eyes, thick eyebrows and a piercing look. He wasn't tall, but strong, much like his father. His muscular physique was impressive, and would serve him well in his later career.

When he was two, he slipped on a wet stone floor and cut his lip. He bled a lot, and his alarmed mother raced him to the local clinic. The doctor on call was a lazy guy, and instead of mending the split lip, sent them home, saying "it will heal by itself." It did, but left an ugly scar, sort of a reddish, oblique line running from the lip down to the chin. With weather changes it took on different colors: on a warm summer day it stood out in its darkness and in the winter it almost disappeared. And on the rare occasions when Yariv became angry, it became noticeable.

He accepted it as part of his being, without much concern. But his mother always felt guilty that she failed to take him to a more skilled doctor. In those years and considering her background, she wasn't sufficiently assertive. Additionally, the doctor was a man and as a woman from her cultural background, whatever the doctor said, he was right, and there was nothing she could do. Moshe did not intervene. He had heard about the incident, asked Haviva if she took Yariv to a doctor, and was satisfied with her answer. Things of that sort were within the domain of a mother, not a father, particularly a career officer with the rank of Major.

Zahava, Yariv's older sister, helped raise him, and they had a close and warm relationship. Although they were merely three years apart, she was very maternal and paid attention to little things that bothered him.

In grade school, he had a reputation as a physically strong boy with a well-developed sense of justice. He could not tolerate kids who picked on weaker ones, and would defend them. In general, his appearance was sufficient to convince a bully to stop, but occasionally he felt it necessary to intervene physically. One decisive shove or smack was enough to signal his intentions, and no one got hurt. Since incidents never reached the level of real disturbance, the teachers didn't stop this junior "protector of the weak."

Sports were among his favorite activities. He always played soccer, loved to swim, and at age 15 started to lift weights to build up his muscles even more.

Yariv had the personality of a leader: during games he assigned roles, saw to it that equipment was in good shape. Naturally his friends chose him to be referee and arbitrator. He spoke in a soft voice and when he started talking, others fell silent and listened.

At age 17, Yariv met Anat, a charming girl, daughter of an Iraqi family, who worked as a clerk in the neighborhood grocery store. Much to her surprise, Yariv's mother discovered that he suddenly started to notice that the milk was running out, or the eggs, and that he would hurry to the store to buy fresh ones. The enthusiasm that he displayed for grocery shopping surprised everyone, until they learned, and burst out laughing, that a cute girl with a long braid was one of the store clerks. From time to time his sister, Zahava, would whisper into his ear that some staple was running low, and smilingly sent him off to get it. She understood well the magnetic pull that drew her brother there.

When it was time for Yariv to enlist, he already knew about weapons. His father had taught him how to use his personal pistol, and when he would bring home a different weapon, he'd show his son how it functioned, how to take it apart and reassemble it, with eyes closed and racing against a stop watch. So part of basic training was already done when Yariv got to boot camp.

Not surprisingly, he asked to be assigned to an elite unit, and was enrolled in Battalion 890 of the paratroopers. Basic training was tough. Many hours of exhausting physical training, running, jumping, carrying heavy loads, crawling at night, and idiotic commands by a young instructor who exploited his position and screamed even when there was no need, adding ten more exercises at the end of a tiring day, to "toughen up," he explained. But many months later, when Yariv would be near the end of his strength after an uphill chase, those extra exercises helped him to keep going. He did not remember the name of that young commander, but secretly he thanked him.

* * *

"Yariv, come home, quickly."

He recognized his mother's frantic voice over the phone.

"Ima, what happened? Is something the matter?"

"Aba is sleeping and I'm unable to wake him. He's making strange snoring noises and isn't moving. Yarivi, I'm so worried, come quickly."

"I'm calling Magen David for an ambulance right now. It will take me at least half an hour to get home and in between we can't afford to lose any time. I'll be back to you in a minute," and he hung up.

"Ima," he soon returned, "tell me details because you'll have to explain to the EMTs exactly what happened and they are already on their way."

"Aba went to sleep early last night, saying his stomach was bothering him, but I noticed that he was jamming a fist into his chest, like so, in the middle."

"On the heart?" he asked, but immediately regretted the question, fearing he might scare his mother.

"I don't know, maybe the heart. Oy! Perhaps he is having a heart attack? Yarivi, I'm so scared, come, come quickly."

"Ima, I'm on my way, but the ambulance will get there before I do, so tell them what you told me, and after you leave, call me, so I'll know where they're taking him. I'm on my way, Ima, everything will be all right."

Several minutes later Yariv's cell phone rang. "Hello, this is Yariv, who's this?" he asked, in a voice louder than usual.

"This is EMT. We're taking your father to Ichilov Hospital. We think he might have had a heart attack."

Yariv, by then 20 years old, had been out for the evening with Anat, enjoying a leisurely drive in his father's car. But after his mother's call, he began driving frantically, passing cars, slipping through traffic lights and rehearsing a convincing conversation with a potential cop, should he get stopped. The minutes felt like eternity. He felt as if someone had deliberately moved the hospital several kilometers further from where it used to be. Yariv, who did not believe in God, discovered that he was talking to him, pleading for his father's survival; that perhaps He'd give him only a mild heart attack that wasn't so damaging, but, please, not something horrid, or heaven forbid...

At the entrance to the emergency room stood an ambulance that appeared as though it had just arrived, its doors swung wide open. Medics were rolling a gurney toward the entrance. Someone was lying on it, covered in a thin blanket, but it wasn't possible to identify who it might be.

"Park the car, I'm running in" he told Anat, as he tore the car door open, leaving the engine running, and leapt toward the ER entrance. His mother stood in the middle of the room, white as a ghost and trembling. Her hair was unkempt, her eyes wide and her lips moving without uttering a sound, as if praying. Her dress hung shapelessly, a dress she used to wear for housework, never outside.

"Ima! I'm here. What are they saying?" as he rushed over and hugged her.

"Don't know, don't know, they didn't tell me anything, but from the look on their faces, their actions, it doesn't look good to me. God! I so hope that Aba will be well, Oh God..." and she started whimpering quietly, leaning on her son.

Yariv approached the receptionist. "I'm the son of Moshe, what's happening with him?"

"He has just arrived and we're examining him. We'll come out right away when we know anything, please wait here."

Long minutes passed. Eternity. Torture. Fear in the air. Mother crying and pleading, Yariv tense and anxious. He had a bad feeling. For several months he had the impression that dad wasn't feeling well, that he was quieter than usual, and now he also recalled that occasionally Moshe'd press a fist against his chest, tightly. As was typical for him, he'd never complain when asked how he was, just wave his hand, as if saying all's well. Moshe never allowed anyone to get too close to him, to obtain information, even essential information.

The door to the ER opened slowly. A young man in a white smock stepped toward Yariv and his mother in measured steps. "I'm so sorry, so sorry. We tried several times...but it was too late. He arrived here, and was no longer...I'm terribly sorry..." and did not continue.

"What are you saying? That my dad's dead?!" Yariv blurted out, nearly in a scream. His mother jumped off her chair, stood trembling for a few seconds – and as her legs gave way, Yariv caught her in his arms and blocked her from falling to the floor. "Ahhhhhh!!!" a scream emerged from her throat. "Ahhhhhh! No! No! Moshe, Moshe..." and she fell silent.

Yariv was stunned. He understood what had happened, but was unable to comprehend what he heard – that just this very minute he had lost his father, his teacher, his compass, the life model he was emulating, the husband of his mother.

"Ima, Ima...." he attempted to console his sobbing mother, who could barely breathe. He was lost, frozen in place. The doctor stood by silently and reached out his hand, approaching him as if to hug him, but stopped short.

It slowly dawned on Yariv that he and his older bothers were now the men of the family, responsible for supporting their mother emotionally and taking care of their younger siblings. Fortunately, since Moshe had been a career officer with a high rank, the family was set economically, but the emotional gap that he left was huge.

Now in the third and last year of his service, Yariv took a week off to observe the shiva, the traditional period of mourning, but then returned to his unit. In his mind, there was no question that his father, in such a situation, would have held back his tears, absorbed the news, and returned to his post. Yariv did exactly what his father would have done.

* * *

Yariv was now celebrating his 29th birthday, and his wife, Anat, and his two children held a birthday party for him, and invited two families from the neighborhood. They arrived at ten on Shabbat morning, and although Yariv was happy that his birthday was being remembered, the noise the kids made, and their running around from room to room, irritated him. He attempted several times to hold a conversation with the men, but the words got stuck in his throat, and his speech was belabored and superficial. He got up and went to the bathroom, just to get away, even if for a short time. Noise and quick movements made him irritable, and combined with the short-temperedness that he had developed recently, he just prayed for them to leave.

When Anat brought out the birthday cake, he sighed in relief and secretly was grateful that the party was coming to an end. Anat and the friends didn't understand why he said "thank you" only half-heartedly and without enthusiasm, and she was disappointed. She had spent hours in the kitchen preparing traditional Moroccan dishes and his favorite cake. His reaction was lukewarm and even the kids noticed it.

"Aba, don't you like the cake we made for you?" asked seven-year-old Eli.

"Yes, yes, I love it, I'm just not hungry right now," replied Yariv, semi-apologizing.

"But I decorated it in all these pretty colors," Eli complained.

"Thank you, Eli, it's beautiful."

"And me too," added five-year-old Yifat.

"Yes, I saw, this really is a pretty and festive cake, thank you all."

After the guests left, Yariv, as usual, helped clear the table. He behaved differently from his father who never lifted a finger to help his wife, as it wasn't customary for men of his generation to do such a "womanly" task. Yariv was a Sabra, a native Israeli, and it was taken for granted that men help with housework. After dinner, they sat down to watch TV and then put the kids to bed.

"So, Yariv, what was wrong?"

"Anat, I don't know. I felt like crap today. You and the kids made such an effort to celebrate my birthday in such a beautiful way; the cake, the meal, the friends, really nice, and thank you so much, but, I just couldn't. I didn't have it in me. I'm unable to enjoy the things that were once a part of me. I don't know, just don't know."

"What's going to happen?"

"You know that I'm going to that group of psychos, with that leader, in the clinic for psychos...."

"What psychos? What the hell are you talking about? You are not a psycho and no one else there is a psycho."

"I feel like a psycho."

"Why?"

"Look, was I ever like this? Unable to enjoy things? Didn't like good food, the burekas, the other pastries, even birthday cake? Don't like talking to my closest friends? I have no patience for the kids and it takes a lot of restraint not to yell at them when they're running around, making noise. They're allowed to. That's what kids do. It's OK, but it makes me crazy. Isn't that being a psycho?"

"No!"

"I'm going to talk to Zev, the group leader, tomorrow, and I'll ask him," concluded Yariv.

"Great, ask. Just so you know, you are not a psycho. Do you hear me?" protested Anat.

SEVENTH SESSION

At the start of any new therapeutic group, Zev always explained in detail why it was important to be present at every session. With this group of participants, he had done what he always did: he had extracted a promise from each potential candidate that if he decided to join, he would be diligent about attending. He explained the importance of continuity and the mutual dependency and support that always developed among group members. He also told them that there was always a waiting list of people who wanted to join, and so it would not be fair to take a spot in the group and not make use of it.

All the group members dutifully showed up for the first six sessions. But at the seventh, Gil failed to appear. Sessions generally began within five minutes of the scheduled time, and everyone waited just a little longer this time, to see if Gil might have gotten stuck in traffic or was running late for some other reason. They waited expectantly for a call on Zev's cell phone. None came.

There is unrest in the room. Something like this had never happened before, and signs of concern are starting to show on the men's faces. Zev is concerned too, but does not want to react too quickly.

A variety of anxious thoughts are swirling in the heads of Gil's friends, much like the thoughts that buzz in the head of a parent whose child has failed to arrive home at the expected time. *Is he sick? Has he simply forgotten? That seems unlikely, since we've all*

agreed that our weekly session is the most important social event of the
week for us. Maybe he's angry or troubled about something. Was there
anything in the last session that might have particularly upset him? The
thoughts begin to be voiced, to spread into widening circles and in
an increasingly negative direction. At first they mostly reflect
concern for Gil's welfare, but soon feelings of anger start to
intrude.

"This is just like him, that's the way he is."

"What, he doesn't care enough about us to show up?"

"Who does he think he is, just to decide not to come and not
bother to let us know? What chutzpah!"

Zev is both surprised and worried. As captain of the ship, he
feels an obligation to have everything working properly, and this
'no show' is a serious event. He feels a responsibility to calm the
men. From experience, he knows that there could be a thousand
reasons why Gil hasn't arrived. Some reasons turn out to be
benign, but others can be quite significant indeed. Everyone is
caught in the occasional traffic jam and everyone has cursed a
mobile phone that failed to work, or oneself for forgetting to
charge it. These are among the "benign" possibilities.

Then there are the more serious reasons. Could Gil have been
involved in an accident? Could he be so depressed that he
couldn't get out of bed? Maybe someone in the group, possibly
even Zev, said something that upset or frightened him. Maybe he
doesn't actually believe that the group is worthwhile, and he just
doesn't want to make the effort anymore. And the most horrible
thought also creeps in: "Maybe he's hurt himself. Maybe he's tried
to commit suicide."

Zev dismisses this last thought as unlikely, because there had
been no signs that would point to such a drastic action. But he also
knows from experience that no possibility can be excluded.

"Gil hasn't shown up and he didn't call to say he wasn't
coming or that he'd be late, so I'm going to call him to find out
what's up," he announces.

The tension subsides immediately; everyone had been hoping
that Zev would do exactly that. But when he calls Gil's cell there's
no reply, only the sound of Gil's outgoing message. Zev proceeds
to call his house but gets the same result. He leaves messages in
both places asking that Gil get back to him right away.

The tension in the room rises again. "Maybe his telephone is broken?" offers Yariv.

"Yes, but then why isn't he here?" Ido asks slowly.

Zev sums up the situation. "Apparently, we are not going to find out the answer right now. I will pursue it later. But this is a good opportunity to discuss what is happening here and now, to explore our reactions. So, what is happening?"

Uri offers the first answer, saying softly, "I feel that I am an integral part of a close family here, and that someone from the family is missing. I wait all week to meet with everyone, and I think about our sessions from the moment I leave until the next time I come, and it never crosses my mind that everyone won't be here. I miss Gil being here."

"Actually, I'm worried," Ron admits quietly. "Maybe something is wrong. Maybe he is sick and is in such a deep sleep that he can't hear the phone. Can we call one of his neighbors? Or his mother?"

So far, these are the typical reactions that Zev had anticipated, and he doesn't add any of his own.

Yossi hesitantly suggests a plan of action: "Maybe we should wait until the end of the session. Then, if we still haven't heard from him, maybe we can try calling his employer. And if that isn't productive, I could jump right over to his house after we're done here."

Zev is impressed by their concern, but now feels he has to intervene.

"We don't have permission from Gil to call his employer, even if any of us know who that is. Don't forget, we have a confidentiality agreement here to guard our privacy. At the beginning, everyone signed an agreement that stated I am allowed to call your home and your cellphone, but nothing beyond that."

"Ah, right, I forgot about that," Yossi quickly apologizes. "But am I allowed to go to his home?"

"Yes, as a friend you can do that. Just don't reveal any details to anyone about how you know him," Zev explains.

"But what if someone else answers the door. How do I explain who I am and why I'm searching for him?"

"You are a friend of his. You were supposed to meet with him and he didn't arrive, and you just want to make sure that everything is fine. Something like that."

"Ok, I understand. I just hope there's no serious problem."

Avi speaks up, somewhat sharply: "Maybe he's just pulling our leg? Maybe testing us? Wants to see if we really care about him? I'm willing to bet that everything is fine."

"I also thought about that, but didn't want to say it. Now it's like you took the words right out of my mouth," Ido admits.

"Gil is such a…" Avi starts.

Zev jumps in. He senses the shift in atmosphere from concern and disappointment to unfriendliness and suspicion, and he wants to stop it in its tracks to avoid the risk of badmouthing Gil. There are no known facts, and Gil isn't there to explain himself. "For the moment we'll continue as if everyone were here; and right after the session, I'll make an effort to find him."

* * *

The aroma of the coffee is wafting throughout the room. Everyone has become accustomed to the faded color of the curtains, to the limply hanging shades, and to the trees outside the windows, and these simple things have become comforting in their familiarity. They often serve as anchors during moments of emotional turmoil, amid storms of feelings, tough and sad words, confessions of anxiety, and feelings of guilt and shame.

Six weeks have passed since the group's first meeting. And because the world kept on spinning, the light coming through the windows has altered. The sun now sets a little earlier, the lights outside come on sooner, and when members return home at the end of a session, it is twilight.

The noises that used to be heard from the corridor have grown quieter, as most of the staff complete their workday and leave a bit earlier. The relative quiet helps the guys to concentrate on their difficult tasks. They can never anticipate what may come up, which tough issue will be tackled and by whom, what the reactions might be, or where the first sentence might lead.

Zev is always ready to break a long silence, yet he often simply allows things to take their course naturally. He offers an explanation when he wishes to clarify a subject, replies to a question, navigates gently when he senses the wagon slipping off its tracks, and otherwise sits quietly, observing and collecting information that might be useful later in the discussion or at a future session. As the group has matured, it now tends to run itself, and its interpersonal relationships have developed.

Now they all settle themselves in their chairs for the seventh session, and Ido clears his throat and slowly starts speaking.

"Remember the time Nava and I were about to go to a movie and we only made it to the apartment building stairs?" Several nods and yeses answer him.

"Two days ago I saw an ad for a movie I had heard about and thought I might like to see. I came home and went online and got some more information about it, and then I was convinced that I really wanted to see it. It deals with the era of the Romans in the Middle East, one of my areas of expertise. I assumed that it probably wouldn't be historically accurate, but that didn't bother me. When I told Nava about it, she wasn't particularly interested in it; she'd rather see a 'chick flick,' something romantic with sappy music and all that. But I could tell from her expression that she was really surprised I wanted to see it, and hopeful.

"'You want to go out in public, to a movie theatre?' she asked, as if she couldn't believe her ears.

"I said, 'yeah, I'd like to, should we try?' She said, 'sure,' and asked me what time. I told her if we left before six, we'd have enough time to buy tickets and grab a pizza. But then she got a little hesitant. She asked me point blank, 'but what if you suddenly find it hard to get out of here, and we have to work on it, and then we don't have enough time.'

"I told her that I realized my good intentions alone might not be enough, and I said that since it was only four o'clock, I'd start doing some of the exercises I learned in the group to get myself ready to leave. That way, by five o'clock I'd know if I'd be able to go.

"I decided to approach this challenge in the same way that I would prepare for a lecture. I knew I had to do some homework, sort of, and so I began. I started with relaxation, which was easy – deep breathing, muscle relaxation, all of that.

"The second part was harder. I made up a scenario of guided imagery, like we've used here. I imagined step by step how I would get to the door, go down the stairs, get in the car, drive to the movie's parking lot...but that's where I got stuck. The thought that I would have to leave a secure place, the driver's seat of my car, and mix with a large crowd of moviegoers, made my throat dry. I almost told Nava to forget the whole thing, but then I decided that I wasn't going to just give in this time. Otherwise, why am I coming here every week?

"So I took a few more deep breaths, and then I imagined that I was leaving the car, locking it, and walking over to the ticket window. I imagined myself standing on line. At this point, my heart was pounding like crazy. I calmed myself, picturing Nava standing next to me holding my hand, and I reminded myself that I really want to see the movie and that it will only be playing here for two days. I also 'shortened' the line for myself to make it a little easier. I only put a few people in front of me, and then I pictured it moving, and I got to the window and bought two tickets. And then we continued, in my imagination, walking toward the pizzeria and then sitting at a table in the furthest corner."

"Well, did you the see the movie for real?" Sergei interrupts impatiently. All the guys are visibly restless, anxious to know if Ido succeeded or not.

"Wait a minute! I'm trying to get through this, and you're not letting me finish, I need to tell it my own way, and you're so impatient..."

"True. Might you have forgotten that this is one of our symptoms? Can't I be just a little impatient?" Sergei's wry comment provokes a wave of laughter.

Ido laughs too, and continues. "At five o'clock, I notified Nava that we were going to complete the task. We were going out to see a movie. She slowly turned from the sink, and she asked me very deliberately, 'so, I'm not going to make dinner, is that right?' And I said no, we'd go out for pizza and dessert.

"We left at a quarter to six, leaving a little extra time just in case, and everything went smoothly, just like I imagined it. Even traffic was considerate of me, there were no bottlenecks, lights changed smoothly to green in my honor, and we arrived, no problem. Still, my heart was pounding the whole time and I kept wiping my forehead. Nava was very quiet, like she was holding her breath and didn't want to break the flow of things. We bought the tickets and walked over to the pizza parlor, just as I'd planned. And then it happened." Ido paused.

"*It* happened? *What* happened?" Ron asked curiously and anxiously. All the guys hoped that the story would end well, and suddenly there was the suggestion of a hitch.

"I started to sweat profusely, my breathing got faster, I felt tense and anxious and I just wanted to run back to the car and abort the whole attempt. But then, just like the other time, Nava took my hand, squeezed it gently, and walked me into the pizzeria. 'Do you want it with cheese or mushrooms?' she asked, as if nothing was wrong. She was determined to make this evening the turning point for us. And her simple, casual talk set me back on track. 'With mushrooms and a beer,' I finally said.

"And then I started to just calm down. As if nothing extraordinary was happening. We started to talk about this and that, how our day had gone, without a word about the movie. Ahead of me, I knew I still had to face the challenge of entering a closed, dark hall with a limited number of exits, encountering hundreds of people, staying there for least an hour and a half…all kinds of obstacles. But I couldn't believe it would be as hard as I was fearing. Exactly what was I afraid of? I really don't know, but in the end everything worked out."

"You did it, Ido! More power to you," Avi exclaimed.

Zev's smile stretched from ear to ear. He could add another checkmark to his imaginary score sheet. Another hurdle had been overcome, and one of his patients had scored a victory. He didn't want to exaggerate it, but at the same time, he did want to congratulate Ido and to encourage and prod the others.

"Good job, Ido. A relief, eh? It seems that the fear of the fear is worse than the fear itself. Give Nava a warm greeting from me. You're a great team."

Ido also was smiling with satisfaction. He had overcome one of the obstacles that had given him real heartache and had stunted his social interactions. Now that he had been able to go to a movie with Nava, he might also be able to go out with his friends and colleagues. From time to time, there were films at the university that were professionally important for him to attend, especially as there was always a discussion afterward. Since his return from battle, he had always found reasons not to be present: he didn't feel well, he had another important meeting, all kinds of nonsense excuses that his friends clearly recognized weren't true. Finally, it seemed that this burden had been lifted and he could return to normal.

"And there is another interesting development," he added, "connected to what I just told you. Nava was so happy about this progress that she decided to take another step. She decided to try to get together with Uri's wife for a heart-to-heart talk. I had told her that Karnit was the one who had pushed Uri to be in the group, and my Nava was impressed by that. She asked if I would mind if she called Karnit. I said I wouldn't, but that I should check with Uri first. So I did, and he was fine with the idea.

"Turns out both girls were going to be in Tel Aviv on the same day, and so they arranged to meet in a cafe at Dizengoff Center. Nava told me they talked for three solid hours about everything: what it was like for them to be home while we were in battle, their worries and fears and loneliness, the rushed phone calls when we said we were ok but it was obvious to them that we weren't. Karnit talked about how her kids had coped with daddy not being home, how she and the other mothers had to skillfully navigate between calming the kids yet not lying to them. We have no kids, and after Nava listened to all this she started to consider that life might actually be a lot easier without children, especially sons. The two women even talked about the physical distance they were experiencing from us, the lack of lovemaking, which is such an adjustment from how everything was before the war.

"Here in the group we mostly talk about what's bothering *us*, but we don't invest much time on how it's affecting the women at home. We have this support group and we have Zev's help, but the girls are sort of floating alone in space. They have no organized support. It's not right. It's obvious that our wives and girlfriends also need support, and I think it was good that Nava, who never sits on her hands, took the initiative to contact Karnit."

Uri spoke up. "When Ido told me that Nava wanted to speak with Karnit, I suddenly started thinking about how much of my behavior at home is completely self-centered. I always talk about myself, things I experienced and how it is for me now. I almost never ask how she is feeling, how she is managing, or what it was like for her during the war. And I was happy that someone was taking the initiative to talk with Karnit about things. After she got home, she smiled more than I had seen in a long time. And she talked and talked, and wouldn't stop. And she told me that she and Nava had decided to meet again next week, and that this time they were also going to invite Nili, Avi's wife, and Yariv's Anat.

"So I'm just thinking: Yossi, what about *your* wife? And Sergei, how about your girlfriend? What do you think? Would they be interested?"

The room hums like a beehive. This development was unexpected and, looking back, so logical and important.

Zev, too, is surprised. He has heard of two or three girlfriends meeting and talking if they already knew each other, but Nava's initiative is something novel and interesting. The content of their meetings would differ from the men's sessions, being totally without professional preparation or guidance. He has some concerns about how this undertaking might work out, but feels it is not his place to intervene. It sounded to him like the meeting between Nava and Karnit had been fruitful, and while the unexpected transition to a larger get-together might hold some risks, he doesn't wish to suppress a positive initiative that has the intent of one woman helping another.

"An interesting idea, let's see how it works out, and good luck with it."

*   *   *

"Gil? Good evening, this is Zev. Are you okay?"

"Yes, I'm fine."

"What happened?"

"What happened? Nothing happened," Gil sounds as if he is in a rush to get off.

"You weren't at group today, and since you didn't call to tell us that you wouldn't be coming we were all worried about you...especially when you didn't answer your cell or your home phone. We were very concerned."

"Well, it just didn't work for me today." Gil sounds impatient and eager to end the conversation.

"Gil, are you really okay? There is no problem? After all, this is an unusual event. You've never missed a session before, and neither has anyone else. I'd like to know what's going on."

"No – nothing. It just didn't work out for me today, you know? Just didn't work out, that's all."

"I find this explanation a little hard to accept. It seems to me that there is something you are not telling me. You remember that at the beginning, you promised to come to all our meetings and only to miss one in the case of a true emergency, and in any event, to let us know. We thought you might have been unable to call for some reason, but we certainly expected that you would at least return my calls when you got the messages. I left you two of them. So really, Gil, what's the story? It's very important for me to know."

"Look, Zev, I'm sorry, but this whole thing just isn't for me. The group, and all that chatter. There's nothing in it for me. I just feel I'm wasting my time, you understand? Nothing ever seems to come of it."

"I'm sorry to hear that. I'm also a little surprised. So far I definitely had the impression that you were an active participant, that you were dealing with the issues that came up. And you even reported on improvements in your sleep, with fewer nightmares, and a positive change in your relationship with Ilana. Isn't that true?"

"Yes, right, but now, you know, what can I tell you…" Gil's voice trailed off to silence.

"Actually, I don't know. What changed? Did I or someone else say something that bothered you? Are you disillusioned by the fact that progress is slow? What exactly changed for you?" Zev is determined to make Gil understand that he's not hanging up until he hears the truth.

"Don't know. I'm just out of patience. I can't listen to all these stories anymore. This one whines about this, then that one complains about that, I'm sick of it. I'm done. I just don't want to continue, do you mind?" his tone is now aggressive.

"Do I *mind*? Are you serious? Do you think that I'm calling you in the evening because I'm indifferent? Of course I mind. I want to understand what happened here, and if you need something to change, please come in and let's talk about it. And I want to know why you didn't answer your phones. The group was really worried about you. We thought perhaps you were involved in an accident, that maybe you didn't feel well, that you were sick or very depressed, and that you might have fallen asleep so deeply you couldn't hear the phone. And listen to this: one of the guys told us he would go to your house to find you tonight! Mind? We all care about you, you are one of us." Zev's voice was firm. His feelings bordered on anger, but he controlled his tone.

"Oh, really?" Now Gil sounds genuinely surprised. "I didn't think that you would all take it so seriously." He pauses briefly, as if considering this new information. "I'm sorry if I scared you, or the group. I just didn't feel like coming and I didn't think it was any big deal."

"It definitely is a big deal! We meet every week, we explore how everyone is feeling, and suddenly someone does not arrive, doesn't call, and doesn't answer the phone. That is definitely a big thing, and it worries everyone a great deal."

It sounds as though the conversation is finally beginning to make an impression on Gil. He had not understood – or even considered – the significance of his absence to the other members. From his life experience, he thought the other guys would hardly notice; and if they did, he didn't think they would particularly miss him. He hadn't deliberately intended to hurt anyone, and it came as something of a shock to him that the others, essentially strangers until just a few weeks ago, would be so concerned about his wellbeing.

"Will you come to the next meeting, Gil?"

"Yes, okay, I'll be there. Please give my greetings to everyone. Please let them know that I'm sorry, I didn't mean to...." here he hesitated, as if waiting for permission to end the conversation.

"Good, this is good. But Gil, if something happens during the week and you want to talk about it, please just give me a call. It doesn't matter when, ok? I need to know what's going on with you. Can I rely on you for that?"

"Ok, I promise."

YOSSI

Yitzhak Mizrahi, originally from Morocco, had worked at the same supermarket for 22 years. He was a good and loyal worker and took sick days only when he was so sick that he couldn't move. He had started working as a teenager, restocking shelves and checking on inventory levels. He steadily progressed; he loved his supermarket, and after so many years there he felt as though it were a part of him. He particularly loved the produce department, where the aroma of fresh oranges and the vivid colors of bananas contrasting with red apples gave him a great sense of pleasure. He enjoyed arranging the fruit in straight rows, as if creating a work of art, and he hoped to become the head of that department. He was proud to be an employee and everyone who knew him thought of him as an indispensable part of "the Super."

Changes in staffing customarily took place in the summer, in preparation for the New Year that begins right after the High Holidays in September. This year, several openings were announced in management, and Mizrahi felt that with his superb performance record and his years of hard work, the time was right for him to receive a promotion.

He completed an application for the position of produce department head, and handed it to his supervisor, Yakov, who'd encouraged him to apply and promised he'd support his application. He assured Yitzhak that he was one of his best workers, and credited him with the smooth functioning of the fruits and vegetables department.

When Yitzhak shared the discussion and his hopes for promotion with his wife, her response was cautious. "Watch out, Yitzhak, that you won't be disappointed. You know these Shiknuzim – the westerners who discriminate against us easterners: promises, promises. I don't trust them. But, good luck, you surely deserve it and we could also use the extra money."

"What's with you?" he angrily replied. "You don't think they'll give it to me? I spoke with Yakov and he promised he'd support my application. Actually, it's all up to him, because the higher-level bosses have no idea what's happening at the department level, so they rely on him."

Weeks passed, and finally all the appointments to new positions had taken place. Vassily Shmuelowitz got the meat department; Gurevitch became head of the grocery; Shoham beverages. Yet Mizrahi heard nothing.

Worried, he turned to his superior. "Yakov, weeks have gone by and I still haven't received the appointment I requested. Do you know what's happening?"

Yakov reddened and evaded the question. "I have an important meeting to attend right now; I'll be back to you tomorrow." With that, he took off.

Suddenly Yitzhak felt ill. He felt tired and weak, and something inside him told him that things weren't going his way. He thought about Yakov's evasiveness and his wife's words, and a wave of bitterness rose in his chest.

The letter arrived a few days later…

Dear Mr. Mizrahi,

We have carefully reviewed your application to become the head of Fruits & Vegetables. We want to express our deep appreciation for your dedicated work over the years and we sincerely thank you for your loyalty. While we are convinced that your skills fit your request, for reasons beyond our reach, we're sorry to let you know that at this time we're unable to honor your request. We hope that you'll accept our decision in the right spirit, and we encourage you to apply for the position again next year.

Very truly yours,
Eliezer Gibelson, CEO
Supermarkets, Tel Aviv

His heart sank. "These sons of bitches, they did it to us again. Like I've seen them do to others in our family and among our friends. Once again, we've been discriminated against. My wife was right. Women have a much better understanding of these things than men do. I should have listened to her."

The management of the fruits and vegetables department was given to Anton Abramowich, the cousin of the branch manager. He had arrived from Russia a mere two years ago, knew nothing about retail, and could barely speak Hebrew. But he had blue eyes and blond hair.

Yitzhak had learned his lesson. He never again applied for a promotion.

* * *

Yossi was the fourth child in the family, with two older brothers and a sister. The kids arrived one after the other within six years, and soon after, their parents had another girl. Yossi was a skinny kid who, with so many mouths to feed, always looked underfed. Actually, he was amply fed and never knew hunger; his body type was simply narrow and thin. At school the kids nicknamed him "Raisin," but he was shy and if this bothered him, he never showed it. He knew he was skinny, and he also knew that his friends liked him.

He attended a public religious school where male students and teachers wore kippas, and part of each day was dedicated to prayer and Jewish studies. He also learned basic subjects, but little about geography and history. But foreign countries intrigued him, and once he discovered a book about the Far East and read it with rapt attention. Stories about elephants in India fired his imagination.

When hair started to appear on his chin, he observed it with interest and decided not to touch it. Some of his friends started shaving from the moment the first hair appeared on their faces, but not Yossi. He enjoyed the masculine look and continued to grow his beard as he grew older. However his hair was delicate, and just like his physique, always looked thin and fine.

In his teens, he became friendly with Eli, an older man from the neighborhood who owned a truck and made deliveries. He had a number of steady customers, including a small print shop, a woodworking shop, and a few manufacturing plants. Eli took to the shy Yossi. They both were observant and belonged to the same synagogue, they often sat and discussed the weekly Torah portion and the synagogue, sharing gossip related to it, cigarettes dangling from their lips.

Eli was finding that it was becoming more difficult to lift heavy items, so at times he'd hire Yossi to help load and unload the truck. Despite his slim build, Yossi was strong, and lifting packages and delivering them to customers was easy for him. Gradually he learned the business that would eventually become his livelihood. He learned how to conduct himself with customers, and he was willing to go out of his way for a client who was under pressure to meet a last-minute deadline. He learned how to set prices for deliveries, factoring in all the relevant variables like size, weight, distance, urgency, and whether the client was a steady one or just a one-time customer. He became skillful at predicting which customers would be difficult and demand extra service, and which would be pleasant and appreciative of his efforts, most likely rewarding him with a tip.

Yossi enlisted right after graduating high school. His older brother was already in the army, and had recounted his adventures in the special unit he served in. Yossi followed in his brother's footsteps, and was assigned to a special unit where he was taught to deal with terrorists, and to then pass on the training to less experienced soldiers. He was pleased by his military assignments, despite having witnessed shocking events.

One day when Yossi was home on furlough, Eli approached him. "What are your plans after the army?" he asked.

"I thought of becoming a locksmith," Yossi replied, "but I don't have the patience for studying."

Eli utilized the opening. "I've been thinking that you should join me in my business."

"Eli, this is very interesting, very interesting. There were times when I was sitting on base, the submachine gun lying across my lap, and I'm fantasizing what to do after the service is over. And I had decided that I wasn't going to work for any boss who'd screw me and exploit me." He titled his head toward Eli, and in a whisper added: "Like they did to my father. He gave his heart and soul for the Super, and look how they behaved toward him."

"Yeah, I've heard about it, what a shame. But you're young and you have no family obligations and you can do what you want. You have experience from your work with me, are you interested?"

"Yes, very much," blushing from excitement and the implied compliment. "How do you mean?"

"I thought that you'd start working for me and slowly, let's say over a period of a year or two, you'll be buying the business and the truck, and I'll be retiring. That'll be good for both of us. You'll be coming out of the army and will have an immediate income, and I'll be leaving my business, turn it over to good hands and peace on the world."

"Great! Eli, thanks. Good plan. When would you like me to start?"

"A month or two? How's that?"

"Sounds good" mumbled Yossi, and in his minds eye he saw the business developing, with new customers, a shiny new truck, and on its side, huge letters, in green over yellow, proclaiming "Mizrahi Deliveries." He'd have two in help, an office with a secretary, ringing telephones and faxes spitting out orders. He imagined delivering furniture directly from a factory to a warehouse, agricultural equipment hauled in a huge truck, supplies to restaurants, computers and more. His imagination sailed further and further. He'd rescue his father from his slavery in Fruits and Vegetables and bring him into the business. It'll be fantastic.

* * *

Ron swung in his seat, looked at Yossi and addressed him: "According to my calculations, there is a period of about one to one-and-a-half years missing from your history. Where were you after you got discharged from the Special Unit?"

"Why do you care? Are you my mother?" Yossi suddenly snarled.

"Oh, sorry, I didn't mean to pry, it's really none of my business. It's not important," he apologized, but knew that he had opened a Pandora's Box, that he touched an important subject that apparently Yossi didn't wish to deal with.

A strange quietness befell the room. Some of the members sided with Yossi, feeling protective of him due to the invasion of his privacy, but others were curious to hear what it was he was attempting to hide. There were also those who had a strange sense that he wasn't quite frank with them, and they were waiting to see how things developed.

Yossi, in the crosshairs, moved about in his chair, looked here and there, placed the palms of his hands on his thighs, glanced from one to the other, blinked and swallowed –and kept quiet. Tension rose among the men, as it appeared that he intended to reply, but instead he just postponed his response, hoping that he wouldn't be called upon to react.

That did not happen.

The stage was set and Yossi, the main actor, was now exposed to the curiosity and suspicions of the group's members.

"I traveled to India!" he finally blurted out, sounding partly angry and partly exhaling with relief. The cat was out of the bag, at last. It was a secret that very few knew; even his mother didn't. She thought, based on the colorful postcards that had reached her from time to time from other countries, that he was traveling for pleasure, seeing the world and accumulating experience in various kinds of work. She didn't know that he was addicted to drugs, was dealing drugs, that his life had been in danger several times, and that once he had been jailed for two weeks.

Sly Yossi had managed to fool his parents and others by acquiring American postcards, filling them with made-up adventures, and then sending them back to friends in the USA, with the request to mail them to his family in Israel. His parents weren't sufficiently sophisticated to figure out that the phone calls from him, which they cherished, were equally faked, originating in India.

The truth is that he had plans to reach these places and make the money his friends had spoken about. Stories circulated that it was possible to make a mint in all kinds of ways in the wondrous land of America. There were those who sold toys or cosmetic items in malls. There was one who worked as a locksmith, a skill he had acquired in the engineering corps, and who charged astronomical fees to hapless homeowners who had forgotten their key or broken it in the lock, especially during weekends or at night. There were those who dealt in illegal drugs imported from China, which they bought for pennies and resold at 80 times their cost.

And, of course, not being citizens helped them to avoid paying income tax. In addition, most of their incomes were in cash. The problem was "easy come easy go." Huge spending was common among these guys; from luxury cars to expensive restaurants, to trips on luxury liners, entertaining women who collected their fees in jewelry as payment for pleasures of the flesh. And, as might be expected from their frivolous life styles, the use of drugs was rampant. From using to dealing, the distance was short. And from dealing to being caught by the police and wallowing in prison for long terms with the dregs of the earth, even shorter. The 'know-it-all' Israelis, especially the veterans of elite units who had learned survival tactics in dangerous combat situations, did not comprehend that the USA, the land of unlimited opportunities, is also a country that enforces its laws. "You get caught – you pay!" And many did get caught.

Yossi heard all these stories and the idea of using drugs and even getting rich from dealing drugs, appealed to him. But getting caught by a drug enforcement police unit, one that was wise to Israeli and other drug dealers' shenanigans, did not appeal to him at all. Therefore he chose to go to India, the other drug heaven.

India had a reputation of being filthy, with tens of thousands of people pushing against each other like ants in a nest, each trying to carve out a morsel for himself. Its climate was said to be even worse than the blazing sands of Gaza, and the danger to life from crime, gangs and other unpleasant people was high. Yet, the chances of being apprehended by police were low, especially in remote areas, small villages and forests. The risk of spending much time in jail was also low, due to lax law enforcement and the age-old culture of bribery. It was possible at times to get out of trouble by bribing police and other officials with literally the very same coin – drugs.

Yossi called Benny, a comrade from the elite unit.

"Benny! What's up? When are you getting discharged?"

"Next week, and you?"

"I'm already discharged, returned the equipment, I'm a civilian and it's time to start living. Want to come with me like we discussed?" He hinted at a conversation they had had many months ago when they were both up to their necks chasing terrorists, disarming explosive charges, patrolling in frightening inner city enclaves on the West Bank. They swore to themselves that if they came out of it with their bodies unscathed, they'd go to India to live it up.

"I'm with you! When?"

"I still have to finish a few things, help my parents paint their apartment, and then I'm with you on our way."

Three weeks after that conversation they met at Ben Gurion Airport and flew to Mumbai. They had established connections with others who had been there before them in that kind of adventure, and set up a meeting point at a newspaper kiosk, manned by an Israeli.

Within days they boarded a dilapidated bus, the kind that Egged, the Israeli bus company, would have discarded 20 years ago. It brought them to a remote village. The shaky ride on dirt roads, the stench of chickens and sweat-soaked clothes that filled the bus, made them very tired and they fell asleep. Benny woke up from a nightmare and jumped from his seat into a combat stance, as if seeing a threatening enemy. Yossi understood immediately and calmed him down. Benny pulled out a cigarette, lit it and took a long, deep drag.

"I'm fed up with these lousy cigarettes; I'm waiting for something better, for grass, like they say."

"By tonight," assured Yossi.

At sunset the next day, they arrived at their destination. It was a small, smelly village with a multitude of people milling about, as if doing nothing purposeful, with screaming children throwing stones at emaciated and starving dogs. Shouting in a mixture of dialects filled the air, and Yossi and Benny didn't understand a word of it. They searched for their contact person and showed a handwritten note in a local dialect to some passers-by. At last, a youth directed them to a run-down building and immediately held out his hand for payment for his efforts. Benny stuck two cigarettes into his palm but the boy made a dissatisfied face. Yossi shoved two rupees into his hand and waved him off.

The two-story building was dark and the smell of marijuana

permeated every corner. Men and women, wearing rags, sat slumped along the walls, some smoking, others in a fitful sleep.

"You've arrived!"

A young man with a distinct Israeli accent, the "landlord" of this "guest house" greeted them. "I've been waiting for you for two days, where were you?"

"We couldn't get out of there, then there was no bus, main thing is, we're here."

"Let me have one!" demanded Benny, pointing to a rolled-up joint. The young man handed him two.

"Finish this one and continue with the second, you'll get a better high, enjoy!"

Benny practically ripped the reefer out of the guy's filthy hand, lit up and took a long and deep drag. It was obvious that he was a heavy user.

"How much is this?" he asked.

"Pay me with some work, not money. Money isn't worth much around here, but work is, because nobody wants to do any work. They are all too stoned to hold a hoe or lift a package," replied the landlord, himself exhaling stinking smoke.

"Work? What kind of work?" asked Benny.

"You'll help in the kitchen, prepare some food, remove dishes and when you move out of here, you'll be delivering some packages to a friend of mine."

"Ah, that's cool, not a problem," as he continued to inhale the fumes.

Several days passed. They slept until noon, only getting up to pee behind the shack in the middle of the night with great effort, then returning to the sleeping bags that covered the room and doubled as beds. The meals included local flatbread and hamburger-like patties that could not be identified, but tasted good, infused with curry and other spices.

According to the agreement between the landlord and Benny, he helped out in the "kitchen." Between drags he chopped vegetables and discarded rubbish by throwing it out the window. At times he helped serve guests and collect the few pennies they owed. Yossi huddled with the landlord, who did not wish to be identified by name. "Call me Itzik," he said in response to "what's your name?"

The two spoke in whispers, communicated with hand motions and looked at the others with suspicion. It wasn't possible to be sure that there aren't other Israelis among the guests who chose to conceal their background. And there were locals who understood enough Hebrew from the years they hung around Israelis who frequented this place. They might be able to catch what the two were discussing. "Itzik" and Yossi agreed on a plan to transfer large amounts of drugs to another location in exchange for Yossi not paying for his stay.

Yossi also smoked grass but he was not as stoned as Benny. That one moved from one kind of grass to another and kept increasing his consumption. He also swallowed pills that he bought from Itzik. There were many hours that he was out of it and hallucinating. Actually there were fewer hours in the day when he was awake and coherent, than hours of being stoned and blubbering. To Benny's mind, he had reached heaven: all the drugs he wanted, free of charge or for pennies. His dream had come true and it helped him to overcome the recurring nightmares that frightened him and caused him to wake up in screams and battle leaps.

At the end of a week in this interim station, Benny and Yossi set out to their next destination. They had received travel instructions from Itzik, but as he himself was always stoned and sloppy, they assumed that his directions were marginal and not accurate. An old donkey carried their bags and the drugs, and they walked alongside. Had everything gone according to plan, they would have arrived after five days.

After two days with the donkey and an escort who talked incessantly in an incomprehensible language, they sent him on his way with thanks and some money, and continued on foot. Within a few hours, Benny announced that he had to lie down and rest. Yossi was unhappy about it but agreed. Benny did not wake up for many hours, hallucinated in his sleep, screamed, writhed even wet himself. He was not in physical or emotional condition to cope with the task.

At last, Yossi lifted him up and they continued, Yossi carrying all of Benny's belongings. He tried to convince Benny to smoke less and to limit the amount of pills he swallowed. He himself only smoked from time to time, aware of his responsibility to reach the next village and collect the huge amount promised to him by Itzik. After all, aside from a few cheap smokes, the main idea was to get rich quickly and with almost no risk. "India isn't America," he kept repeating to himself when he got tired and doubts crept into his heart. He started to think of ways to get rid of Benny. It turned out that Benny would be solving the problem by himself.

At the end of the third day, the two arrived at a tiny inn, one room, no toilets, a kerosene lamp for lighting, and a huge Indian who rambled on rapidly, swinging his long arms.

After they went to sleep, Benny started to snore heavily. His breathing was uneven and unstable. He sat up, mumbled something incoherently and threw up. Yossi became alarmed. Benny's condition was clearly not good and there was of course no possibility of getting any medical help. He gave him a tranquilizer and water and moved all the drugs out of his reach and then sought the help of the Indian. The innkeeper didn't care; he'd witnessed things like this by his drug-addicted guests on many occasions. After some time, Benny returned to a deep sleep. Yossi, exhausted from the day and night's unsettling events, dropped off into a coma-like slumber.

When Yossi woke up, about 10 in the morning, Benny was quietly lying next to him. He did not snore. He did not breathe. He had died in his sleep from drug poisoning. His muscular body, the body of a soldier in an elite unit who chased terrorists in the hills of Jerusalem, who waded knee-deep in mud, loaded with weapons and equipment, who scanned the horizon from the top of the Beaufort Castle in Lebanon on freezing nights – could not stand up to the drugs.

The huge Indian flung his arms even more vigorously and anxiously, and spoke even faster than before. A death in his inn might trigger an investigation even in this god-forsaken place. He was determined to get rid of the body as soon as possible. Somehow he managed to reach a friend who arrived in an ancient car. The Indian and Yossi loaded Benny's body into it and disappeared in the direction of the village they had set out from several days ago. Itzik, alarmed as well that his drug dealings might be investigated as they no doubt contributed to Benny's death, bribed the village manager not to ask too many questions, and one way or another Benny's body was returned to Tel Aviv.

Yossi was shaken. Not only did he mourn the death of a friend, he felt a degree of responsibility for his death and he anticipated that Benny's family would ask many questions, as well as the Israeli police, the Ministry of Defense, the army, and God-knows-who-else. He wrestled with the idea of returning to Israel to be at Benny's funeral, but immediately decided that this would be the equivalent of jumping into a lion's den, and didn't go. "Go find me," he mumbled to himself.

For several days after Benny's body was shipped back, Yossi stayed with Itzik to nurse his wounds and regroup. He felt badly that Benny had finished his once admirable life in such a sad way. He was aware that Benny was not the only victim of drug-induced deaths among discharged Israeli soldiers. He knew it was a serious problem, affecting hundreds each year, including other deaths and suicides. He was determined not become the next statistic.

He didn't touch any more marijuana or any other drug. He set himself a goal to make $500,000, and then to return to Israel and start a business. For a year he moved about in the area, buying and selling drugs, transporting suspicious packages from one place to another. He spoke sparingly, observed his surroundings, was cautious and avoided making too many contacts. He kept himself away from others and concentrated on his goal. He earned the reputation of a reliable and fair person, and his word was his word.

* * *

"Who are you? Where are you from?"

A booming voice emanating from a beard-surrounded mouth woke Yossi up from a deep sleep. He leaped up, ready to do battle, when it became clear that he was surrounded by police, at last having been caught trafficking in drugs. Fortunately Itzik was aware of what was happening and had a vested interest in helping out.

Yossi was taken into custody and awaited a trial which could have resulted in years of imprisonment, the very reason he avoided going to the civilized, clean USA. He cursed himself for being sloppy, not covering his tracks sufficiently to evade capture.

He was thrown into a holding pen together with riffraff. There were men of all colors and ages, thin and heavy. He did not understand a word they said. Fortunately, one young man recognized that Yossi was clearly a foreigner and, since he spoke English, befriended him. Turned out that he too was dealing in drugs, as were many of the others. Food was served twice a day with a huge ladle, sleeping was on the floor, and bathroom facilities were best not described.

Yossi stayed there for two weeks, having once been pulled out for questioning for ten minutes. He answered basic questions and cleverly dodged others posed to him by a British-sounding magistrate. Then he was sent back.

On day 15, a guard sprung open the door, called his name "Yussee Mizrakee" and told him to follow. He was brought outside and told to get lost. Itzik was waiting in a car and they took off.

Itzik had been petrified that if Yossi were put on trial he would reveal too much, jeopardizing Itzik's operation and possibly his life. He bribed anyone who might have any influence and managed to get him freed on some technicality.

*   *   *

Yossi grew a Sikh-looking beard, filling in thin spots with dark coloring, moved to a different location much further away, adopted local clothes, learned some phrases in the local language and continued to operate very cautiously. He made all the deliveries by himself, not trusting anyone, but after several months of great success he became careless. By then he had managed to accumulate hundreds of thousands of dollars, and others became aware of it. He managed to transfer some of it to his account in Bank Hapoalim in Israel, but was careful to dole these deposits out in small amounts, spread out over weeks and months. The money arrived from different sources and in circuitous ways.

Yossi kept a considerable amount on his body to have enough available to enter deals on the spot, and also because he could not safely transfer all of it.

One night, sitting with a few people he got to know, he drank enough to fall into a deep sleep, deeper than usual. When he woke up, he discovered to his horror that the money he was carrying, as well as a large package of drugs for which he had already paid, were gone. He decided to quit before someone took not only his money, but also his life. It was the end of that chapter in his life.

Cleverly, he had stashed away enough emergency money to buy a ticket to Tel Aviv and, just as he had arrived anonymously 16 months earlier, he disappeared from the horizon and landed at Ben Gurion Airport. No one came to greet him.

* * *

"That's my story. That's what happened in the year to year-and-a-half that is missing in my story. Your calculation is remarkably accurate, Ron. More power to you."

It seemed to the others that they heard a sigh of relief in Yossi's last sentence, as he leaned back, shifting the weight of his body onto the back of the seat.

Ron pressed: "So what happened with old Eli? You practically promised him that you'd join his business and would let him retire comfortably?"

"True. I'm ashamed about that. After I made the arrangements with Benny to leave the country, I went to Eli and sat down with him. I told him how stressed I was after everything I had lived through in the West Bank and Gaza, how unable I was to concentrate, how irritable, how I'm unable to sleep at night and need to wind down. I told him that I'd planned a trip to the US to live it up a bit, as I'd also told my family, and that in a month or two, I'd be back and then we'd do the deal."

"And how did he react?"

"I knew he didn't believe me. He was an old, sly fox and knew how to distinguish truth from tale. He had heard of IDF veterans who traveled abroad to exotic places and never returned. He liked me and cautioned me to be careful as to what I was going into. He knew much more than I did. But he was also a gentleman and understood that he wouldn't be able to change my mind, so he wished me a good trip, and that was it."

"But now, you're actually working in that business. Did you

return to him?"

"No. During the time I wasn't there, he passed away. I heard about it only after I had returned, and I was sad and ashamed. I'm grateful to Eli for everything he had taught me, and when I came back, I really didn't know what to do. I still had no interest in further studies, and dealing in drugs, in which I'd become an expert...surely not. I had a pile of money, bought a used truck in good condition, for cash, as well as a smaller delivery van for lighter loads, also in cash, no payments, not bullshit, and I returned to the same environment where I was well-known, and started to build my business. No one had moved in after Eli passed away, so it was easy for me. But now, as you all know, I can't get out of bed in the morning, and all that...."

EIGHTH SESSION

Zev opened with a question: "We've talked about all kinds of topics and made progress with many. Yet I have the feeling there are still some important subjects we haven't touched, either because there was no opportunity, or maybe because they are too 'hot' and no one was quite ready to discuss them. Is that the case?"

Gil, returned to the group but sitting slightly apart, made no response.

Yossi responded eagerly: "Yes indeed. There's an issue I've been meaning to deal with for some time, but I always felt too embarrassed to bring it up." Here he hesitated briefly, then continued with visible effort and determination.

"Sometimes I just become very irritable and impatient, until I find myself lashing out at people around me. Afterwards, I can't find any good reason why I acted that way. I'll have these furious outbursts, where it looks like I just don't care about anyone else's feelings. It's especially bad with my parents. Later, I feel miserable, and ashamed of myself.

"I'm particularly upset about the way I behave toward my father, because I love him, yet I have absolutely no patience for him. We have very different ways of dealing with life, and I get crazy when I see how people humiliate him at work and he just keeps quiet about it. I would have blasted them, probably even quit by now if I were in his job. And my mother also makes me nuts. I know she loves me, but she still talks to me like I'm a child:

'It's cold outside, don't forget to take a coat' and that kind of thing, and I tell her I don't like it, and she doesn't stop. Please! I just got back from a war, I survived dangerous situations, I managed to be on my own for months in a foreign country, and she's on my ass about a raincoat. And sometimes I explode, I just can't help myself, and I'll scream at her, pound my fist on the table, slam the door, and leave home without a coat, on purpose, even if the wind is howling and it's pouring. Then when I return home, I'm thoroughly ashamed of myself. I can't look either of my parents in the eye, because I know I hurt them and insulted them. God, these are my parents! I'm wearing a kippa, and the commandments tell us 'Honor your father and your mother,' and look what I'm doing. Look how I behave."

"Yes, we've seen some of this here," Ron confirms. "Often you'll just cut in, right in the middle of somebody else's sentence and you're very short-tempered, and sometimes you seem to have no patience for someone else's explanations. I know you have a good heart and good intentions, and you've really helped some of us several times, but I can see what you are talking about. The question I have is, were you always like this? Or did it start happening after you got back from the war?" With a serious look, Ron sits back in his seat.

Yossi blushes, clearly taken aback. "Truly? It's that obvious? Here I'm really trying hard to be quiet and polite and listen to everyone, and in the end I still come across like some wild beast?"

"No need to exaggerate. You're far from being a beast, but short-tempered, yes, we can all see and feel it. You also sit very tensely and you're probably not even aware that your fists are often clenched. Did you know that?"

"No, I didn't know. But in the morning when I wake up, my jaw aches, and my mother once commented to me that I grind my teeth in my sleep. Perhaps it's related. And there is something else; when a driver cuts me off on the road, I blare my horn like crazy, smack the steering wheel with my fist, scream and curse and I try to overtake him, to teach him a lesson. It's frightening. What if he is as crazy as I am and pulls out a gun or something and tries to take revenge? God forbid!" he concluded with a sigh.

Zev: "We are discussing here one of the well-documented symptoms of PTSD, it's a common one, and not only when interacting with family and friends. Is there anyone here who experiences it at work or school?"

Yariv: "And how. Do you remember the birthday party that my wife prepared for me, how I had no patience for the children? I'm crazy for them, my kids, they are terrific, good kids, but when they run around the house, squealing, I feel the blood rising to my head and I want to scream 'Quiet!' but I don't say a word. I escape into another room, or into the yard, or even get into the car and take off. I was never like that.

"And now to the work situation: I'm an independent metalsmith. My income depends on the jobs I manage to get. Many people know me and appreciate my good work. When I weld something, it lasts forever. When there is a problem, I solve it, I have good ideas and my prices are reasonable, so it makes sense to give me the job – except that I have become so short tempered, cutting people off in mid-sentence, and they look at me like I'm who-knows-what. I know for sure that recently I've lost several jobs due to this. One is a restaurant owner in Tiberias, for whom I've done work many times, and I was sure the job was mine. We started to talk and he wanted a small change. I started yelling 'What do think? Do you know how much more work is entailed!?' and he looks at me with astonishment. A minute later he says: 'Maybe next time, be well.' And that was the end of a job that never started. And I had a talk with another guy and he asked if a gate could be repaired in a different way, and I start screaming. I saw that he was looking at me like I'm insane, shortened the conversation and said 'I'll get back to you,' and of course I haven't heard from him. The quality of my work hasn't changed, but my behavior puts people off and it's costing me money. Worse, my good reputation is getting ruined. People in the north know that 'Yariv is an excellent craftsman, punctual, doesn't cheat you on price, he's the man,' and I'm spoiling that reputation. It's very worrisome."

"That's clear, isn't it? Anyone else?"

"Yes" and Ido pulls his body forward in his seat. "Recently I've had problems with the department head where I teach. It has implications because he is important in my career advancement. He drags his words, repeats himself and I'm sitting on pins and needles. I'm unable to listen to his chatter and there is no doubt that he senses my impatience. That's very bad, because if I piss him off, he won't support my promotion. We also have less than pleasant discussions about the article I owe him. We've already discussed this here, remember?" Several heads nod. "These discussions are tense. I know I have to finish the article, but when he brings up the subject, my answers aren't polite, and that's a mistake. The trouble is that it feels like ants are crawling under my skin, I have no patience, I'm tense, I bite my lip. That's something new for me, and not typical."

By now, Yossi had overcome his blushing and embarrassment and felt encouraged that he wasn't the only one struggling with this issue. He had been trying for some time to overcome it and had invested hours in thinking, trying to understand why he was behaving in such an aberrant manner. "You know what? Recently, after I've thought about this many times, I'm beginning to understand what has happened here. I scream instead of talking in a civilized manner, cut people off in mid-sentence, even make faces and leave in the middle of a conversation, really awful behavior. There are even people who've known me for years, and when I arrive, I notice that within minutes they aren't there anymore. They keep away from me, I think, because they anticipate that there will be some altercation with me, and they don't want that. The conclusion I've arrived at, and I'm not sure that there is any substance to it, is that when I was in those traumatic events, which I'll describe in a minute, I had to shut up, hold my breath, keep myself from screaming – and now that the situation is no longer so, I allow myself to behave like I just described."

"I'm curious to know how you've arrived at your explanation?" wondered Ron.

Yossi straightens out in his seat, coughs lightly and tells: "We were in an ambush in the area of Jenin. It was about 2 AM, pitch dark, no moon, and an ominous silence. It was cold, thin rain drizzled down and was annoying, getting into my eyes and obscuring my vision. Tiny drops dotted my goggles and it was difficult to wipe them every minute. We were waiting for a group of militants that intelligence had notified us were roaming in the area. There was terrible tension. I was tired from the lengthy walk to our hideout, the M-16 was gaining weight every fifteen minutes like it was pregnant, the knapsack was slipping around on my back, and even the helmet refused to stay in place. It was maddening. In front of me sat this stupid guy, who, out of fear, started to talk again and again, and I had to smack him in the back to shut him up, as the tension kept rising. We sat there for about an hour and a half, and suddenly, there was a noise in the bushes. My heart jumped, my pulse went berserk, I could hear it pounding in my ears. I thought, 'that's it, just don't let us be discovered. We'll have 30 seconds to eliminate them, or they'll eliminate us.' Every muscle in my body was tight. God, I never knew how many muscles I have. The fist grabbing the weapon, jaws clenched, eyes narrowed trying to see even a bit in that damned darkness. The noise goes on and on. In reality, it might have lasted just three seconds, like slow motion in a movie. Nothing happened. No militants, no fire, nothing. The tension continues. Suddenly I hear breathing next to me, like a gurgle, and nonchalantly a goat – a goat! – is trotting past me, looks at me and continues on. I almost burst out laughing, but bit my lip. Just because there's a goat here doesn't mean that the enemy isn't here as well, or could be arriving any minute. My pulse slowed down, the muscles relaxed, but I felt anger. That bastard of a goat almost caused me to have a heart attack. I wanted to put a bullet in it, but instead, I changed the way I was sitting…and my gun slipped out of my hand and hit the rocky ground. My muscles stiffened again and I held my breath. What if the noise I just caused would reveal us? Compared to what I just did, the chatter of that stupid guy in front of me is nothing. I worried that my commander would lace into me, that I'm endangering everyone, and suddenly I got the urge to pee, but I didn't dare to move."

Nobody reacted. Things like had happened to everyone at some point, and all understood, even though he had endangered others' lives.

"And there were other ambushes, many of them. Sometimes night after night, and there wasn't enough time to rest and unwind. Every time we went out, my stomach was in knots, I was nervous, tense and fearful. One of these days it won't be a goat, it will be the real thing, I thought, armed guys looking for us just as we were looking for them. We knew them to be courageous and not likely to shun a fight. I have a wife at home, and a two-year-old, what am I doing here? And that tension kept building up.

"I once spoke to an army friend, but he had a desk job and didn't exactly understand what I was talking about. He quickly changed the subject, I think, because he was ashamed about how he was 'fighting' paper on his desk while I was fighting in ambushes at night, in deadly danger. Since then I've never discussed it with anyone."

"Yeah, many of us had similar experiences, but you've announced that you've discovered the reason for your nervousness, the impatience, the crass speech. What is it?"

"Ah, yes. According to my thinking, I was in situations that – in order to save my life and the lives of my friends – I had to shut up when I wanted to scream, I had to sit quietly and in an uncomfortable, even painful position when I wanted to get up and run away, I had to hold it in instead of peeing and relieving myself, I had to be super-disciplined and yield to the demands of the moment. Now, as a civilian, I don't give a shit! Let them think whatever they want. I don't effing care what they think and how they look at me. I explode, and that's all there is to it!"

"Very interesting," mumbled Yariv. "It's a logical and reasonable explanation. The trouble is that your mother, who worries about you not getting a cold from the rain, has no idea what you are concealing; she just worries about your well-being. She doesn't deserve a slammed door, and your father, who's slogged for years in a miserable job, hasn't changed, but you did. As for me, customers always want a little more for their money and say 'do this and do that,' nothing new, just that now I don't have the energy and the desire to hold back, to be polite, to be a good boy. If they knew what you had to endure in those night ambushes as they were slumbering in their warm beds, they wouldn't dare to challenge you...." as his face twisted in anger.

Everyone had similar stories. Either fear-provoking ambushes or another horrifying event where it would be logical to scream, burst out, curse, cry or run, just that under the circumstances it wasn't possible to react freely. It was necessary to be disciplined, suffer, hold back, no complaining, and bite one's lip. In civilian life this control failed. When a mouth opened up, it was difficult to close it. When there was a slight complaint, it turned into a major confrontation. When there were differences in opinion, even insignificant ones, they turned into a quarrel, at times loud, even vile. Such behavior did bring about a lessening of tension, but at a high price.

Uri: "So, Zev, you've heard it. Probably nothing new to you. What does one do?"

"Right, not new and very common. Everything you've described is known and I've heard it many times. That's the bad part. The good part is that we can add a few tools to our tool box, to help with this problem.

"First, the mere fact that someone is aware of the issue, is very important. Yossi seemed to have been surprised by how much his behavior was obvious to everyone. He knew in a limited way, but not fully. Secondly, the desire to bring about a change is vital. If someone is aware of their behavior but not interested in changing, chances are that there will be no change. If the approach of 'I don't give a damn' continues, it will have unpleasant reactions from others. Parents will mostly protect their son even if he is 40 years old, but an employer will show him the door. Clerks in government offices will place his file at the bottom of the pile, and a doctor's receptionist who is being yelled at, won't find time for an appointment. Is this picture clear?

"And for those who are married, or have a partner, the suffering is huge. And the same is true for children. How many times have you heard about marriages that fell apart, or the girlfriend left? And the children are caught in the middle. They are unable to get up and leave. They are just disappointed that Aba no longer talks to them with affection and love, isn't helping with homework, doesn't play ball, and even yells about minor things, like normal playtime noise. They look at Mom with the question: 'What happened to Aba?' and she's stuck with a legitimate question but no good answer.

"What to do? One must internalize the difference between 'something terrible happened to me and I deserve a world that will forgive my behavior and pamper me' and reality. The reality is that most of the world really doesn't understand, and worse, doesn't give a damn what happened to you. You have to find the way back into society without the screaming. Not easy. Makes you angry. Irritating, but doable. One of the ways is to guess up front who you are dealing with. Mostly we deal with people we know: family, friends, employers, colleagues, customers and local shopkeepers. The number of people we deal with and *don't* know is relatively small. And many times we have some choice as to who we wish to interact with and whom to avoid. Those whom we know, we also know their quirks, what's important to them, how sticky they'd be about a particular issue, very important information that allows us to plan.

"Yossi, for example, knows that for his mother, as any Jewish mother, it is very important that he'll take his coat. He could lay money on it that she'll pester him about that, for sure. Doesn't matter how many times he'll ask her to stop, she probably won't. It's in her blood. The same thing with his father, who, every time he lends Yossi his car, admonishes him to be careful about scratches, even though Yossi never ever put a scratch on it.

"And what does Yariv know? That his customers will want something for nothing, something extra, and will haggle over the price. And what does Ido know? That his department head drags his words and will, for the hundredth time, remind him that he needs to complete the article. There are no surprises here. Right? And the wives and partners? What do they want?"

Yossi jumps in: "Attention! Attention. Why don't you pay attention to me? You are neglecting me, you forgot about me and words like that."

"Sound familiar? And the kids?"

"Aba, come play with us. Ilan's father plays ball with him every Shabbat afternoon."

"The surprises come from less well-known sources, for example the bureaucracy of the Veterans Administration, that can make even the most patient people in the world go mad. And sometimes salespeople in stores who don't want to be there and are rude to customers. These are the kinds of people who can cause a problem, because we don't know them and their particular quirks. They constitute a relatively small number in our lives.

"In order to reduce the tension and the number of outbursts and unpleasantness, you can also prepare a number of expressions and phrases that can be pulled 'off the shelf' in a moment of confrontation. The advantage is that at a moment of anger, or a short fuse, one doesn't have to search for the right words, or worse, say something that would have been best not said, and might even require an apology."

Yossi, at the edge of his seat, is awaiting a magic wand to solve this embarrassing problem. "For example?"

"When your mother is pestering you about the coat, and you may be sure that she will, put your hand on her shoulder, and in a calm voice say 'thanks for reminding me. When it's cold I'll take it, right now it isn't needed' and leave the room with a smile. Don't yell, don't slam doors, and don't make impatient faces at her. Confirm for her that you heard what's concerning her, and that you are willing to heed her advice when you're ready. This sentence has to be etched in your mind so it will roll off your tongue. If you have to start searching for words, it's almost certain that you will yell or say something insulting, like 'get off my back, cut it out,' and words you'll regret in a minute."

"Got it. I'll practice."

"Quick relaxation and deep breathing will also help, like down-shifting at the approach to a steep hill, for extra power. The fact that you know what's coming and how irritating it could be; allows you to almost turn it into a joke, like 'I knew what she'd say and I was ready for it.'"

Yariv now adds the implications for his situation. "I'm coming to my client, I have my price in my head, I know that he'll want more for his money and I don't want to lose this job. I don't raise my voice; I tell him something funny, take a deep breath and give him some of what he wants. Actually it isn't different from any daily transaction just that this time I have to leave the anger behind and being short-tempered is out of the equation. At the end, the anger just adds to the tension I live with anyway, so I'll be gaining doubly; I'll get the job and we part with a smile."

"Look, I'm not minimizing for a second the challenges of irritability. Such emotions can be draining, and despite Yossi's elegant explanation, there isn't, as yet, any good scientific explanation why this happens. There are researchers who claim that trauma causes physiological changes in the brain tissues, it's not so clear. Until we'll know for sure, we'll use the tools at our disposal, and there is much evidence that there are good results."

"I'm going to come home and I'll give my wife a kiss…and she'll fall on the floor from surprise…" and a wave of chuckling and laughing sweeps the room.

"All joking aside, if you'll actually do it, you'll be surprised at the dividends. It isn't a manipulation. She deserves to get a kiss from you, that's part of the marriage deal, to protect and honor each other, and she has been suffering together with you this whole time. You remember that Uri arrived here because his wife practically pushed him through the door."

Ido got the message. It's not that he was unaware before, but the simplistic way that Zev demonstrated with Yossi and Yariv propelled him to think out loud. Uncharacteristic of his reserved nature, he turned his thoughts into a parody: "Dear Mr. Head of Department; What a pleasure it is to meet you this morning," and bowing deeply, continues. "Would it be too much to ask for your thoughts this very morning, and I shall be just too delighted to add some of mine...." and everyone roared in laughter.

The message was clear. The phenomenon of irritability and short-temperedness, even among people who are usually even-tempered, is very vexing. It gobbles up a huge amount of emotional energy, causes confrontations that take even more out of you, and nearly always ends up with negativity. It is avoidable on many occasions, and every encounter with another person that is pleasant, or at least neutral, improves not only the healing from trauma, it might even bring practical, positive results. A pleasant conversation with a VA clerk and a brief explanation why something is urgent might move the folder from the bottom of the pile closer to its top.

* * *

There is heaviness in the room, a strange and atypical quiet. It seems no one has a thing to say. For several weeks now, sessions have been lively; it seemed that participants could hardly wait for their turn to talk. Now, for unclear reasons, *nobody* is talking.

Eyes glance furtively from one to another and an air of uneasiness and tension blankets the room. Although there have been silences before, this one is longer and somehow, different.

Zev thinks he understands what is happening. *"We have reached the phase of the revolt against the leader."* This phenomenon is well-known to therapists who run therapy groups, but certainly not to participants, unless they are veterans of other groups.

In Zev's broad experience, a new group always begins with participants who are cautiously groping to find out who their new comrades are, and whether they – especially the leader – can be trusted with one's most intimate and painful secrets. They wonder and worry about the psychologist, who hasn't been with them to those places and through the difficult times that everyone else has. Can he be trusted to navigate this ship through the storms? So much depends on his skillfulness and empathy. And there is always the hidden fear that develops, that "he doesn't like me, he prefers someone else."

After these fears have quieted and an atmosphere of trust has been established, a prevailing feeling spreads among the members that it is ok to have faith in each other, and that the leader is indeed competent to navigate the troubled waters, that things are visibly progressing. Yet gradually, under the surface, doubts still creep in. They remain unconscious for a time, but one day someone utters a remark that implies doubt, perhaps the belief that the leader is not completely genuine, that he is "in it for the money," that he really doesn't care deeply about the members' well-being.

And the doubt expressed by one person stirs up the unconscious doubts of the others. Feelings that one is being neglected, that the leader likes and cares more about someone else, that nothing is really helping, that "this whole thing is bullshit," and other thoughts of mistrust bubble up and intensify. And then a revolt begins.

Old patterns of interaction with parents and siblings enter the picture, both silently and out loud, and the psychological phenomenon of "transference" arises: interacting with someone as though he were somebody else; and "counter-transference," where a member may elicit certain feelings from the group leader that may cause the therapist to perceive that individual incorrectly. All these occurrences can join in a kind of a conspiracy that expresses itself in a revolt against the leader, which is played out in different ways. One way is extended silence, another is total non-participation, and things come to a screeching halt.

Everyone in the group is obviously thinking, but no one allows a thought to leave his lips.

As he has done before, Zev sits quietly and does not intervene. He feels it is important for the men to arrive at a conclusion as to what is happening on their own. This is different than earlier silences, when the conversation became stalled due to the heaviness of the subject under discussion; because of a flood of emotions; or by the search for a solution to a challenging problem. This time the atmosphere felt different, and there was no issue on the table.

An uneasiness is growing, and everyone senses it.

Sergei throws out, "What's happening here? Why isn't anyone talking?"

Silence. Even this invitation to break it makes no difference.

"Does anyone wish to respond to Sergei?" encourages Zev, gently.

"Don't know. Guess we've just solved all our problems, and we can get up and go home, and that's it." Gil breaks his silence, his voice heavy with sarcasm. "Finished, we're all healed, no more nightmares, no more flashbacks, work is a pleasure, explosions do not disturb us, sex is fantastic, studies are a piece of cake...."

"Oh, really? Or is it that everything is so extremely *not* ok, that we don't even know where to start," retorts Yariv darkly. "What is so awful, so insolvable, that the group has come to a full stop?"

"Well, I don't know exactly how to say this without...hurting someone's feelings, or sounding ungrateful, but...." Yossi begins, but stops short.

"Whose feelings?" prods Zev, certain that it is himself who will be the target.

Yossi reddens and squirms a little in his seat. "You know what I'm thinking, don't you?"

"Yes, I think I do. And how would it be hurting my feelings? You mentioned sounding ungrateful. What are you feeling less than grateful about?"

"Now look! Stop playing mind games. You know what some of us are thinking." Yossi has decided to be the one with the courage to say what the others are thinking. "We feel that you haven't been through the things we have, so you can't really be very helpful. That most of us are still suffering from the same problems we started with, and that this whole business of group therapy is just a scam."

"For what goes on here, I don't want to keep asking my boss for the favor of leaving work early, then taking a long, hot, crowded trip on a bus, then getting home late, hungry and tense from all the things we talk about. I could just as well meet two or three guys from here at that café on the corner, Café Aroma, have a cup of espresso and a nice piece of chocolate pie with whipped cream, talk about whatever we want and have a better time. It'll be so much easier, and we wouldn't need a leader to do it." Tough words come from Uri's mouth.

The revolt is in full swing now. One after another, the guys express objections, voice doubts about the efficacy of the treatment, hint about negative personality traits of the group leader while avoiding being too specific, and enumerate various issues they feel Zev didn't handle well. If anyone had been listening from the outside, he would have thought that this was a group of unruly, discontented people, full of complaints and lacking any direction.

"So, really, next week why don't we just meet at some café and forget about coming here," Yossi concludes defiantly.

But no one reacts to his provocative suggestion to abandon the group. It seems they have some hesitation about leaving Zev and the place they've become accustomed to over the past weeks, where they have faithfully shown up (with a single exception) in the face of rain, competing demands and pressures, and fears about what will arise during the sessions.

"I've been feeling like that for some time, but I always pushed it away. I thought I was the only one who was feeling kind of disappointed and frustrated. But now, hearing that I'm not the only one, this is actually calming for me. And now that it's come up, I'm also thinking that some things did happen here that are positive. To meet in some café…I don't really think that's the solution," offers Ron.

"Positive things? What positive things?" challenges Yossi, clearly positioning himself as the revolt's leader.

"Look," Ron responds, "when we first met, nearly all of us were suspicious of each other and only a few were able to talk about our most painful issues. We did speak about some of our problems, like how some of us weren't able to pick up the phone – which was frustrating – but not really our most painful problems, and it was only after we became a real cohesive group, and developed more trust, that the real demons started coming out of the closets. That's when we started talking about night terrors, about weeping, about feeling ashamed and guilty, about complete lack of sexual desire even when a wife or girlfriend was inviting us, and other really tough problems. And the sky didn't fall, and Zev did guide us, sometimes quietly but sometimes more obviously, and he helped us to keep grappling with a painful subject, and he didn't allow us to gang up on any member whose point of view we disagreed with. And sometimes he was silent, but I think he was mostly doing that to allow us to find our way, which we did. And there were also all those coping methods he taught us, which we used, which helped some of us overcome some very real problems. What would it have been like without a leader? I also enjoy cafés, and espresso, and a piece of chocolate cake topped with whipped cream, but, really – that isn't the idea, after all, is it?"

The expressions on the guys' faces suggest that they understand him and agree. Everyone is struggling and frustrated that the healing process was so lengthy, slow, exhausting, at times disappointing, but all are inwardly aware that there have been undeniable improvements, some small, others more significant. And all inwardly acknowledge that without the group sessions, everyone would probably be in exactly the same place he had been before joining – perhaps even a worse place, with a divorce or broken relationship, total social isolation, maybe even an attempt at suicide. Some had been suffering for years from their demons, and for some, the awful event they lived through was still fresh in their mind. Sitting at home and keeping quiet couldn't solve any of these problems.

And something else had happened, quite unexpectedly: a sense of camaraderie had developed among strangers. A group of men who had felt isolated in their suffering had coalesced and become comrades in battle. This battlefield boasted no firearms, no shrieking mortar shells hurtling in their direction. These fighters sit in simple wooden chairs, in civilian clothes, in a room with a coffeemaker and some cookies and a soft-spoken guide.

And although there is no dangerous enemy lurking behind olive trees, an enemy is very much present in the room, powerful and terrifying. It is an enemy that can rob even these fierce fighters of sleep, make them shed bitter tears, and force them to battle with feelings so heavy that at times they wished they could flee, maybe even die. But nobody had fled. They've stayed to help themselves and each other. Even those who often don't allow another to finish sentences, who always "know best," who brag about their accomplishments and sometimes even engage in aggressive confrontations – all of them have, more often than not, listened patiently to each other in rapt silence. They would hand a tissue to someone whose tears were uncontrollable, and they made sincere efforts to help each other solve problems. They offered ideas and shared thoughts that others found to be helpful. They cared about each other.

"Do you remember that time when Gil didn't show up and we didn't know what had happened to him, and we were all so anxious it made us crazy?" Ron continued. "And how we tried so hard to contact him and even offered to go look for him? Just a few weeks earlier we didn't even know that he existed."

Gil reluctantly acknowledges their concern with a slight nod.

Zev leaned towards them a little. "So, next week then, at Café Aroma?"

Smiles slowly appeared. The revolt had ended. It seemed clear that the group had needed to pass through this phase, to air internal tensions, express complaints, and finally conclude that with all the frustrations, there was something dear and precious here that no one wanted to lose.

GIL

When he was four years old, Gil already loved to draw. He would search for pieces of paper and make simple yet recognizable sketches. He drew houses, flowers, and trees, like most children his age, yet it seemed to his parents that he derived special pleasure from doing so. His mother bought him a sketchpad and a box of colored pencils, and he drew every day. Gil's sensitivity to beauty, and his interest in a pursuit as aesthetic as drawing, stood in sharp contrast to other aspects of his personality.

Gil's hair was black and curly, his eyes dark brown and piercing. His body was of average proportions, but almost always tense and in motion. He gave off an air of nervousness – penetrating glances, quick, jerky movements, constantly shifting from one leg to the other. It was difficult to be in his company and not be affected by his agitation. His speech was awkward, too. Aside from the use of street language, laced with juicy curses that he blurted out at inappropriate times, his sentence structure was unusual. It was possible to understand what he said, but his speech caused raised eyebrows, especially among those who didn't know him. Those who did know him grew accustomed to his style and didn't even have to look up to know who was talking.

Gil's mother was the daughter of immigrants from one of the Eastern Bloc countries. She had arrived in Israel with a group of children and lived on a kibbutz for the first several years. She then moved in with relatives in one of the new immigrant towns. She completed high school, and after serving in the army, registered in a secretarial school where she learned to operate a computer. She then took a job in an import-export company. At age 24, she met Yoram, a *Sabra* (Israeli-born) from Afula. Following a courtship of several months, they married.

Yoram was an auto mechanic – a "tough guy." He spoke loudly in an unsophisticated manner and had a short fuse. He played around with the idea of being "observant" and wore a *kippa*, but the truly religious did not take him seriously. From time to time, he would appear at synagogue on Friday nights, but he couldn't be counted upon to come for prayers, to make the *minyan* – the ten men required for prayer – and when he did appear at synagogue, he acted as if it was his. He spoke loudly to others during services and angered the regulars.

Yoram served as an auto mechanic in the Ammunitions Corps. Although he was an unpleasant guy, he was an excellent mechanic and everyone knew that when there was a problem with a vehicle, Yoram was the man to see. He managed to repair just about anything, accompanied by grumbling, protests, and procrastination that left the person who asked for the repair feeling guilty for bothering him.

Some aspects of his father's personality stuck to Gil: the piercing look, the unusual manner of speech, the tension radiating from him, were all reminiscent of Yoram. The relationship between father and son was warm, but looking at it from the outside, one wouldn't guess so. The two rarely spoke to one another, yet they spent hours together. Yoram always kept some old, disassembled jalopy in his yard which he rebuilt and restored to life. Gil observed his father working and, as he got older, he started to participate: initially just handing his father a hammer, pliers, wrench; eventually taking part in the repairs. By 15, after years of tutelage, he knew more about cars than most junior mechanics.

School was not a happy experience for Gil. He lacked the patience to sit quietly during lessons. He had concentration and attention problems. His handwriting was essentially unreadable, one scribbled letter colliding with the next, ink from his ballpoint pen smudging the words. At times his homework looked as if he had wrapped a sandwich in it, its curled corners and creased paper stained with grease.

Repeated attempts by his teachers to correct this situation during his first years of school were unsuccessful, and Gil was promoted from one class to the next while still having the same problems. His teachers were aware that he was not stupid, and despite his memory problems, his grades were decent. There was never sufficient reason not to promote him.

Through all those years, despite his terrible handwriting and his rough-edged personality, Gil continued to draw. His technique consistently improved, and he drew particular subjects hundreds of times until he had developed his own style. And just as one could immediately identify him by his voice, it became possible to identify him by his drawings.

At age 12, he filled an entire sketchpad from front to back with drawings of strange animals, monsters, vehicles, mechanical contraptions, and wilderness scenes. Until then he had preferred to draw in black and white, only occasionally adding some color. Now this changed. Gil started introducing a hot red color into his drawings that added a measure of violence. Red sparks appeared in the faces of his mythological creatures, as if they were exploding. He began adding words in frames, such as: *"Zbang! Bang! Fuck him!"* It wasn't hard to discern that inner tension was being expressed in his drawings, but Gil no longer shared his drawings with his parents. On the one hand, he was afraid they wouldn't like them; on the other, he realized that his strange drawings could upset the viewer, especially his mother. He only shared his drawings with one classmate, Yossef, and he swore him to secrecy. Yossef was an introverted boy who liked Gil, and there was a quiet understanding between them, like the one between Gil and his father, expressed not in words, but by spending time together.

One day, Gil accidentally left his sketchpad in his classroom, and the custodian who found it placed it on the teacher's desk. The next day she saw it and innocently opened it. She was shocked by the content of the drawings, and by the anger and violence they expressed. Shaken, she called the school psychologist and requested a meeting. The psychologist took one glance at the drawings and speculated that here was a disturbed child with the potential for dangerous aggression. She decided to arrange a meeting that included herself, the classroom teacher, a social worker, and the principal.

At the meeting, the principal opened the discussion, observing, "These are the kinds of drawings that after some terrible event, everyone would look at them and say, 'it was obvious that the boy was disturbed, so why didn't he receive help?' I'm referring to incidents where a student suddenly goes wild and attacks classmates and staff, as has happened in several different countries – in France, the USA, England. Students and teachers have been murdered and only then it turns out that someone knew or suspected, but nobody intervened. We must not allow such a situation to develop."

"What would you suggest?" inquired Gil's teacher, frightened. Scenes passed through her head of instances when she had corrected Gil or admonished him for certain behaviors, and she immediately identified herself as a primary target for his wrath.

"Anna, what do you think?" asked the principal, turning to the psychologist.

"We have to invite the parents in, tell them what we've seen and gently explain our concerns, then advise them that Gil needs psychological help. I can give him some help myself, but if he requires more, we'll give them the names of clinics where he can receive treatment."

The classroom teacher asked, "Should we show them Gil's drawings?"

"No. That would be an invasion of his privacy. The drawings are his personal property, and he has not given us permission to show them to anybody else," the psychologist replied.

"What if the parents demand to see them? It's obvious they will want to. If I were summoned to my son's school with a story like this, I would immediately insist on seeing the drawings, and then I would decide for myself." This came from the social worker, who'd had a lot of experience with therapeutic interventions with families and all the difficulties stemming from them. "Parents instinctively protect their kids; they view any organizational structure with suspicion, even the educational system, and they don't like others meddling in their private lives, especially if it causes shame or fear."

"First we need to talk with Gil. It's possible that he hasn't even realized yet that he left the drawings at school. He might be searching for them like crazy, his anxiety and anger rising. We have to talk to him right away, tell him that his sketchpad has been found, and ask him gently if these drawings have any significance," continued Anna.

"He'll explode with rage. I know him," pronounced the teacher, her anxiety breaking through.

"Possibly, but he will also experience relief that they aren't lost. It can be assumed that these drawings are dear to him. It is also possible that he has quietly been *hoping* that someone would notice his feelings, that he might welcome assistance – even if he doesn't admit it – with his unhappiness," added Anna.

"Anna, meet with Gil, do as you said, then come back to us and we'll determine what we should do next," concluded the principal.

When Gil arrived at school in the morning, he was even more tense than usual and didn't speak. The teacher hadn't slept all night. She was fearful of meeting with him, but gathered her strength and took him aside.

"Gil, I think you might have lost something the other day that is important to you, and you'll be happy to hear that it's been found. I have your sketchpad," she added quickly, having endlessly rehearsed in her mind how to say that in the most appropriate manner.

"Where is it? It's mine, I want it!"

She handed him the pad and immediately asked, "These drawings have meaning, don't they? You are expressing something. I don't understand them, but they seem to show some anger, is that right?"

To her surprise he didn't respond, just tilted his head slightly.

"Come, let's talk about it with Anna, you know her." And she immediately started walking toward Anna's office. Gil held the pad in his hands and walked quietly behind her, dragging his feet.

Anna spoke with him behind closed doors. Gil insisted that these were just ordinary drawings, that they had no particular meaning, and that he just loved to draw. He refused to allow his parents to see them. Anna mustered all her clinical skills to convince him that showing them would in fact be a good idea, hinting that children who create drawings like these might possibly be sending a message to adults that something is bothering them. "And just in case there *is* something that is bothering you, it's worthwhile to talk about it." When Gil did not answer, Anna took it to mean that he was agreeing.

Anna reported the results of her meeting to the principal, Gil's teacher, and the social worker. After a brief meeting, they decided to invite Gil's parents to come in, to explain to them why they were being asked, and then to explore what might be going on within the family. The situation was delicate, as Gil's father's reputation as a "hothead" and an impatient fellow was well known, and they suspected he had little insight into his son's soul. They anticipated that he would react with anger and possibly humiliation, perhaps feeling that his son (or his family) was being "ganged up" on. Despite these concerns, the phone invitation went smoothly and the parents came in the next day.

"Vat's de prublem wit' my son?" asked Yoram.

"We aren't sure there *is* a problem. But it is our responsibility to bring to your attention that we are a bit concerned by his drawings. You know that he draws beautifully, and often we enjoyed his drawings and praised them and hung them in the classroom. This time, though, they seem to have a different character, and we're seeking your help to see if, by any chance, you might be aware that there is something that bothers him," explained Anna.

"Vat could be bothering him? The home isn't good? No food? Ve don' love 'im? Vat?!" replied Yoram in a whining tone, his voice rising.

"That's just it. We don't know what's troubling him, but his drawings hint that he is struggling with something he's not talking about. We asked his permission to show them to you – he didn't want to do it himself." With that, she handed the sketchpad to the couple, opening it to a neutral drawing of a landscape.

"A pretty picture, and there is nothing worrisome in it, but look at this one, for example." She turned the pages to one she had earmarked earlier. "This angry one with fire spewing from a monster's mouth and these words in the frame. It's a little different, don't you agree?"

The parents nodded and Yoram's irritation subsided.

"Look here, I'm no psychologist, you guys know better than me vat needs to be done. Should ve be vorried?" he asked as his wife sat quietly, tears gathering in the corners of her eyes.

"I'll meet with Gil a few times and I will try to clarify what's happening with him. And I'd like to ask that – at home – you don't reprimand or punish him for this, because he hasn't done anything wrong, and we definitely don't want to frighten him. Okay?"

Yoram and his wife both agreed to this, although it was clear that it was Yoram who called the shots.

The meetings between Anna and Gil were positive. He opened his soul and tearfully explained that sometimes kids mocked him about his manner of speech, and that this embarrassed and angered him. After a few sessions, he hinted that his father was not an easy guy, and although he loved his father and was proud of how well he could repair all sorts of things, he was also a bit fearful of him but afraid to reveal this to him or to his mother.

Anna was fond of Gil and felt a closeness develop between them. She was empathetic to his troubles, like his awkward speech, and decided to continue the counseling. She worried that if she suggested sending him to a clinic, his parents would terminate the treatment too soon – possibly not even begin it – and that even if they did follow through, there was no way to predict who would be treating him. The mere fact that the counseling took place within the school, that he could always approach her when something was bothering him, offered a measure of reassurance that nothing truly aggressive would happen there. She taught him anger-management techniques, ways to avoid unpleasant confrontations, and how to speak more softly, and she continued to encourage his artistic pursuits. New colors entered his drawings, and fire no longer spewed out of raging monsters' mouths. He learned to express his feelings in a more sophisticated manner. At times his mother would contact Anna to find out how things are going. Anna did not go into details, but asked what his mother had noticed at home. The answers were usually encouraging. There too, Gil was quieter, less disrespectful, and he even smiled. The inner tension persisted, but Gil now had tools to cope with it.

Gil and Yossef continued to meet after school. Gil liked going to Yossef's home, where he felt that the atmosphere was more serene. Yossef's father was at work, his younger brother and sister played with their friends, and his mother, a calm woman, was happy to see that her son had a close friend. She left juice and cookies on the kitchen table.

Yossef and Gil built things out of wood, Gil leading, as he was the expert on using tools. Among other things, they constructed a wooden scooter, managing to find some wheels for it. They would study for tests together, this time with Yossef being the leader. His technical skills were minimal but he was a good student and helped Gil to understand confusing material. They rehearsed historical events until Yossef was convinced that Gil knew enough to pass. Were it not for Yossef's help, Gil might very well have become a dropout.

When middle school ended, Gil transferred to a trade school. Academics were of no interest to him, and everyone agreed his technical knowledge and skills, and his interest in this area, were perfect for tech school. He loved roaming through the workshops, smelling the engine oil and peering into the bowels of disassembled motors. He was able to pass his theory classes somehow, but was always waiting for the moment the bell rang, indicating the beginning of periods spent among machines. His teachers liked him, and he was the kind of student men enjoyed talking with: robust, masculine, and possessing the ability to understand the soul of a machine or a roaring engine. If it were permissible, they would probably have gone out for beers together.

Toward the end of the school year, recruiters from different companies appeared at school, seeking well-trained workers. Among them was a rep from Caterpillar, a company producing diesel-powered bulldozers. The rep interviewed Gil and noticed the teacher winking at him, hinting that Gil was a good candidate. Gil was hired and worked there for six months, between graduating from school and joining the army. The plan was that he would return to Caterpillar at the conclusion of his army service, having learned to operate machines like the giant D-9 armored bulldozer. Gil's boss assigned him to the engine department. The knowledge he had absorbed from his father since childhood, together with his training at the Ort technical school, gave him a special standing. He was considered an "expert" and enjoyed his unique position.

* * *

Ilana was 14 when she met Gil, and he fascinated her. He was different from other boys. It might have been his quietness, his strange way of talking, or some other personality trait that was difficult to identify, but she felt drawn to him. Although she was shy, one day she gave him a long, intense look that captured his attention. Her frank expression and obvious interest in him was a new experience for him, and created a physical sensation that a 14-year-old boy could not ignore. He was struck by the intensity of emotion that overcame him.

Gil was inexperienced and uncertain about how to react. He also feared rejection. Finally, after a few agonizing days of emotional confusion and hesitancy, he managed to approach her. He invited her to join him in a trip downtown for some ice cream. She quickly said yes.

Gradually, a friendship developed between them and they began spending more and more time together. One evening as they were saying goodbye, Gil hesitantly bent down to kiss her cheek. Ilana turned her head toward his, pulled him toward her forcefully, and kissed him on the lips with surprising desire. They stood there holding each other for several long minutes without words.

After six months at Caterpillar, Gil enlisted. Despite his apprehensions about the unknown, he adjusted quickly. But his prickly personality, strange manner of speech and unusual personality traits caught the attention of his comrades and instructors. Initially they did not react, but in one of the martial arts lineups, someone laughed just after Gil identified himself. Gil became furious, leapt from his spot, and pummeled the private in the face with his fists. The soldier fell to the ground, dumbfounded and perplexed, and the others formed a ring around them to see what would happen next. Gil was not actually interested in a fistfight. He had always disliked confrontations, particularly physical ones. He was court-martialed, and accepted his punishment with quiet chagrin. Yet he believed that the private had deliberately provoked and embarrassed him, and he really couldn't understand why he, Gil, should be the one who was punished.

Upon completion of his days in detention, he returned to his platoon and to training. The incident that landed him in the brig sent a message to others not to provoke him and after that, there were no further incidents. To the contrary, his response had aroused admiration among his comrades and the story made waves in the platoon and the battalion. At the end of basic training, he was assigned to the Army Corps of Engineers, and in one of those rare instances in the IDF when someone with special skills is actually assigned to an appropriate task, he was sent to a course for D-9 operators in the framework of a Field Engineering Unit. It soon became clear that Gil knew more than the instructor, both about driving and repairing. He knew the hydraulic system, the nerve center of the machine, backwards and forwards, and was able to discern aberrant engine sounds even before the warning light began to flicker. He could operate the machine deftly on slopes and on slippery rocks. In one of his training sessions, the instructor was driving and the machine almost flipped over. Gil responded with lightening speed, dropped the shovel, and stabilized the machine, preventing a disaster. From then on, he no longer received instruction: he was promoted to the level of corporal and became an instructor himself.

In the evenings he'd call Ilana on his cellphone. "Sweetie, what's up?"

"I miss you. When are you coming for furlough?" she'd answer.

"In a week, for two days, we'll have a ball."

"I'm sending you a kiss, and don't fool around with the girls, Gil!"

"I promise," and he snapped the phone shut.

He dreamt about the end of service, his return to Caterpillar, a giant wedding with Ilana. People from both sides of the family would attend, friends from both sides, work friends, everyone they had ever met. His overwrought imagination sailed even further – he'd resign from the company and become an independent operator. He'd develop a countrywide reputation as "The Expert" for heavy earth-moving equipment, and desperate owners would stand on line with their broken machines, pleading for his services.

Gil was deployed to the Gaza Strip at the end of his third course as an instructor. Operations against Kassam rocket launchers brought him to the other side of the fence that surrounds "the Strip." The bulldozer's wide tracks dug deeply into the soft sand and Gil propelled the machine forward with no hesitation. Houses and orchards that hid militants became targets for the D-9's large shovel. With a shrieking engine he'd storm ahead and topple them, but did not always feel good about his actions.

"It took thirty years for this olive tree to reach this height, and I'm decimating it in 30 seconds." Thoughts of that sort battled inside his head with competing ones: "This majestic tree that produces thousands of olives also hides cells of murderers who launch deadly Kassam rockets toward the town of Sderot…let it fall! It will be much more difficult for them to launch rockets from an open area. The children of Sderot have the right to go to school without hearing constant sirens and warnings of 'Red Dawn, Red Dawn!' that send them into bomb shelters within 30 seconds."

Gil had an even harder time destroying homes. He'd complete the "leveling" of a house, see the smashed furniture peeking out of the rubble, a demolished dining room table, half a sofa pointing skyward as if in protest, and he would turn his head away. He didn't wish to see any more than he had to, and tried to concentrate on his task. Gil knew who was hiding in those houses, and had heard from his friends how a floor covered by a rug in the bedroom hid the entrance to a tunnel that led into Sinai. He knew what passed through these tunnels: cigarettes, drugs, people, and worst of all, dismantled rockets made in Iran. Rockets that were too large to be smuggled assembled were dismantled and delivered in pieces, only to be reassembled again in Gaza. Gil knew they had the capacity to reach Ashkelon, and eventually Tel Aviv. Kiriyat Gat was already within their reach. Thoughts of this kind accelerated his engine's roar, and with it its speed, assuring that not one stone would remain of a house that was suspected of hiding rocket launchers or the opening of a tunnel. When thoughts about the family whose house he had just demolished came into his head, he'd turn away, gazing at the horizon, far away from the heap of rubble he had just created.

Operating the D-9 was dangerous. Gil sat in the armored cabin, three meters high off the ground, the plastic windows protecting him from small-arms fire directed toward him. At times, a militant would sneak up to the bulldozer and throw a Molotov cocktail at it or shoot at it. At such moments he experienced the fear of death, would crouch deep down in his cabin and wish to escape, but he continued. The sound of striking bullets shook him. Fortunately, no bullet managed to pierce the plexiglas windows; they glanced off to the side, causing no harm. Even the incendiary devices did not stop him, but the clanking of metal on metal shook him and alarmed him.

Ilana enlisted just a few months after Gil. At the end of her basic training she was deployed to a unit stationed far north, a great distance from the Strip. It became more difficult to arrange the casual meetings she and Gil used to have during his brief furloughs, and the phone calls increased in number.

"Gili," she'd start, "when will I see you? I miss you; I can't go on without you."

"Don't know what to tell you. I can't leave here, its 'hot' here...there is a lot to do," he'd reply.

One morning Gil's platoon departed at two a.m. in total darkness, headlights off and moving slowly to keep engine hum and the squeaking of the tracks to a minimum. The platoon commander led them, equipped with night vision goggles, and they followed at a distance. The destination wasn't far, less than one kilometer, inside the Strip in the vicinity of Beit Hanun.

The mission was to destroy houses that gave shelter to units of militants, and to attempt to do it without attracting attention. The column drove slowly and cautiously. Gil was in charge of three bulldozers, his heart was pounding, and his eyes strained to see in the dark. Suddenly, a sharp explosion was heard and his machine shook and veered sideways. Gil attempted to straighten it out, but couldn't. When he pulled the steering lever its reaction was different than usual: it moved too easily, with no resistance. Gil immediately understood what had happened: a track had been ripped apart! Now he and his machine were sitting ducks, vulnerable to attack, unable to maneuver, to escape, to reach a safe hideout behind sand dunes. The smell of gunpowder rose in his nose and his fellow soldier in the cabin panicked and started screaming: "Evacuate! Let's get out of here, we must *evacuate!*"

Thick smoke poured into the cabin, and the little that was visible a minute ago, was no longer visible. Gil felt a dull pain in his knee and when he reached for it, he felt a warm, sticky flow on his pants. Gil kept his cool, got on the radio, and announced "Commander one, commander one, we have a problem."

The platoon commander had already grasped what had happened from the explosion and the veering of the bulldozer, and had contacted the evacuation unit that wasn't far away. The unit arrived within minutes, and despite the darkness, attached steel chains to the bulldozer and dragged it back across the fence. Amazingly, they were not attacked and the incident passed without casualties. But the event etched itself in Gil's memory.

News of the incident found its way to all ranks of the army throughout the country: that a bulldozer had triggered a roadside bomb, damaging its track, and had needed to be evacuated.

Ilana called him in panic. "Gili! Gili! Are you okay? Did something happen to you? I heard that something happened and I got so scared, are you ok?"

"Nothing, nothing happened," he said soothingly, "we just tore a track and we're back now, nothing to worry about." Yet inside his head a different scenario kept flashing: *What if we'd been unable to evacuate? If I had choked on the smoke? What if we had been sneaked up on and kidnapped?* The thoughts that filled his head terrified him. The realization that his injury could have rendered him disabled, that he might easily have lost his bright future with Ilana, preyed on him relentlessly. Reality suddenly seemed to have hit him in the face.

Gil was taken to a hospital, where a piece of shrapnel was removed from his knee. He was bandaged and released. He returned to his room, pulled out his sketchpad and box of graphite pencils, and drew a picture in black.

NINTH SESSION

Zev opens the session by announcing that he has received an email from Gil. It arrived two days before the meeting, but from the date on it, it was obvious Gil had written it immediately after the last session. And clearly, he had sent the email instead of being here in person. There was silence in the room as everyone waited with great anticipation to hear what it said.

"Dear friends and Zev:

I'm writing now after I have thought about the issue a lot, hesitated and postponed. I started to write several times but I never finished, so I didn't send it.

As you know, I didn't come to one of the sessions because I felt I wasn't getting anything out of this group. And you made an effort to contact me, and you even tried to find out where I live. Zev contacted me and convinced me to come back. Your concern and caring really made an impression on me that I should continue, and that perhaps I am a little too impatient.

But, it's like this: I don't feel right. I still have the same nightmares and I still don't contact my friends. I noticed that for some of you things are going quite well, but not for me. I just don't fit in, in this group. And maybe I'm a lost cause.

I know, Zev, that you've tried in all kinds of ways to help but it hasn't helped. I'm sort of in the same place I was before, and it's hard for me to listen every week how this one is progressing in that issue and another with something else, and I'm stuck.

So, it's time I cut out this nonsense.

I felt badly that if I were to leave the group it's like being a traitor, or something, so I didn't leave earlier, but now I really don't care anymore about what you might think.

All the best to all of you. Be healthy, things should be good for you and you should return to normal lives. And thanks for all the help you gave me when I was down, and to you, Zev, for trying.

Gil."

"Wow! He's really down," reacted Yossi.

"What do we do? Just accept that he is pulling out of the group? If we accept that, it's like we're agreeing with him that he's a lost cause, and that's not right," says Ron.

From the faces of the others, it appears as though some don't care, or may be concerned but aren't eager to wrestle with the problem.

"Does anyone else have a reaction?" asks Zev.

"Yes," Yariv says promptly. "I've felt for some time that Gil doesn't belong in this group. He kept himself apart, contributed little, and gave me the feeling that he didn't really want to be here, sort of from the very beginning."

"I don't agree that if we accept his desire to leave, then we're agreeing that he is a loser," Ido put in. "He's an adult, and if the group isn't good for him, he has the right to look out for himself and stop coming."

"And what if he feels that we were neglecting him, or really weren't concerned about his welfare?" Ron argues.

"What are you talking about? He says himself in his good-bye note that we cared about him, and looked out for him, and that Zev contacted him and brought him back to the group. How many times do we have to pursue someone who doesn't want to be here?" Yossi adds adamantly.

"Sounds to me that the group was a burden for him, as he saw it, that it was good for everyone else but not for him, and that he was suffering," Ido adds.

"Sounds a bit whiny, doesn't it?" adds Avi.

"Do you really believe that Gil didn't derive any benefit from his participation here? That not one of his problems improved, even a little? Don't you remember him saying that travelling

215

south, toward the Gaza Strip, was no longer a problem? So what does he want – everything?"

"Why didn't he have the balls to come here and tell us himself? And why is he hiding behind an email, eh?"

"Well, maybe he was afraid that we'd all jump on him and try to convince him to stay, and he had actually made his point and wanted to avoid a confrontation."

Zev, sensing that the conversation was likely to slide into an increasingly disagreeable tone, decides to alter its course.

"I will, of course, call him again this evening and see if he has anything to say. I'm sorry that he has decided to leave, but at the same time, he explains his decision, and I respect that. Perhaps he is correct in feeling that this group isn't for him. That happens, but there are other groups, and there's also individual treatment, which fits some people better. I'll offer him that as well.

"Is there anyone who'd like to add anything? Anyone wish to contact him? Sometimes group members feel better after they've had the opportunity to say good bye to a fellow member, even if he has chosen to leave."

"Yep. I'm calling him tonight. I want to see what's up with him," Sergei announces, and falls silent, which signals that the matter is closed.

At least, formally.

Gil's claim that "things are going quite well" for everyone else, and his suggestion that he alone is suffering, has evoked a mixed bag of emotions. Some members simply dismissed it, as Avi did with his observation that Gil sounded "whiny." Some felt a sense of betrayal, as one might feel after having been stood up by a date. Some of the more sensitive members were feeling some guilt; perhaps more could have been done in the sessions to let Gil know that he was liked and his presence was welcomed. Others simply felt sad. Here was a friend who was suffering like everyone else, but feeling that he wasn't getting any better, was disappointed, and perhaps – even worse – depressed. At least one group member felt that Gil was not a sympathetic person from the very beginning, and that his behavior had probably been unpleasant his whole life, not just here. Surely, it wasn't the first time Gil was dodging a challenging task and didn't want to work hard, like everyone else was.

Zev, having had two days to digest the email, had decided to hold off on responding until he had gotten the group's reaction. Now he could feel that there is a sense of failure in the group, a sadness that the tightly-knit group hadn't completely held together. He noticed the men's reluctance to change the topic and deal with things that didn't pertain to Gil. Finally, though, everyone seemed to conclude that the subject had been exhausted for now, and after a few uneasy minutes of hesitation and nervous glances, Uri raises a new topic.

"As you know, Nava and Karnit met a week ago, and there has been another meeting in which Yariv's wife Anat and Avi's wife Nili also took part. The other wives and girlfriends were also invited, but not everyone could make it. It seems that the meeting was a success, and they exchanged thoughts and advice, and they agreed among themselves to keep things confidential."

"Did you get any clues about what they discussed?" asks Avi. "Something that might give us an idea about what we are not doing but should be, or about what things upset them?"

"Yeah, I did. I got the feeling that they all share one major complaint: that we don't involve them enough with what's happening in our heads. This isn't news, we all know it, but apparently we're still persisting in doing this, in keeping things to ourselves, in shutting them out a little. Perhaps, because this was their first chance to talk with each other, this came up as a big issue."

"After we spoke about it here, I actually did tell Nili things I hadn't told her before," Avi reveals. "You remember my failure in the ER, when I couldn't stay there with my little daughter, and had to get Nili to relieve me? When we all had returned home that night, and both kids were sleeping, Nili looked at me sadly. And she said, 'So, one day maybe you'll include me again? I want to help you with what's bothering you, and I didn't ask a single question when you called me. I just called my friend Zipora, and asked her to take care of Shlomo, and I flew to the ER to relieve you. But I'm living in this house with a kind of a shadow, someone who acts differently than before, and I'm unable to comprehend what's moving or stopping you. And you won't help me. Could you perhaps include me a bit more? I don't want to push you to remember those horrible incidents, but just give me a hint. Occasionally I can connect a remark you make with another and draw a conclusion. But the truth is, even then I don't know if my conclusion is based on fact, or my imagination.'

"She was so logical and sincere, and so gentle, that I gathered up my courage. I started to tell her many more details about what happened with Rami. I described how he looked when he was hurt, what I did to try to save him, and how I failed. I even told her something that I hadn't spoken about here, something I had forgotten that suddenly came to mind. She was silent the whole time, stroking my hand, nodding to show she was listening. She didn't interfere in the story, didn't ask for clarifications. I think she was practically holding her breath, afraid she'd stop the flow of my words if she were to ask anything. I assume there are probably a few things in her mind that aren't clear, and maybe one day she'll ask me about them, but when I was finally opening up to her, she just listened. At last, after so many months, she got the details about what had happened to me. She can understand a little why those events are affecting my daily behavior. And she should be told. After all, she wasn't there and she didn't experience what I experienced, but she bumps up against the consequences every day, without understanding the reasons."

Zev, who has been sitting quietly and just listening intently, now turns to Avi and asks, "What was it that you shared with Nili that you haven't told us?"

"I was born in a kibbutz and I spent my first years essentially in two locations: the children's house and school. I didn't see much of my parents, but since all the other children there were living in the same way, I had nothing to compare my situation with...except occasionally, when we went to Tel Aviv to visit my cousin, David. There I saw that his room was next to his parents', and that most of the time, except when he was at school or playing outside, the family was together. They slept in the same apartment, ate their meals together, and if something were bothering him, or he didn't understand something, his mother was always there to answer him. I slept there a few times and I felt envious that he was so physically close to his parents and that there was no caregiver looking after him instead of his mother.

"One day, when I was seven, I got terribly sick during a particularly bad winter. I had a high fever; I vomited; I was coughing uncontrollably; and I felt horrible. It wasn't life-threatening, just miserable. And the caregiver at the children's house was such a tough, no-nonsense woman, with such a cold, deep voice – she just gave me pills and warm drinks. What I wanted more than anything was my mother, but I couldn't let myself cry 'Ima, Ima,' I couldn't ask her to bring me my mommy, because it wasn't acceptable, you'd be looked at as a crybaby. So I swallowed it, and just cried quietly under the blanket. I lay there, shivering with fever and shaking, with a splitting headache, and felt like the loneliest kid in the world. I wanted to die, or exchange places with my cousin. I knew that if he'd been that sick, his mother would have been sitting at his bedside, stroking his head, putting a cool compress on his forehead, and saying soothing words.

"Instead, what I had was an iron bed, a stiff mattress, a scratchy wool blanket and a caregiver who acted like a drill sergeant, without a visible drop of empathy. According to her, there was no need to notify the mother or father of a sick child. Looking back, I'm convinced she abused her authority, and if it happened today, there might have been an inquiry, but in those days, nothing happened.

"When my mother finally found out what had taken place, she lodged a complaint, and my father too was furious, but obviously it was all over and done by then. After their complaints, it never happened again. But I have a miserable memory of that illness, and it still makes me sad to think about it."

"And you recently told Nili this sad story?" asked Zev.

"No. She had known this story in detail. We always tried particularly hard to be sensitive to the needs of our children. But I'm telling it to you now, because I only realized recently that it is the background for what happened to me in the service."

"Oh, I see. So what happened that is connected to your illness at the children's house?"

"We were in an operation in the territories. It was a wintry night, quite similar to the night in the children's house. I had a cold, my nose was stuffed, I probably even had a fever, the beginnings of flu or something like that. My joints ached, I was exhausted and the equipment was heavy and stunk from the wet. We were moving in a line and still had a good distance to go before reaching our destination. We spread out, keeping a distance from one another to minimize casualties, afraid that we might be discovered. This was after a disastrous commando operation we all knew about, in which 12 fighters had been lost, partly because they crossed an exposed road in a cluster instead of being spread out. The media had made a big thing out of it.

"I'm hauling myself along, boots sinking in the mud, and I'm so congested it's hard to breathe. Suddenly, I slip and fall into a ditch I didn't see. All of a sudden, there's a burst of fire. Huge noise, tracer bullets, dogs barking menacingly, and I'm lying in that ditch alone, unable to move. I fell on my shoulder, my rifle is stuck in the mud under my body and I can't get it out. I have a wicked headache, my temples are pounding, and I'm terrified. I'm calling to the guy in front of me who was supposed to keep eye contact, and he can't hear me or just doesn't answer. I'm alone in the muck, freezing, shivering from cold and fear, and I feel completely abandoned.

"And as I'm lying there, I suddenly get an image of myself in the children's house, lying under a stinking wool blanket, no mother, no father, only that damned caregiver. And I feel like screaming, 'Ima, Ima' but I don't; if someone were to hear me, they'd think I was a crybaby, like when I was seven years old."

"Sad and frightening, Avi. No wonder this story was buried deeply in your soul. How did it end?"

"The guys ahead of me managed to finish off the attackers; there had only been three of them, but they had serious firepower. Then someone noticed that I was missing. They started searching with flashlights and found me in the ditch, half-submerged in the mud, unable to get myself out. Avram, a very sweet guy, plucked me out, stood me up, wrapped me in a thermal blanket, and then carried me to the local medic station."

The guys looked at Avi with pity. Nearly everyone had a similar story, some less severe, some more, but without the background of neglect at an early age making it worse.

Zev added, "You had a tough experience that came on top of an even worse background. We never know exactly what causes one person to react in a particular way and another person in a different way, to the same event. Every one of us has fallen into the mud and experienced exhaustion, but for you this event carried an immense emotional load. The fact that you hadn't told us this story until now is also significant. You've spoken of some lesser issues in great length, but this story has special meaning for you. You're probably aware that there has been much criticism of the pedagogical methods used in the kibbutzim, and that children no longer sleep in the children's houses at night."

"Yes, I know. We had many discussions about this in the kibbutz. My mother to this day hasn't forgiven that idiot caregiver, who undoubtedly caused some emotional damage to me and to others. It's just unfortunate that it crossed with an event during the service. At our first session, I wasn't sure whether I wanted to stay or leave, but a powerful thought for me was, 'I'm never going to be left alone again,' so I said to myself that if there was an opportunity to receive emotional support, encouragement and camaraderie, I'm grabbing it. And I'm glad that's what I decided to do."

"How did Nili react to everything you told her?" asked Uri.

"She cried a little, and she hugged me tightly. She was quiet, but her actions said it all. I believe that the next time I show some irritability or sadness, she won't be taken so much by surprise. I see now that I really owed it to her to talk more about my experiences, no matter how hard it is, or how sad it is to relive them. I think we have to share our stories with our loved ones; they are putting up with a lot of shit because of everything that happened to us."

"Agreed," Zev responded with emphasis. "Everyone ought to share as much as he can and at the right time. Avi told these stories after his disappointment with himself at the ER, and after an explicit request from his wife. But you don't have to wait for a special event. If the atmosphere feels right, it's also possible to sit in a quiet room, a glass of wine in hand, and tell. Avi, what are your feelings now toward Nili?"

"We are closer than we've been in many months. I no longer carry around that heavy load of secrecy, and I feel she understands me. She's part of me, and part of my story. It's very different. It's better."

"And what about the kids?" questions Yossi.

"What about them?"

"Did you tell them about your experiences?"

"Not exactly. I don't think that kids should be burdened with frightening descriptions. It's enough to tell them that I have had difficult moments, but that I always thought of them and of Ima and about coming home, and that helped me to get through those moments. They know that I lost a close friend, they know his name was Rami, but they don't need to know that I tried to save him but failed. That's too much for them. Nili also tries to help them to understand why Aba is sometimes tense or sad."

"Have you told your parents about this event and its connection to the children's house?" Ron wonders.

"God forbid! Imagine what feelings that would awaken in them – especially my mother. I know that to this day she is angry with herself for accepting the doctrine of the children's house. In her heart she always knew it was faulty, and regretted going along with it. My father, who toed the party line even more than she did, never openly objected; I'm actually not sure what his feelings are about it."

"Anyway, sharing the story with Nili is a big step forward, I imagine. And from your words, it seems like a big burden has been lifted off your shoulders."

"Yes."

* * *

Many of the men were nodding sympathetically to Avi's story. But Yariv seemed tense, actually irritated. He sat stiffly in his chair, rocking slightly from side to side. The others noticed that something was brewing. Ron turned toward him, looked in his face and said: "So? What's up with you? Say it."

"We still haven't dealt enough with flashbacks. We've mentioned them, and you say it's been reported that their frequency has diminished, yet there's no good answer on what to do when they *do* occur. Avi just talked about having one, and yesterday, again, I had one. It was very unpleasant!"

Zev responds: "True, we dealt with flashbacks previously and I said that we'd revisit the issue. So, in the light of Avi's and your experiences, let's talk about it now. From your own experience, when does it happen?"

"Could be during a nightmare, when I find myself suddenly

waking up as if it's happening right then and there, as part of the dream, but it can also happen in the middle of the day and I never know why. I'm unable to connect it to anything in particular. I've experienced flashbacks in all kinds of situations: at home, in the street, sitting by myself or being in the company of others."

"And how long do they last?" inquires Zev.

"An eternity! The feelings are so intense that I want to scream and run away. I've never checked it with a stop watch. People tell me that it lasts only seconds. But, when I'm in the middle of the experience, the feeling is that it'll never end. It's so intense, the content, the vivid colors. And the noises - like explosions, or disgusting odors. It's impossible to describe how real it feels, so real and terrible. I always dread the next attack."

"Your description sounds accurate. I've heard such words from others as well," confirms Zev.

"What does one do?"

"First of all, it seems to be true that the frequency is subsiding over time, and that's a partial consolation.

"Secondly: the mere fact that there's a good chance that the experience will recur, allows one to prepare mentally for it, and that cushions to some extent the element of surprise and the startle reaction when the flashback does happen. In contrast to other health issues such as a sudden and unexpected pain, instead of being taken by surprise, being disappointed and angry, say to yourself something like this: 'Well, it's here again. It's very unpleasant, but I know what will happen, and in a short while it'll be over.' True, it's easy for me to say because I've not experienced what you've been going through, but try it.

"Third: instead of trying to avoid the experience, a natural reaction, here's another way: look the beast straight in the face! Experience the event, and then immediately switch the image with another one, a pleasant, soothing and calm one.

"Fourth: Remember the session when we discussed intrusive thoughts? A flashback is similar in a way, a continuation of the same theme, just much more intense, with a suddenness that causes a startle effect, and in extreme cases, even dissociation – a loss of a sense of reality. The visual image and the physical sensations are so intense that it is possible to truly believe that it is happening right now. But you can use the same methods for dealing with intrusive thoughts, and try to shorten the flashback.

"Fifth: Shake your body vigorously, similar to a dog shaking off water when coming out of a lake. The purposeful intense physical movement returns to you the sense of control that the flashback robs. The researcher Peter Levine, an expert in trauma treatment, talks a lot about the physical movements that many animals do after being attacked – a vigorous shaking. This shaking releases the tensions that had built up in those moments of intense danger. And therefore, he claims, animals do not have the same delayed post-traumatic reactions as people. When you are experiencing a flashback, apply this technique – shake the flashback experience off vigorously, and return yourself to the actual presence you're in.

"And sixth: Similar to the way to handle intrusive thoughts, have an alternate activity planned that you can immediately switch to."

A sigh of relief was heard. The frightening subject has been attacked head-on, with several ideas that sounded interesting and surely worth exploring. Zev was also able to strip some of the mystery off the nasty subject and simplify it.

"What happens if, after everything you've suggested, I'm still flooded with feelings of dread?" Yariv asks.

"There are people in the mental health field who advocate the use of medications, such as anti-depressants, which, as you remember, take a while before they work, and must be taken in a prescribed manner, daily, and usually for some length of time. Regarding anxiety, a useful method is to keep an anti-anxiety pill in your wallet, and if the anxiety persists, to take it as prescribed (such as 'As needed'). Most likely the anxiety will subside within 20-30 minutes. The mere thought that you're carrying a 'spare tire' in your wallet may be sufficient to calm you down without actually taking it."

"You've nailed it! I now have an arsenal that I can use to combat this scrooge, phew!" sighed Yariv in relief.

* * *

Ron, like the others, had listened intently to Avi's and Yariv's stories, but so far he hadn't talked much about a big source of personal stress: living so far away from the people he loved most. While the other men had wives or girlfriends, and families who lived a mere bus ride away, Ron's parents, his siblings, and his girlfriend Alice are all a 12-hour flight away, in Boston. Although he feels warmly toward his uncle and his uncle's family in Tel Aviv, they weren't close enough to discuss truly intimate issues. He would visit them occasionally, sleep over, and then return alone to his modest apartment. He had no one nearby with whom he could talk freely, even when he wished to.

He particularly missed his dear mother and his sister Ruthie. Both of them had supported and understood his decision to make *Aliyah*, moving to Israel, when his father had been so opposed. From time to time, Ron would call to speak with them. Conversations with his mother were affectionate and encouraging, laced with moments of laughter and loud, exaggerated kissing sounds. When he spoke with his sister, she was also loving and supportive of his activities, and glad that Ron had chosen to continue with higher-level studies. She was convinced he'd succeed. Ron's attempts to talk to his father, however, always ended up as a failure; despite all of his father's knowledge about Jewish history, he still couldn't accept his son's desire to live in Israel. After exchanging a few clumsy sentences, their conversations always ended with Ron feeling that his father's attitude was "I tried to warn you but you wouldn't listen."

The situation with his girlfriend Alice was more emotional and complex. She was still attending college and about to graduate in a few months, pondering what she would do after. She had taken liberal arts, which didn't prepare her for any specific occupation, but gave her a broad base. She was thinking of teaching, nursing and law, but hadn't settled on any. She missed Ron terribly and thought of him every day, often gazing at their picture on the dresser, both suntanned and in swimsuits, smiling happily. She called him at least once a week, and he called too. The emotional bond between them had continued to grow stronger despite the distance between them, and they realized that they could not continue to sustain it unless they could see each other.

"I have an announcement to make," he said, after some hesitation. "I haven't talked to the group very much about my girlfriend, Alice. Well, she's about to graduate from college and, in a few months she'll be coming here to live. I've found her an *Ulpan*, an adult Hebrew school, where she can learn more Hebrew – she knows some already – and after she's a little more fluent, she'll decide what to do about working. I'm counting the days until she gets here."

"Wow! That's big news, Ron. I don't think you'll have much time for studying. That ability to concentrate on your studies that you've been working so hard at will give way to concentrating on something completely different...." and the guys roared with laughter. "There will certainly be an improvement in your knowledge of anatomy...." More peels of laughter were heard. The solemnity of the session gave way to teasing and laughter. The laughter was needed; a cathartic reaction to Avi's tense and emotional story.

Yossi cleared his throat.

"We were in the Casbah in Ramalla. We patrolled and searched for armed gunmen. I was on guard duty one night. Being a sharpshooter, I had to lie there for long hours waiting quietly in case I had to shoot, and it started to get cold at night. My joints hurt, so I tried to stretch to move my legs, quietly. It was hard.

"Suddenly, we heard shots and a scream. We didn't know who was shooting or at whom, but since there was no radio communication about casualties, we concluded that the scream didn't come from one of us. We didn't know if someone was hit and escaped, or was hit and was evacuated, or perhaps just screamed and nothing happened to him.

"In the morning, I'm looking over my shoulder high up at the building behind me, and I see an armed man; head slumped but I can see his face, hands dangling, blood dripping from him. He was motionless. I looked through the binoculars for signs of life, but didn't discover any, so I concluded he was dead. And I guessed that it was he who screamed last night. It puzzled me that no one would have come to his aid, that no one made an attempt to evacuate a comrade. From what I saw, it appeared that he had bled to death, alone up there.

"Two days passed and no one came to retrieve the body. From time to time I'd glance at him, hoping that someone would have come to redeem this fighter from his makeshift grave, hanging there grotesquely from the building's crevices. The look on his face started to bother me. He was so alone; fought for an ideal he believed in, sacrificed his life and no one among all his friends or commanders made the minimal effort to redeem his body. If they had turned to us to request permission to retrieve him, they would have received an affirmative answer. The Israeli army respects life, even that of an enemy fighter.

"Two more days passed and the body started to emit the stench of death. His face looked crinkled, parts of his clothing starting to fall off. The sight was sad and horrifying. The stench reached its peak in the late afternoon hours and toward evening, with the sun baking the corpse.

"I began to feel pity for my enemy. Arab or no Arab, he was a human being. Perhaps he was a husband; he certainly was the son of his mother and father. Perhaps he had children and what about his grandmother and grandfather? I was grateful to whoever eliminated him, otherwise he would have been able to eliminate me, but the disregard and lack of respect for this fallen warrior haunted me. After all, he gave his life for them, so where are they? Are they going to wait until he disintegrates and falls off the building piece by piece and dogs devour him?

"During the next several guard duties, I had to wrap a cloth around my nose as the stench of the decaying body was unbearable. And the sight of the rotting corpse, of a fighter who fell and was not brought to burial, for which no attempt was made to rescue him from his slow and agonizing death, continues to haunt me at night."

"And how are you coping with it?"

"I'm not coping. I'm just suffering. I can't get that picture out of my head, it wakes me up at night, torments me, and believe it or not, I even feel...don't know how to say it...you'd think I've gone mad..." and he fell silent.

"Is it difficult for you to say what's on your mind? Say it, we will understand and won't judge," Zev encouraged him.

"I feel as if...it's going to sound crazy... sort of a feeling of... guilt."

"That's not crazy at all; it's very understandable and reasonable. Your religious background is in conflict with the disgracing of this unfortunate person, even though he's your enemy. By your belief, a person is created in the image of G—d, and the lack of humanity towards him simply doesn't reconcile with your own humanism."

"Exactly! You got it right. That's what I feel, but I never dared to talk about it because I feared that I'd be seen as a traitor or crazy, and therefore I always kept quiet. But it's been tormenting me for years and I don't know what to do about it."

"I have an idea that perhaps to you and to others might sound peculiar. People will say that 'Zev has lost it,' but here is my thought. You have to reach closure with this horror, and what's missing for you from the point of view of your morality and respect for humans, is kind of a burial ceremony, even though the deceased is your staunch enemy. Crazy, isn't it?"

"I have thought of it, but obviously never said a word. Aside from the fact that I don't have a body, years have passed, and I have no name, nothing."

"True, but it doesn't matter. The closure for you is moral, not physical. The 'burial' that you must conduct in order to achieve peace of mind is strictly symbolic. Perhaps all you have to do is say a short prayer or conduct a ceremony inside your heart. That's not so crazy. Here is something sort of similar. Does anyone remember that famous picture of two women hugging and crying on Ammunition Hill in Jerusalem after the Six Day War? Turns out that they were a Palestinian and an Israeli woman, two widows, who each lost her husband in the same battle, they were enemies. Yet, they are both hugging and consoling each other. If you were to conduct such a ceremony inside yourself and bring your desecrated enemy to his well-deserved rest, there is a good chance that you might reach peace and that the torturous image might fade. Try it."

"You have no idea what burden you took off me. I never dared talk about it, or even think about something like it, but now I can."

* * *

Zev watched the group, waited for a pause, raised his eyebrows and said: "For some time I have noticed that a certain subject has not come up in our discussions, an important subject that is embedded among the words but isn't given a name. But now with Yossi's story, this may be the time to discuss it."

Sergei cut him off: "What are you talking about? You are being so mysterious. Maybe you can include us in this riddle?"

"Okay. I didn't mean this to be a riddle or a mystery; I am referring to the subject of grief, Grief Work."

Uri joined: "Grief work? What is grief work?"

"The mental energy that we need to process mourning a person who was dear to us is tremendous," explained Zev. "Anyone who has experienced such an event knows how much energy it consumes, how feelings surge and how grief comes in waves – rising and ebbing, rising and ebbing. Grief is not a straight line; one may also laugh while grieving, wipe tears of sadness only to be replaced by tears of laughter when recalling the deceased, their jokes and pranks. It's a complex process that requires extended time, but at the end, if brought to conclusion, the mourner gets to the point where he or she can remember the loved one with affection, yearning and love, but not necessarily with crying. The process requires much work, and that is why in the professional literature we refer to it as 'Grief Work.'"

"The Swiss psychiatrist Elizabeth Kubler-Ross has researched the topic thoroughly and discovered that there's a fairly consistent process with a number of steps that nearly every mourner experiences. Not everyone in exactly the same sequence, but close. And there are people who will repeat a stage they had already passed, only to work through it again."

Ron, who was staring at the floor, added, "I've experienced something like that and the things you are mentioning sound familiar, very familiar."

Zev, softly: "Do you think you could share with us what your experience was?"

Ron, nodding his head, slides back in his chair, clears his throat slowly, blinking, starts: "When my grandfather died," his eyes turning reddish. "I came home from school, in first grade, I think, so I was probably six years old, and I see my mother in the kitchen, leaning against the table, and crying bitterly. I got very scared, ran over to her and asked, somewhere between asking and screaming; 'Mommy, mommy what happened, why are you crying?' She raised her head and started to say something but she was crying so hard that I could not understand her words.

'Mommy, mommy, tell me!' She regained her composure, again lifted her head, and slowly said: 'Grandpa....grandpa...grandpa is no longer with us.' I didn't understand what 'Grandfather is no longer with us' meant, I thought that he had traveled to a far place. 'So what? He'll come back,' I blurted out, still not understanding why Mother would be crying because Grandpa traveled to some distant location. 'No, Ronnie, no, you don't understand, he passed away' and her head sunk again.

"A wave of anxiety swept over me, I felt cold all over, I started to shake, and I was stunned. Grandpa died? How could that be? He was healthy as an ox. Just last Shabbat we played ball in the yard and he ran as fast as I. What does that mean 'passed away'? Impossible, there is a terrible mistake here. Mom certainly didn't mean what she said. Mistake! Nonsense! Come Shabbat, we'll have another ball game. 'Ima, why do you say such things? It isn't true, he didn't die, he's well and is coming on Shabbat to play with me.' My mother bent down and enveloped me in her arms. She hugged me with her body that shook from her sobbing. 'No, Ronnie, my sweetie, I am not telling tales, it's the truth. Grandpa will no longer come to play ball with you, he pass.....' and she was unable to finish the word. We were wrapped in each other's arms. I felt I had to console her just as she was consoling me, as Grandpa was her beloved daddy. 'What happened, mommy, what happened?' 'He had a heart attack in the street and dropped to the ground. Passersby tried to save him, but it was too late. They couldn't save him.' And then I started to cry.

"And I cried, and I cried, and I ran from the kitchen to my room and slammed the door with such a bang that I almost broke the glass panel on it. Only then did I start to understand a little, but I still rejected the thought. I cried, and I had my doubts. Perhaps Mother was wrong after all. There are many guys who look like him – chunky, with a belly, an endearing smile, thinning white hair – perhaps they made a mistake and it was someone else who looked just like him, and tonight they'll call and tell us that it was a mistake, and that after all it wasn't Yehuda but someone else. That poor family, of the other guy, but MY grandpa? No way. But suddenly I cried again. I retold myself the whole story but I didn't believe my own words. I just couldn't believe what Mom had said, it was just too terrible.

"After the funeral we returned home and started to sit "Shiva'a," and all kinds of guests came, and family, and friends from his work and from his circle of retirees. He had retired from his previous job but had taken a part-time job and developed a new group of friends. And people were sitting around, nibbling on snacks, some had even brought entrées, it felt like sort of a party in his memory that lasted for days. I would enter the room and see them all eating and drinking and even laughing, and that made me mad. My grandpa is dead and they are coming here to eat and drink and make merry and laugh – what the hell is this? Don't they understand that Grandpa will no longer come on Shabbat and play ball with me? Idiots! I was furious and walked out. From my room I would hear people asking; 'Where is Ronnie, we don't see him?' And Mom, in her quiet voice, would answer; 'He's angry, so we don't push him to be here with everyone. It's hard on the boy, he needs time to digest what happened; he and Yehuda were very close.'"

Ido joins: "And after you were angry, did it pass? How long did that anger last?"

"Several days, and then I was terribly sad. I didn't cry anymore but I had no appetite, and I didn't feel like going into the yard to play ball. And my friends, some came to see me but I had no interest in being with them, I had no patience and I talked not so nicely, even to Mom. I was fresh to her and to Dad, but they understood me and Mom gave me hugs and kisses."

Ido continues, "And then?"

"The Shiva'a concluded, Shabbat came and I understood that Grandpa Yehuda wouldn't be coming to play ball with me, that he would never come again, and I felt terribly sad, but I also accepted that there was no mistake, that he really had died. It wasn't somebody else, it really was my own grandpa, and after a few weeks I returned to normal life. I hung a picture of us playing ball – Mom gave it to me – in my room and I looked at it often and even laughed when I remembered the fun we had."

Ron settled back in his chair. He looked relaxed as if he had just completed a challenging task and was pleased with its outcome.

"Thank you, Ron, for allowing us to share in your sad experience from childhood. You described wonderfully what happened to you, your love for Grandpa Yehuda, and how you coped with your loss. You might not believe it, but you did indeed describe the stages of Grief Work, without even being aware of it," concluded Zev.

"Really? Could you explain that?" asked Yossi.

"Yeah, it's like this: at the beginning when Ima told Ronnie that his grandpa had passed away, he was in shock. He had the shivers, his body shook, remember?"

"Yeah, yeah."

"In the second stage he was convinced that there had been a mistake – that's the stage of denial, something like 'it's not possible.'

"And after that Ron fled the room and slammed the door so hard he almost broke it, and he was disrespectful to his parents. That was the stage of anger.

"There is still another stage – according to Kubler-Ross – which we did not talk about, and that's bargaining, and it goes something like this: let's say that someone gets very bad news about his health or the health of a loved one, and refuses to accept it. The bargaining expresses itself in words like: 'If you, God, or some other higher power, will spare me, or my loved one, I promise that I will make a contribution to the Association of Sick Children, or my temple, or I'll give up smoking,' or do something else that's hard to do, kind of a bargaining with God. In Ron's case there was no room for bargaining because his grandpa had already died and it was not possible to change that fact, but it's important to know that there are times when bargaining could take place."

"So, for example, if my friend had already been killed, then there is no room for bargaining, but if he was critically injured and was in mortal danger, then there would be, right?"

"Exactly."

"And there is the last stage: that of acceptance. Accepting the bitter facts and then returning to normal life. Life that, albeit, has sadness and yearning for the loved one who passed away, yet at the same time continues to function normally. Here, Ronnie hung a picture of his grandpa in his room, looked at it and even laughed, and as he said in his own words 'returned to normal.' He didn't forget his grandpa, but he didn't deny that he had died. He no longer talked freshly to his parents, didn't avoid being with others, the way he acted during the Shiva'a, and he returned to normal living."

"We will return to this subject again, now that we are aware what Grief Work is. Everyone here has surely had such experiences both in civilian and military life," and at that Zev announced that the meeting was over for today.

Yariv leaned forward, and whispering, added: "I imagine that from now on, when we discuss our events, we'll be paying attention to the stage we're in."

ZEV'S DEMONS

Zev entered the grocery store. He was hungry after a long and tense day's work. He'd just completed five individual sessions with clients, followed by his weekly group therapy session in the late afternoon. Although he'd run similar groups many times before, this one seemed to be especially taxing. He started to select some plums and apricots, when he was suddenly surprised by a tear that crept down his nose and dropped onto a plum. He ignored it and continued choosing his fruit. When the third tear plunged and splattered on some apples, he knew it was time to leave. Quickly wiping the salty liquid from the fruit, he left the store.

A wave of unbearable sadness swept over him. He didn't understand why. He continued on Herzl Street, crossed it, made a sharp turn into one of the side streets and then, convinced that no one could see him, he allowed himself to burst out crying.

Finally, he suppressed the sobs erupting from his throat, and mopped up the tears gushing from his eyes. He was grateful that he had walked; had he been driving, he wouldn't have been able to see the road.

"What's happening here?" he asked himself. *"After all, selecting plums isn't a sad task."* He was stymied, thrown completely off balance. His mind went to the day's sessions. He had felt satisfied with the progress that had taken place in the individual sessions and with the bonds that had formed among the group's members. He felt well physically, had no headache or aches and pains he

was aware of, and his life and his work generally seemed to be moving along well. Yet at this particular moment, he was definitely not functioning well.

When he reached his apartment, he immediately lay down on his bed fully clothed and pulled the covers over himself from head to toe, barely taking time to slip off his shoes. Not having eaten dinner made no difference to him; he had lost his appetite. He was just sad. Terribly sad.

He fell asleep and slept for 11 hours.

* * *

By this time, he was six weeks into treating his group of post-trauma patients. In addition, every day he met with several individuals for an hour or more. He continually swallowed the horror stories that rained down on him, keeping his cool, displaying the empathy he felt for his patients. He knew that it was very painful for soldiers to talk about the horrifying events they had witnessed. Just getting themselves to the clinic was a major accomplishment. While the initial part of the first session was usually easy – Zev gathering such straightforward information as serial numbers, addresses, telephone numbers, and the answer to "who referred you" – the moment it reached "The Story," tension rose on both sides.

New patients always had doubts. "Will he really understand what happened to me? He wasn't there. No one could possibly comprehend what took place if he wasn't there. One has to feel it on his skin. What does he know? Why should I trust this stranger? What if he doesn't believe me? Mocks me? Will think I am a coward, someone who is weak? That I blew it, that I couldn't rise to the occasion?" A thousand unspoken questions, fears, and hesitations always preceded the opening sentences of "The Story." Patients often admitted, after telling Zev what had brought them to the clinic, that they had never before told anyone about the traumatic events they lived through, not even their wives or girlfriends. Occasionally, some of the younger soldiers had shared a horrific event with their mother, but they often found themselves more reluctant to discuss it with their father. And if they were older reservists, they had often just kept it inside.

In that first session, there were those who sat for long minutes without uttering a sound. Zev would sit quietly, allowing them the space and quiet they needed to feel secure and trusting enough with a stranger – that unfamiliar listener – to start pouring out their painful stories. It was vital that he not inadvertently say or do anything that might suggest he was untrustworthy, that he could not be relied on completely, or that he was unsympathetic. He was always nervous about what he was about to hear, wondering whether he would be able to handle it without displaying undue emotion, without crying. Frequently – almost always – the story was revealed in a stream of details that were out of sequence, confused, sometimes illogical, and Zev had to focus hard to make sense of it. He was excruciatingly careful not to interrupt the flow of the story until there was a natural pause by the patient. He felt a sense of deep respect, almost of holiness. Something was happening here that had to be honored and revered down to its tiniest detail.

"This man is entrusting you with the story of what happened during the most terrible moments of his life," Zev would remind himself. The soldier would recount how life was almost snuffed out of him, how he witnessed the death of his closest friend, how he listened to shrieks of agony during the last moments of someone who died right in front of him, someone he wasn't able to save even though he desperately wanted to. Zev might hear how the soldier lay there, shivering with fear, even wetting himself; how he thought of running away or maybe did run away, how he feels like a coward. How he lost all faith in his commander and even wanted to kill him. How he questioned why he was there at that moment instead of with his loving family. He might confide his hatred and rage at the sophisticated and courageous enemy that inflicted such terrible losses among his friends. He might rail at the unbelievable stupidity of comrades-in-arms who caused unbearable losses due to "friendly fire" (accidentally shooting at your own people.) He would tell Zev about the intolerable fatigue after hours of marching in the hills, carrying heavy loads of equipment and arms, the hunger and thirst, the conflicting orders, the disorganization, the lack of supplies. How the machine gun jammed at a critical moment, the horror of knowing you are a sitting duck, unable to defend yourself or your comrades. And

about acts of heroism performed by friends who had sacrificed their own lives for others, about the dulling of one's senses, about despair, depression, and helplessness, about the fear of confronting the enemy.

And then there was the suffering that continued long after the events were over. Chronic neck and back pains, heartbeats going amok at the sound of clanking metal, the loss of all interest in family, in sexual desire, in activities that were once enjoyed; the irrational rages and outbursts of temper against loved ones as well as strangers, the flashbacks, night terrors, and panic attacks.

All this pain Zev listened to day after day. The feelings of terrible insecurity about things one used to be highly skilled at, feelings of shame and guilt, the loss of any ability to act rationally, persistently negative feelings, repetitive and troubling obsessive thoughts. Stiff and jerky body movements, restlessness, and anger: tremendous anger at society, the government, the army, the commander, life, and everything and everyone else.

And the patient would talk of the difficulty and hesitation about coming to the clinic, the postponements that sometimes went on for years, the insistence that "I don't need this" finally answered by a loved one's angry retort, "If you don't get treatment, I will leave you!" All these painful events are summarized in sentences that were, for so long, impossible to utter.

"And that's it. That's what happened" a teller would conclude at last.

After the story is told, the soldier's tension starts to subside. He has finally found the courage to begin to confront the demon that has been haunting him for months, sometimes years, making his life miserable, depriving him of the solace of sleep, distancing him from friends and family, destroying his marriage, making it impossible to concentrate on work or studies, being re-experienced in vivid flashbacks of gruesome scenes, the smells of burnt flesh, the cries of the wounded, causing a rage he cannot control. Now that it has finally been let out, it may be possible to clip the demon's wings, to curb its power.

But now the tension that has subsided for the soldier has landed full force on Zev. The burden is now on Zev to relieve the suffering that has been revealed. It is up to him to generate solutions, to guide the soldier back toward a more normal life. Zev must help him repair the wrecked marriage, bring him back to his children, enable him to study and progress at work. He must ease his fears so he can listen to the news again, travel to places he is terrified to revisit, pick up the phone to call a friend or the father of a fallen comrade. And more, much more, has to be done. It is an awful burden, an awesome responsibility.

So it is understandable that Zev sometimes has to escape, to retreat home and sleep for 11 hours. But more than usual, with this group Zev feels he is drowning in a sea of sorrow, loss, destruction, and inconsolable grief. And more than usual, he feels overwhelmed, knowing he is responsible for rebuilding shattered worlds, lessening the effects of wrongdoings, restoring ruined psyches to normalcy.

Zev is no stranger to the phenomenon of "secondary traumatization": instances where therapists themselves become traumatized by the very crises they are attempting to relieve. The professional literature is full of articles, anecdotes, and warnings stating that a therapist must be prepared for this onslaught, and should seek help from others and not try to absorb all this alone. Zev thought he was intellectually prepared for secondary traumatization, but now he found himself sinking in a quicksand of sorrow and despair.

"I'm not able to help them. Who do I think I am – God? All the years of study, the internships, the seminars, the articles I read and wrote, the professional meetings with experts, all the years of treating hundreds of patients – all of these become nothing when I look into the eyes of the suffering man sitting opposite me, mourning his dead friend. I feel helpless, paralyzed. What can I possibly do in the face of such an enormous loss? Can I give him back his dead comrade? Can I erase all the horror he has seen and will never forget?"

Now his paralysis gradually spreads over him like thick glue. He feels a weakness in his limbs and is engulfed by a sickening feeling of hopelessness.

"Helplessness…it's one of the cornerstones of post traumatic stress disorder (PTSD). It has happened to them, and now it is happening to me! I must confront it; I must not allow it to overpower me. If I sink into despair, what good can I do them? I will fail those who have turned to me for help."

Ultimately, Zev's determination and self-discipline, his experience, and his soul-deep desire to help the men who have sought him out, enable him to make the enormous effort to extricate himself from the black feelings that threaten to derail him.

"This is all part and parcel of the work with post trauma: to develop the tools to overcome precisely these feelings of helplessness and paralysis, and in doing this, to become a model for others. My suffering is a drop in the bucket compared to theirs, yet having feelings similar to theirs can help me to help them."

The day after his long sleep, he picks up the phone and arranges a meeting with one of the few therapists he knows who is familiar with combat-related PTSD. He also writes a lengthy email to a childhood friend, a psychiatrist, and pours his heart out to him. He does not expect or need a response that will offer solace, but the very act of writing is calming. It is as though he has reconstructed a traumatic event that he himself had experienced, and then jettisoned it from his mind.

In the evening of his next day at work, and after meeting with his colleague over coffee, he returns to the supermarket and selects plums with the steely determination of one ready to do battle with great challenges.

"Obviously I may not be able to help every single one of them. And those I do have success with may not be completely healed in every area of their lives. None of this detracts from the tremendous value of helping them regain some of their former joy, their ability to function normally and well. Even the greatest surgeons cannot save every patient; but they can save many, and can improve the lives of many others. And I can do the same."

As long as the group meets, Zev will continue to reel under the heavy responsibility of treatment. And when he encounters additional difficult situations, and is unable to magically solve every problem, he will feel saddened and disappointed. But with every slight improvement in the condition of his clients, he feels relief and encouragement. With every session, he feels hope that there will be an additional morsel of success, of progress toward healing.

And he is comforted by the knowledge that he will be helped

in his work by the simple passage of time. While time alone does not heal all wounds, piercing sensations do lose some of their sting. Many horrible fears will soften to the level of a mere unpleasantness, and successes in life, both spontaneous ones and those due to his assistance, will help bring his clients closer to more normal lives. And that is enough.

TENTH SESSION

Yariv and Yossi arrive at the clinic earlier than usual. They huddle in the corner and look out the window, gazing at the meadow that has started to show signs of spring. A lone anemone bends in the wind, and clumps of grass peak out of the ground. The awareness that today is the tenth session is bothering them. Everyone in the group has benefited from participating, even Gil, who tried to claim otherwise. But the time remaining to solve pressing issues is becoming shorter at a frightening pace, and they are concerned that someone will get into a lengthy story about an unimportant issue and consume valuable time.

Yariv and Yossi, although from different backgrounds and experiences, had a bond from their shared battle experiences. And over the course of the meetings, they'd gotten closer to each other, and now often understood each other with a single glance.

From the very first session, Yariv, the commando with Moroccan roots, has stood out as a natural leader, just as he is in his life outside the group. His solid body, calm voice, and relaxed gaze transmit the sense of a man one can count on, someone you can trust when you find yourself in difficulty. But he never pushed himself on the others, and had no wish to run the group. He was open to receiving direction from anyone, not just Zev.

Yossi was very aware of his gifts. During the chaos of fighting, Yossi had observed his ability to command and was impressed by his cool-headedness and logical decisions under such difficult circumstances. When the group first started to meet, Yossi was worried that Yariv might use his unique abilities to secure a special role for himself. But when Yariv made no such attempt, and was open and sincere with everyone about his own pains and demons, Yossi had relaxed.

On the surface, their camaraderie is not easy to explain. Twenty-nine-year-old Yariv, tough-looking and athletic, an officer and a born leader, had simply developed a fondness for skinny, unsure, Yossi, the private with a poor, Middle Eastern background. What attracted him to Yossi isn't obvious. Perhaps it is his humility, the modesty in his voice, or maybe it is Yariv's sympathy for the discrimination against Yossi's family that held them back economically while Yossi was growing up. It troubled Yariv that while his own parents, immigrants from North Africa, had succeeded and moved up in Israeli society, Yossi's parents, who had been residents here for many generations, continued to remain at the bottom despite all their hard work. This kind of socio-economic discrimination always infuriated Yariv, who had a strong sense of fairness.

He saw Yossi's deeds in India as a brave attempt to do something unusual, dangerous, and adventurous in order to break out of the cycle dictated by society's norms, a courageous – if reckless – effort to make money and improve his social standing. The fact that Yossi's actions were illegal didn't trouble Yariv for two reasons: first, they took place in a country where drug-dealing is rampant; and second, because Yossi brought money into Israel, not drugs. And from that money he bought trucks that contributed to building the country. In this way, Yariv managed to rationalize Yossi's deeds and overlook his methods. He liked Yossi, and the feeling was mutual.

Perhaps the strongest connection between the two was the horrible event they had experienced together in the Lebanese village of Debel – the "Story" that they had not yet shared with Zev and the group.

Now Yossi whispers to Yariv: "What do you plan to bring up first today? I'll reinforce whatever you say so we can stay on track. Actually, I'm not sure if anyone will waste time, now that Gil isn't here any more – but Uri might. What do you think?"

Yossi's remark reveals some of the dynamics that have developed among group members. On the surface, everyone takes care of the others, but under the surface there are, of course, differences in character and points of view that sometimes clash. Generally, potential attacks and aggression among members have been staved off by Zev's skillfulness and by the mutual respect the men have for each other. The fact that they are all "in the same boat," that they have all experienced traumatic combat events, and are all suffering from many of the same symptoms, unites them and creates a spirit of mutual sympathy and cooperation. Yet, in the innermost parts of their hearts, some who had been part of the most horrific events felt a degree of contempt and dismissiveness toward those whose experiences seemed less extreme. Although they never expressed these feelings out loud, a facial expression or a tone of voice sometimes exposed them.

By now, everyone had assembled. Without delay, Yariv brought up an issue that still troubled him.

With a glance at Yossi, Yariv says, "I think that we haven't dealt enough with the issue of intrusive thoughts. We touched on it a few times, but it still bothers me a great deal. I know that it's also true for Ron, who isn't saying much but who I think is silently suffering, and Sergei too. So far I haven't been able to overcome this. Several times a day, no matter what I am doing, upsetting thoughts come into my mind, take a position and dig in, and I can't dislodge them. What about you, Yossi?"

"Similar. I keep thinking about Benny, how that courageous fighter pissed away his life in a godforsaken Indian village. He had a brilliant future. A handsome guy, brave, smart, from a good home, and look what the service did to him. Once, when we talked, he hinted at things that tormented him, but he chose not to get any treatment which might have helped him cope. He just drowned his guilt feelings in alcohol and covered them up with a cloud of marijuana smoke. In the end, he committed a kind of passive suicide. It's painful for me to keep thinking about him. Sometimes I think that if I hadn't agreed to go with him on our adventure, maybe he'd be here with us in the group, or would have found some other help, and could have returned to normal life."

"What did he say was tormenting him so?" asks Yariv. He's curious, but mostly hoping to help Yossi, his friend, minimize his feelings of guilt.

"He didn't reveal too many details. Once he started to talk, it was kind of like he was in a trance. He said he'd been an interrogator for the secret service. He and another interrogator were under terrible time pressure to get information from armed men who'd been apprehended and were planning a suicide mission, and they did things to them that they knew were against the rules. He started to mumble some other snippets related to that event, but then he just went back to sucking on his reefer. He drank half a bottle of that crappy Indian alcohol, and sank into one of his gurgling sleeps. It was obvious to me that he was tormented by his actions, and that he was trying to escape from an event that caused him deep feelings of remorse and guilt."

"Sad, very sad," Yariv responds. "There are moments when you feel such rage at the enemy that you're ready to throw away the values you were raised on, and when the opportunity arises, tough things can happen: the terrible incidents in the villages of Deir Yassin, Kfar Kassem, the My Lai massacre in Viet Nam – horrible events you know about, and probably others that haven't been made public yet.

"People who were involved in these events suffer in silence because it's too dangerous to talk. They know they'll be judged by those 'pure hearts,' people who never had a gun pointed in their face, people who sat in a safe place that makes it easy for them to pass judgment on others. Benny was under tremendous pressure to save lives, and it's not that I condone what he and his buddy might have done, but under no circumstances would I pass judgment on them. There is no shortage of veterans, especially from elite units, who were in horrible situations and didn't always use kid gloves in their dealings with the enemy. And these are guys who become so convinced that they're invulnerable..." Yariv shook his head sadly. "They survive all that, and then travel to places like the Amazon, Central America, India, they dismiss warnings, get themselves in trouble..." He fell silent for a moment. "Benny had to deal with his guilt, and if you hadn't gone with him, he'd have found someone else. You didn't cause anything that happened to him. It was his choice and you did what you could. You went with him without knowing what was lurking behind his need to escape. And it wasn't *your* crime, Yossi; you served in the army without doing the things he did."

Ron jumped on the opportunity to chime in. "I also want to talk about the issue of tormenting thoughts. Yariv's right: although we have dealt with it, it isn't getting any better for me. There isn't a day that I don't think about the wounded soldier I lost. Logically I might know that I couldn't have done anything more, but emotionally the feeling of having failed continues to torment me. I sit and study chemistry, and the picture of him floats up before my eyes. I erase it, move on to something else, and he reappears. It's as though he's accusing me: 'you're here, but I'm not.'"

Zev intervenes. "What's happening here is 'survivor guilt.' Ron, as the medic you did everything that could be done, including risking your own life, but to no avail. Sadly, when the soldier arrived he was no longer alive, but you couldn't know that. Survival guilt is a well-known and troublesome phenomenon. It can be summed up in a single phrase: 'Why him and not me?' and the more joy there is because it *isn't* 'me,' the more guilt there is. In order to get rid of this feeling, you need to examine the event objectively, rationally, to verify for yourself that you did the best that could honestly be asked of you. There may be other situations where there is some legitimate responsibility, and they are dealt with differently. But that is not the case in your situation. In fact, it's just the opposite. You did everything you possibly could in a totally hopeless situation."

"I know, but I'm still struggling." He nods, settles back into his chair, and looks around for someone else to speak.

From the giddly, almost child-like expression on Uri's face, it's obvious he has something momentous that he wants to share.

"I don't know exactly when and how this changed, but remember the problem I was having with Karnit – that even though I loved her, I didn't want to go near her? I had no sexual desire. She tried several times to get me interested, with a kind of half-sexy, half-funny dance, but it was always useless, and finally she gave up. Well, somehow, things started to shift, and I'm happy to let you know that in about seven months, you'll all be invited to a party to celebrate the birth of our first child!" Uri exclaims.

"Wow! The group's baby!"

"The ninth member of our group!"

"Mazal Tov!"

"In seven months? Truly fresh news. Best of luck to both of you."

Zev smiles broadly, feeling that an important victory has been scored. And he feels as happy and proud – as grandfatherly – as when his own daughters announced they were pregnant. He now has seven grandchildren, and Uri and Karnit's baby feels to him like an eighth. He gets up from his chair and gives Uri a quick hug, not saying a word.

Uri continues, excitedly. "And that's not all. I've almost completed the composition for my final. You may remember that I had a beginning and an end, but the middle, the longest section, was a large hole. I've been pondering this part every day. Every time a melody came into my head, I immediately jotted it down in the small notebook I always carry. Once, in a restaurant, I didn't have it with me so I wrote a melody on a paper napkin. Turns out that this was the most moving tune, maybe because the sun was setting at that moment, creating a nostalgic atmosphere, reminding me of my first meeting with Karnit on that beach at sunset. Every day I've added a few bars. Sometimes I sit at the piano for an hour not touching a single key; other times I try one tune after another. I'm almost sure I'll have it finished by the end of the semester."

"That's great Uri. We all knew you'd make it," says Yariv.

Zev smiles again, makes an encouraging remark, and in his mind gives himself another point.

*　*　*

The number of unresolved issues is shrinking. Zev had expected to hear at least a little bad news from someone, but today, none seems to be coming up. He worries there may be someone who isn't doing well but just isn't talking about it. In his head he reviews the list of symptoms the members have described, and he finds himself repeatedly bumping up against nightmares and sleep disturbances. He has heard about some improvements from a few of the members, but not from everyone, and these are symptoms that every one of the eight members had complained about.

He knows from both experience and the professional literature that disturbed sleep is a stubborn and persistent problem that can cause a lot of suffering. He also knows that, while there are many effective medications for sleep disturbances, anxiety and depression, which can offer great relief, there are people who are reluctant to take them. It is a source of frustration for health-care providers when they are faced with clients who complain bitterly about nightmares and the inability to sleep, but who refuse to take well-proven medications. All kinds of reasons are offered: "I don't believe in drugs," "drugs are for crazies, and I'm not crazy," "I've heard about terrible side effects"; and other excuses. In the end, all a therapist can do is throw up their hands and say: "It's your choice; do what you want." Clients who come in week after week with the same complaint, yet are unwilling to change, are a source of sadness and exasperation. Zev didn't want to delve into this issue; he merely wanted to raise everyone's awareness about it and give the members food for thought.

Zev turns to Ron. "We've heard that Uri has made progress with his ability to concentrate and his composing. In that context, what is happening with your studying?"

"Oh, I really should have mentioned it; I'm sorry. I started with the kitchen timer like you suggested, using it to break time into manageable bits, and it rang every few minutes, until I arrived at the conclusion that I didn't actually need it anymore. What's helping is that I passed an exam with an acceptable grade, and feel encouraged. It's like a car that has finally come out of deep mud and is starting to move at a reasonable pace. I'm still not concentrating as well as I used to: I get up, drink some water, peek out of the window, play with the TV remote, toy with the phone; but essentially I'm keeping pace and I'm managing much better."

"That's good progress, Ron."

Yariv raises his hand and starts talking. "There is this issue I've been sitting on for a long time, but we're running out of sessions, and I don't want to wait any longer. It's about what happened in Lebanon. It's been preying on my mind, and I need to see if getting it out will help me to get past it.

"When we received the order to enter that village, Debel, there was total darkness and confusion. We were supposed to enter under the cover of darkness, but every time we suited up and started to move, a new order came: 'wait.' The idea was to enter quietly on foot, in the dark. We'd move three kilometers toward the village, settle in, and be ready to attack by daybreak. But after all those delays, we didn't start out until two o'clock in the morning. We were already exhausted from all the tension; there were rumors and the sounds of artillery in the distance, and we figured that if we started out now, we'd never make it there before sunrise, and we'd be exposed. And that's exactly what happened.

"While we were still approaching the village, we were discovered and a heavy barrage of mortar opened up. One shell after another fell around us. One fell only five meters from me, it didn't explode, but I was badly shaken. Other shells exploded about 20 meters away, and shrapnel was flying all over. Fragments of rocks were catapulted about and striking people. One soldier was hit in the eye and was screaming.

"The equipment, which was heavy to begin with, felt even heavier. I was terrified, exhausted and thirsty, and all of it was robbing me of energy. And it wasn't even clear what our task was, so we just sat there, absorbing mortar fire and not returning any! Holding our fire added to our feeling helpless, and guys started whispering, 'What the hell are we doing here?' We were losing confidence in the Battalion Commander, while mortar shells were landing all around us. It was scary as hell.

"I don't remember exactly what happened. There was a ton of dust and smoke, the shrieking of shells. Missiles and pieces of rocks were hitting the side of a house in which we tried to seek shelter, with terrible sounds. Actually, staying in that house made us an easy target, and it was obvious that there were far too many of us in one place, which increased the danger. The enemy was sophisticated and I imagine that they saw exactly what was happening with us. Then there was a huge explosion – we were hit by a missile, a direct hit! The house filled with smoke, the walls shook, and people were shrieking, 'I'm hit, I'm hit!'

"I was stunned. The blast threw me against the wall and I smacked my head and was confused. I knew that something bad had happened, but had no idea how terrible it actually was."

Yariv sighs, leans back, swallowing hard. He looks anxious, and everyone waits quietly for the rest of his story. Some are thinking, "Yes, this happened to me, too." They feel a sense of solidarity with Yariv, and at that moment they're experiencing what he is experiencing. Yossi and Avi drop their heads, hiding contorted faces, on the verge of tears. There is a heavy silence.

Yariv gathers his strength and starts talking again. "Now, finally, I need to bring it all out into the open, this awful burden that I've been carrying." But again, he falls silent.

Silence and tense anticipation fill the room.

A moment later Zev turns to Yariv, and asks gently, "Burden?" but does not elaborate.

Yariv shifts in his chair and continues. He has been pondering for months how to talk about this event, how to admit to the awful feelings of guilt that wrap around him like a suffocating blanket, and how to say it without looking like a coward to the others. He has rehearsed the words in his mind dozens of times, like an actor practicing his lines. Sometimes, he'd begin the story positively, then move on to the part he was less proud of. At other times, he would start by blurting out his feelings of guilt, and then explaining what took place. Now he was groping for words, hoping that after he uttered them, he'd get some relief. But he couldn't be sure, and he hesitated again. A word that is spoken cannot be taken back. Until this moment he'd believed – and hoped – that he had been the only one in the world who knew exactly what had taken place in Debel. Now he was on the verge of confessing.

He was afraid that after speaking the words out loud, his comrades in the group – and Zev, too – would see him differently. That after he told his story, he would no longer be accepted by them. In his imagination, he saw their looks of disdain, and he thought he might never again feel able to show his face in the group, would be scorned by men he had come to love. He took a deep breath, then slowly looked around, making eye contact with each member, as if trying to make a secret deal that after he spoke they wouldn't throw him to the wolves; that they would accept him, with all his warts. That they would still think of him as a fighter, as one of them.

With a painful effort, he continued. "Then it got quieter. I noticed that some of the men who had been crying out were silent now. Some were just whimpering in pain. There were no more screams. I knew there were a great many wounded and that I would have to assist with the evacuation. It was too dangerous to stay in the building, such an easy target. I had to leave. But before I could even finish this thought, a second missile hit the house. Now new shrieks filled the air, mingling with the smoke and the horrific smell of burning flesh. I was still near the wall where I had been tossed by the first missile, still hadn't moved. I felt the blast on my chest and I was having trouble breathing. Then the thick smoke and dust started to clear, revealing a horrible landscape: broken bodies, torn off limbs, blood everywhere. The last moans of the dying filled the air. I was in shock, terrified. I didn't know where I was, it seemed like a horrible dream that couldn't possibly be real.

"At my feet lay a soldier whose belly was ripped open. Blood was gushing out of him and he was pleading for someone to help. I bent down, wanting to help, but he went silent, his eyes wide open, staring at the ceiling. He just died in that second. Next to him was a man with blood bursting out of his arm, and no hand at the end of it. I applied a tourniquet, tossed him over my shoulder, and started to exit the house, with no idea where I would go. Suddenly, my legs gave way and we both fell on top of dead bodies. I vomited. I got up, hoisted him over my shoulder again, and managed to get out and hide behind the building. I thought that if we got hit again, the rear wall would offer the best protection. Inside the house, the air pressure alone could kill you. I called for a medic, but I don't know if anyone heard me."

"You probably saved his life!" called out one of the guys.

Yariv didn't respond. He was staring into space. "I had to go back into the building to retrieve the others. But I froze! I couldn't move! There were so many injured men in there that I could have saved from bleeding out, like that soldier with the tourniquet. But...I was frozen. I was terrified of going back inside that hell. I was selfish! I saved one soldier and I saved myself and then I didn't want to go back in! I was afraid I'd die if another missile hit the house...and I didn't go back. I heard cries coming from the room, and I didn't move. I knew what was going on, everyone bleeding, wounded, and I couldn't get my legs to move. I was stiff with fear. I stood there for some time, I don't know how long, maybe a minute, maybe more...and that whole time, the wounded are crying out and I'm staying outside. I'm fine, except for that blow to my head, and I could have helped, and I *didn't*." And with these words, Yariv burst into bitter tears.

There was silence. You could hear the sound of the men breathing. The room is filled with a mix of feelings, an air of respect for Yariv's experience, feelings of horror – and of sympathy. His colleagues understand his feelings of guilt and misery all too well. Some had been in similar situations, and they understand the confusion, the smoke, the awful fear, the sense of obligation to rescue and evacuate, as well as the instinct to survive.

Some others, with different experiences, are hearing the adage in their minds: "Don't judge another until you are in his place." Under such conditions, no one knows exactly what he would have done.

"That's the burden?" asks Zev, gently.

"Yes. That's the burden. It's been weighing on me ever since, and I can't get rid of it. I look at myself as someone who failed, who didn't act responsibly, who didn't do what he was obligated to do. I never thought of myself as a coward, but after what happened there...I hate myself. I don't deserve to feel happy. What did I do?" he was weeping.

Zev speaks again, quietly: "Are you fully aware that you saved the life of a fellow soldier?"

"And what about those I let bleed?"

"Under those terrible conditions – the confusion, the fear, the smack on your head from the blast that threw you against the wall...you did what you could. You are your own worst critic. True, you might have done more, but under those terrible conditions...."

"Don't make excuses for me. You, like everyone here, understand exactly what's tormenting me, and now I just have to live with it." His voice was stronger now.

Avi turned toward him. "Yariv, I do understand what took place there. I was in a battle just like that, with smoke, choking, chaos, but there were no injured so there was no one to rescue. I understand that you wished you had done more, but you did the best you could. Do you hear me? So, how are you planning to cope with it?"

"That's the problem. At least now I'm not alone with this knowledge. I'm not the only one who knows what happened there. At least I brought this horror out in the open. Now you can be the judges."

"Nobody here is a judge," Zev says emphatically. "We are not doing an inquest. Our aim is to bring fighters back to living normal lives, to reduce the burdens, to calm down, to restore normalcy to troubled lives." He had been anticipating for a long time that besides Avi's failure to save Rami, and Uri leaving his men to die in the tank, someone else was sitting on a similar event, and had not yet dealt with it – a situation in which someone blames himself, or someone else, for a failure in battle, whether real or imagined – and he would have to be ready to help resolve their dilemma.

"And how do you feel now, Yariv?" asks Yossi, looking his friend directly in the eye.

"A little bit better. At least I got one other soldier out of that hell; maybe I can focus on that. I don't know who he is, but I really hope he survived. Whenever I thought about this, I always got stuck on what I did *not* do, always kind of suppressing the part where I did something good. I think I could have done better. I wish I had. But it's also true that I didn't run away, I didn't abandon *everyone*."

"And what will you do with these feelings now?" inquired Zev.

Yariv is silent. He isn't sure how to answer the question. He doesn't want to give a stupid answer, but he is still not quite sure he knows how to cope with his feelings of guilt. He brought it to the group hoping for a miracle, a magical wave of the hand that would distance him forever from the feelings of shame gnawing at him daily.

He hadn't chosen to be in that damned village, in that damned house, in that damned war; circumstances of life had landed him there. He had tried to do the best he could with what fate had delivered to him. He was starting to feel a glimmer of calm, of relief.

"Yariv, you can give yourself a pat on the shoulder for what you did accomplish, and forgive yourself for what you didn't," suggests Zev. "We have an unrealistic expectation that under any circumstances, any place, any time, we'll always function at our very best. There are a tiny number of outstanding people who manage to do this, who truly are heroic, who receive medals of valor. The fact is that they are unusual, these heroes, people about whom books and articles are written. Most of us are just average, normal people, we do what we have to do and what we are able. We don't stand out, either in civilian or military life. Otherwise, everyone in uniform would be donning a medal of valor, and the fact is that most fighters don't. Think again of your actions in that horrible place, and what you accomplished. Medal of Valor? Perhaps not. Failure? Also not."

"You are putting it in perspective, and that's helpful. I'll make an attempt to discover who that soldier was – the one I applied the tourniquet to and carried out of the house. I feel like it's important for me to know what happened with him. Meanwhile, I really do feel less pressure now than I did before, when I was guarding my secret, carrying that in silence." Yariv sinks back in his seat.

ELEVENTH SESSION

Everyone in the room has one thought on their mind. Yossi is the one to voice it.

"Hey, guys, today is session eleven. We're getting close to the end." He shifts uneasily in his chair.

Some nod, some sit quietly. All eyes rest on Zev.

"That's correct. Only today and next week," Zev confirms. "And, how should we best use the remaining time? One way might be to take an inventory, like seeing how many jars of vinegar remain and how many jars of honey..." Laughter greets his words, taking some of the nervous edginess out of the air. The comparison to food is humorous; yet underlying the words there is a deep and significant meaning.

"The vinegar can represent those symptoms we still have not overcome, and the honey comprises the coping tools we have accumulated in our toolbox over the course of our sessions. If we look at the vinegar bottles as the symptoms that are still on our shelves and as stuff we don't want, everyone could make his own list. I know with certainty that the number and intensity of the symptoms have subsided since we started. I also know that the shelves have not been emptied of every bothersome occurrence.

"If we view the honey jars as our coping tools, I hope that they are heavily laden and that each one of you grabs a jar and uses it as needed."

"I do the relaxation exercise several times a week, when I'm not too tired or too lazy," Uri responds.

"And do they help you?" Ido inquires.

"Yeah, they actually do, especially when I'm anxious or irritated."

"Do they ever put you to sleep?"

"Interesting that you should ask. At times I do nod off, but just for a few seconds. When I wake up, I feel refreshed and ready for action."

"If you fall asleep, is it really helping?" asks Yossi, doubtfully.

"Yes. I start with the relaxation, and at a certain point, the anxiety subsides, and when I wake up it isn't as intense as it was, and I can continue with whatever I have to do. For example, the other day I was home, preparing for a lesson I had to teach at school. The subject was somewhat complicated and I wasn't really familiar with it. And I was starting to get a little stressed about it. Then, all of a sudden I noticed that I wasn't thinking about the lesson anymore – I was thinking about the tank, how I was caught in that high-pressure situation, and that lead to thinking about running away from my current situation. I was suddenly so anxious that I wanted to call my principal and tell her that I was sick, but I knew it was ridiculous to let myself get panicky and start making excuses and that I needed to just concentrate and face up to my task. I started the relaxation, the anxiety receded, and maybe I even dozed for a few seconds. When I awoke, I was more alert and less anxious, I prepared what I had to do, and was able to complete the lesson."

"That's impressive. Are you sure you're not bluffing?

"No, why would I? It doesn't work all the time, but at times it works well."

Yossi continued. "Well, I admit I'm a bit afraid about what happens after next week. In the last ten weeks, I've gotten used to getting answers to my questions, to Zev's input, the connections among us, and the support of the group. Sometimes, at night, these thoughts float up, sad and heavy, but I always think, 'I'm in the same boat as everybody else, with the same anxieties and fears. Come Tuesday I'll get help, we'll all support each other, and I won't feel isolated.' What will happen in two weeks when I'll know I don't have that anymore, scares me." All around him there are nods of agreement. Everyone in the room shares these worries.

Zev had anticipated this anxiety, having experienced it

numerous times as each short-term group came to a close. He, too, had to cope with the loss of this group of men to whom he had been personally connected for two and a half months. His weeks had been filled with thoughts revolving around them and their well-being. Often, between sessions, his time was taken up with concerns about one person or another, or he would find himself wrestling with a bothersome issue for which he had not yet been able to come up with a good solution. Often he worried how a week would go for a member who was especially troubled by a particular symptom, and who was relying on him to solve the problem. He delighted in every turn for the better, and was disappointed – in himself and in the circumstances – when things didn't go well, when there were setbacks and disappointments, or when someone promised to try something in connection with an issue, but didn't, or couldn't.

Of course, he was still bothered by having lost Gil. He understands that Gil had a myriad of emotional problems that preceded even his military service and its traumatic events, but it saddens him that he had been unable to maintain Gil's participation or to give him what he needed. It may have been an impossible goal, yet he's unable to erase Gil's sad face and obvious suffering from his memory. Zev had wished for something that he could have used to solve Gil's problems. He remembered the confrontational phone call they had when Gil failed to show up and didn't understand, at first, the implications of his own behavior. How he had convinced him to return, and then lost Gil after all. He knew it wasn't his fault that members sometimes drop out of groups, and it isn't a rare event, but in his gut there's a gnawing feeling that he failed.

Zev experiences in his heart, even if just a bit, the same feelings of misery and guilt suffered by members of the group who had tried to rescue a comrade and not succeeded. He fervently hopes that his professional colleagues, with whom he reviews his work, will confirm that he did all he possibly could for these men in their difficult circumstances.

"May I reveal something here?"

Everyone turns toward Ron with curiosity. "A few weeks ago, Ido and I started exchanging text messages. We began communicating between sessions, in anticipation of the group ending, knowing we did not want to be left floating in midair. And after a few times, Yossi and Yariv joined in."

Quiet descends after this surprising revelation. Although there was no agreement not to be in touch between sessions, this new infrastructure catches the other three by surprise. Zev was also a bit surprised, but not very. He has experienced this in previous groups, and sees it as a positive development. This kind of connection points to a close relationship among members, and preparation for future times, when someone might need help after the group has disbanded.

"You've shown foresight in planning for the future, more power to you," Zev notes encouragingly. "It would be great if everyone who wants to, could be part of this network. How about exchanging cell numbers with everyone? Aside from this, you should know that you may contact me any time. I promise to respond promptly. I cannot promise that I will be available for a great length of time, but I can always make a referral to other skilled therapists." With this assurance he reinforces things he'd said previously that might have been forgotten.

"I'm sure that I'm not 'done,'" Avi states. "This was a great beginning, and I got a lot out of it, and I also learned that I have other issues unrelated to the events that took place during the war. Those events fell on fertile ground. Years ago, when I was 16, my mother actually dragged me to a therapist to deal with some socialization issues, but I thought the therapist was an idiot. She talked down to me like I was a child, and I fled. She probably said some relevant things, but we had no rapport. Now that I've grown up a little, and after having a positive experience here, I'd like to find someone good, and continue. Can you help me with that?"

"Of course. I'll give you several names. Set up some meetings and find someone you can relate well to. Does it matter to you if they're a man or a woman?"

"Actually, no. As long as the therapist has the personality and skills to help, it doesn't matter."

"Ok, that's good; it broadens the possibilities." Zev says with a smile. "This offer is for everyone, obviously."

Relief is visible on many faces. Avi's opening of the subject was well received; he's not the only one who has considered the issue of further treatment, whether immediately or sometime down the road. A few of the men feel that they've gotten sufficient relief for the present, and are in no hurry to continue. Still, it's comforting even to them to know that there's an emotional spare tire in the trunk.

"Is there a plan for a concluding party?" This from Sergei, the expert on catering.

"There's no fixed format. Every group does what it wants. Anyone interested?"

"I've been thinking about it. After all, it was the custom in the military to have a graduation ceremony at the end of every milestone, and we are a folk that loves eating and drinking. What do you all think?"

"Of course. Why even ask?"

Sergei had been waiting for an opportunity to demonstrate his skills in preparing delicious dishes for his friends. "I'm bringing several surprises, come with a good appetite," he says with an impish grin. "Someone has to bring beer to wash down the delicacies."

"Not a problem," Yossi assures him.

"I'll bring a cake," offers Ron. "And coffee we have anyway."

"Seems we'll be having a party," concluded Zev. "Not much hesitation about this."

Yet Yariv looks uncomfortable, as though something is still burdening him. "Now that we've concluded all that, let's get back to some of the main issues, please. Let's get back to the things that still torment us. There is something in particular that I haven't been able to cope with. There's an issue that persists, and it's concerning food, and now that we're talking about this, and I don't know what Sergei will surprise us with, it may present a problem for me."

The room immediately quieted. In one fell swoop, Yariv has returned the group to the reality of its purpose, obliterating the festive atmosphere that had spread throughout the room. There were still two meetings left, and there was still work to be done. Consistent with his always-practical approach to issues, his words were reminders that they should use the precious time remaining to do serious work.

"What is it that you haven't discussed yet, Yariv?"

"I've mentioned a few times the issue of scorched flesh, but I never went into details. I can't eat or smell or even look at seared meat or chicken. It nauseates me. It awakens sickening memories."

"Can you share with us what created this situation?" Zev asked gently.

"It's time, isn't it? It's bad for me to sit on it forever; it's just that it's so hard for me to think about. So, here it is.

"It relates to that event of evacuating the wounded and the dead from the Lebanese village. After the first missile penetrated the house, there was almost total darkness. My eyes were tearing; I nearly choked from the dust and smoke in the air. I tried not to breathe, but obviously, I couldn't hold my breath for more than a few seconds. I was trying, but suddenly I took in a deep breath and all I recall is that nauseating stench of burnt flesh, of scorched clothing. I opened my eyes and just below me lay the corpse of a soldier whose body was blackened and charred, and his entire face was burned off. I couldn't recognize any human features. The burnt skull and the deep holes where the eyes had been, told me that this was once a human being. I gagged, turned aside and vomited; I felt such shame. Ever since, every time I see a plate of food, I quickly glance at it to see if there is any meat on it. If there is, I turn away and refuse it. Anat understands this and doesn't prepare meat dishes anymore. My kids sometimes ask why we don't grill like our neighbors, and Anat explains that I don't like that kind of food. They're always disappointed and sometimes they keep at her, asking 'If Dad doesn't like eating grilled food, then he shouldn't eat it, but why can't we?' Obviously, I can't tell them why I can't eat meat. Even Anat only knows that it is associated with some horror I witnessed, but I've never told her the details that I just told you."

The silence in the room was as dense as the darkness that enveloped Yariv after the missile explosion.

"Tough story...a very tough one."

Ron offers, "How can we help you, Yariv? Do you want to return to where you can eat anything that comes to the table?"

"Yes, sure. It affects my relationships with my own children and with friends and I'm even filled with anxiety about next week here. I'll be worrying about it all week, and planning all kinds of machinations as to how not to look, not to smell, how to hide in another part of this room, in case any grilled meat appears. I do this anytime I'm invited for a meal, and if anyone catches on that I'm avoiding something, or having some kind of problem, I give some idiotic explanation, that I'm allergic, or some other lie. It's very difficult."

After a brief silence Avi rises up and approaches Yariv. He places a hand on his shoulder, leans over him, and speaks reassuringly. "I had a similar situation, but I worked on it. I'm not enthusiastic about grilled meat, but I can manage now if I have to, when I'm with friends or strangers, without having to get into any explanations." He goes back to his seat.

"How'd you do it?"

"The guided imagery helped me a lot. I created for myself an exercise where I visualize entering a room that has a plate of grilled meat on skewers. I approach, slowly, I look at them, and eventually, I smell them. Remember that method of pausing if an imagined situation was too intense? And marking that point by lifting your finger, like you're pointing and saying 'wait a second'?"

Yariv nods, remembering their past sessions.

"You can't imagine how many times my finger jumped up, trying to go through an imaginary encounter with shish kebab – until I mastered it. When the thoughts are coupled with the smell, I neutralize them with beautiful visions of the seashore with fresh breezes, colorful flowers with soft scents, and delicious aromas like apple pie – all sorts of counter images. Would you like to work on that with me now?"

Yariv's grateful for this information and Avi's offer. He agrees to work with him, and the others sit quietly while the two men do the visualization exercise for the next 15 minutes. Zev observes without intervening, impressed by the thoroughness with which Avi goes through the procedure.

"Let's see how this will work for you," Avi says, after they complete the exercise.

"I'd like to discuss something," Sergei starts hesitantly. "My problem is not that I remember, but that I can't, there's holes in the events that I went through."

"Tell us about them," Zev encourages.

"It's about a battle – I don't remember what happened there. Every time I think about it, it's different. In my head it's never the same story twice. One time I recall that I'm coming out from behind the jeep and hear the explosion, and the next time that I think about it, I'm convinced that I first hear the explosion and then jump behind the jeep. Yehoshua who was with me, remembers something altogether different. He claims that there was an explosion, that we both froze in place and only after we saw our comrade, Itzik, lying there motionless, we both jumped from behind the jeep and dragged him to safety behind the house.

"Itzik, who thank God has recuperated and returned to driving his cab, tells us that he was blown away by the blast and that he saw two guys running like crazy toward the house, and that only after he screamed 'Ay! I'm hit,' they turned around, and one of them, maybe I and maybe Yehoshua, leaned over him and dragged him to safety behind the house.

"I'm unable to recall which of these versions actually happened. I'm lying at night and trying to reconstruct the story. Every time it's different. And also, there is a piece missing altogether, I simply don't remember what happened after I, or perhaps we, dragged Itzik behind that building. He was covered with blood and I couldn't identify him. Imagine, I have known him from our reserve duty for years, and suddenly, I couldn't identify him! Perhaps I fainted, because I have no recollection of how I came to be in a sitting position in the second house, not the one where we dragged him to. I don't recall if someone carried me there or if I got there on my own, all I know is that I was in the second house and someone stuck a water canteen in my mouth and screamed "Drink! Drink! You're all dried out." I remember drinking but my hands shook and half of the water spilled on my face and my vest, and down to my pants. I remember that I started to walk and the guys looked at me as if I had pissed on myself. I was too confused to understand what they were looking at and I didn't know how I got there. It was only after I arrived at the hospital and they took my clothes off and I saw that my pants were wet, only then I understood. I haven't felt so ashamed since I was a kid...."

Sergei stopped talking as if in the middle of the sentence, a sentence as truncated as his description of the event.

COPING WITH THE DEMONS

"The confusion that you experienced," Zev said gently, "is typical of several others who suffered from 'holes in the story.' According to them, every time they thought of the story, they were unable to recall all of it, even if the event lasted only a minute or less. The inability to control such a basic function as the recollection of an important event in their lives shook their self confidence and caused confusion and shame. Consequently, they preferred not to talk about it at all, fearing that listeners would think of them as out of their minds, or worse, if they'd told the story more than once and the two versions didn't match, they'd be considered fakers. They'd be thought of as people who made up stories of heroism that never happened, and therefore untrustworthy. It was better to just keep quiet and suffer silently. Only in the framework of the group, where it was obvious that they were not alone, did they dare speak of this troubling phenomenon."

"You can't imagine how grateful I am that you had the guts to say what you did," said Avi. "You can't imagine how many times I have already attempted to deal with this problem, but couldn't close the gap."

Yariv entered the conversation: "Of course I can! The two of you are not alone, I have the same problem. I spend hours thinking of that battle, trying to remember just what happened, and I don't have the courage to talk to others about it. They'd think I'm psycho. This movie runs through my head for hours, over and over, and I can't finish the scene. I reach a certain point; smell the scorched flesh, see the tank exploding, see the gun turned backwards, see people running all over – and then it's a blur. I don't know where I am in the midst of all that bedlam. It's maddening. I know I was there. Not long ago, I met a guy who was also there and he said to me: 'Boy, you were lucky to have gotten out of that tank just in time. A second after you leaped off the turret, it took another missile hit, and there was nothing left of it. You lucky guy.' And I had no idea what he was talking about. I dropped my head, and mumbled 'Yeah, lucky, lucky.' And then I took off quickly, afraid he might want to talk more and I wouldn't know what to say to him. I didn't want to ask: 'So, what happened to you?' because he'd surely think that, just as he remembered what happened to me, I'd remember what happened to him, and I just don't remember."

Zev straightens out in his chair. All eyes are turn to him, awaiting direction like musicians looking to their conductor.

"Being unable to recall an important part of a traumatic event is one of the best-known symptoms in post-traumatic stress disorder. We have heard about it from people who've been raped, accident survivors, victims of armed robbery, natural disasters, and of course from soldiers in battles. It isn't clear what causes this phenomenon. Some think it's a psychological defense mechanism, not remembering a frightening and horrifying moment; others think it's a physiological occurrence, a system's overload, sort of a 'short circuit,' but at the end of the day, there's no definitive answer. Much like other subjects we're talking about, what's important is how to deal with it.

"Gil and Avi already tackled part of the solution but rejected it: talking to someone else in order to close gaps or fix distortions. The problem they raised is the shame of asking someone else and being perceived as psychos, confused, or some other negative perception. This rejection also emanates from the feelings and thoughts that anyone who experienced a difficult situation would surely remember it, and if not, there must be something wrong with him." Several men nod their heads.

"Let's start with the fact that it's a well-known phenomenon, widespread among trauma survivors, and that there's nothing to be ashamed of. But it's easier to say that here, in this room, then out there in the big wide world. We must therefore find the best routes to closing the gaps."

"What? Place an ad in the paper: 'Hey guys, I don't remember'…" added Yariv with a sarcastic tone.

"Not exactly, but similar. Nearly every event has witnesses and in that way they're partners to the trauma even if they were not physically affected. And asking a witness may not be as difficult as asking a total stranger. There's a good chance, as we heard from Avi, that someone else who was there might remember details or a sequence that's different from what you remember, or don't remember. It may be possible, for example, to pose the question in a slightly pointed manner."

"Give an example," asked Yariv.

"Here. You are talking to someone who was also there and you tell him something like: 'After the evacuation, I was so tired that I fell asleep in the helicopter,' and the other guy says: 'Well, you missed the part where...' and he fills in all kinds of details for you that you didn't remember, without you even telling him that you forgot. And a conversation ensues in which each one is filling in details. Depending on how it evolves, you might say; 'I forgot some details,' or not even mention it. It is quite possible that he, too, doesn't remember it all and you can help him."

"Makes sense," agrees Ron.

"One of the best methods is the reconstruction of the event. For example, I worked with a soldier who didn't remember what had happened in a certain battle in which he was involved. The battle lasted less than two minutes, but it was very significant for him. I pulled out a piece of paper and a pencil and we reconstructed step after step how the room looked, where he was, who was crawling in front of him, from what side did fire open, and in what direction was the evacuation. Within minutes, things became clear to him that were shrouded in a fog of forgetfulness."

"He agreed to do something so frightening? Such a thing would flood you with difficult memories," asked Yossi.

"Yes, he agreed, after I had first asked him. The suffering he endured from the missing part was worse for him than the reconstructing and when we finished, he was relieved. But, one has to be prepared for it and it has to be the right person for it."

"Wow!" was heard from Yariv's corner.

"Another way is to ask straightforwardly. I spoke to a soldier a few months ago. He'd been involved in an incident that bothered him a great deal – he almost killed an innocent elderly Palestinian man at a border checkpoint. The old man's face haunted him every night because it reminded him of his own grandfather's face. The soldier didn't remember what had happened to the old man and he was steeped in feelings of guilt. I suggested he contact his commander and find out what actually happened to that grandpa. It turns out that the old man got away from the incident unscathed. It was a huge relief to the soldier, and since then he stopped obsessing about him."

"Great, but that's if you are willing to talk straight with no shame."

"Correct, but let's remember that we're here constructing a

toolbox that has all kinds of solutions. Not every tool fits every task. And, while we are at it, let's examine whether or not it's justified to feel ashamed about not remembering. It might be better to confront the issue straight on and without hesitation and say something like: 'You know what...I'm missing some details from that incident in which you were also present. Do you perhaps remember...and can you fill them in for me?' No apologies! The chances are good that the other person would feel good that he does remember and be happy to help.

"And, it's also possible to ask circuitously via a third person if it's too hard to ask directly."

"Are there any other ways as well?" asked Yossi.

"There are. There are news reports in the papers about events, battles, incidents and training accidents. The weekend supplements often go into great detail. Military correspondents have access to sources, and they are often present when things happen. Many books are written about incidents and wars, and the author often interviews participants. Memorial assemblies to the fallen are filled with details. Archives of the IDF and veterans organizations, groups for disabled vets, TV programs, movies, photo exhibits and written material are replete with information. Sometimes one has to conduct a mini research project about an event, and the chances are good that material can be found. These days, with the Internet, there's a ton of information, Israeli and foreign. All that might not help you to locate exactly where you were at a given moment, but background material with indicated times, direction of movement of personnel, names of fighters and commanders, might very well help you to know, for example, whether the jeep passed before or after the tank was paralyzed. It is quite likely that some military correspondent described the incident in great detail and suddenly a light bulb will light in your head."

"So, there really are ways," muttered Uri in a calm voice.

Zev concluded: "With the passage of time and sometimes for unclear reasons, there is suddenly an association to something and the missing piece slips in, like the last piece of a puzzle. And when there is general calming down and improved functioning, there is a chance that the gap in memory of the event will fill in spontaneously."

* * *

Four days after the session, Avi's cellphone rings. An upbeat voice responds to his "hello."

"Hi, Avi, Yariv here."

"Hey! How goes it? What's up?"

"You won't believe this. I was in Tiberias, I go there often in my work. I'm in the street, and I pass a kiosk with skewers of grilled meat. I always keep away from it. But this time, I decided not to cross to the other side of the street, I just continued, even glanced at it, and nothing happened. It's not that I stopped to buy or anything, but I didn't try to escape. If anyone had been walking with me, they wouldn't have noticed anything unusual.

"Thanks so much for your help in the last session. You know what? When I was speaking during the session, I saw Sergei's worried face. He looked disappointed, and I'm afraid I might have spoiled something for him, something he had planned to cook for us. I'm gonna call him and tell him that he can prepare whatever he wants. I don't think that I will be eating any meat by next week, but I'm definitely not as put off by it as before. I really think I can be around it without being upset by it."

"Bingo! So happy to hear it. Fascinating, isn't it? How things can change in one shot if you go at them correctly. That guided imagery, that's something, really something."

Several minutes later, Yariv's phone rings. "Yariv, hi, it's Ron."

"Hello! What's up?"

"You remember how Zev suggested that everyone should have everybody else's phone numbers?"

"Sure. Great idea," Yariv said, cutting him off.

"So. I just wanted to verify that what I have for you is correct."

"It is. You're fine."

"Do you by chance have Gil's number?"

"I don't. But that's a great idea; we should bring him back into our circle. I'll see if I can get it for you."

TWELFTH SESSION

At about four in the afternoon, half an hour before the starting time of their weekly meetings, the guys began to arrive. They quietly slipped into the room, as though no one wanted to be identified as the earliest to arrive. Whether by agreement or simply spontaneously, they wore nicer clothes than usual, signaling that something special, festive, was about to occur, however deep their sadness about separating and their concern for the future. By now the interpersonal network via texting and cellphones was in place, and the informal network among the wives and girlfriends was percolating as well.

Zev, too, had dressed up a bit, wearing a white long-sleeved shirt with a thin brown sweater and matching gabardine slacks.

As promised, Ron appeared with a huge chocolate cake. Not satisfied with the simple paper plates and cheap napkins they had used during the sessions, he brought cheerful, colorful plastic plates and blue-and-white striped napkins.

Sergei arrived, accompanied by his sister Miriam and laden with chafing dishes from which wonderful aromas of prepared food wafted. He'd brought his sister partly to help carry the food, and partly to show off the chef who was instrumental in creating all these delicacies (he being merely her sous chef). After they had arranged everything on the tables, she gave him a hug and headed off.

The water heater hummed as usual; the tiny red "ready" light glowing. Beer had arrived, as well as a bottle of Cognac with a dozen small glasses, but until the session was over, coffee was the beverage of choice. And this time there was a line in front of it, as some of the men's nervousness was expressing itself in increased consumption.

By four-thirty, the designated hour, everything was ready. It was going be a difficult transition, this final session: the conclusion of their group treatment, the assessing of results, the evaluation of their progress, the saying of goodbyes to each another and to Zev.

It was possible that the connections that had been forged among the seven warriors – men who twelve weeks ago didn't know each other's names, much less their intimate troubles – might last for years. It might persist as a bond that would make it possible for a member to pick up a phone at three o'clock in the morning for an emotional, intimate conversation about a frightening or vexing situation. Even Gil, who had only been part of the group up to a point, had not been completely forgotten. He was still part of the system, as others knew his cell number. Some of the members still thought of him and wondered how he was managing.

For Zev, the last session is always like receiving his grades at the end of a school year, only in reverse: as a student, his grades were presented by the teacher and indicated – more or less – how well he learned. Today, a group of "students" will be handing him his grades, reflecting how much *they* had achieved as a result of his work; about his effectiveness in teaching them how to cope with their conflicts.

All along, Zev had been assessing how things were progressing, culling remarks from the members that gave him clues. But today was the summation. Had he succeeded as a group leader? As a therapist? He had been their moderator, teacher, fatherly figure, and supporter. Had he met or exceeded their expectations, or had he fallen short? Where had he failed – and why? When had he made a mistake, said something he shouldn't have said, failed to intervene when he should have?

And as with any parental figure, he became closer to some of his "kids" than to others, although he made a sincere effort to be neutral in his approach to all. Today he hoped to hear that he had succeeded, and was worried that he might hear a remark implying favoritism, real or imagined. He was more concerned about that possibility than about a comment like, "You didn't help me enough with the nightmares."

Questions like these were always floating in his head at the close of each session, but with the knowledge that there'd be an opportunity next week to fix an error. Today, this opportunity would be shut down once and for all. While he might be able to straighten something out with an individual over the phone, the group dynamic officially terminated today, and this was a heavy burden.

For him, these were eight people to whom he was responsible to offer help with their lives. After a period of time, he might forget their names, while paradoxically continuing to remember important issues in their lives.

Next week, he will start running a new group, there will be eight new unknowns in one equation. And twelve weeks later, he will find himself being "graded" again.

Running a group was, objectively, a job, a temporary task. But it was an essential one, one he loved to perform, and he deeply hoped that he improved each time he did it. Today's "grades" would give him feedback on this question. He had studied for years to gain the skills to perform it, learned from his mistakes, and made a great effort to be fair and neutral. His empathy for people whose lives had been adversely affected had been the driving force that pulled him into this unique area of "fixing things," instead of becoming, for instance, an automobile mechanic. For both these professionals, a client would come with a problem to be fixed. But a mechanic generally won't form an emotional connection to a car (with occasional exceptions). A therapist does form emotional ties with a patient.

So for Zev, the last session was always an emotional, highly-anticipated event, associated with both tension and satisfaction. He knew, before anyone uttered a word, that he had made some significant improvements in the lives of these fighters who had been so severely affected by horrible events, and this pleased him. He knew that many problems had to be resolved, and that some might never be solved completely. And that there were skeletons in the closets that he still did not know about, which he might hear about today, and that gave him a sense of anxious anticipation. Before the final celebratory meal, there would be serious business.

All the men had seated themselves, and the room was shrouded in the heavy silence that so often fell between subjects, marking the beginning or end of a sad story. This time, what hung in the air was the question "Who would be the first to speak in the last session?" Would Zev offer a concluding summation? Would someone in the group take on the role of spokesperson and evaluate what had – or had not – been accomplished? Would someone want to tell some as-yet-unheard story?

The silence didn't last long, and as he had in the first session, Ron started to talk.

"Like everyone, I have been thinking of this moment. This last session is for taking inventory, as we said last week, and I know that I've done that for myself. I assume this is true for everyone. I've been thinking how to cover the subject: maybe each of us could say what improved and what did not, what requires further personal work. To me, the issue is much larger than individual symptoms. It's true that one can count the changes in symptoms, but what seems much more important to me is the quality of life after this time we have spent together.

"You all know about the injured soldier I lost. At first I was convinced I was responsible, then I learned here that it wasn't so. What's most important, the feelings of sadness, the fatigue, my problems with concentration, my bleak outlook on life, that's where the big difference lies. I didn't forget the white face of the dead man; I'm still being tormented by his parents' question – which actually never took place – 'Why didn't you save our son?' but I'm able to put it aside, dive into a chemistry book and look forward to studying medicine. Perhaps some time in the future, I will even find a way to save somebody who today has no chance of surviving. And the second important subject for me is the camaraderie that formed among us. There is nothing in the world, at this moment, that is more important to me."

Ron had broken the ice. Even more, he had said what the others felt, but were unable to express in such an orderly fashion, and they were grateful to him. So was Zev.

Yossi, wearing a new *kippa*, eagerly took up the thread. "Do you remember how in the first session someone said 'girly talk' and you all jumped on him? That was eons ago, and the fact is that I've never heard a single word that was 'girly' or weak. Nothing that was said here was meaningless. Everyone here has an important story to tell, one that gets into one's soul, whether it's about a dead friend, or the rotting body of an enemy fighter. After the first session, I wasn't sure I wanted to continue with the group. I was trying to protect myself from the unknown. I thought it would be dangerous to touch old wounds. But it turned out to be just the opposite. We opened up and felt supported, not isolated anymore. I feel like I've traversed a long trail in a brief period of time. It's hard to believe how many changes have occurred in just three months. I now arrive at meetings on time, and as some of you know, I answer the phone. I'm no longer avoiding everything."

"Absolutely," agreed Yariv, and others nodded.

"The problem I still haven't solved is controlling my impatience. I still lash out and I don't talk nicely to my parents. I truly try. I take a deep breath, and prepare a sentence in advance, like Zev says, 'from the shelf,' but what comes out of my mouth is different somehow. Even if the words are correct, there's tension in my voice whenever I respond to them, and I can see in their eyes that they're often upset by my reaction. Then I feel remorse, I'm ashamed, I slither away. The problem may occur less frequently, but it still exists," says Yossi with a sigh.

Yariv chimes in. "You know, Yossi, we discussed this. Not all our problems are related to the events during our military service. We all have personality traits that predate the events. It isn't realistic to expect that after 11 sessions every troublesome behavior will just disappear, and that all our bothersome personality characteristics would just go away. You were always a bit hot-headed, and you explained why: that it had a lot to do with the discrimination your family – especially your father – endured. I don't think you should expect that such an important aspect of your personality is going to change in just two months. It will take a long time, and perhaps some of it will always be there. What you could change, if you really want to, is your behavior. Do you still blow up every time your mother is on your case about the raincoat?"

"No, no. I talk to her much more calmly. I smile and leave. The

271

truth is that I hear much less from her about the raincoat. I think that she, too, has made progress in her relationship to me; sees me as more grown up, not just her little boy. But with my father...heaven help me. I do speak to him impatiently, like he's a child."

"Don't you think this goes a little deeper? What do you suppose would happen if he suddenly got a promotion and became a manager in the supermarket?" Yariv shrewdly challenged Yossi with something he knew would resonate with him.

"Yeah, I get it, I get it. It has nothing to do with the service or what happened in Gaza. I've always had a problem with him, I'm just more aware of it now. Actually, I haven't even told you, but now I go with him to his synagogue on Shabbat. I hadn't been there in years, and he appreciates it a lot that I go with him."

"So isn't that a real change?"

"Actually, yes," Yossi acknowledges.

At this point, Zev joins. "You may all have noticed that Yossi is describing not only a change in his own behavior, but a change in his mother as well. It seems to me that this is the result of a better understanding between them of what had happened to him in the service, instead of the groping in the dark that preceded the talks here. I assume that such relationship changes have happened, or will happen, with others of you as well.

"But, there is also another issue here. There are people, and Yossi you may be one of them, who have great difficulty dealing with anger. That's a separate matter, not necessarily related to PTSD, and there are excellent methods of dealing with it, which come under the category of 'Anger Management.' I can give you names of experts in that field who can help you with it."

Uri slides forward in his chair, eager to speak. "I wanted to talk about a similar situation. Since I've been more open with the people around me, they've changed in dealing with me. I can see in their eyes that they're sad about what happened to me, but they don't look at me anymore like I'm some strange person, difficult to connect with, carrying a heavy and mysterious burden. When I suddenly wake up at night screaming, confused and incoherent, Karnit isn't terrified, or off running to another room. She hugs me and says, 'Uri, wake up. It's a dream, open your eyes.' Her voice is calm and she's already turned on the light, and within a few seconds I'm back to reality and the episode is over. These episodes used to happen often and last longer. The improvement is that they are less frequent and end quickly. It's true that I'd like to get rid of them once and for all, but they are stubborn."

"My nightmares *haven't* improved," puts in Sergei. "It's difficult for me to fall asleep because I worry about having nightmares, and when I finally do fall asleep, mostly during the day, I still often wake up with a start. I've tried different things to deal with it. I don't watch war movies, as we decided here. I keep a journal, which you are familiar with. I've even written some poems, a short story – but nothing is of much help. The cries of the wounded still haunt me; I'm unable to silence them. It's also possible that I'm not *allowing* them to stop. I worry that if I silence them, it's as though I'm betraying them, and that's why I'm not letting them fall silent."

Zev explains: "Your thinking is not unusual, and perhaps you're right. But I don't imagine that continuing to deprive yourself of sleeping at night is what your fallen friends would wish for you. Find another way to think about them, and try to broaden your circle to include others who may think of them. If I remember correctly, one of them was active in sports. What would you think of organizing an annual sports event in his memory, with a trophy that has his name engraved on it? Such commemorations are not unusual, and in this way every year, on a designated day, young students will learn about your friend. Since it will be you who has organized the commemoration, you will not feel like you have abandoned him. To the contrary, thanks to you, his name will be on other peoples' lips for years to come, and perhaps then you could 'allow' yourself to sleep."

"I've actually thought about that, and I've even begun to check it out with his family. His mother is enthusiastic about the idea, and I'm working on something for the next Day of Remembrance for the fallen."

Yariv raises his hand, and turns to address Sergei. "For a while now, I've noticed a change in you, Sergei. Perhaps someone else has also noticed. For the last several weeks, you haven't been grabbing your throat between your fingers. You used to make this grabbing movement" and he demonstrated it with his hand, "and clearing your throat, numerous times during each session, and that's all disappeared. Have you noticed?"

The others all look at Sergei, who blushes and admits, "You're right. I'm aware that it's disappeared – but why was I doing it in the first place? What's happening here? What does this mean?"

"You have great powers of observation, Yariv. Did anyone else notice? I was also aware of it, but choose to not comment. What do you think caused this behavior, and why did it change?" Zev asks Sergei, but his gaze invites them all to tackle the question.

Heads shake. No one has any idea why such a behavior would develop, or what would make it disappear. It's obvious that it was an involuntary reaction to some emotional stress, but there is no obvious answer as to why or how. Zev decides to outline his own thinking.

"Do you recall Sergei's frightening descriptions? For several months, he would don his helmet, his flak jacket, and all his other equipment, and then drive to the Gaza Strip in an unarmored jeep, following that dirt road on his way to the tunnels that border Egypt. He would pass Palestinian villages and there was always the fear of snipers. Sergei told us how he would fasten the helmet's strap really tightly, as protection from the unexpected, and the strap would hug his throat, under the chin, at exactly the same place he used to grab with his hand. For a long time after the danger had passed, putting pressure on that spot had a calming effect, possibly symbolically, magically. Only now, after becoming completely convinced that the danger has passed, has this habit disappeared. Could that be true?"

"Wow!" blurts out Sergei. "Was that the reason? I've been wondering about that habit for a long time. I couldn't understand it. I tried to stop it, but couldn't. At best, when I really tried, I could restrain my hand for a minute or two; but then, sure enough, it would creep back. I was aware that for the past week or two I'd stopped doing it, but didn't understand why. It's a magical improvement, Zev! And you, Yariv, thank you for your power of observation."

Yariv smiles, somewhat embarrassed. "Thanks. I always pay attention to small things and this particular gesture just caught my attention. I'm happy that you got rid of it, and Zev's explanation sounds very reasonable."

* * *

Three-quarters of an hour had passed since the session began. Yossi, glancing at his watch, is becoming hyper-aware that only three-quarters of an hour remains before the group will come to an end. He rises to get a last cup of coffee. There is a gurgling sound as a few last drops of water attempt to fill his cup. He removes the cover and refills it with fresh water, carefully and intently as if performing holy work for the last time. He is grateful to find an unexpected task to attend to that does not require coping with feelings, divulging hidden secrets, or sharing struggles. He is listening, of course, to everything that is being said, and feels happy that he can do something helpful for his friends. When the process is complete he returns to his seat and waits, like everyone else, for the humming sound and the little red light to go on for the last time. Everything is becoming "for the last time."

Zev looks at every member, his eyes passing from one to the next. He is estimating the degree of improvement, the failures, and the disappointments.

"As in our first session," Zev gestures around the circle, "we've heard from some of us, and now we'd like to hear from everyone else. Uri, Ron, Sergei and Yossi have shared their personal 'inventory-taking.' I'd like to hear from all of you as to what you got out of being here, as well as what requires further work." He sits back in his chair and expects the unexpected.

Yariv leans forward in his seat and takes up the request. "I've seen many changes for the better. Next Purim I don't expect a problem joining my kids in a party with firecrackers, and fireworks no longer disturb me like they used to. I'm slowly overcoming the feelings of guilt, and I also understand that I did what I could, and did it well. As you know, I tell my wife everything, no more secrets. Whatever you all know, she knows as well, and as the kids mature, I will also tell them more than I have. We now visit friends without a problem, and my aversion to grilled meat has lessened. If my nose isn't playing a game with me, it seems that Sergei's brought a surprise that might once have alarmed me, and I'm ready for it." A sigh of relief is heard from the section of the room where Sergei is sitting. "He called me during the week, otherwise I wouldn't have prepared that particular dish," Sergei explains.

Yariv continues. "The experience here was very positive, and I'm grateful that I was given the opportunity to participate, and like Ron already said, the friendship among us is worth even more than some modest improvements, and thank you all, especially you, Zev, for the help. You're great."

Glances are sent toward the two who have not yet spoken.

Ido says, "Remember my hesitations? I said that I'm a careful person who doesn't enter things quickly, but I did, and how! I wouldn't hesitate for a moment to recommend someone else to join such a group – with Zev, of course. Actually, I've already started talking to a friend of mine from the battalion who's in bad shape. It's the same, familiar story: he doesn't sleep, doesn't contact his friends, and all the rest. He, too, was in Lebanon. I started talking to him after about our fifth session, telling him how things were moving along, and he started to show an interest. Zev, I hope that you'll get a call from Sami; so now you'll know who he is."

Zev nods. "I'll be happy to talk to him, thanks."

"So, what's left?" Ido continues. "The irritability and impatience have improved, but I have not fully returned to the way I used to be. But I think I'm on my way. I get along well with the head of my department, and I finally completed my article. It probably isn't written at the highest level I'm capable of, but it's certainly acceptable. And by the way," he adds impishly, "mark your calendars, because next Fall you'll all be guests at the wedding of someone you just met this year."

The sound of clapping fills the room.

"So, you and Nava will take the big leap, eh?"

"You're going to move beyond the joint cooking and the excursions? The voices of the bride and groom will be heard in the streets of Jerusalem. And we know how this came about!" Here Uri enthusiastically cites the ancient blessing, "Mazal tov!"

The somewhat reserved and formal Ido willingly accepts the hugs his friends give him, while Zev looks on, beaming with satisfaction; another "V" sign for his mental chart.

Now Avi starts his summation. "The nightmares have

improved, and I don't have any more flashbacks. I can't even remember the last time I had one. My ability to sleep has also improved; if I do have a bad dream, I get out of it quickly. I made an agreement with Nili that if there is ever a need to go to the clinic or the ER, she will do it, unless there is no other option. I believe I could probably handle it, although I'm not jumping at the opportunity. The experience here was excellent. It's hard for me to believe that 12 weeks can bring about such a change. I believe that the fact that we shared the feelings that we had been sitting on, and talked openly about such awful things, and also heard from others about their reactions to noises, to blood, to TV news, and absorbed that these things are not unique to us – all that helped a lot. And you, Zev, are a great navigator in troubled waters. Kudos to you. We must certainly have given you some moments of indigestion, but you never let it show. Your evenness gave us a sense of calm and security. And I'd like to add a word about Gil. It's too bad that he left the group. I believe that he actually was helped in a few things, but I think he probably has problems that are much more complex than could be dealt with here. But in Gil's name, I offer thanks from him as well."

The time has arrived for Zev to give his own summary and impressions. Everyone has been anticipating it. He has rehearsed his words in private for some time.

"In the first session, I was concerned that we might have some problems here. For one thing, the hesitation some felt about keeping confidentiality took a little longer to overcome than usual. But it soon disappeared. I was very impressed by the rapid development of mutual trust and caring for each other.

"There were stories here that were hard to talk about, very sad, horrifying, and at times embarrassing, and you dealt with all of them. I'm very happy about all the improvements that you've listed, while I'm clear that we did not solve every problem. I never had any illusions about that. And you will all remember that my goal was to bring the symptoms to a manageable level, and to improve daily functioning, and from what I hear, that has largely happened. Nightmares are a common problem and a stubborn one. I wish I had a magic wand to erase them for you. For those of you for whom the problem persists, please don't hesitate to use sleeping medications or tranquilizers, and continue to consult with mental health professionals to help cope with this issue. There are some newer methods of treatment, such as Somatic Experiencing (SE), that look promising. Be sure to consult with doctors who understand PTSD, because not all do. Some of you have said you would be interested in another round of group therapy, and we can certainly talk about that. Others might want to go into individual therapy, a good idea. The more normally you live, the more you will notice that the soul will continue to heal itself and the other symptoms will become marginalized. None of you will forget the traumatic events, but they'll take their place as memories and will no longer take center stage.

"Some of you already said this, but I'd like to emphasize how much the mutual caring among all of you will continue to help. Although today is the last session, if anyone of you has a question, just pick up the phone, I do answer it." There were smiles and some laughter at Zev's little joke.

"Judging by these wonderful aromas, it's time to see what Sergei and Miriam have prepared for us."

The guys all rose up from their seats. Sergei had already set up the room for a party. The chairs were in a wide arc, and the side table and coffee table were side-by-side, draped in a white tablecloth. On it was a bountiful variety of foods, a generous buffet, with fancy labels: *"Romaine Hearts with Tomato and Tofu, Roasted Chicken à L'Orange, Puréed Celery and Sautéed Green Beans, Fettuccini with Basil and Tomato and Grilled Vegetables, Pan-Seared Sole in a Butter and Caper Sauce,* and for dessert, *Parve Ice-Cream with Noisette Sauce and Strawberries.*

Bottles of beer were opened, and the cork popped out of the cognac bottle. Yariv stood up, holding his glass in the air. "On behalf of all of us, I'd like to thank you, Zev, for the professional and humane manner in which you ran our group. *L'Chaim,* and we wish you the best." Everyone clinked their glasses, and Zev blushed with pleasure and surprise.

He was about to be surprised again.

Ido stood up, positioned himself in front of Zev, and with a flourish, pulled a flat package wrapped in colorful paper from behind his back. "And this is for you." Zev took the package from him, mumbling, "What's all this?"

"Open it and see."

Zev removed the paper from the package, slowly and carefully, making the moment last. Finally, he revealed a shiny wooden frame in which was mounted a certificate of appreciation, which read:

> To Zev, with thanks and appreciation
> for your work in returning us to
> "the way we used to be."

> Yariv
> Ron
> Avi
> Yossi
> Ido
> Uri
> Sergei

EPILOGUE – TEN YEARS LATER

Gil's condition continued to deteriorate. He sank into a deep depression, stopped going to work and lost his clients. He was under psychiatric care, took anti–depressants, and was eventually hospitalized for a long time. He took part in treatment groups for months, and eventually his condition stabilized. Yet, he never returned to full health. His childhood emotional problems worsened. His lawyer claimed that he suffered an irreversible mental trauma in the service, while the Ministry of Defense brought proof that he had had mental problems since childhood. After a long and exhausting legal battle, they compromised and he received a large disability compensation. His marriage fell apart, but his parents continue to have a close relationship with him. He frequents the Disabled Veterans club of the IDF, where he has befriended some guys with similar difficulties. Some of his old friends keep in touch, and from time to time, Yariv calls him or they meet for coffee. Gil participates in a bowling club and has managed to become a top-rated player. He paints in gouache and oil, and his paintings are dark and sad.

Ron graduated from the Sackler medical school and specialized in trauma medicine. Today he heads the trauma department of a major hospital in the southern part of the country, fulfilling his vow to save lives. He married Alice, who graduated from law school at Tel Aviv University and specializes in matrimonial law. They have a son and a daughter. Ron's father, who retired and continues to write articles and books, finally made peace with his son, and even apologized for his stubbornness. His mother continues to work and was awarded a prize by the Boston medical establishment for her success in medical genetics research. Ron and his brother, Bill, communicate by e-mail, Facebook and phone calls, and at times compare professional knowledge, being in similar professions. To this day, Bill has not visited Israel because he is "too busy." His sister, to the contrary, visits often and her daughter is preparing to celebrate her Bat Mitzvah in Jerusalem. The parents visit every year for two months, staying in an apartment they had purchased in Jerusalem.

Avi's oldest daughter married an IDF air force pilot. He expanded his metal shop into a factory that produces precision instruments, an extension of his father's genius in inventing and improving agricultural machinery. He still sometimes suffers from frightening dreams. His relationship with his parents is close and they visit each other often. One evening, sitting with his father over a glass of wine on the terrace in Avi's home overlooking a valley, the conversation evolved into what his father did during the Yom Kippur War on the Golan Heights. Only then did Avi learn why his father had been awarded his own Medal of Valor.

Ido signed up for further service in the standing army and stayed for another eight years, reaching the rank of lieutenant colonel. It was sort of a "loan" arrangement with the university, which caved in to pressure from Military Intelligence. After he completed that stint, he returned to teaching at the university. All through his time in the service, he continued to do historical research, and his articles appeared in professional journals in Israel and abroad. Ido and Nava have two sons and a daughter, and they moved to Modi'in, where other IDF officers live. On Sabbaths, they often take day trips, introducing their kids to the places they themselves explored.

Uri and Nili had a bad time in their marriage, and received years of marital counseling before reconciling. He now heads the music department in the school where he had been teaching for many years. Uri composed a short opera about the war, which received mixed reviews. He continues to enjoy playing the piano and has started teaching his two sons. He still suffers from anxiety and takes anti-anxiety medication. He also had several years of individual therapy, which helped to some degree. Recently, he did some family history research and unearthed programs from concerts his grandmother gave in Vienna before World War Two. He framed them and they hang on his wall above his piano.

Yariv and Anat left the kibbutz due to their disagreement with the new ideology of privatization and social changes, and moved to the town of Arad in the Negev. They have a huge farm where they raise sheep for milk and chickens for eggs, a continuation of Yariv's love for animals. Yariv also owns a hardware and building supply store in Beer Sheva. Consistent with his belief in nondiscrimination, he employs a mentally-challenged teenage boy, whom he teaches about building materials. The boy also spends much time in Yariv's home, learning to care for animals, and often goes home with fresh eggs. Yariv attends the annual get-together of Battalion 890 of the paratroopers. Despite an improved tolerance for eating grilled meat, the family decided to become vegetarians, reasoning that it was healthier anyway. Yariv keeps in touch with Gil, and they have met several times.

Yossi continued to develop his company. He now owns five vehicles – four trucks of various sizes and a small pickup. He liberated his father from his hateful supermarket job, and Itzhak is now doing light deliveries. Yossi's hot temper still causes him difficulties, and his wife, who runs the office, often has to intervene and calm down infuriated customers. They are kosher and have five children, all studying at a religious school. He keeps in close contact with Yariv, and once a year hosts his family for an elaborate, delicious Middle-Eastern feast. In return, Yariv's family hosts an annual kosher summer picnic in a national park. The kids know each other and some have become friends.

Sergei completed his studies in cinema. He never married because he found it difficult to form a long-lasting relationship with a woman, and feels attracted to men. He left the catering business and directed three documentaries. The first was about children from broken homes, for which he received prizes; the second was a documentary about Israel's most famous films; and in the third film, "Freedom Fighter vs. Terrorist," he showed both sides of the Arab-Israeli conflict and was heavily criticized and demonized. Peace Now, an activist organization, adopted it as a document that objectively reflects the complexity of the situation. He lives in Tel Aviv, has a comfortable life, and often travels to Paris and Berlin for artistic ideas and inspiration.

Zev was blessed to see three of his grandchildren get married. Shortly after the completion of the group, he retired. Forty years of treating others had exhausted him, and he had many other interests. He decided to dedicate his remaining time to oil painting. Some adorn the clinic in which he worked for years, and he donated some to public buildings where they are on permanent display. He and his wife took several trips to foreign countries, and when his health became a challenge, he wrote two books. One is an autobiography and the second is a collection of short stories based on his professional experiences as a psychologist. He always remembered his work in running the PTSD group as the crowning achievement of his professional career, and often lectured about it. He also participated in the Bar Mitzvah of Yariv's son, Rami, named in memory of Yariv's friend who fell in battle.

~ *** ~

GUIDE TO THE SESSIONS

This is a general guide to the problems and therapies of PTSD that are discussed in this book. It is meant to help readers locate sections that may be of particular interest.

	Symptoms of PTSD	Therapeutic Techniques
Session 1	Avoidance; not talking	What is PTSD; symptoms
Introduction to Zev, therapist Introduction to group members	Shame	Confidentiality of group Commitment to group
Session 2	"Not how I used to be" Lack of desire Unable to talk about events (Gil)	Ron's story Goals of therapy Cognitive vs Dynamic Therapy Cognitive-Behavior Therapy
Session 3	Sleep problems	Learning to relax Headache elimination
Session 4	Nightmares Tried to save others (Avi) Concentration problems (Sergei, Uri) Memory problems; missing appointments	Guided imagery Feelings of failure
Session 5	Ignoring friends (Gil) Social contacts (Yossi, Yariv) Shame (Uri) Loss of memory of event Noises (Uri)	"Cashing in" favors; getting help from others Grieving: its stages and "Grief Work" (Ron)

	Symptoms of PTSD	Therapeutic Techniques
Session 6	Noises – fireworks Dreams	Making progress (Uri) Setbacks (Avi in the ER) Other peoples' reactions What to tell children Challenging questions
Session 7	Neglecting spouses	Missing a session (Gil) Group dynamics Social progress (Ido)
Yossi	Drugs and escaping	Handling social discrimination
Session 8	Irritability (Yossi)	Revolt against therapist Handling ADD
Session 9	Flashbacks Dealing with children	Leaving the group Spouses' meeting Fear of abandonment "Lone soldier" – those without family (Ron)
Zev's demons		A therapist's perspective
Session 10	Intrusive thoughts Guilt – interrogation Survival guilt Return of desire Confusion, low functioning	Friendship (Yariv, Yossi) Medications Perception of others Revealing secrets
Session 11	Disturbing smells Fear of future	Summarizing Planning for future
Session 12 Final party Zev's summary	Flashbacks, nightmares Physical symptoms Irritability	Spouses' support "Somatic Experiencing"

GUIDE TO THE CHARACTERS

All characters are fictional, and are composites of the hundreds of patients Dr. DeLevie has treated.

Name	Background	Personality
Zev	Married, 3 children, grandchildren; European background	Psychologist; calm, reserved, artistic, problem-solver
Avi	Married, 4 children; Bulgarian parents emigrated to Israel in the '60s; raised on a kibbutz	Shepherd and metalworker; strong, quiet and sensitive; emotionally scarred by radical child-rearing practices
Gil	Married; heavy equipment operator and mechanic; tough father	Attention-deficit disorder from early childhood, irritable, artistic
Ido	Steady relationship; college professor, researcher, urban explorer	Reserved, serious, cautious, intellectual
Ron	American immigrant; scholarly Boston family; moved alone to Israel in his teens against their wishes	Spiritual; looking to connect with heritage and religion, and to gain his father's approval
Sergei	Russian immigrant; broken family; caterer and film student	Quiet, adjusting to different culture
Uri	Married, wife Karnit is Iraqi; Eastern European (mostly German) background; professional / musical family	Initial difficulty fitting in; very good jazz and classical musician
Yariv	Moroccan background; father and uncles are career officers, father died of heart attack	Seen as leader, strong, fair, serious
Yossi	Married, children; Middle Eastern background; father suffered discrimination	Impatient, irritable, used and dealt drugs

Military Experience	Problems
Medical corps	Secondary traumatization due to job stress
Infantry; ambushed in Kasbah night operations, attempted to rescue friend, failed	Can't tolerate smell or taste of meat, can't tolerate sight of blood; guilt
Equipment operator; bulldozed houses in Gaza Strip, injured and almost suffocated	Avoids contact with people and locations
Intelligence officer; operated behind lines, sought by Hamas	Unable to concentrate, procrastinates, avoids crowds
Combat medic; tried to save injured soldier in Gaza Strip, failed	"Not the way I used to be," guilt, sense of failure, unable to concentrate
Paratrooper; dodged snipers and mines in Gaza Strip	Nightmares, headaches, unable to concentrate
Tank commander; tank battles in Lebanon, abandoned his command	Nightmares, difficulty maintaining relationships or interest in music, shame and guilt
Infantry; ambushed in night excursions, tried to save friend and failed	Fear of loud noises and fireworks, survivor guilt
Commando; pursued terrorists in dangerous, secret missions	Irritable, disrespectful of parents, suffers flashbacks, has hole in his story

ABOUT THE AUTHOR

Dr. Ari DeLevie, born in Haifa, Israel, is a clinical psychologist with forty years' experience treating children, couples, families, and trauma patients, individually and in groups.

He worked with Vietnam War vets (at the Bronx VA hospital and at Castle Point, Montrose, NY) and with the Department of Rehabilitation for the Israeli Ministry of Defense after the Six Day War of 1967, where he treated soldiers suffering from what was later termed Combat-Related Post Traumatic Stress Disorder (PTSD). Following the Second Lebanon War (2006), he volunteered at the Unit for Combat Reactions, an Israeli Army mental health clinic, where he worked with veterans who had been suffering from PTSD for as long as 40 years.

His professional orientation is Cognitive-Behavioral Therapy (CBT), described as problem-focused and action-oriented, not exploring the past at length, but being in the here and now. He enjoys solving problems in a practical manner but has no illusions that every problem is solvable.

Dr. DeLevie is retired, lives in NY. He has three daughters and seven grandchildren, loves drawing and writing, foreign travel, classical music, and humor.

Made in the USA
Charleston, SC
17 July 2014